THE DRAGON AT NOONDAY

Edith Pargeter

A TANDEM BOOK
published by
WYNDHAM PUBLICATIONS

A Tandem Book

Published in 1976
by Wyndham Publications Ltd
A Howard & Wyndham Company
123 King Sreet, London W6 9JG

First published in Great Britain by
Macmillan London Limited, 1975

Copyright © 1975 by Edith Pargeter

Made and printed in Great Britain by
Richard Clay (The Chaucer Press) Ltd,
Bungay, Suffolk

ISBN 0426 17718 5

THE DRAGON AT NOONDAY

"Do you remember," I asked, "what David said to you after the field of Bryn Derwin, when he stood unhorsed and bruised and at your mercy? *'Kill me!'* he said. *'You were wise!'* Not defying, not challenging, rather warning and entreating you for your own life. He knows himself and you. As often as his right hand launches a blow against you, his left hand will reach out to parry it, and his voice will cry: *'Kill me!—You were wise!'* "

"You read this," said Llewelyn darkly, "as a reason why I should not kill him, who betrays me and Wales together?"

"Far be that from me," I said. "It is warning enough of perpetual danger, and the best reason why you should. But it is also the absolute reason why you never will!"

CONTENTS

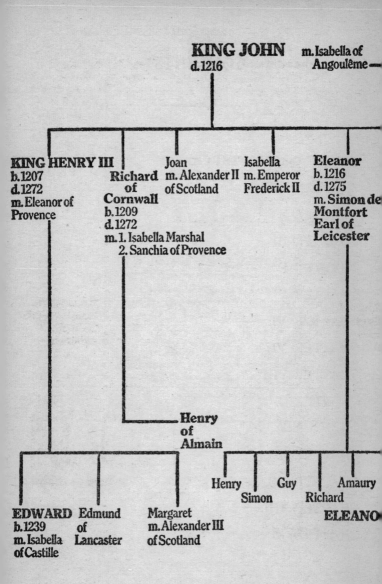

KING JOHN
d. 1216   m. Isabella of Angoulême —

KING HENRY III
b. 1207
d. 1272
m. Eleanor of Provence

Richard of Cornwall
b. 1209
d. 1272
m. 1. Isabella Marshal
2. Sanchia of Provence

Joan
m. Alexander II of Scotland

Isabella
m. Emperor Frederick II

Eleanor
b. 1216
d. 1275
m. Simon de Montfort Earl of Leicester

Henry of Almain

Henry   Simon   Guy   Richard   Amaury

ELEANO

EDWARD
b. 1239
m. Isabella of Castille

Edmund of Lancaster

Margaret
m. Alexander III of Scotland

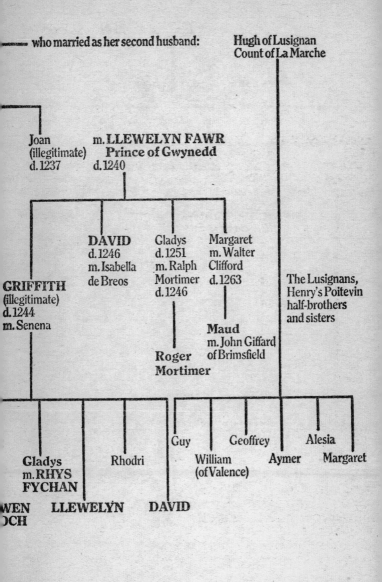

who married as her second husband:

Hugh of Lusignan
Count of La Marche

Joan
(illegitimate)
d. 1237

m. LLEWELYN FAWR
Prince of Gwynedd
d. 1240

DAVID
d. 1246
m. Isabella
de Breos

Gladys
d. 1251
m. Ralph
Mortimer
d. 1246

Margaret
m. Walter
Clifford
d. 1263

GRIFFITH
(illegitimate)
d. 1244
m. Senena

The Lusignans,
Henry's Poitevin
half-brothers
and sisters

Maud
m. John Giffard
of Brimsfield

Roger
Mortimer

Gladys
m. RHYS
FYCHAN

Rhodri

Guy

William
(of Valence)

Geoffrey

Alesia

Aymer

Margaret

WEN
OCH

LLEWELYN

DAVID

The chronicle of the Lord Llewelyn, son of Griffith, son of Llewelyn, son of Iorwerth, lord of Gwynedd, the eagle of Snowdon, the shield of Eryri, first and only true Prince of Wales.

CHAPTER I

Still I remember that homecoming we had, when we rode back to Aber from the assembly of all the chieftains of Wales, in the spring of the year of grace, one thousand, two hundred and fifty-eight. We came at the season of the rising of Christ from the dead, when all things rose gloriously with him, the meadow flowers in the grass, the larks soaring from under our horses' feet, the fortunes of Gwynedd, and the star of our prince Llewelyn, no longer prince only of the north, and hemmed in by English power on all sides, but the overlord of many vassals and the entire hope of Wales.

For at that assembly every chieftain of the land but one only had sworn the oath of fealty to my lord and friend, and done homage to him as suzerain, and for this while at least our long-dismembered land was one. Indeed, I think that was the first time in all our history that Wales had been one, no small glory to him who kneaded all those several fragments into a single rock within his hands.

So we came home at that Easter with great elation and lightness of heart, to match the season and the wonder. When we rode between the mountains and the sea into the royal maenol of Aber, the women came out with flowers and singing to meet us. Not the woman I would most gladly have seen, for she was a long ride south out of my ken, and wife to another man. But, even wanting her, I will not deny that I, too, was carried aloft on the wings of that exultation, and the inward grief I had, pierced through and through by her absence, I lifted up in my heart to the glory of God, and as an entreaty for the safe-keeping and blessing of Llewelyn's lordship, and the crowning of his endeavours for my land. For I, Samson, his clerk, the least and the closest of those who loved him, desired most of all things then left in my life his triumph and happiness.

We celebrated the feast as never before, having so much reason for thankfulness. As I remember it, the weather was kind and fair upon the Good Friday, when all we of the prince's company kept the long vigil of grief that the season and our own hearts belied. And after, when the day of the resurrection was come, we were very merry in hall those nights, and very drunken, at least some of us below the fire. For Llewelyn himself never drank deeply, his intoxication coming rather with the draughts of strong mead the bards provided him. They had fuel enough to their fires that spring, and sang his whole life's achievement before him, and all their hopes of him for the future.

'He took up the fallen sword of his royal uncle,
David, to whom he was faithful from his childhood,
And made it more glorious far, a lightning against the invader,
A terror to kings, a rod of justice against treachery.
Who is like him in the field of battle,
And in the council of princes who can match him for wisdom?
In the council of princes the first and greatest,
He took diverse and warring clans into his palms
And fused their fragmented metals into steel with the fire of his longing,
A sword of swords to defend Wales, from Montgomery to the sea,
And from Ynys Mon to the farthest reaches of Kidwelly,
No longer many but one, this Wales of his making.

2

More glorious than his glorious grandsire, whose name
   he bears,
He has thrust back the English from our borders,
Given us ships and engines of war, taught us the uses
   of unity,
Held up before us the vision of freedom, never
   henceforth to be forgotten,
And we bereft of it never again content, so bright is its
   beauty.
He is the lion of Eryri, the bright falcon of Snowdon,
The red-gold dragon in the noonday,
So radiant, the eyes dazzle....'

So sang Rhydderch Hen, the chief of the bards, and
Llewelyn listened with a sceptical smile, though for all
his suspicion of flattery it was heady wine to him.

David, his youngest brother, left his place and came
and sat down beside me, leaning with an arm about my
shoulders. And stooping to my ear he said, in his voice
that was tuned clearer than Rhydderch's harp, and never
so sweet as when its matter was bitter: 'As I believe in
hot ice and cold fire, so I believe in Welsh unity.'

'You have seen it,' I said, taking him, as I always took
him, warily but not too gravely. 'New-made and puny,
but alive. God forbid we should ask too much of it at
birth, but at least we have seen it born.'

'Into a kindred of litigants and fratricides,' said David
no less sweetly, 'where its chances of surviving infancy
are slender indeed.'

'God knows,' I said, 'they have seldom brought such
a miraculous child to birth before, what wonder if they
make inexpert nurses? Yet you are newly come from a
prodigy, do not turn your back on it yet. They have all
taken the oath of fealty, have they not?'

'All but Griffith de la Pole,' owned David, mocking
himself with the name, for so the English called Griffith
ap Gwenwynwyn of Powys, who alone held out from the

3

Welsh confederacy, and in using the same style for him David acknowledged that this Welshman born was so drawn into the Englishry of the marches as to be no longer a true Welshman at all.

'For Griffith we are not accountable yet. His time will come. Did you ever know the rest of them at one until now, bound in one oath to one man?'

I looked along the high table then to see that one man at the height of his achievement. The smoke of the torches and the candles made a soft blue mist within the hall, and in that mist the light shot rings of colour and sparks of fire, as sometimes the sun will strike these wonders out of rain. So I saw Llewelyn sit mute and upright within a halo of tinted darts that sparkled like stars, and his face was bright and sharp as crystal, and his eyes looked far. He was not accustomed to waste much thought upon being splendid without, all his intent fixing upon an inward splendour, but this day he had made himself unwontedly fine in honour of the feast, and very fittingly he shone. Not as David, who wore jewels as his right and meed, being so beautiful, but with a strong, brown, warming splendour, full of hope and force and fire. He was twenty-nine years old, at the full of his growth and strength, more than average tall, and broad of bone, but lean and lissome of flesh. Brow and visage, he was brown always, the winter and indoor living doing no more than pale him into gold, a ruddy gold fitting for the dragon of which Rhydderch sang. His hair, too, was but the same brown darkened, and the close-trimmed beard that outlined his bones and left his mouth bare was like a goldsmith's modelling for a coin, such as the English strike of their kings. And that night in hall he wore the golden circlet of his rank, the talaith of Gwynedd that had become the talaith of Wales.

'He would need,' whispered David in my ear, 'to be more than man, to hold those oaths together. We shall see, we shall see, who will be the first to fall away.'

4

At that I turned sharply, drawing back my head to have him the more clearly in my sight, for he hung upon my shoulder with that half-mocking and half-rueful affection he commonly used towards me. There were always galls to be found somewhere sharpening the sweet of David's converse, and I could not fail to catch an echo here, for it was but three years since he himself had fallen away from his fealty to Llewelyn, and risen against him in arms, in company with Owen Goch, their oldest brother, then partner with Llewelyn in the rule of Gwynedd. For which unjustified assault Owen still lay in close confinement in the castle of Dolbadarn, though David, whom Llewelyn conceived as the victim of his elder's influence and eloquence, was restored to grace and favour, and indeed had earned both in action since. Yet often in this time of his restoration I had known him make allusion of his own wayward will to his default, like one probing with the point of a dagger in idle malice, towards whose heart it was hard to guess, though always he exposed his own. Some such prick, and aimed surely at me, I looked for here. For David knew how to hurt as he knew how to please, and his real and hot affection was a rose with many and long thorns.

'Oh, no, my sweet Samson,' he said in the softest of breaths, 'not I! Not this time! Never again in that fashion, whatever else may follow. Set your loyal, loving, clerkly mind at rest, I stay my brother's man. I do but reason from what we have. A great handful of irreconcilable princes, hungry for land, accustomed to contention, so suddenly assaulted by my brother's vision of a Wales as whole as England, able to stand against England and match as equals. All this they feel and desire, like some epic of the bards. But nothing of it do they understand, and nothing of it can they will, with any charged purpose. Oh, while Llewelyn is there among them to lend them his vision it goes well enough, but as soon as his eye is off them they'll look again at their neighbours and kin,

5

and see them as before, not allies, but rivals, and the manor allotted unfairly to a brother, or the boundary-mark moved by a neighbour, will loom larger to them than the sovereign power of a Wales they've never known.'

He looked up then and caught my eye, no doubt studying him very warily. I would rather he had not, but there was never any way of hiding from him what I was thinking. He laughed, a little hollowly, but without any bitterness or blame. 'You are right,' he said. 'Who should know the way of it better than I, who first began it?'

Nevertheless, as April ran its course in sunshine and sudden squalls of rain, after its fashion on our northern coast, I began to disbelieve in that danger, at least while the oath of alliance was so new, and had brought nothing but good to any of those who joined in it. For it was Llewelyn's power that had set up his liegemen in their own lands, and his influence that held them secure in their tenure, and had even added to their holding newly conquered lands in the march, snatched back from the barons of England. What reason, then, had any to turn away from him?

Yet self-interest need not always be informed by intelligence, and the habit of generations dies very hard.

It was late in April, after we had sent out the last of the prince's deeds of protection and support to his new vassal, that Meurig ap Howel, Llewelyn's best scout from the middle march, came riding into Aber, a little, wrinkled dealer in ponies who traded as far as Oswestry and Montgomery, and regularly brought back to us word of what went on beneath the hangings even in Westminster. For our intelligencers were as wide-ranging and efficient as the king's, if less exalted. King Henry had at least one Welsh prince to be his spy, and that was Griffith ap Gwenwynwyn of Powys, that same man known to his English masters as Griffith de la Pole, from his castle of

6

Pool, by the Severn town of that name. But we made better use of humbler men, Welsh law students and clerks and merchants, and notably our well-established horse-doctor in Chester, who was familiar and respected about the garrison, and on whom we relied for details of the king's muster and plans in his regular summer campaigns against us.

This Meurig was a dried-up little man, well on in years but hardy as a gorse-bush, so grey and so light of weight that he seemed to drift into Aber like a shred of thistle-down blown by the silver shower that came in at the gate with him. Goronwy ap Ednyfed, the high steward, brought him in steaming to the brazier in the great chamber, to Llewelyn, for he was bursting with his news.

'You've had no word yet from Rhys Fychan?' he asked; and being told that we had not: 'I can be no more than a day ahead with it; he'll have a courier on the way to you this moment. My lord, the reconciliation you went to such pains to bring about along the Towy last year is broken. Meredith ap Rhys Gryg has accepted King Henry's peace, and forsworn the oath he took to you barely a month ago!'

At that there was a great rumble of anger and outrage from all those around, and Llewelyn chilled into stone for an instant before blazing into indignation.

'Meredith!' he said. 'He, to be the first traitor! He of all people who owed us the most, who came here a fugitive, ousted from all his lands. And after I set him up again in everything he had lost!'

'I doubted him then,' said David roundly. 'When we took Rhys Fychan in and embraced him, that stuck in Meredith's gullet like a burr. For all he gave him the kiss of kinship like the rest of us, I felt then it had a sour taste to him. He could not stomach that we should accept and approve, and take him into the confederacy on equal terms. But most of all,' he said, 'he could not stomach that his nephew and rival should stand equal with him in your love.'

7

'And what use,' Llewelyn asked of Meurig, 'has Meredith made of the king's peace? For peace will be the last thing he desires of it.'

'My lord,' said Meurig, 'the very use you expect of him. King Henry has granted him leave to possess himself of Rhys Fychan's lands to add to his own, and has lent him the aid of the seneschal of Carmarthen and the royal garrison there. And they have seized Rhys Fychan's castle of Dynevor and manned it in Meredith's name, while Rhys with his family was at Carreg Cennen. All that you did a year ago between those two is to do again, restoring and reconciling if you can.'

'Not all,' said Llewelyn grimly, 'and not as it was done before. Restore we will, but reconcile? For him to break his oath again as lightly? A pity!' he said. 'I had a great liking for the man.'

And that was not strange, for Meredith ap Rhys Gryg was a great, squat, powerful bear of a fellow, old enough to be the prince's father, a notable drinker, singer and fighter, very good company in hall and on the battlefield, except that it seemed he could change sides faster than most. 'And what of Carreg Cennen?' Llewelyn asked.

'Well held and well victualled, and safe as doomsday,' said Meurig. 'Rhys and his wife and children have nothing to fear inside it.'

This Rhys Fychan of Dynevor was husband to the prince's only sister, the Lady Gladys, a match made by their mother when she and all her children, with the exception of Llewelyn himself, were in the protection (or custody, for so it was, however sweetened) of King Henry of England. A hard struggle Rhys Fychan had had of it to get command of his own inheritance against his ambitious uncle, Meredith, who had kept him out of lands and castles as long as he could. No wonder, then, that when, under the king's protection, Rhys got possession of his own at last, he turned on his uncle and drove him into exile in Gwynedd. Thus those two had

8

taken turns to harry each other, according as the fortunes of the time ran, and it was but chance that when Llewelyn made his bid for the freedom of Wales it should be Meredith ap Rhys Gryg who rode by his side, and Rhys Fychan, the ally of England, against whom he was forced to fight.

In the past summer we had seen the climax of that struggle, for Rhys Fychan had sickened of his subservience to England, and come over at his testing time to the side of Wales. And Llewelyn had been the first to vindicate, accept and welcome him into the alliance, making peace between those two enemies. In that southern part of Wales were many such instances of bad blood between kinsmen, and fratricide and worse were not unknown, chiefly because of the old customary law that all land was divisible, and where there were many sons their portions must be equal, and therefore equally meagre.

In Gwynedd we had some measure of reform from this debilitating system, and out of no princedom but Gwynedd could a prince of Wales have emerged.

'This example,' warned Meurig, 'if it continues unpunished, may sway certain other feeble trees. They say there are some who bend.'

'The wind may blow them to bend the other way before long,' said Llewelyn. And he said to Goronwy, who waited to know his will: 'Send out the writs for two days hence, and have the captains muster in one hour. I stay here. Meurig has yet more to say.'

'There is more,' said Meurig, when Goronwy had gone about his errand. 'This I heard in Shrewsbury, where I ventured without safe-conduct, the garrison wanting horses. There was a royal official lodged at the abbey, on his way between London and Chester, and he had Welsh servants in his train. One was a clerk, in good odour with his master and with other functionaries about Westminster. I was lucky to meet with him. By his tale, my lord, King Henry has been wooing your traitor

Meredith ever since last year, when Rhys Fychan repented his servility and turned to Wales. The uncle was a handy way of striking at the nephew. That very month he offered him seisin of all his own lands and all his nephew's for his fealty and homage, and two commotes belonging to his neighbour Meredith ap Owen into the bargain. So easy it is to give away what you have not, if you are a king, my lord!'

'This is sooth?' said Llewelyn. 'Your Welsh clerk has seen this deed?'

'Not that, but he has spoken with one who has. The man he quotes is in the king's own chancellery, and the assault on Dynevor bears him out. Moreover, there is another detail. I believe you will recognise the note! Meredith has held out for safeguards on his own terms. King Henry promises that he will not take into his grace and peace either Rhys Fychan or Meredith ap Owen of Uwch Aeron, without first consulting his new vassal. And for you, my lord – he promises further that he will never receive *you* into that same grace and peace, without the courtesy of getting Meredith's leave first! The traitor fears both you and his kinsmen, he will have the whole protection of the royal writ against you.'

'He has good need to fear me,' said Llewelyn grimly, 'and if he thinks the king's forces along the Towy can stand against mine he has yet something to learn. And you say King Henry has been trailing this lure before him ever since last autumn?'

'The document of grace, remitting all Meredith's past transgressions against either the king or the Lord Edward, is dated the eighteenth of October, and letter patent, at that. And the charter granting him the commotes of Mabwnion and Gwinionydd, in the teeth of their proper lord, bears the same date.'

'He has the devil's own impudence,' said David, with a shout of angry laughter, 'give him that! He has known all these months what he meant to do, and he came to the assembly with the rest and took his oath like a man, and no doubt swallowed it down without gagging. I could almost admire the man his brazen face!'

'He lives in the past,' Llewelyn said, for Meredith was indeed of an older generation, and came of a stormy line. 'Give him the grace of the doubt, he may not have made up his mind when he came to the assembly. Oaths to him are meant at the moment of swearing, but the heat of a quarrel or the smart of being slighted are sanction enough for breaking them a day later. If the offence had been only against me I might have let it pass, but he betrays what he cannot grasp, the common cause of Wales. For that he shall pay. And for the gross offence against my sister's husband, who has kept the peace with him loyally.'

'We march, then?' said David, his face bright at the offer of action, and his eyes alert and glad, for when we took the field, and he had all the fighting his heart craved, that restless energy that festered into mischief when he was curbed had a channel for its flood-tide, and ran violent and clean, sweeping all before it, and he fought and laboured, and gave and took wounds, and went hungry and weary, all with a child's zealous innocence.

Llewelyn looked not at him, but at Meurig, and asked: 'How long have we?'

'King Henry sent out his writs on the fourteenth day of March. The host musters on the seventeenth of June at Chester. "To go against Llewelyn!"'

This we had expected. The brief truce the king had made to tide him over the winter, when campaigning in Wales was too hard and costly, was drawing to its close, and certainly his constant intent against us had not changed. It was a matter of course that he should again attempt a summer war.

'Six weeks is all we need,' said Llewelyn, 'to teach Meredith the meaning of treason. We'll call the fullest muster we may in two days, and go south and make it plain to him that he has no right in Dynevor, that his neighbour's lands are not in King Henry's gift, and that from henceforth any who break their oath to Wales and betray the common cause will pay a heavy price for their treachery.'

'Do we take engines?' asked David, glowing.

'Not this time, we cannot move them fast enough. We must do as much as we may, and be back in time to meet the king's muster. For Dynevor we may hope, but even Dynevor may have to wait a better opportunity if he has it garrisoned too strongly. No, we can do more and more profitable hurt to Meredith by harrying his lands and lopping him of all we can. We'll send to Meredith ap Owen, too, and bring him into the field. He has a score of his own to settle, for those two commotes of his. And now let the captains come in,' he said to Goronwy, 'and, Meurig, we'll talk further when you are rested and fed.'

So we went every man about his particular business in preparation for that campaign, the first stroke of Llewelyn's power as overlord. With the spring so fair, and the land fresh and drying after the passing of the last snow and the early April rains, going would be easy, and at all times we could move so quickly, and needed to carry so little provision with us, that we could pass from north to south and back again, and appear in many places where no man looked for us, all within the space of two or three weeks.

Afterwards, when the council was over, Llewelyn had another hour's talk with Meurig, for he would know more of what the Welsh clerk from Westminster had to tell about affairs at court. For many weeks seething rumours had been reaching us of a growing dissension between King Henry and his magnates.

'It is true enough,' said Meurig, 'the king has troubles at home, and they are growing fast. As I heard it, some of the greatest earls of the land, and some high church-

12

men, too, have been driven to despair by the chaos the king has made in his rule, bankrupt of money, beset with all the brood of his Poitevin half-brothers, and in particular burdened with this bad bargain he has made with the pope. With the last pope, true, but this one pursues it just as inflexibly.'

I was brought up in the old Celtic tradition of the saints, and I confess the distant actions and arbitrary decrees of popes were always alien to me. Popes drive hard bargains. Of this trouble that plagued King Henry, and yet promised him so much, I knew by rote, yet the image of Pope Alexander, who held out the bait and the trap, remained to me as a strange heraldic beast on a blazon, no kin to my Welsh flesh. The papacy, for reasons but half-known to me, had long hated and desired to be rid of the imperial house of Hohenstaufen, and spent years beating the bushes for a champion to overthrow them and dispossess them of the kingdom of Sicily. And King Henry, when the prize was dangled before him for his younger son, Edmund, could not resist the lure. He had taken the oath, and under pain of excommunication he was pledged to bear the whole vast burden of the debt past popes and present had incurred in this contention, and to carry their banner to victory.

'The king's magnates detest and regret the business of Sicily,' Meurig said, 'but most reluctantly they feel that for his honour, and England's, and their own, they have no choice but to help him out of the pit he has digged for himself. They'll grant him aids, since needs must, to try to win this throne for his boy, and fulfil his obligations under oath, but they want something from him in return, the better ordering of the country's affairs, or why pour their efforts into the void?'

'And what of his parleys with France?' Llewelyn pressed him keenly. 'Whether the pope abates his terms or no, the king cannot get far in this enterprise without making his peace with King Louis.'

'He still desires it, and it becomes ever more urgent. But that, too, may be a long tussle unless fate cuts the knots. At his last council the king had to tell his lords that the pope has refused any change in his demands; the agreement must stand, in full. That means there's interdict hanging over the land and excommunication over the king unless he stirs himself. But desperate ills make desperate remedies, and it may be a dozen earls and barons of England can change the pontiff's mind, if the king cannot. There's no sense in even emperor or pope demanding the impossible.'

'Or prince of Wales, either,' said Llewelyn, and smiled. 'So it stands, then. Not yet resolved on methods or means?'

'So it stood. Like a hanging rock lodged on a mountain-side. By now it may be in motion,' said Meurig, blinking his shrewd old eyes. 'Once launched, who can guess where that fall will come to rest?'

'Not in Wales,' said Llewelyn, slowly considering, and increasingly sure of what he said. 'Can he fight that battle, and ours as well? He may get his muster into arms and harness, but can he get them to Chester and into Wales? Not this year!'

'It is not impossible, though I would not say it is *likely*. But when a mountain slides,' said Meurig, twining a finger in his silver beard, 'I have known men felled who thought they walked out of range. And I have known nuggets of gold to be picked up by fortunate souls who kept their wits about them.'

'You say well,' said Llewelyn, and laughed. 'Pray God I keep mine!'

There was then no clarity in our expectations from that landslip that quivered above England. We rode from Aber, in rapid but orderly muster, two days after this visit, still ignorant that the first move had been made in the avalanche. For after the council at Westminster, seven great lords met and conferred, on the Friday after the fortnight after Easter, that is, the twelfth day of April of that year twelve hundred and fifty-eight, and compounded among them a sworn confederacy, every member taking a solemn oath to give aid and support to all the others in the cause of justice and right and good government, saving the troth they owed to king and crown. And then these seven, doubtless, sat down together to define what they desired for England, as we dreamed and argued and fought for what we desired for Wales. And, having defined it, they set out, even as we, to encompass it. For on the last day of April, while we rode south to the avenging of Meredith's treason, those seven led a band of earls, barons and knights, all armed, to confer with King Henry in the palace of Westminster. And disarming at the door, in token of their plighted loyalty, they went in to him and with all reverence but with great firmness set before him the body of their complaints and the sum of their remedies. To take or to leave. And the king, half-reluctantly and half-thankfully, and Prince Edward, his heir, with deeper suspicion and affront, perforce took them.

It was not known to us then who those seven were who set the mountain moving. But soon we knew them, and here I set them down, for fear they should some day be forgotten.

There were among them three earls:

Richard de Clare, earl of Gloucester,

Roger Bigod, earl of Norfolk and earl marshal,

Simon de Montfort, earl of Leicester.

Also to the fore, for he was a man of clear and individual mind, was Peter, Count of Savoy, uncle to Queen Eleanor of Provence, and counsellor to King Henry. And the remaining three:

Hugh Bigod, brother to the earl marshal,

John FitzGeoffrey, of whom I recall little but the name, for he died later the same year,

15

Peter de Montfort, lord of Beaudesert, no close kin to the earl of Leicester, but head of the English family of that name – for Earl Simon was French, and inherited through his English grandmother, the male line being exhausted.

These seven, hardly knowing themselves what they set in motion, were the beginners of that great ado between crown and baronage that shook the kingdom to the heart for many years, and drew my lord into its whirlpools, to his blessing and his bane.

But as for us, we were about our proper business in the vale of Towy, exacting from Meredith ap Rhys Gryg the full price of treason.

We made south by fast marches, halting but twice on the way, the second time at the abbey of Cwm Hir, and so came over the bare, heathy hills skirting Builth, and struck into the upper valley of the Towy above Llandovery. At that town the castle was securely held for Rhys Fychan, there was no stirring of Meredith's men in those parts, and we were assured our coming was not yet expected. There, too, a body of archers and lancers came east under Meredith ap Owen of Uwch Aeron, the loyal one of our two Merediths, to join us in that enterprise. For though his two commotes were in no great danger, for all King Henry's impudent gift of them and Meredith ap Rhys Gryg's more insolent acceptance, yet the insult from both was sharp, and not to be borne without reprisals. This other Meredith was a quiet, steady, grave man some ten years older than my lord, slow to anger and cautious in council, but staunch to his word and resolute once roused, and Llewelyn set great store by his opinion.

From Llandovery we swept on down the river valley, and did no harm to any holding that was not the seisin of Meredith ap Rhys Gryg, but from what was his we drove off the cattle and burned the barns, and where

16

any holding was fortified we burned that, too, laying his lands open as we passed. All along that green, wide valley we spurred faster than our own report, until we came where the castle of Dynevor, that was Rhys Fychan's principal seat and the heart-castle of his royal line, loomed on its green mound among the flowering meadows, with the river coiling round its southern approaches. There we made a testing assault, but it was plain that the place was very strongly held, for the prestige of conquest no less than for its real worth, and so we made but one night halt there, deploying a small force of archers to occupy the hills around and plague the garrison, so that they would hardly dare venture out of the gates, to test the numbers of those who held them in siege. For this castle, strong though it was, was open to archery from the hills enclosing it, which were well wooded and gave excellent cover. Unlike Rhys Fychan's second castle, which by its very situation was almost impregnable, being built upon a great crag, with sheer cliffs on three sides, and only one ridge by which it could be approached. There in Carreg Cennen the Lady Gladys, with her three little sons and her household, was safely guarded. For which I gave thanks to God, for there was one among her women who drew me by the heart, and whom I dreaded to see as greatly as I longed for it, Cristin, Llywarch's daughter.

But at this time I was not to be put to the torment of looking upon her again, for we had no call to go to Carreg Cennen. Our business was with Meredith ap Rhys Gryg in his fortress of Dryslwyn, a few miles downstream along the Towy valley.

In the night we heard repeated calling of owls across the river, from the woods on the southern side, and knew that Rhys Fychan had brought his own muster from Carreg Cennen to join us. But we made no move as yet, nor did he, beyond sending out a runner who made his way to us safely in the darkness across the open water-

17

meadows below the castle. A little, gnarled, bow-legged knife-man he was, as dark and seasoned as a blackthorn bush, and wise in every track in his native region. We uncovered our turf-damped fire for him, for he had swum the river to come to us, and by night this glimmer would hardly be seen as far as Dynevor for the thick growth of trees between. He said that his lord had left Carreg Cennen well held and his lady in good heart with her children, and, if the lord prince approved, Rhys proposed to join his forces with ours not here, but well downstream, at the easy passage which the messenger would show us, so that the garrison in Dynevor might have no way of judging what numbers we had, or what part of them we had left to contain the defenders within their stolen fortress.

Llewelyn approved him heartily, but said that if Rhys Fychan knew the ford of which he spoke, and knew it passable at this time – for the river was past the highest spring flow, but still fresh and full – there was no need for us to leave cover, and we might await him in the forest. For until now we had run ahead of our legend, and trusted to strike at Dryslwyn before they knew we were anywhere near. The messenger grinned and shook his head.

'My lord, by our advice it's you must cross, not we. Well I know Dryslwyn castle is on this side of Towy, but Meredith ap Rhys Gryg is not in Dryslwyn. He has wind of you. His castellan here in Dynevor got a runner away to him before you closed the ring, and he's in Carmarthen by now, and if you want him it's to Carmarthen you must go. The force that took Dynevor for him is still in arms there, and the king's seneschal has brought a fresh muster in haste from Kidwelly to strengthen Meredith's hand. We had a man there watching when they rode into the town, not two hours before midnight.'

'Then they'll hardly have had time to order their

18

ranks,' said Llewelyn, 'and we had best move fast.' And he questioned the man closely what numbers the seneschal might have with him, for it seemed that King Henry felt obliged to give all possible aid to his first renegade client, as well he might if he wished to attract others.

'If Patrick of Chaworth is leading Meredith's allies in person, and in such force,' said Llewelyn, 'it behoves us to make as notable a demonstration of our own power, or there'll be more waverers. This bids fair to be the feudal host under another name.' For de Chaworth, lord of Kidwelly and king's representative over most of south Wales, did not commit his forces lightly in defence of even a well-disposed Welsh chieftain. Plainly he had his orders from the highest. Meredith ap Rhys Gryg was to stand or fall as a symbol of what King Henry could do for those who came to his peace.

'At what hour,' Llewelyn asked, 'should Rhys Fychan be ready for us beyond the ford?' For it was agreed that the cover was better on that side of Towy if we wished to drive straight at Carmarthen, and though the town lay on this hither side we did not wish to meddle with the town, where we might well be tangled in too long and confused a contest against so strong a garrison. If we could set up an untimely alarm and bring them out over the bridge to us before their order was perfected or their commands properly appointed, we could do them much damage at little cost.

'He is on the move now,' said the man, 'leaving archers to mark Dynevor from the woods. Unless we march within the hour he'll be waiting for us.'

'I suits well,' said Llewelyn. 'I never knew a town yet that liked a dawn alarm. With luck the folk may cause enough confusion to do half our work for us.'

So within the hour we marched, traversing the slopes of the hills among the trees until we were well clear of any eye or ear in Dynevor, and then moving steadily down into the meadows. It was still dark when we crossed the river, the guide going before in a darting, mayfly fashion, for the firm passage was complex, and flanked by deep pools. When he had shown the whole crossing and brought the prince safely over, he stood thigh-deep on a spit in midstream, and guided the rest across. This is a broad valley and green, and even in spring the flow is not dangerously fast. But still I remember the cold of it, and the way my pony quivered and shook her mane as she waded it.

From this on we pressed hard, to be upon them in Carmarthen before they were aware of us, and the meeting with Rhys Fychan's muster, in a clearing among the woods on the southern bank, was accomplished in near-silence and almost on the march. There was little time for greeting of friends or avoiding of enemies when those two war-bands joined. They moved forth from the darkness of the trees, we out of the shrub growth and alders along the river bank. Rhys rode forward and leaned to Llewelyn's kiss, and he was no more than a slender, bearded shape outlined by the gleam of his light mail hauberk in the late moonlight. There was barely four years between those two, Rhys being the elder, and though they had been friends but half a year they had a great understanding each for the other, and needed few minutes and few words to have their plans made. Then we rode, rushing upon Carmarthen as vehemently as we could, for there was already a faint pre-dawn light that made speed possible.

Yet on that ride, though Rhys's lancers were but shapes to me, being helmed and mailed, still I looked about me covertly in constraint and dread to find among them a certain fair and lofty head, and a comely, easy face ever ready for laughter. No friend to me, though he willed to be, and I had no just reason for resisting. And no enemy, either, for he wished me well, and I, if I could not do as much for him, at least prayed earnestly in my heart that I might keep from wishing him ill. For Rhys Fychan's knight, Godred ap Ivor, was my half-brother, though he was not aware of the blood tie as I was. He was lawful son to the father I had never known, and who had known my mother but one night of her life, the night that brought me into being.

God knows that was not to be held against him. Had he come to me otherwise, I might have welcomed a brother. But he had a wife, and his wife was my Cristin, whom I had found in innocence when he was thought dead, and in innocence loved, and in anguish resigned to him when he returned from the dead. God so decreed that it should be I who discovered and restored her her lord. In my life are many ironies, but none greater than that. And three kinds of brothers have I had, and he the only one bound to me by blood, and the only one alien in my heart and mind. For Llewelyn was my star brother, my twin born in the same night, and David was my breast-brother, my mother being his nurse from the day of his birth. And to both my love flowed freely, but to Godred it would not flow. He had but to come within my sight and it froze, and was stilled, proof even against the warmth of hand or breath. For Cristin's sake I could not love him.

In this country I was always aware of him, even as I was of her. On that night ride I looked sidelong at every man who drew abreast of me, and the hairs stood up on my neck like hackles as I peered after the features of faces half-glimpsed under the stars. But he was not there. That was not asked of me, that I should suffer his gladness at sight of me, and bear to ride beside him in the bitterness of fellowship. Surely he was left behind with the garrison in Carreg Cennen.

I gave thanks to God, too soon. And God visited me with another torment, I doubt not well-deserved, seeing how ill I used a harmless, well-intentioned man. It was but nine months since I had turned without a word in the bailey at Dolwyddelan, and left those two together. Just enough time for a child to be conceived and carried and brought into the world! And man and wife reunited after parting and sorrow commonly beget and conceive in the first joy of reunion.

With such piercing thoughts I tore my own heart, well knowing that with her it was not so. For there had been no joy. It was my ultimate grief that I had bestowed on her no blessing, but a curse. For the last glimpse of her face had told me clearly enough where Cristin's joy lay, and where her love was given.

It was ill thinking of these things for which there was no remedy, but I had not long for fretting, there being work to do very soon. For in the haste and turmoil of an alarm at earliest dawn, Meredith ap Rhys Gryg and Patrick of Chaworth brought their armies fumbling and hurtling out of the town of Carmarthen to fend us off, just as we massed and moulded our first charge to shatter them.

The light, everywhere but in the east, was still dove-grey and secret, the eastern sky was a half-circle of palest primrose, with a drop of molten gold at its centre. We came out of the gentle slopes of woodland and over the meadows, driving at the end of the bridge, and across the river from us lights flared and flickered in the town. We saw the half of de Chaworth's host spreading like spilled water from the narrow bottle of the bridge, and galloping wildly into station to hold us off, turgid with haste and confusion, but so many that the heart shrank, beholding them. We saw their numbers multiply, pressing across the bridge. We saw Meredith's banner, and found his thick, hunched body in its leather and fine mail, leaning forward into the thrust of his lance before he so much as spurred to meet us. We struck them while they were no more than half poised, and recoiled, and massed to strike again, before they were well set to stand us off.

That was no very orderly battle, but a violent assault and a rapid withdrawal several times repeated. For a brief while we stripped the bridge-head of its defences, but we had no will to cross, for their numbers, as well as I could estimate, were nearly double ours, and those are odds not acceptable for long to a wise captain. Nor did we want Carmarthen, no doubt rich and profitable to sack, but we had other business, and in this land, where we were welcome to live freely off the tenants, we had no need and no incentive to plunder the townspeople. Many of them might well be of our party, if they had the means to show it. We aimed rather at those persons we most needed to disarm and unman.

For my part, I did my best to keep always in that place I had made my own, at Llewelyn's left quarter, another shield covering his shield. I drove with him against Patrick of Chaworth, whom he singled out from all. And it seemed to me, as I kept station beside him, that he saw in Patrick an image of the king, who was England, and held status as the enemy of Wales. He could better tolerate Meredith, the seduced, than Henry the seducer. It was left for Rhys Fychan, who had the best right, to level his lance at his uncle, and in the shock of their meeting Meredith went dazed over his horse's tail, but his mounted men flowing round him covered him long enough to let him remount, and in the mêlée, which was tight and confused for a while, those two enemies were forced apart. So was I separated from my lord's side, for our two hosts had meshed like interlaced fingers and clung fast, and even at the command of the horn we had some ado to draw off and stand clear to strike again.

It was in this pass, while we heaved and strained with shortened swords and axes at close quarters, that I saw from the corner of my eye Rhys Fychan's livery ripped sidelong from the saddle and crashing to the ground among the stamping hooves, where there was scarcely room to fall. And, wheeling that way, I heard the felled man cry out, clear and shrill in terror even through the clamour that battered our ears, and saw his body, young and lissome, slide down between the heaving flanks, catching at stirrup and saddle and finding no hold. And I saw that the stroke that swept him from his horse had burst the thongs of his helm and torn it from his head, and the hair that spilled out over his face was fair as wheaten straw, or barley-silk in the harvest. So I saw again my half-brother Godred, and terrible it was to me that he should appear to me only at this extreme, for his every danger was my temptation. Once I might have slain him, and no one any the wiser, and I did not. But this time I had only to let him be, and he was a dead man, and my hands unreddened.

So the mind reasons, even in an instant briefer than the splintering of sunlight from a sword. But happily the body also has its ways of thinking, which are all action, too fleet for the mind to turn them back. So I found that I had tugged my pony's head round and urged her with heel and knee, and like the clever mountain mare she was, used to riding tightly with hounds, she straddled Godred and stood over him without trampling so much as one pale hair of his head, while I swung left and right about me to clear a little ground for him to rise, and having won a meagre, trampled space of turf I reached down a hand to him to pull him to his feet.

He rolled from under her belly, heaving at breath, and grasped my hand and clung, leaning heavily on my knee a moment before he lifted his head and knew me. The spark of recognition lit in his round brown eyes in two golden flames. There was time then for nothing more than that, for the mêlée had broken apart, and we made good haste out of the press, he clinging by my stirrup-leather and running beside me, for my pony could not carry the two of us. He was unhurt but for the bruises of his fall, and quick to borrow the first advantage, for when a riderless horse trotted by us close he loosed his hold, clapped me on the thigh by way of farewell, and caught at the trailing bridle. The beast shied from him, but not for long, for by the time I was back at Llewelyn's side and poised for a new assault I saw him come cantering and wheeling smartly into the line. Bareheaded he went into battle with us that time, and so contrived that he rode close to me, and from his place saluted me with raised hand and a flash of his wide eyes as we leaned into the charge.

In that bout we struck them from two sides, sharply but briefly, for there were new reserves still crowding over the bridge to their support. So we drove in vehemently wherever we saw a weak place, to do them what hurt we might while we might. Rhys Fychan sought out Meredith ap Rhys Gryg yet again, and that time I saw the sword cleave through his shoulder harness and into his flesh, and he was down again in the lush grass of the river bank, turning the bright blades red. When we obeyed the prince's signal and quit the field, we turned before dissolving into the cover of the woods, and watched Meredith taken up and carried away in his blood, over the bridge and into the town.

'Not dead nor near it,' said Llewelyn, lingering to see the last of him. 'The old bear will live to fight again many a day.' And I think he was glad. But for this long while Meredith's right arm would strike no blows in battle, and as I knew, having seen him in combat many times, he had but an awkward use of his left, like most men who have not strenuously practised the exercising of that member.

A few dead we left behind us there, but no prisoners, and, though we took some minor wounds away with us, none were grave. We reckoned it, in its measured fashion, a victory, as we rode back towards Dryslwyn from the bridge of Carmarthen. With de Chaworth's hands full, as they surely were, with the salvaging of wounded men and scattered horses, and the shattered order within the town, it was the best time to test out the defences of the castles along the Towy.

Well I knew that I could not escape company on that ride. From the moment we formed and marched, Godred took his captured mount out of the line, and watched our ranks pass until he found me, and then fell in at my side. His yellow head was bared to the early sun falling between the trees, and though his face was bruised, and bore a pattern of shallow scratches over the cheekbone, where the metal of his helm had scored him as it tore free, his youthfulness and brightness were no less than when last I had seen him, the greater part of a year ago. No, they were still more marked because of the lifting of the passing shadow of death. I had heard him cry out against it; I knew he had recognised it as it stooped upon him. I have heard a hare scream so before the hawk struck.

I do not know if he looked sidelong at my face and found in it something that made him approach warily, or whether it came naturally to him at all times to touch lightly and turn gravity to gaiety, even in matters of life and death. For he leaned down first from his taller mount and patted my mare's moist neck, fondling along her mane.

'I owe you as good a fill of oats as ever a pony ate,' he said to her twitching ear. 'Remind me to honour the debt when we halt at Dryslwyn.' And to me he said, no less lightly and agreeably, yet with a note of carefulness, as if he felt some constraint: 'And to you, Samson, I owe a life. When will it please you claim it back from me?'

I could not choose but think then how I had once been tempted to take it from him unlawfully, and how I had now but rendered him in requital what I owed to him, leaving him no debt to me. But I said only, I hope truthfully, that I was thankful indeed to see him none the worse.

'Faith,' said he, 'you come always to be my saving angel. I thought my last hour was come and, I tell you, a good clean lance-thrust would have been welcome, rather than be pounded to pulp among the hooves. Make as little as you will of it, you cannot make it less than a life to me, and I shall follow you round with my gratitude until I can repay you, though I promise to do it without overmuch noise or importunity. I know you have no appetite for being thanked,' he said, watching me along his wide shoulder with a gleaming smile, 'or you would not have ridden away from Dolwyddelan without a word, and left Cristin and me to hunt you in vain, last year when you brought us together again. That was a great grief to her.'

He had a gift for double-edged words. Surely if he had known of my grief he would not have probed my heart with hers. He spoke of things he believed he understood, though he knew no more than the surface. And that was his strength and my weakness, that he could prattle by my side of Cristin, and the time of her loss, and the bliss of her recovery, without one tremor of pain or uneasiness, while every shaft he loosed pierced me to the soul. All his honey, which he poured innocently and assiduously, was gall to me. And in my agitation of mind I began to suffer another disquiet, for now I could not be sure whether I had indeed wheeled my mare astride him on the ground to save or to trample him. Such doubts he never failed to arouse in me, because he sought and praised and affected me, and trusted in my returning his kindness, while to me he was hateful, and his presence a torment. That undoubted guilt tainted all my dealings with him, even those which were clean in intent.

He rode beside me all that day, as good as his word in pursuing me with attentions and thanks which were

27

more than I could bear. Even the work we had to do could not long shake him off from my neck. We circled Dryslwyn castle in cover, hoping the garrison would think us departed and send out some party we could pick off, perhaps with profitable prisoners. If King Henry could persuade Welshmen to his peace, so, perhaps, could Llewelyn recover the fealty of some thus handed over against their will. But the castellan continued very wary, and clearly had no lack of provisions within.

'We should have brought siege engines,' said David, scanning the towers and fretting for an opportunity lost. 'There would have been time.'

'With de Chaworth calling in reinforcements from as far as Pembroke by now?' said Llewelyn. 'Never think he'll hold still in Carmarthen for long. One week, and he'll be moving this way against us. And we have still work to do in Gwynedd before the seventeenth of June. No, let's use our time here on Dynevor, since it may well be short.'

So we marched on, and camped for the night about the uplands that overlooked Dynevor upon the north. Here we could not have used siege engines even had we brought them with us, for Rhys Fychan wanted his castle restored undamaged, if that were possible, and in particular did not wish to risk the life and limb of those of his men now prisoners within. So we gave free rule to the archers, and let them pick off any of Meredith's men who showed themselves too rashly about the walls, and any who ventured out, giving them no rest, and no chance to bring in further supplies for the garrison. By such means a castle may be taken, given time enough, but our time was running out. Whether the king's muster came to fruit or not, it behoved us to be ready to receive the shock.

In the second week of May our scouts sent back word from Carmarthen that reinforcements were moving in from the south in some strength, and it appeared that a massive attempt against us was being prepared. It was high time for us to turn homeward.

'A pity to go with the work half-done,' said David, chafing and burning. 'Leave me here with my own men, and Rhys and I between us will go on with this harrying. With Carreg Cennen to fall back on we can well avoid battle at the worst, and still do Chaworth and Meredith damage enough, and keep them from re-victualling Dynevor. If King Henry gets his muster into motion, you have only to send for me, and I'll be in Gwynedd before him.'

Which was true enough, for the royal army could move but slowly among our forests and mountains, while every hidden path was at our disposal.

'I grieve,' said Llewelyn, frowning upon the distant towers of Dynevor, with Dynevor's lord at his shoulder, 'to leave your castle still in other hands. I promise you it shall not be so long.'

Rhys Fychan, who had sworn fealty to him less than a year ago, pledging it as the last fealty of his life, and never went from it again, made no complaint, but reassured him.

'Lend me David, and between us we will take and hold more land than Dynevor could buy. For the walls and towers I can wait,' he said.

So David remained, making his headquarters with Rhys Fychan at Carreg Cennen, and entered gleefully on a campaign of pinpricks against the king's seneschal, while Meredith ap Owen, true man namesake to our traitor, retired to his own country along the Aeron, and we turned back into Gwynedd to receive whatever manner of blow King Henry might launch against us. As for Meredith ap Rhys Gryg, according to the reports we had he was nursing his wound in Carmarthen still, and was not likely to stir from there for many weeks, so we had no hope of getting him into our hands at this time, and he small hope of meddling with us.

I was not sorry to be turning my back upon that region where I knew my love so near and yet by the width of the world out of my reach. This time of year, with the ripening spring so sparkling and fair, brought me the sharpest reminders of her. Once I saw her coming down the fields at Bala at the Easter feast, with a new-born lamb in her arms. Well for me that I should go back to labour and possible danger, for there was no other remedy to medicine me from my longing after Cristin, excepting only my devotion to Llewelyn.

We made our last night camp in the woods, intending to march before dawn. Rhys Fychan had already withdrawn his foot soldiers on the way to Carreg Cennen, and all that day I had not seen Godred, until towards midnight I sat wakeful by the last fading ashes of our fire, and he came silently through the trees, stepping lightly as a wildcat. I saw the faint glow from the live embers catch the glitter of his eyes, which were always wide and candid to all appearances, like a child's. He smiled on me with his warm, ingratiating smile, that was like a tentative hand laid affectionately on my arm.

'Did you think,' he said in a whisper, for there were sleepers all round us, 'that I would let you go away without a word of farewell?' And he sat down beside me in the grass, and told me the events of his day, how duty had kept him from me until now, as though I had a right to all his company and devotion, and he a need to excuse himself. He said it was a grief to him that the time had not been right for Llewelyn with all his force to visit Carreg Cennen, so that Cristin might have had the joy of seeing me again, and adding her gratitude to his. For they owed me, he said, so much, more now than she yet knew, and her thanks would have had a grace he could not match, and given me a pleasure it was not in his power to give.

So he chattered softly into my ear, and I was chilled and fretted by his nearness so that at first I hardly noted his words, or looked deeper than their surface meaning. Then it was as if a curtain had been drawn from between my understanding and his matter, and I heard clearly the light, insinuating urging of his voice, very cheerful and winning, as though he held out to me certain delights by the gift of which he hoped to win my somewhat morose and difficult favour. And what he was holding out to me, with discreet invitation, was Cristin.

Shallow and easy I had known him from the first, able to live as well without his wife as with her, able to make do with other company wherever it offered, and to make himself comfortable under any roof and at any table. But that he should value her so little as to parade her before me like a pander, and think it an earnest of the great value he set on me into the bargain, this turned my blood so curdled and bitter that I could not abide to sit beside him. And in this same moment I realised at last that to this man, pleasant, well-intentioned, born with only a thistle-down mind and a vagrant heart, I was bound by more, much more, than the blood in our veins. I had plucked him back from death, and I was committed to him, the body of my act for ever hung about my neck. He might escape me, as the receiver of benefits may forget lightly, but I should never escape him, for the giver can never draw back his hand from the gift.

He saw me shiver, or felt it, perhaps, for our gleam of hot ashes was almost dead. He leaned confidently close against my side.

'It grows cold,' he said quickly. 'I am keeping you from your sleep, and tomorrow you march.'

I said yes, that it was time I slept, glad at least of this help he offered me, for the one good gift he had to give was his absence. And I rolled myself in my cloak, to hasten his going. He rose and made his farewells in a whisper, wishing me good fortune and a smooth journey home. And even then he seemed reluctant to go without

31

some last insinuating proffer of goodwill, for as he withdrew into the darkness of the trees he turned to look back at me. I saw the pale rondel of his face, and seemed to see again the winning, intimate smile.

'Can I carry any fair message for you,' he said softly, 'to my wife?'

CHAPTER II

In the last days of May, when we had been home barely a week and were busy about our preparations to meet the king's muster, a young man with one attendant came riding into the llys at Aber, and asked audience of the prince. Very young he was, barely twenty years, shaven clean and with his thick brown hair cut short in the old Norman fashion. There was a Norman look about him altogether, for he had the strong, prominent bones of cheek and chin, and the sturdy build, and the wide way of planting his feet, as though no wind that ever blew could overset the rock that he was. And yet it was the face of a clever and venturous child, and he looked upon Llewelyn, when Tudor brought him into the high chamber, with great eyes of David's own blue, but unveiled, lacking that soft, deceptive haze that shielded David's thoughts at all times.

He spoke, this young man, in declaring his errand, with a largeness, and as it were piety, in his cause which said much for those who had sent him, and the purposes that drove him, and he had a kind of purity very apt to those purposes, possessing it in some natural way, as swans possess whiteness, even among the mire of ponds.

'My lord,' he said, when Llewelyn had greeted and made him welcome, 'I bring you letters from King Henry of England and his council of the reform, and am to take back your reply when you have considered the matter put forward. And I am commanded by king and council to answer whatever questions you may put to me concerning this embassage, so far as is in my power. And that you may know my credentials, my lord, I am the eldest son of the earl of Leicester, and my name is Henry de Montfort.'

So for the first time we looked upon one of that family whose name was to sound so loud, glorious and lamentable a fanfare in the fortunes of England and Wales. But the boy, having delivered the official part of his message, suddenly softened and smiled, abating the severity of his stance like one stepping from a dais or a throne. And a little he blushed, submitting to his own diminished humanity.

Llewelyn looked upon him with some pleasure and much curiosity, for this was not the ambassador he would have expected from King Henry, nor, indeed, had we looked for any communication from him at this time but the ominous news of the first contingents reporting at Chester. He accepted the scroll, thanked the messenger for his errand, and promised him due consideration and an early reply to take back with him. Then he commended him to the chamberlain, to see him well lodged and his man and horses cared for, and desired his company in hall at supper and the pleasure of a long talk with him afterwards. When the door had closed behind him, and only Goronwy and Tudor and I were left in the room with Llewelyn, he broke the seal and unrolled King Henry's letter, and all we watched him read.

When he had done, he let the opened scroll lie spread on his knees for a long moment, while he pondered it still, and then he looked up at us, and smiled.

'Will you hear what King Henry writes to us? The seal is the king's, the style is the king's but the voice speaking has another sound. He writes that he has called a parliament at Oxford on the eleventh day of June, and that he invites me to attend there, or to send proctors in my place with full powers, to discuss the making of a new truce between England and Wales.' He laughed

34

for pleasure at the startled and calculating joy in our faces. 'Meurig was a good prophet, and the rocks have fallen, not upon us. We may put away our plans; there'll be no need to pit the fords or break the bridges this year, and nothing to interfere with the harvest or the stock. England wants truce. Now tell me, does that sound like King Henry speaking?'

'Not to my ears!' said Goronwy. 'There has been some mighty persuasion used upon him, to bring about this change of tone. You might well question the messenger, my lord. It seemed to me he was instructed to be open with you.'

'If that was his meaning,' said Llewelyn, 'we'll get what understanding of it we can. But make use of it we surely will, whether or no. We are offered a truce, we'll take it. More, we'll carry it to the issue of a full peace if we can, and not grudge paying for it, if King Henry wants for funds for his Sicilian venture.'

'You will not go yourself, my lord?' said Tudor doubtfully.

'We'll let the council speak as to that. But I think not. Not at the first summons, as though we had done the suing, or were in haste to get rid of the threat of this June muster. No, we'll choose grave and reverend proctors and do credit to this parliament. Surely one of the most auspicious of King Henry's reign,' said Llewelyn, marvelling, 'at least for us, if not for him.'

So in great elation, though still cautiously, we went about the business of calling the council and preparing letters of accreditation. And at supper in hall young de Montfort sat at the prince's right hand and was pledged from the prince's cup, and his bearing continued open, friendly and serious, though his eyes grew rounder with wonder as he looked about him, and listened to the unfamiliar music of the Welsh tongue, and the singing of the bards. Doubtless that was the first time that he had ever stepped into our country. Now and again, confused by the strangeness of an alien language, he stumbled from English into French, for he spoke both freely. His mother was King Henry's sister, and most of his young life had been spent in England, though his father the earl still had lands in France also.

Afterwards Llewelyn took the boy with him into his own chamber, and kept only me in the room with them, for he wished to talk without formality, and make his own judgment, as yet uncomplicated by any other advice. And that I could be a silent witness he knew, and so had used me many times.

'You know,' he said, 'the content of the letter you brought?'

De Montfort said: 'Yes, my lord, I do know.' And he watched his host's face with his candid eyes and said: 'I hope you will accept the offer made. And I am to tell you that as soon as you have made your mind known, his Grace's council will issue letters of safe-conduct for you or your proctors to come to Oxford, and provide you an escort from the border.'

'His Grace's council are very considerate,' said Llewelyn with mild irony. 'And very anxious to have me quieted and still, at some cost, it seems.'

'I think,' said the boy steadily, 'it suits us both to have truce.'

'I don't deny it,' the prince said. 'Yet it did not suit King Henry last year, upon much the same terms. We do know something of the troubles under which he labours. Now tell me, and I shall trust your account, how do things stand between king, magnates and people at this coming parliament? It is not in my interest to add to England's difficulties, and I covet nothing beyond my own borders. The better I understand, the more likely are we to come to a mutual understanding. What has befallen since the great council of April, to bring about this realisation that war between us is more than either of us can well afford?'

And Henry de Montfort answered him, with confidence and address. How the seven magnates, of whom his father was one, had drawn up and presented to the king their aims and ideas for the reform of the state, with the promise that if he would accept their guidance on these matters, then they would stand by him to the best of their power in the matter of the Sicilian adventure, would raise an aid to help him, and send envoys to persuade the pope to abate the severity of his demands, and withdraw the threat of excommunication if they were not met. And the king and his son, the Lord Edward, and even the Poitevin nobles had agreed to what was rather an offer and appeal than a demand. Twelve councillors chosen from the king's adherents and twelve by the magnates formed the new reform council, which was to meet for the first time in full session at Oxford.

'And what has been done thus far?' Llewelyn asked.

'First, a group of envoys, my father among them, is now accredited to King Louis' court, to negotiate peace between England and France. They make good progress, my lord. Then letters have also been issued for proctors to go to Rome. Besides pleading for an abatement of the heavy terms under which his Grace labours in the Sicilian agreement, they will also ask for a papal legate to come to England, to help and guide us in all the adjustments that have to be made. And thirdly, as my errand proves, we desire a relationship of tolerance, at least, with you, my lord. The greater enterprise is England itself,' said this youth of twenty with noble solemnity. 'It is a duty to extricate the country's honour and the king's from this unhappy affair of Sicily, but also to amend the many things that are wrong in the realm, where we lack a fit system for hearing the pleas of the lesser people, and labour without a justiciar, and with sheriffs irregularly appointed and not easily displaced. I see no reason,' he said, 'to conceal that your forbearance on our borders is necessary to us, if we are to have time to create a just order in England, and a right relationship in Christendom.'

'You speak,' said Llewelyn, a little laughing at him, and a great deal admiring, 'with the tongue of prophecy. Whose is the voice? Your father's? For we have heard, even in Wales, something of the earl of Leicester.'

'The voice is my own,' said the young man, with a fleeting and impish smile. 'My father's is less voluble. But louder!'

'Yet of all voices,' said Llewelyn, 'I think it is not King Henry's.'

The boy leaned to him earnestly, and jutted his rugged Norman chin at him half in offence and half in amiable resolution to convince him, as past question he was himself convinced. He might have practised reserve and recoil very fastidiously, but deceit was not his gift. 'You mistake, my lord,' he said, 'we are all of one mind. King Henry has accepted with relief and gratitude the goodwill and help extended to him. Well I know there have been dissensions enough, but they are put away. One of the greatest of our French noblemen, Peter of Savoy, the queen's uncle, is among the movers of the reform. The magnates, the bishops, are earnest for it. The king, who is always good though not always wise, admits his need of it and embraces it. His Poitevin half-brothers accept it. Oh, my lord, you who have been praised – yes, even in England! – for uniting all the warring clans of Wales, you of all men should be moved by the singular unity of England at this pass. Two unities can rest side by side, to the enrichment of both.'

'If it lies with me,' said Llewelyn, touched and amused, 'they shall.' And he made much of the young man, and talked with him freely of lighter and more personal things until he dismissed him, already yawning, to his lodging. Among other things I remember Henry talked affectionately of his family, of his four younger brothers and his little sister, then five years old, on whom he doted, she being the only girl and the youngest child. Very close and loyal were these de Montforts, thus poised between England and France, and choosing England. No more deliberate choice ever was made, though I think it was made by divination of blood and bowels, and not by conscious will.

After the young man had left us, Llewelyn looked after him for a long moment, thoughtfully frowning, before he asked of me: 'Well, what do you make of him?'

'He is patently honest,' I said, 'and someone has certainly shown him a vision.'

'That I believe,' he agreed. 'But are you telling me King Henry, at his time of life, has taken to seeing such visions, too?'

I owned that was unlikely, but argued, none the less, that what the boy said might well be true, in that the king had known himself in difficulties from which he saw no escape, and might indeed be profoundly glad and grateful if his barons had banded together to attempt his rescue. Without their stern purpose or this boy's fervent exaltation, after his own fashion he might be equally sincere in his adherence to this new-found unity. But whether we should fear it or hope for it was more than I could yet determine. Their mind to us at this moment, it seemed, was clear enough, and we would do well to take what advantage we could of it, while we could.

'So I think, too,' said Llewelyn. 'Though we have seen already how long the unity of Wales remained immaculate, and can England do better, with so many warring interests? A pity if this boy's faith were shattered too soon! I tell you, Samson, I wish it were politic to go myself to Oxford. I should like to see this new council at work with my own eyes, and see what manner of men I have to deal with, if they can mould and master the king's actions as it seems they have done. And I should dearly like,' he said, 'to see the oak that dropped the acorn from which that sapling grew.'

On the day following, the council of Wales met and formally approved acceptance of the invitation to Oxford, and Llewelyn issued his letters of procuration for the parliament, appointing Anian, abbot of Aberconway, and Master Madoc ap Philip, his most trusted lawyer, to attend as his proctors, with full powers to negotiate peace or truce. And Henry de Montfort departed, I think very well pleased with his visit and much interested in all that he had seen at Aber, with the reply to king and council in England. He took leave of Llewelyn with due ceremony, mindful of the dignity of his office, but also with a fresh warmth that was pleasing to see.

I had thought no more of the prince's regrets that he could not be his own envoy and go to observe the procedures of these reforming earls for himself, but after the messenger was gone he came to me with a bright and resolute face.

'Will you go with Madoc and the abbot,' he said, 'as clerk and copier? I shall have as good an account in its way, perhaps, from the two of them, but they will be preoccupied with law and arguments and bargaining, and in any case it will be impossible for a Welsh student or groom to approach them while they are about the court. But while all eyes are on them, you can move among the humbler sort and use your eyes and ears, and you, I know, will be quick to think and feel as I, and settle on the details I should best like to know. Will you do this for me?'

I said I would, and gladly, if I was indeed the best instrument to his purpose.

'You are,' he said. 'You know my mind as you know your own, and your judgment of men I will trust to measure very close to mine. And, see, I have sent word

40

to Meurig in Hereford, concerning that Welsh chancery clerk of his acquaintance, and told him you will be in attendance on my proctors. Besides what you can observe for yourself, he will find some means of coming to you with all he knows of what goes on among the king's officials. If they will abide by this concern with procuring good orders at home, then I will keep any truce I make, and pay any indemnity I promise, and take care of my own household. But I greatly need to know.'

So I promised, though with some misgiving, for I had not been in England for twelve years, and had not thought ever to return there. And the memories I had of that time, long overlaid with the business of living here in Wales, were disturbing when they moved in me again, full of reminders of my dead mother and her most unhappy husband, and the imprisonment and death of my lord's father. Old tales, but not so far removed into the past as to be kindly hearing and easy tears. But I fretted vainly, for I was going where I had never been, and into a changed and seething land, frantic with new ideas and hopes, like a pot boiling, and in the event there was nothing to tug me back into the past, and everything to urge me forward towards the future.

On the second day of June the letters of safe-conduct were issued to us from the king's court and some days later were received at Aber. And then we set out, the two proctors with their body-servants, and I as a clerk to them, and crossed into England at Oswestry on the day following. And there we were met by a very gallant company as escort, more nobly led than I had expected, for we were to be accompanied to Oxford by one of those very seven lords who had begun this new enterprise of England.

This name came ever new, like a charm, the name of de Montfort. For our sponsor and escort was none other than Peter de Montfort who was head of the English house, the lord of Beaudesert near Warwick. No close kin to the young man Henry, and of an older generation, I suppose well into his fifties, but almost a neighbour, his Beaudesert being none so far from Earl Simon's Kenilworth, and certainly a loyal adherent and true friend, as after he proved. Thus in all that followed I could not keep from thinking of him as one of that same splendid and fatal family, and so I think of him still.

He was a tall man, of commanding figure but unobtrusive presence, his gestures spare and few, and his voice quiet. His colouring was florid, and his hair and clipped beard a rich russet red, as yet only touched with threads of grey, and he had very grave and considerate eyes which spared, rather than avoided, observing us too closely on that ride together, as also he said no word of the business on which we rode. His courtesy, though doubtless habitual with him, nevertheless underlined for me yet again the importance they set upon this agreement, and I grew ever more certain that our proctors would be able to secure truce at least, if not peace, for a merely nominal sum.

Very pleasant it was, in that warm June weather, riding through the western parts of England, where the gently folded land was softer, the rivers bluer and the watermeadows greener than in our harsh and rocky homeland. Again we rode through Shrewsbury from the Welsh gate to the English bridge, and passed by that great abbey where first I set eyes upon England's king. But after that I was upon unknown ground, as we followed the Severn southwards to Worcester.

Riding behind my masters thus, and having before me the baron of Beaudesert's long, erect back, and his russet head courteously inclined now to his guest upon one side, now on the other, I saw him as greater even that he was, for both our proctors were meagre men to view thus from behind. Face to face was another matter, and I think de Montfort was in no delusion concerning the tough quality of those two with whom his fellows would have to deal.

Abbot Anian was an ascetic of the old, heroic kind, worn to spirit and bone but very durable, and where Llewelyn's interests were at issue, his grey and gentle face was but a weathered scabbard for a steely and resolute mind. For Llewelyn was sometimes at odds with his bishops, whose first loyalty was to the church, and who were in any case more worldly, quarrelsome and litigious men, insistent on rights and privileges which often clashed with those of the prince's under Welsh law, as well as quick to shake the threat of religious sanctions at any who crossed them even on very trivial secular matters. But with all the orders, whether the great Cistercian houses or the older blessed foundations of the clas and college, and the solitary hermitages of those withdrawn from the world, he was always on terms of love, trust and deep respect, like his grandsire before him. To the bishops the vision of a united Wales was in some degree offensive, even heretical, since they drew their authority from outside Wales. But those who were rooted in the land and had chosen the place of their ministry once for all, whether born Welsh or no, had no such severance within them, and were at one with us.

And for our other proctor, Master Madoc ap Philip, he was elderly and a little crabbed with learning, but equally devoted to Llewelyn's cause, and very well able to chop legal arguments in any court, whether by Welsh, English or marcher law. Out of court he tended to be taciturn, and it surprised me to see him warm almost into loquacity with de Montfort, perhaps because that considerate man never touched upon law, but left it to the lawyers, and instead pointed out along the way whatever was notable, like the noble towers of Worcester cathedral soaring above the waters of Severn, placid and sunny now in their summer flow, or the great Benedictine abbey at Evesham, making a halt purposely for us to see this latter, since we did not intend a stay overnight. And both these I remember now by reason of what befell afterwards, and marvel that I did not then feel my heart either soar or sink in contemplating them, beyond what was due in admiration or pleasure.

Thus briskly but without haste we came to Woodstock, where once Llewelyn had attended King Henry's court and done homage to him for a shrunken princedom, since gloriously restored to its old bounds. Thence in the early evening of a fine day we reached Oxford.

The king's hall lay outside the north gate of the city, a very spacious and noble dwelling, well fitted for large assemblies. But we were accommodated at the Dominican priory, among the backwaters of the Thames. And a very busy and teeming city I found it, this Oxford, crowded as it was with all the king's chief tenants and their knights, for they had come in force and in arms, as though King Henry's intent of moving against Wales still held good. Yet it seemed rather to me, when I had walked among the people in the streets and the retainers in the stables and halls, that every lord came ready in harness and brought his muster with him for fear of needing them in defence of his own head. I would not say they truly felt fear. But they did not intend to be taken by surprise.

Castle, friaries and halls were all filled, and one or two of the schools had sent their scholars and masters home, partly in expectation of an air too disturbed for fruitful study while the parliament lasted, partly to make room for those flooding in. But the streets were still full of the schoolmen, of whom, as I was told, there must have been at this time some thirteen to fifteen hundred enrolled there. It was told to me also, though I cannot vouch for its truth, that the king's hall was built outside the gate because St Frideswide, whose tomb in her great church was a place of pilgrimage and still is so, had no wish to be visited by kings, and it was bad fortune for any crowned monarch either to enter her town or approach her grave. Yet in spite of this prohibition I believe King Henry had done so, with proper reverence, and come away none the worse for it.

Peter de Montfort made himself responsible for presenting the Welsh proctors to the king on the third day after our arrival, when all the council and parliament were fully assembled. Then for a few days I was required, for the proper justification of my presence if for no other good reason, to attend the meetings held with the English representatives, at first with King Henry himself present, though that was but a royal gesture, perhaps not even his own, but prompted by his advisers. These meetings were held in a chamber in his great lodging outside the gate, and there I saw, at one time or another, many of those fabled figures who had been until now merely names to me.

King Henry at this time was fifty years old, his face unlined, his features fair, his person very elegant and well tended. He had that willowy youthfulness of pliable people, that kept him somehow from breaking even in tempests, while stronger trees crashed to ground. His image had long faded in my mind, yet when I saw him again it arose fresh as of old, and scarcely changed. He had a certain strangely appealing honesty even in his side-steppings, that disarmed his opponents and expunged his offences. I could well understand that those lords of his old enough to have witnessed his coming to the throne, a child of nine, pretty and trusting, might still feel the old emotion, and the same helpless need to take responsibility for him, and help him out of all the pits he dug for himself by his simple cunning and cunning simplicity. And in spite of all that followed, I do believe that was how this enterprise began, that ended in civil war and tragedy. But not for Henry. In all tempests the willow is a born survivor, and springs erect after the wind has passed, none the worse for a few shed leaves. It is the oaks and cedars that fall for ever.

After the first few meetings, which were concerned with the ceremonies and courtesies, all those learned men tucked up their gowns and set to work on the real tussle, Abbot Anian and Master Madoc bent on procuring not mere truce but, if they could, a permanent peace, and the king's men, as far as I could see, not themselves absolutely opposed to this course, but quite unable to get King Henry's agreement. For like all pliable men, he could also, on occasion, be immovably obstinate. Then everyone was banished from the sessions until there should be a point of agreement ready to be recorded, and I was set free to make my way about the streets and schools and markets of Oxford, and listen and observe.

I was standing just within the gate, one among a crowd of people watching the lords of parliament ride out to the session at the king's hall on the fifteenth day of June, when one standing close at my back said into my ear in good Welsh: 'As fitting a place to meet as any, Master Samson!' And seeing that I stood sturdily and made no start he commended me in English, mentioning Meurig's name freely, for there were Welsh scholars in Oxford as well as English, and we were surrounded by so many other loud conversations, and so little to be distinguished from those about us, that openness was the safest method. He moved forward a little to be at my side, and so for the first time I saw that chancery clerk whom Meurig had encountered at Shrewsbury.

He was younger than I, and very well found, in a good gown, and his hands ringed. It was a sharp, clever, smiling face, shaven smooth as an egg, and lit by wide-open but guarded grey eyes.

'I have been following you,' he said, 'for a day and a half, to make sure no one else was following you. To be honest, I think they are so intent on their own business they have no further interest in ours. At least no one has shown any in you. We may walk together, two clerks with minor business about the court.'

His name was Cynan, and he was in very good repute with his masters. We walked together as he had said, elbowed by the Oxford crowds, among which we were anonymous and invisible, and I told him how far the discussions had progressed, and he told me what went on in parliament itself, for momentous things were happening, there in the king's great hall.

'Behind the scenes,' he said, 'the council of twenty-four, the king's twelve and the barons' twelve, are hard at work on plans for a new establishment to replace their own temporary power. What form it will take I cannot yet tell you, but before you leave it must come to a head. For the present, I can tell you that the envoys are back from Paris, with the terms of the French peace settled and agreed, but for a lot of complicated details, no doubt most concerned with money. It's a family quarrel and a family peace, and that means not one of them is going to part with a grievance or a claim without getting paid for it. But since they all want it, so it will be. You may tell your prince there will be a treaty with France within the year.'

I asked what had been said in parliament concerning the Welsh truce, for I knew it could not be pleasing to those marcher lords who had lost land to us. He hoisted his shoulders and smiled.

'You may say so! There are those who came to this town armed and ready, believing still in the king's writ and pointing their noses towards Chester. Now they find that is a dead issue. If there ever was union in this land, as some truly believed, Wales may be one factor that breaks it apart. Come,' he said, suddenly quickening his stride and drawing me towards the gate, 'I will show you one enemy at least, inveterate and venomous.'

So I went with him, and we joined the gapers about the precinct of the royal hall, watched the lordly arrivals,

47

saw the horses led away by grooms, and the nobles of the land striding into the hall one after another, the rulers of this realm of England.

Cynan said: 'That one, the burly man with the frown and the measured stride and the harassed air – no, he's no enemy to any man, he wills well to all, too well! That is the new justiciar, Hugh Bigod, brother to the earl of Norfolk. Yes, they already have the first thing they demanded, a justiciar. And this one following, this is Gloucester.'

Earl Richard de Clare was a debonair person in his middle thirties, handsome and fair. And I had thought of the earl of Gloucester as a looming thundercloud over the southern march of Wales. Surely men are magnified and diminished by the circumstance into which they are born, and I wonder if they themselves are not malformed and even broken by that accident of birth, being forced into forms for which their hearts and minds have no desire. I looked upon this man and was drawn to him. He had a proud but not a vicious face, rather troubled and open to wounds.

'He is here!' said Cynan in my ear. 'Observe him!'

It was a man of much the same age as de Clare who came stalking into the doorway, dropping his bridle into the groom's hand without a glance, and discarding the retinue of three or four squires and valets who rode behind him. He was of middle height, slender and sudden of movement, with a narrow, fierce, arrogant face, made to look still more elongated by a trimmed and pointed beard and a thin, high-bridged nose, and the sweeping glance of his black eyes was like the circling of a sword, so that I hardly wondered that men made haste to step back out of its range.

'That is William de Valence,' said Cynan, 'the eldest of King Henry's Lusignan half-brothers, and the most dangerous. And the hottest enemy of your prince in this land, if words be any guide. It seems he has been the latest to feel the goad – the men of Cemais have plundered and raided his earldom of Pembroke, that he holds through his wife, and he blames the example and encouragement of the prince of Wales for all his trials. He came here all whetted and ready for the muster and his revenge, to be told the Welsh war is already a dead issue, and a truce in the making. He got up in a fury and told parliament it had no business to be haring off after domestic reforms that could well wait a better day, that its proper work was to march into Wales and avenge his wrongs on Llewelyn. And when he found but lukewarm backing, he turned on the new council and the prime movers of the new order, and denounced them as little better than traitors. That went down badly with many, but it was the earl of Leicester who answered him, and it ended in a burning quarrel. Valence is well hated, by English and Welsh alike.'

'And yet,' I said, 'when they cry out against the foreigners, are they not striking at Earl Simon no less than at Valence?'

He shook his head. 'Never look for logic, at least among crowds, you shall not find it. Aliens, they say, but it means more than being born in France. The earl of Leicester after his fashion is as French as King Louis himself, but when he came here to take up his earldom – and it came to him through an Englishwoman, fairly and honestly – he took up the burden of Englishness without undue self-seeking, and put down roots he meant and means to send deep. Count Peter of Savoy has not even that degree of native blood, but no man rails at him. He puts into this land more than he takes from it, and gives honest counsel to the king. But the Lusignans came to make their fortunes when their house fell into some disfavour in France, they marry land, they accept church office, wherever there's money and advantage, there are they, and all their Poitevin hangers-on come flooding in after them. They see themselves somewhat at risk now,

49

since King Henry feels them to be a liability to him at this pass. But they will cling tooth and nail to what they have, and if they feel it threatened they will not hesitate to break apart this present consent and unity. For what is being said and thought and hoped concerning the earl of Leicester, you may hear it around you.'

And so I did, after we had parted, going about the streets and keeping my ears open. Surely those I heard talking had but a hazy idea yet of what the reform of the realm could mean, or how it was to be brought about, since the makers of the new England were even then only beginning their own consideration of ends and means. But they had suffered for want of a just order, or so they felt, and they had grasped the promise of it now that it was mooted, and their hope was real and urgent and would not be easily satisfied, or easily quenched. Oxford, perhaps, was peculiarly alive to such issues, by reason of the schools, but even in the countryside it impressed me greatly that the simple were following with fierce intelligence the turmoil in the state, and from this troubling of the waters looked for a miraculous cure.

Thus far I had seen many of the great men engaged upon the enterprise, bishops, barons and knights, and those great clerks – for truly some I think were most able men – who served the king. Once I caught a glimpse of Henry de Montfort riding out from the town gate, and with him a younger boy, by the likeness his brother. But I had not yet set eyes on their sire, whose name I heard ever more frequently and ardently on the lips of the people.

It was two days after this first encounter with Cynan that Abbot Anian again took me with him into the final meeting with the English negotiators, for they had secured the best terms they could get, and the agreement was ready to be copied, sealed and exchanged. Peace we could not persuade them to, King Henry stubbornly resisting, but a truce was ours, to run until the first day of August of the following year, thirteen months of grace for Llewelyn to consolidate without hindrance all his gains. And a mere one hundred marks to pay for it! Not one foot of the ground won were we called upon to surrender. The only concession was that the king's officers in Chester should have unhindered access to the Lord Edward's isolated castles of Diserth and Degannwy, to provision and maintain the garrisons, and that we took for granted. For if the truce prohibited us from taking them by storm, then someone had to feed them meantime, and better at the king's expense than at ours. Such were the terms the abbot was taking back to Llewelyn.

King Henry himself appeared for the ceremonious sealing of the agreement, somewhat forcedly gracious, still with one wistful eye on the war of conquest he had intended, as the possibility passed from him. Then the proctors withdrew together, and we clerks were left to gather up all the documents and exchange the needful copies. Master Madoc and the abbot were to stay yet some nine or ten days in Oxford, until all the personal contracts had been prepared, and the letters of guarantee for the payment of the indemnity, and various other details for which their approval was necessary, and that afforded me time to meet again with Cynan, whose account of how things went in parliament would be more exact than what could be gathered in the streets.

I was still in the chamber where the committee had met, copying the last 'datum apud Oxoniam decimo septimo die Junii', when the door opened behind me, and someone came into the room. I took it to be one of the royal clerks returning, for they, too, had left documents lying, and had still work to do. But when the incomer first stood a moment motionless, and then came round between me and the open window-space, then I did look up, and with a start of something like alarm, for this being loomed so large that he cut off the light from me, and the June day was suddenly dark, and my vellum overcast as though clouds had gathered for thunder.

He was a good head taller than any I had seen about the court, head and shoulders above the middle make of man, with broad breast and long arms, and narrow flanks that tapered strongly into long, powerful legs. He stood and looked down at me with a wide, brown stare, unwavering and undisguised by either smile or frown, and the unthinking arrogance of that look said that he had the right to stare so upon any in this land, and ought not to be evaded. His forehead was massive, his features large and regular and handsome, and his dress, short riding tunic and chausses of fine brown cloth stitched with gold, all carelessly royal. But his size alone would have told me that I was looking at the Lord Edward, the heir of England.

I rose and louted to him, and waited his pleasure, since he did not at once lose interest in me and withdraw. And as he looked upon me, so did I upon him, for in many ways he was startling and strange to me. It was thirteen years since I had seen him, and then he had been but six years old, a tow-headed child, already very tall for his age, following our David like his shadow. Now he had hair very darkly brown, almost black, a curious change, and, whatever he might still retain of youthful awkwardness and inexperience, most markedly he was already a man. I made him nineteen, and astonished myself by recalling, out of what hidden place in my memory I cannot tell, that this very day, the seventeenth of June, was his birthday.

It was not until he turned a little, and drew away from the window, and the light fell brightly upon his face, that I saw that this splendid creature was flawed, for as soon as the roundness of his stare was relaxed, his left eyelid drooped over the brown eye with that same dubious heaviness always so noticeable in his father. It gave me a shock of wariness and surprise, for though in the father it seemed fitting after a fashion, in this grand countenance such an ambiguity had no place. It contradicted all that glow of openness and boldness and nobility that he projected about him. It was one more minor shadow after the sudden stormcloud his bulk had cast upon the day.

When he had looked his fill upon me he said, in a voice youthful and light of tone, but measured and assured: 'You are the Welsh clerk the abbot brought with him, are you not?'

And when I owned it: 'I saw you pass with him the other day, and thought that I should know you,' he said. 'If I remember well, your name is Samson. You were David's groom and servant when he was a child in my father's care.'

I said: 'Your memory is better, my lord, than I had any right to expect. I am indeed that Samson. It is kind of you to keep me so long in mind.'

'So, you are still in the service of the princes of Gwynedd,' he said. 'I trust all goes well with the Lady Senena? And David – I pray you, when you return, commend me to him. He will remember that we were good friends in childhood.'

'I thank you, my lord, Prince David is well, and so is his mother. He has not forgotten the time spent with you. If he had this opportunity your Grace has afforded me,' I said, 'on this day of all days, he would wish your Grace all happiness and blessing for your natal day.'

He was surprised and disarmed, and the sudden smile was strange and brief on that monumental countenance. 'I see there is nothing amiss with your own memory,' he said. And he looked at the parchment I had before me, and said, with an unreadable face: 'I trust it may be a day worthy of celebrating for both of us. It should be so, since it is also the day we were appointed to muster at Chester.' And with that, as suddenly as he had come, he withdrew, and left me to finish my work.

Such was the Lord Edward at nineteen, sufficiently

gracious to one so insignificant as myself, yet with something ominous about him. I made my way back to the Dominican priory in no very settled mind about him. That he had truly felt affection for David I knew from of old, that the memory of that affection might still warm him I could believe. But always I saw again the left eyelid drooping and veiling the brown eye, and that could not but remind me of King Henry benevolently promising what afterwards he never fulfilled, as though he closed that eye to be blind to his own double-dealing. A small thing of the body, but so slyly apt. In the father, a weak and amiable man by and large, it could be accepted as no more than a timely warning. But if strong men and giants study also to close one eye to their own false intents, then where are ordinary human creatures to look for refuge?

The last meeting that I had with Cynan was on the last day of June, for we stayed the month out in Oxford. And that time we met in the meadows by the river in the cool of the evening, when many scholars and townspeople were strolling there for enjoyment at the end of the working day. Something of what had befallen in the assembly was already common knowledge, criticised and commended in the town. As, that the form of government had been remade in a practical shape, and still by general consent, which was achievement enough. These agreed principles came to be known as the Provisions of Oxford.

After the election of a justiciar, some twenty of the royal castles had been put in the hands of new and trusted castellans. Out of the king's twelve in the council, two had been chosen by the magnates' twelve, and from the magnates' twelve two by the king's men, to elect a new permanent council of fifteen. King and council were to rule together and respect each other. The dates of three parliaments were laid down for every year, though others could be called at need. No one found fault with all this. Since unity had called us there to make truce instead of dispatching the host to Chester to make war, it seemed that for the moment English unity was as great a benefit to us in Wales, and I could be cautiously glad that it continued unbroken.

'No longer,' said Cynan. 'The shell begins to crack, and what will hatch is hard to guess. This reform was never meant to raise the cry "Out with the aliens!" but the winds are blowing it in that direction, whether or no. There's been the devil to pay in the assembly, and the Lusignans have refused the oath that's being required of all the baronage. Those who drafted it added a clause that has frightened away more than the Lusignans. It was all very well holding men by consent, but it stuck in their gullets to have to add at the end: And he that opposes this is a mortal enemy of the commonweal! All the timid and moderate are taking fright, and some have fallen away besides the Poitevins. But there's another solid reason for their defection – with the king so short of money, the lords of the reform have ordered the return to the crown of certain royal lands and castles he has given away to others, and who holds more of them than his half-brothers? Whatever the cause, they have not only refused the oath, but tried to persuade King Henry to break his, and abandon the new Provisions. I've heard, though God knows yet if it's true, that Aymer of Lusignan, the one that's bishop-elect of Winchester before he's old enough to hold the office, has run off and shut himself in his castle at Wolvesey, and rumour says his three brothers will not be long behind. Now the magnates have no choice but to deal with this dissident brood somehow, and whatever they may do will please neither king nor pope. Aymer is, after all, a bishop-elect. If they try to rid themselves of him, that's hardly likely to endear them to Pope Alexander. And they need his goodwill sorely.'

'But they still intend,' I said, 'to send a delegation to

Rome to try to get easier terms for the king? And to ask for a papal legate to come over and help in the settlement?'

'They intend, yes. But the pope has shown no relenting yet, and if Aymer is turned out of his bishopric that won't sweeten him. On the whole,' said Cynan with chilly cynicism, 'the pope has done very well out of holding our poor wriggling king to his bond. If he has not ousted the Hohenstaufen from Sicily, he has got half his crippling debts in the business paid by English tenths and aids. Never trouble about English pockets and English grievances, but leave them to it, take your truce home, and hope to keep it refurbished every year at their expense. What has Wales to do in this dispute but profit from it?'

That was good enough sense, but either I had outgrown my own ideas of the world and the state during this stay in Oxford, or else some disturbing new vision that troubled our content had journeyed to Aber with young Henry de Montfort, and caused both Llewelyn and me to sicken with the same obscure longing. For surely those weighty men who had tried and were still trying to amend the England they lived in had seen a vision that had application even for us in Wales. True, our society was utterly different in its organisation from theirs, yet it could not remain utterly separate. The England we rubbed shoulders with in the marches was an abrasive force, and it mattered to us what manner of England it was. All the more since we must, in a changing world, adapt to it and borrow from it, for no border severs man from man, or one manner of living totally from another.

So I asked what was ever on my mind: 'And the earl of Leicester? What is his stand?'

'His stand is upon the whole reform, and nothing less. He sees an England remade, where all members work together for the common good, guided by a ray of the spirit emanating from the pope, and one in a Christendom made in the same mould of service and selflessness. Never stare so,' said Cynan, smiling somewhat bitterly, for indeed I had turned to examine him narrowly at this unexpected utterance. 'I can recognise a saint when I see one, and a demon, too, and Earl Simon is both – or just falls short of both, and fits together the two halves of him into something unique among men. This is a man who will be cheated of a hundred marks rather than owe one. But also he will exact the last mark owing to him, or, even more strenuously, to his lady, or die still dunning the debtor. He has had saints to his teachers, like Bishop Robert of Lincoln, and both his saint and his demon have drunk deep of them, and been exalted. He is all pride, and all humility. The king dreads him, and Friar Adam Marsh reproves him for his moods and his depressions, and is heeded as reverently as by a raw novice. But what can the common human experience do with a force of nature but take refuge from it? He will stand fast, but in the end he will stand alone.'

I said: 'And I have never seen him!' Almost I added that I had never seen Cynan until now, for he spoke with a tongue not his own, inflamed by the spirit. And I had thought him a clever, loyal, limited exile, holding fast to an ideal of home for his own self-respect. 'I must see this man,' I said, 'before I leave Oxford.'

'You shall,' said Cynan.

He took me – so simple it was – to the great church of St Frideswide, to the chapel where her tomb was, forbidden to kings. That same night we went there, the light already failing, and the lamps about the tomb made a clear reddish radiance. We stood in the darkest corner of the chapel, and there were others going and coming, so that we were in no way significant, and no man marked us.

A man came in from the evening, through the dark of the church into the ruddy light of the lamps, and went without haste to kneel at the tomb. Though he was unattended, there was no need to question if he were noble, and though he was soberly clad, dark-coloured and plain, his plainness had its own splendour. And when he was kneeling, upright and still with linked hands before his face, I had him in profile and saw him clearly. He was no taller than your middling tall man, he had thick shoulders and a powerful body, compact and at peace with itself, at least at this hour. For all his movements, and after, his stillness, were whole and harmonious. When he was not at worship, I could well imagine that same sturdy body knotted into tensions lesser men never know. The linked hands held so still I saw every sinew. They were large, strong and intense, of a braced sensitivity that caused my own hands to clench and quiver. And the head was a bronze head, cropped, naked, marvellous, like a Roman emperor of the nobler sort, with large, bright bone thrusting through flesh and skin and brown, glowing hair, that clung like a beast's rich fell upon the quiet skull. His face was shaven clean like a monk, and it seemed that it could not be otherwise, so pure was the line that framed it, and so fiercely still. He had great, loftily-arched eyelids closed over large eyes, like a prince already carven on a tomb, and a wide, austere, feeling mouth that formed the measured phrases of prayer with fine and private movements, and under this generous mouth a generous jaw graven in gold by the lamps about him.

Cynan said in my ear: 'You have your wish.'

It was not needful to tell me, the print of his legend was deep and clear upon him, and the young Norman vigour I had seen in his son Henry was but the lesser and lighter promise of what I saw now, yet the likeness was marked. Once seen, even at a distance there could never again be any mistaking this man for other than the earl of Leicester.

We watched until he ended his prayers. When he opened his eyes, the great lids rolling back from them into the burnished sockets of bone, they were so large and so straight of gaze that they seemed prominent, though they were deeply set. Their colour could not be determined there in the church; what they had was rather a burning clarity. If, as they said, the king owned he was afraid of him, I think what he meant was rather the holy dread that small, spiral men feel in the presence of the towering and upright. And surely it was the king's saving grace that he could not only feel but confess it. This man might have fears, too, an obligation failed, a principle lowered, a point of honour in doubt, but never of another man.

So we watched him rise from his knees, not with the spring of youth, for he was approaching his fiftieth year, but with a solid, powerful thrust, and pace firmly out of the chapel and out of our sight. And Cynan said: 'Who knows but some day men will make pilgrimages to his tomb? They might get a better hearing from him than from St Frideswide!'

I saw Earl Simon again, the day we rode from Oxford, for he came in courtesy to bid farewell to the envoys. Seen by day, his eyes appeared a deep and luminous grey, more daunting than the blue gaze of his son's innocence, because the father was not innocent, but pure, and that is a more terrible and wonderful thing. Strange to be seen, there followed at his elbow one more accustomed to be followed, and hung attentive on his words and looks at every move. And that was something I had not looked for in the Lord Edward, the heir of England. When it was fixed upon Earl Simon's face, even that veiled left eye opened wide, and the lofty stone face quickened into warmth. Then I understood that the spell the earl had cast upon me by St Frideswide's tomb, and upon Cynan, I know not where, beforetime, was nothing particular to us, but the enchantment he exercised upon most young men, even this royal giant who stood dwarfed beside him.

And I thought then that this might be a bond more dangerous to the earl than to the prince, for unless I greatly mistook him the Lord Edward would not take kindly to being spellbound for one moment longer than the reflected magic flattered and enhanced him. And what he had once loved and admired, and then found proof against his possessive affection, he might resent and hate no less fiercely.

Then we rode home with our truce and our thirteen months of grace, and told all that we had seen and heard in Oxford to Llewelyn. And Llewelyn, having put in order all the practical moves the report required of him, brooded long over the shadowy grandeur that hung over the future of England, like a morning too brilliant to promise constancy until nightfall, and ended saying, as I had said: 'I must see this man!'

CHAPTER III

From this time we set to work to make the parchment gain effective, for even when a truce has been agreed by both parties with goodwill, it is no easy matter to guard a long and difficult border from infringement. No prince can be everywhere, or have his officers everywhere, and there are always plenty of roving men of independent mind on both sides of the barrier to make the occasional raid a tempting prospect. There need be no planned offence, either; it is enough if a hunted deer crosses into alien territory.

The order went out to all Llewelyn's allies, castellans and bailiffs immediately the truce was ratified. But there were certain complications in the south, for Meredith ap Rhys Gryg, now healed of the wound he got at Carmarthen bridge, was not fully bound by the truce, being Welsh and not English. Insofar as he was vassal to King Henry he was bound, but in his own lands he had his own rights, and was in no mind to sit quietly after the knock he had taken. But he had David and Rhys Fychan keeping close watch on him from Carreg Cennen, and their power was enough to temper his grievance with caution. And as to Patrick of Chaworth, as the king's seneschal he was obliged to respect the king's truce, and was no longer free, at least openly, to aid his ally. His was a delicate situation, for even when all action between the two sides was halted, it was a matter for exact definition what territory each held, and the need to separate the armed bands was urgent. As long as men have weapons in their hands and an enemy within reach, peace is hard to preserve. But there was nothing to prevent de Chaworth from keeping close company with Meredith, and in force, too, so long as his avowed concern was the procuring of a sensible agreement on boundaries and the disengagement of the armies.

Still, by the time July was past and August well forward, and still the king's seneschal kept the field with a formidable host, it began to seem as if he was more concerned with maintaining a presence in arms than with getting a settlement. Meredith and Patrick were at Cardigan, with a large force drawn from all the marcher lordships, and David and Rhys Fychan were joined by Meredith ap Owen in the cantref of Emlyn, though even so their numbers were much inferior to those Meredith ap Rhys Gryg could field if de Chaworth chose to risk aiding him in a quick assault.

Llewelyn gnawed his knuckles over this threat, and was in two minds about what he should do, for he was unwilling to leave Rhys Fychan exposed to more loss by withdrawing David and his men, and yet a little apprehensive of David's high temper and taste for audacity if he remained on the spot, with the king's men close and ready to provoke him.

Their mother, the Lady Senena, also felt strongly enough about affairs to leave David's maenol at Neigwl, which she controlled in his absence, to the steward's care, and come visiting to Aber, a thing she did less often as time passed. She was well beyond fifty now, and a little slower in her movements and more stooped in her person than of old, and very grey, but her thick black brows were as formidable and her spirit as imperious as ever, and still she gave orders to everyone with the same expectation of being instantly obeyed, except that from Llewelyn she never truly looked for more than the easy tolerance with which he listened and then did as he would. Yet at least he listened, for the Lady Senena, in spite of some past mistakes, had sharp good sense.

'You should fetch the boy away from there,' she said, rapping her stick smartly on the ground for emphasis, 'before he puts your truce in peril, and his own head after it.'

'I have been thinking the same thing myself,' Llewelyn owned, 'though it's rather Meredith I distrust than David, as long as they stand there forehead to forehead like two rams.'

'You should go yourself,' she said roundly, 'and see the peace enforced, and the men brought home.'

'Not for the world!' said Llewelyn. 'I gave him the command, and I would not snatch it back from him. But I may go so far as to send him a mere suggestion, a word of advice. How if we ask Samson to be the courier? No one will know better how to manage David.'

So we went to work and prepared formal copies of the truce, for David to send to both Meredith ap Rhys Gryg and Patrick of Chaworth, as a courtesy to men standing against him in arms when the agreement was made. 'Put it into his head,' Llewelyn said, 'if he has not thought of it for himself, to demand a meeting face to face to settle the details of separation, a meeting with both, mind, for de Chaworth will be a check upon Meredith if he does his proper duty. Since they hold off from the first move, we'll make it for them, and force a response.'

So I was his courier, and rode south alone. It was late in a hot August when I made my way into the commote of Emlyn, and after some enquiry found where the allies were encamped. In that summer weather they had no need to seek a roof at night, or far to go for food; campaigning was a pleasant and even an idle life while everyone held off from battle.

David came out, brown and hard and burning with health, to embrace me heartily, and made no ado about welcoming his brother's counsel. Though Llewelyn did well to move considerately with him, for he could be haughty and quick to take offence when the mood was on him. Nor was it the first time I had been used to make some gesture of guidance acceptable, my privilege with him being curiously strong.

'We are tangled in a net of legal quibbles,' he said, 'and to tell truth I have been looking for a way to bring the thing to a head. But one false move from us, and Meredith may very well cry breach of truce and drag in Chaworth, who by all we have seen is ready and eager for it. Let's try this means! As the king's proxy, Chaworth will be hard put to it to find an excuse for not attending to see fair boundaries drawn, when the parties are the king's vassal and the partner in the king's truce. Let's challenge him! We'll call him in as arbitrator.'

So we sent out those two invitations to conference, with the copies of the royal agreement by way of probe. And David chose to send me as courier to de Chaworth in the castle of Cardigan, to underline by my embassage as Llewelyn's clerk the royal nature of the agreement to which I had been a witness, and the penalties for breaking it. Which I greatly approved in David, in that he was willing in Llewelyn's interest to make use of the personal weight of Llewelyn's name. Every such evidence of the right relationship between the brothers of Gwynedd was sweet to me.

'And a clerk,' said David, sharply teasing me as he sent me forth, 'is half-holy in all circumstances, and may go safely into Cardigan and come again. Still, keep your sword about you. I cannot spare my half-priest.'

I doubt I was more swordsman than priest by that time, having fought so often beside my lord, and never having gone beyond the first stage of seeking orders. But I went as he bade me, and bore myself neutrally and modestly in the halls of Cardigan.

This Patrick the seneschal was a big, fine-looking, black-avised man, very gracious but with uneasy eyes. He had got his great lands, like many another of his kind, through marriage to an heiress, his wife Hawise bringing him not only the lordship of Kidwelly, but also the castle of Ogmore, in Glamorgan. These gentry who held through their Welsh or half-Welsh womenfolk kept always a tighter and greedier hold on the soil than those born to it by right, and Patrick was little better liked than William of Valence in Pembroke. Still, he received me into his hall with ceremony, so I gave him back good value in the dignities and styles of those I represented. There were plenty of his officers and knights about him, but no sign of Meredith ap Rhys Gryg. But I had kept my eyes open in the baileys, and I knew Meredith's Welshmen when I saw them, even if they wore English arms.

'My lord,' I said when I had delivered him the scroll of the truce, 'I am commissioned by my lord Llewelyn, prince of Wales, and by his brother Prince David as his lieutenant in these parts, to present you these letters, in token of their acceptance with a whole heart of the contents thereof, and their confidence that you, as the seneschal of the king's Grace, will hold to the agreement as faithfully as they undertake to do. It is in the interests of both parties that there should be peace between us here as elsewhere. You know that this is complicated by the position of the lord Meredith ap Rhys. We desire that an impartial judge shall define where the line of demarcation between us is to be drawn, and we hold that there can be no fairer voice than the king's seneschal, in an issue between Welshman and Welshman. In the name of the prince of Wales, Prince David invites you to preside at a conference to settle all disputed claims and bring about peace between our arms. And he sends, through your courtesy, this same invitation to Meredith ap Rhys Gryg. The time may be as soon as you will, and the place wherever you find just and convenient. If you will, we will move halfway to meet you.'

I could think of nothing I had omitted, to convince

him that he had no choice but to accede. And if he
accepted, then Meredith had no choice, either, since he
was completely dependent upon the English muster to
counter the force we could loose against him. It seemed
to me that Patrick was relieved at being offered this way
out of an uneasy situation, and brightened very thoughtfully as he read and considered. He took the scroll that
was superscribed to Meredith, and did not deny that he
knew very well where to find him. For all I know, he
may have been behind the hangings of the dais that
moment, with both ears stretched.

Patrick said what it was incumbent on him to say,
paying lip service to the king's will and the sacredness
of the king's peace, and after some pondering named
Cilgerran as the spot where we should meet, as being
between our two stations along the river Teifi, and to
that I agreed.

'And as to the day,' he said, 'it is now the last day
of August; let it be the fifth of September, then, if that
is agreeable to your lord.'

'In his name,' I said, 'I close with that day. At Cilgerran
on the fifth of September the conference shall be, and
there shall be nothing attempted in arms before that day.'

Thereupon he offered me refreshment while he dictated
a letter of acceptance on his own part, and a guarantee
that the like would be forthcoming from Meredith ap
Rhys Gryg as soon as possible. And before evening I
rode back into our camp with the fruit of my embassage,
and reported everything to David and his council.

'The castle of Cilgerran is held for the Lord Edward,'
said Meredith ap Owen cautiously. For the heir of the
Cantilupes, whose stronghold it was, was still only a boy,
and Edward was his guardian during his minority.

'That should be a guarantee,' said David. 'Edward may
not like the truce, but for his father's sake he will not
break it. And surely de Chaworth will never dare misuse
a castle Edward holds.' Then he asked me of all I had

seen in Cardigan, and I told him as best I could judge what numbers they must have, by the great plump of knights he had about him there, all the more as Meredith ap Rhys Gryg had kept himself and his men well out of sight.

'Double our numbers they may be,' said David, 'but double our worth I doubt. But we'll be first in Cilgerran and choose our ground.'

So we marched in time to make camp on the evening of the third of September, and chose a raised site among trees outside the vil of Cilgerran, with a sweep of the river to cover our right and rear, and good lookout spots from which the approaches from town and castle could be governed. Our forward scouts brought word that de Chaworth himself was not yet in either, though the town was full of his first companies. And early the next day the leaders rode in, for we were now but two or three miles from Cardigan, having gone more than halfway to meet them. A courier came before noon, a middle-aged squire of de Chaworth's household, to appoint our meeting to take place next day in the meadows before the town, where they were setting up tents to give the council shelter at need.

'Patrick has a mature taste in couriers,' said David, frowning after the rider as he departed. 'No sprightly page, but a seasoned man-at-arms, and with his eyes wide open and roving. What need was there for this visit at all but a gesture of courtesy, the prettier the better compliment? The hour was already set in advance.'

Nevertheless he shrugged off this doubt, and we sat out the day with strung patience. When the late dark came down David and Rhys Fychan circled the camp and made sure all was well, and every outpost wide awake. A dark night it was to be, without a moon, but on such summer nights there is always a glimmer of stars. It was very silent and still, the freshening wind of evening already dying, barely a rustle of leaves to be heard.

'My thumbs prick,' said David, straining erect to listen, and shivered, not with fear, rather as a hound quivers, snuffing the wind after quarry. And he sent forward two more men, well beyond the limit of the camp on the road to the town, to lie in cover, and two more in our rear along the river-bank. Nonetheless he let the camp take its rest as though he felt no qualms, only ordering that every man should keep his weapons and harness close to hand while he slept.

Our fires were turfed down to a glimmer, and it was almost fully dark, as dark as it would be that night, when David lay down in his cloak to sleep. It was hard to know if he believed in his own precautions, for he had done off all harness, though he kept it by him, and stretched himself out in comfort to his rest. There had been no call from our outposts, no movement from the town. The first owl I heard calling, called from upstream, well in our rear, and I like a fool took it for a real owl, so hushed and still was all the night about us. But David, who, I swear, had been fast asleep, started up out of his cloak and was on his feet in an instant, stretched and listening, his eyes two pale blue flames, and when the call came again he kicked out at the turfed fire and set it blazing high. Men boiled silently out of the grass and the bushes, reaching out for sword and knife before they were well awake, and David's squire sprang out of the shadows into the glare with his lord's hauberk and sword in his arms. And but for the crackle of the fire the silence had barely trembled as yet. We waited, but facing up-river, away from Cilgerran.

'They cannot be there,' said Rhys Fychan in a whisper.

'They are there,' said David, just above his breath. 'They have spent this whole day making a great circle about us, while we watched them deck their tents for us in the fields. A great circle through the forests on this side the river, to come round on our quarter. And a great circle on the other bank, to cross again upstream from us. The rest will come out from the town to help them finish the work. So they think!'

'Shall I sound?' asked the boy with the horn, quivering.

'Not yet. Between us and them every man knows already. It's only those towards the town may need an alarm, and they are not threatened yet. Let them close in.'

It was long minutes more before they struck the eastward rim of our camp, expecting to fall upon sleeping men, and clashed hand to hand among the scattered trees with men armed and waiting. The first shuddering clang of metals and shrill of cries went through the dark like lightning tearing it, and then David cried: 'Sound!' and the horn pealed higher above the confused din, and we surged forward like leaves blown by its breath, towards the attack, while behind us, back and back to the rim of the open meadows, our comrades started up to keep our circle unbroken. There, at the first advance across the meadows from the town, the archers would have their targets clear. For us it was swords and knives, and every sense sharpened to pick out friend from foe.

They had their night eyes then, as well as we, but we closed our ring to hold them out, and so fought pressing forward rather than giving back, for as long as we could keep our ranks. They were very many, and they came in heavy waves against us, but the shock of surprise was lost. All these who had spent the day closing their trap round us had gone on foot; we were spared the horrid confusion of mangled horses threshing among us and turning our cover into bone-breaking hazards. Man to man is fair odds, night or day, and if they had sent a spy out to view our dispositions, still we had possession of the ground we had chosen, and to take it proved beyond their power.

I kept at David's side as well as I might, as always it was my custom and privilege to keep Llewelyn's left flank when we were in the field together. And hard and hot work it was to keep pace with David, for he was so violent and agile there was no matching him, and in the wildest of the labour I heard him laughing, and a sound like light singing that spilled out of him much as a cat purrs, for pure pleasure, not in the killing itself, though indeed we had not sought it and had no need to feel shame at it, but in his own readiness and skill and prowess, and the mastery of his body. And I also exulted in him, for he was like a living fire in the darkness and din and chaos of the night.

There was then no time to beware of anything beyond arm's-length, the range of a sword or dagger was all the room each man had. But after a while I knew that we had moved forward, while they had made no advance, for we were trampling the dead and wounded, and that frightful floundering, and the cries from under our feet, and the gushing groan of breath as we trod the air unwillingly out of a living man, these were the worst things of that night.

It lasted until the east, towards which we faced, began to grow pearl-grey before the dawn, and then we could see more of what we had done and what had been done to us, and then men began to turn from us and run, slipping away between the trees and plunging into the river. As for the expected attack by mounted knights from the town, we did not know until full daylight whether it had ever been ventured or no, and found it then but a minor part of the battle, for it had been designed only as the final blow, and the archers had dealt with it by starlight before ever it reached our encampment.

So the dawn came, and what was left of the chivalry of de Chaworth and the English lordships of South Wales broke away from us and fled back into Cilgerran to lick its wounds there. And we went somewhat wearily and numbly hunting among the trees for prisoners worth taking, for Welsh worth retrieving and grafting into our own forces if they were so minded, and for our own wounded and dead. As the light brightened we saw that of the enemy the number left here was great, and among them many knights. And it seemed to me that Meredith ap Rhys Gryg, who surely had persuaded de Chaworth to this disastrous madness and treachery, had also let the English bear the brunt of the assault, and kept his own men in reserve. For it was the English who had suffered worst. The tangle of them in the broken and ravaged undergrowth was full of bright devices now smutched and bloodied and buckled, like the flesh beneath the surcoats. We made up the tale of them as well as we could. And combing the soiled grasses low towards the river, David came suddenly to a halt before me, and leaned, gazing long at the ground.

He came, God knows how, always so clean and bright out of every testing, as though the elements that bruised the rest of us had no power over him. In that dawn he should have been streaked with sweat and smoke and blood, if not his own blood, and wearied to stumbling, and here he moved immaculate and light, his black hair only a little damp on his temples, and his eyelids a little heavy over the jewelled blue of his eyes. And close at his feet, where he stared thus ungrieving and unexulting, there was the wreckage of a man, broken and trampled, with a slashed face turned up to the morning light, and a caved breast holding a pool of blackened blood. A tall man once, handsome and dark, with black brows touching, and black beard finely pointed. And very nobly equipped, if so many had not fought over his accoutrements in the dark.

David looked up at me, his eyes like blind blue stones. 'This is he?' he asked. For he had never seen the king's seneschal close before.

I said: 'It is.' I had spoken with him but a few days since; even at this pass I could not mistake him.

71

So we took up Patrick de Chaworth, persuaded to his death, and had him borne away under flag of truce into Cilgerran.

'A pity!' said David, grim. 'It should have been the one who talked him into this betrayal.'

But though we searched the whole day among the wreckage of that night's work, we found no trace of Meredith ap Rhys Gryg. Could Rhys Fychan have laid hands on his uncle then, I believe he would have killed him, though he was in general a temperate man. But though we found some dead of Meredith's following, the man himself was escaped clean, and the next we heard of him was that he was barricaded into his castle of Dryslwyn with the strongest garrison he could muster, and braced ready for attack, and very unlikely to show his nose out of those walls again until the echoes of Cilgerran had passed away on the wind, men having such short memories.

I think David would have been happy to attempt the storming of Dryslwyn, but Meredith ap Owen and Rhys Fychan said no, and reluctantly he owned that they were right, and there was no credit in breaching the very truce we had just asserted and defended. So he contented himself with sending into Cilgerran, to the dead lord's lieutenant, a formal protest against the breach of faith, and a flat statement, for want of the promised conference, of the demarcation he proposed to observe, and to recommend to the prince of Wales and his chief vassals in the south. And so demoralised were the survivors in the fortress, and so willing to bury the unhappy and unblessed venture, that they accepted David's proposed line hastily, grateful to get out of it so lightly.

David raised his brows and laughed when he read the reply, somewhat startled by his own success. 'So we have come out of it with our own demands met, with limited losses, and with little prospect of further trouble in these parts while the truce lasts,' he said. 'But I wish we could have taken Meredith ap Rhys Gryg back with us in chains, to stand his trial for treason. Small chance of that now. He'll lie still in Dryslwyn like a hare in her form, the rest of the year. We must wait another opportunity.'

Then the canons of Cenarth came and ministered to the dying and buried the dead, doing their merciful office humbly and sadly. And we, declining Rhys Fychan's pressing invitation to linger at Carreg Cennen on our way, made by the shortest route for Gwynedd, keeping company with Meredith ap Owen through his lands along the Aeron, and so coastwise into Merioneth. I think David was sorely tempted to pay the desired visit to his sister, but Carreg Cennen would have taken us too far out of our way, and he wished to render full account to Llewelyn as soon as possible. Therefore he excused himself. And I was mortally glad, for by the grace of God I had been spared Godred's close clinging on this occasion, he being left with the castle garrison, and I had no wish to seek him out when I was delivered from his seeking of me, much less to see him in proud possession of Cristin whom he did not truly value, and had dangled before me, unless love had made me mad with suspicion, like bait to some personal trap in which he essayed to take me. My desire was never to see him again. And truly it should have been, no less, never again to see her, but that I could never quite command.

Howbeit, David would go home, and home we went, to recount to Llewelyn all that had passed. And he, though without any great surprise or expectation of exacting redress, nevertheless made a point of sending a letter of protest to King Henry over his seneschal's faith-breaking, that it might be known what were the rights and wrongs of the matter, and any attempt to put the onus upon the Welsh by a crooked story might be forestalled.

The reply he got was conciliatory, and professed strong

disapproval of de Chaworth's unaccountable act, of which neither the king nor any of his officers had had prior knowledge, nor would have countenanced it if they had. The unlucky lord, being dead, could not suffer further from being disowned, yet some of us wondered.

While we were busy in the south, in England, it seemed, the dispute over the oath and the Provisions, so far from being reconciled, had begun to split the ranks of the baronage apart in good earnest. All four of the Lusignan brothers had refused the oath, and being offered in default only a choice between exile for all, or exile for the two who had no land claims or office in England, and safe-custody for William of Valence and the bishop-elect, who had, they had chosen all to leave, and sailed for France along with many other Poitevins. Certainly not to renounce their claims peacefully, to judge by Valence's temper, but rather to recruit sympathy among the powerful in France and from the pope in Rome. While we were fighting the battle of Cilgerran in the first days of September, Pope Alexander was sitting sourly entrenched against all the exalted arguments of the delegation from England, suspecting their ideas and aims of all manner of treason and heresy, and flatly refusing them countenance, or what they most earnestly asked of him, the despatch of a legate to preside over and regulate the re-making of the realm of England. They came home empty-handed.

Nonetheless, the reformers continued their labours undaunted, and the great council worked tirelessly on the measures of renewal. And one thing at least Earl Simon had procured for the king, and that was the agreement with King Louis. Though the treaty was not yet signed and sealed, the long-awaited peace between England and France stood ready at the door.

Until December I do believe King Henry still piously held to his oath, and meant to go hand in hand with his new council and his magnates, in spite of all the choler of his half-brothers. But in December came the bitter blow that soured his heart ever after against the lords who had forced his hand. Pope Alexander, seeing no hope of getting his way over Sicily with his present candidate, cancelled his grant of the kingdom to young Edmund, withdrew with it the threatening clerical penalties, and began to look round for a more effective claimant. If ever the time came when England could repay the papal debts in full, then Edmund might ask to be restored, but not before. And even so his application could only be made, naturally, if someone else had not been set up in the pretendership meantime.

No doubt this came like a blissful release to most of the lords and barons, but it was a desolating shock to King Henry. He had agreed to the proposals of reform only because they were linked with the promise to help him succeed in the Sicilian enterprise. Now he was committed to the reform, but had for ever lost Sicily. Being Henry, and the man he was, this was worse than an irony, it was deceit and treason, for he could never be subjected to humiliation and embarrassment without looking round in fury for a scapegoat, and now he blamed the reformers for his loss, and was convinced they had deliberately wrecked his great project while pretending to assist in it. If he had ever been sincere in accepting the reform, and I think he well may have been, he ceased to be so from that moment, and began to burrow secretly after his freedom and his revenge.

But for us in Wales this period of truce was quiet and prosperous. We tended our country and harvested our resources, and kept our ears pricked for the news from England, and one eye upon Meredith ap Rhys Gryg, still skulking in Dryslwyn, but growing weary now of his own caution. To do him justice, it was never fear that kept him quiet, but only a solid, practical sense that warned him when the stake was not worth the risk. But at last he judged that his part, without doubt the leading part, in the treachery of Cilgerran had drifted far enough down the river to be forgotten, as old grudges easily are where there are always new to be savoured. And he came forth from his seclusion and hunted and raided as was usual with him, leaving the king's new seneschal well out of his plans, and no doubt confident that such private inroads as he could make with his own Welsh forces on territory friendly to Llewelyn would not be at all displeasing to his patron, King Henry, provided the crown could not be implicated in any way.

In early May a rider came into Bala from Rhys Fychan in Carreg Cennen, one of the lancers of his household, grinning so broadly his news could be nothing but a good joke. He was brought to Llewelyn in the mews, where the prince was busy with his hawks, and bent the knee to him very perfunctorily in his haste to get to his message.

'My lord,' he said, 'I bring you brotherly greetings from Rhys Fychan, and sisterly from the Lady Gladys. And I am bidden to ask you where it will please you to take delivery of the person of your traitor, Meredith ap Rhys Gryg, to be tried by his peers?'

There was a general outcry then of astonishment and triumph, and everyone within earshot dropped what he was about and listened without concealment.

'What, has Rhys got the old felon into his hands at last?' said Llewelyn. 'Now how and when did this come about? I thought he had gone to earth for life, and we should have to dig him out with siege engines.'

'My lord,' said the man, broad-smiling with pleasure, 'after the lambing Meredith began raiding our stock, and we lost a few yearlings to him and made no sign. Then a week ago Rhys Fychan pastured some of his best ewes with their lambs not far from Dynevor, where they could be seen from the towers, for we knew Meredith was there, the first visit he's paid there since Cilgerran. There was none but the shepherd with the flock, but we

76

had a good strong company in cover close by.'

'And he took the bait in person?' said Llewelyn, marvelling. 'He has herdsmen and lances enough. You might have got but a poor catch for your trouble.'

'Ah, but, my lord, Meredith's hatred to Rhys is such, he grudges letting even his knights into his feud. Rhys knew him well enough, he came himself to make his choice, he must show his hand in any stroke against his nephew. And he brought a pretty little company in attendance on him, good men, but few. We took them all, with no loss, and no hurt but a few scratches. It was brisk, but we had their measure. And we took Meredith. He is in Carreg Cennen, and he is yours to do with what you will.'

'Come,' said Llewelyn, and helped him away to the hall, 'we must share this with Goronwy and Tudor, and send word out to the rest. This is not my quarrel, but the quarrel of Wales.'

So they debated and made their plans, more gravely once the jest had been enjoyed, and rightly enjoyed, for it was bloodless and just, and there was no killing in any man's mind, as Meredith had brought about all that killing at Cilgerran. There was no doubt but that Llewelyn must move against Meredith as any monarch moves against the traitor, else his claim and style as prince of Wales was of no value. Also the time was approaching when our truce agreement would run out, and we knew that the formal summons to the summer muster against Wales was already issued, and thus far remained in force. We knew, or it came very close to knowing, that this was a matter of form, and the muster would never take place. But for all those who had not our knowledge of the pressures and persuasions in England, the demonstration of genuine power and confidence was essential. So was the right use of Meredith, my lord's first traitor, deep in his debt and absolute in ingratitude. We did not want him slain, we did not want him hurt, we wanted him disciplined, curbed, spared, and brought to submission.

On the twenty-eighth day of May all the great vassals of Wales assembled to sit in judgment. Even Rhodri, the third of the princes of Gwynedd, came from his manor in Lleyn, where commonly he tended to hang aloof between scorn and jealousy, half minding his own lands, half envying the prowess of David, his junior, and wholly resentful of what outdid him, while he spared to attempt rivalry. He read much in Welsh law in those days, privately and secretly, and brooded on Llewelyn's admitted departure from it. But he said never a word.

Before this great assembly Meredith ap Rhys Gryg was brought and charged with treason. And in this matter there was none, not even Rhodri, could charge breach of law against the prince. He presided, but he took no accuser's part, and the verdict was left to the assembly.

Meredith was brought in pinioned, but loosed in the court at Llewelyn's order. He looked in bright, aggressive health and untamed, that square, bearded, loud-mouthed, lusty man, fatally easy to like, and indeed his liking had proved fatal to more than one. He made no submission, and very volubly and fiercely defended himself by accusing all opposed to him. But he could not deny his oath of fealty, for most of those present had witnessed it. Nor could he well deny his breaking of it, which all had seen. The assembly convicted him and, against his obdurate refusal to submit, committed him to imprisonment at his lord's will in the castle of Criccieth.

'Let him stew a while,' said Llewelyn, after he had been taken away, 'and he may come to his senses and his fealty again. I would not let so gross an offence pass, for the sake of Wales, but I cannot altogether forget how he fought at Cymerau. If he returns to his troth it shall not be made hard for him, but securities I must have.'

But for a long time Meredith ap Rhys Gryg maintained

his obstinacy in his prison, while his men in the south, led by his sons, held fast to all his castles but otherwise lay very low, not anxious to provoke an attack which the king, in time of truce, could not prevent or censure. Perhaps he hoped that King Henry would refuse to renew the truce now that it was about to lapse, and would come to his vassal's rescue in arms. If so, he was soon disillusioned, for very shortly after he was shut up in Criccieth the expected approach was made on the king's behalf, and Llewelyn sent out letters of safe-conduct for the royal proctors to meet his own envoys at the ford of Montgomery, at the hamlet called Rhyd Chwima, chief of the traditional places of parley on the border. There the truce was extended in the same form for another full year. Once again Llewelyn offered a large indemnity, as high as sixteen thousand marks, for a full peace, but King Henry remained stubborn, and refused the wider agreement.

The king's mind was then on France, rather than Wales, for in the winter of that year he set out for Paris, and there the great treaty between France and England was sealed at last. After, they said, much haggling over family details, just as Cynan had foretold. But signed and sealed it was, and King Henry duly did homage to King Louis for those Gascon possessions he held on the mainland of France, and became a peer of that country.

Now it was while the king was still absent in France, and laid low with a tertian fever at St Omer, that the thing happened which was ever afterwards railed at by the English as a breach of the truce, but which we saw in another light. Truly the truce was broken, but not first by us. And this is how it fell out.

Early in a hard January a messenger came riding into Aber from the cantref of Builth, where the royal castle was held for Prince Edward by Roger Mortimer, the greatest lord of the middle march. Roger, through his mother, who was a daughter of Llewelyn Fawr, was first-cousin to my prince, and there was a free sort of respect and even liking between them, though they seldom met. But inevitably they were also rivals and in a manner enemies, and neither would yield a point of vantage to the other, or to the relationship between them. Indeed it was impossible they should, Mortimer being on his father's side, where his inheritance and his obligations lay, all English, and the king's castellan into the bargain, while Llewelyn was utterly bound by his duty and devotion to Wales. But between them there was no ill-feeling, each acknowledging the other's needs and loyalties. But no quarter, either. An honourable but a difficult bond.

The messenger came in a lather and a great indignation, clamouring that Mortimer had expelled from their holdings the Welsh tenants of Meredith ap Owen, our loyal Meredith, in the cantref of Builth, desiring to have English holders about the castle there. Granted he was responsible for the trust he had taken on, but he had no right to turn out local tenants who had done no wrong.

'Be easy,' said Llewelyn to the envoy from the injured Welshmen, and clapped an arm about his shoulders. 'Go eat, and rest, and follow us at leisure; you shall find your homestead ready to be occupied again.'

'Not so!' said the fellow, burning and happy. 'If you ride, my lord, so do I ride with you.'

And so he did, when we drew in the muster at short notice, left orders to the outlying chieftains to follow, and rode south into Builth in the January snow.

They were never prepared for the speed with which we could move, and that even in the winter. We burst into Builth like the blizzard that followed us, and swept it clear as the north-west gale drove the frozen snow. Those raw English tenants of Mortimer's tucked up their gowns and ran like hares, and the exiled Welsh farmers – for that is land that can be farmed, not like our bleak and beautiful mountains – came flooding back on our heels with knife in one hand and wife in the other, and the children not far behind, padding through the drifts with their dogs at heel. In every homestead and holding from which they had been driven, we replaced them, restoring a balance that had been violated in defiance of troth. Where, then, was the breach of truce?

It was not any part of Llewelyn's plan, when we rode out from Aber, to attack the castle of Builth, or to go beyond the violated territories. And thus far we had not set a foot outside our rights, or infringed any part of the agreements to which we were sworn. Whether we were entitled to do so at this point is a delicate question. I know whose hand set this tide in motion, and it was not ours. But to stay it, once launched, was not so simple a matter. Tides must run their course before they turn, and so did ours. Llewelyn swept by Builth on an impetus that could not be stayed, dropped, as it were a calf ripe for birth, a third of his following to encircle the castle, and surged westwards into Dyfed, halting only when the town of Tenby was in flames. Then we withdrew homewards, without haste, consolidating as we passed. But the noose about the castle of Builth remained close and deadly behind us, twined by the men of the cantref, who had their own revenges to take, and drawing ever softly and tenderly tighter as the year wore into spring.

Now, though we did not know it until many weeks later, this action of Llewelyn's, like a fire in the underbrush, ran unseen and broke out in distant places long after we were already satisfied with our expedition and on the way home, intending nothing further against the peace, and believing the flames already put out. As we pieced together the story from Meurig's messages, and from certain word-of-mouth reports gathered from Cynan himself at the ford of Montgomery in August, when in spite of all the truce was again renewed, this was the way of it:

King Henry in his shivering convalescence at St Omer received the news of the Welsh attack upon Builth and Dyfed, doubtless omitting or glossing over the reason for it, and was greatly alarmed. He was obliged by the Provisions, which laid down the dates of the three parliaments, to be back in England for the second day of February, when the Candlemas session should begin, but he was held in France not only by his sickness, but also until he could get from home the money necessary to pay his temporary debts in France. In his fright over Builth he wrote to Hugh Bigod, the justiciar, and ordered him to postpone the Candlemas parliament until he came home, and in the meantime to put aside everything else, and turn all his resources to relieving Builth and guarding the marches. There was to be no parliament without the monarch.

To do him justice, no doubt he expected to delay the proceedings no more than a week or two, but in the end the delay was longer, and its effects more serious. For the earl of Leicester, also on his way home from that prolonged and courtly convocation in Paris, reached England at the end of January, and took fire when he heard of King Henry's order. The dates of the three parliaments were a sacred part of the agreement to which king, prince and nobles had voluntarily set their seals and given their oaths, and here was the king, after his old arbitrary fashion, countermanding parliament on no authority but his own, and trampling his oath underfoot.

It seems a somewhat small infringement, but in truth I think it was not so. For what was dismaying was that the king should feel perfectly at liberty to take back power into his own hands without a word, almost without a thought, never even considering that any man might object so lightly his oath lay upon him, and always would. And the force of the earl's reaction showed that in his heart, whether known to himself or not, he had never trusted that oath to be heavier than thistledown,

82

and knew that if its breach was passed over now in a little thing, it would be useless to attempt to enforce it later in many great things. At any rate, he took a high and angry line in the meetings of the council, protesting that the king had no right to interfere with the proper calling of parliament, and refusing to countenance the despatch of a money aid to him until it could be done in the proper manner, through parliament.

Thus Henry in St Omer sat and fretted over ever more frightening reports from home, that Dyfed was in flames, that the earl of Leicester was at odds with the count of Savoy and in defiance of the royal orders, and that Edward was much in Earl Simon's company and much under his influence. Which was certainly true, but the king saw in it more than I think was there to be seen. Other and worse rumours haunted him in his convalescence: that ships bearing armed men and barded horses had set sail for England without royal licence, that the Lusignan brothers were collecting mercenaries in Brittany, that Simon himself had sent for foreign troops. Which last was certainly untrue. It seems that Henry's tormented mind went in terror of civil war in England, and was even inclined to believe that his son, under the guidance of the earl of Leicester, was about to make a bid for the throne, and depose his own father. The king was a sick man, and very easily frightened when he felt himself threatened or forsaken.

Forced still to sit biting his nails for want of the money to pay his debts and leave, even when he felt well enough to make the crossing, he wrote to the justiciar again, sending him secret orders to summon a picked force of lords with their armed followings to London by a day late in April. The order came just before Easter, and Cynan said afterwards that the chancery clerks worked day and night to get the writs out in time, all the more desperately because they had to cease all their labours for Good Friday. And what was most marked was that the name of the earl of Leicester was not upon the list of those summoned. Henry had heard by then that Edward was with Earl Simon, and that in protest against the rupture of the parliamentary order they intended to hold a parliament in London in the teeth of Gloucester and the more timorous or orthodox of the council. In a frenzy of suspicion King Henry ordered that the city of London should be closed against his son and his brother-in-law, and strong forces recruited to keep the peace. And the minute he could clear his debts and redeem the jewels he had pledged for money meantime (doubtless he had King Louis' help in that matter) he sailed for home and rushed to Westminster.

As soon as he knew the king was come, Prince Edward hurried to him to pay his respects and make his peace, whether in truly injured innocence or having thought better of a folly I should hesitate to say, but that his associate in the affair was Earl Simon, and of him I could not believe that he nursed any intent against the crown, or would ever have encouraged it in the young man who followed and worshipped him. So I hold Edward innocent of anything more than standing fast on the absolute observance of the Provisions concerning parliament.

But so did not King Henry. They say he refused to see him at first, afraid of weakening out of love once he set eyes on him. Later he relented and, if he did not altogether believe the young man's protestations of loyalty and love, he forebore from saying so, and they were reconciled. But the King, still suspicious, thought best to send his son out of the kingdom for a while, to busy himself in running the affairs of Gascony.

Much of this we did not learn until the middle of the summer, by which time we ourselves had added one more anxiety to the king's troubles. For in July the castle of Builth, round which the men of the cantref were still squatting happily like hounds round an earth, was taken by night, and almost without a blow. There were some among the guards there who hated their overseers far more than they hated the Welsh and, though they gave out that the gate had been stormed by a surprise assault while a foraging party was being let in, the truth is that they opened to our men wilfully, and stood by to see the fortress taken. Rhys Fychan came in haste with his forces from Carreg Cennen, and razed the place to the ground.

Yet in spite of this offence, the royal muster, called as usual about the time of the ending of the truce, was again countermanded, and late in August Bishop Richard of Bangor and Abbot Anian of Aberconway met the English commissioners again at the ford of Montgomery, and this time procured a truce for two years instead of one. If we could not get a full peace, we managed with the next best thing, peace by stages, a year or two gained at a time.

It was while the commissioners were conferring, in a camp in the summer meadows on our side of the ford, that I got the greater part of the true story of that Easter alarm from Cynan, who was there in attendance. On our side the river the ground rises gradually in many folds, on the English side somewhat more steeply into the wooded hills that hide the rock and castle and town of Montgomery, a mile or so distant. There are plenty of quiet thickets there where men may talk privately, as we did.

'I tell you this,' said Cynan, 'the king has a feeling for the shifts of other men's minds, and though he may be too easily hopeful, yet he is often right. This clash has shaken a great many of those who felt themselves touched with suspicion by contagion, and they are busy withdrawing silently, every day another inch or two away from their sworn devotion to the reform. The balance swings gradually King Henry's way. Some were affrighted, a few were truly shocked, none of them want to risk such a tussle again. The king feels the bit between his teeth, and when his confidence is high he can be desperately bold.'

'He swore to the Provisions himself,' I said, 'he cannot say any man forced his hand.'

'He swore in order to get his way over Sicily, and now that he has lost Sicily he feels himself released from his oath. The bargain's broken. It makes no difference that they did their best for him, however reluctantly, even if he believed that, and he does not believe it. Did I tell you he wanted to put the earl of Leicester on trial for acts of treason? But for King Louis he might even have done it, but Louis has far more sense than ever King Henry will have, and sent the archbishop of Rouen over to intervene, of course on some other excuse, but that was the reason for it. So it all passed off into a private clerical enquiry, and they found Earl Simon innocent of any wrong act or intent. Just as well, for he made a strong and calm defence. Strange, that man can take fire at a private quarrel over anything, even money, but when he is under grave public attack he turns quiet, reasonable and patient as any saint. So the quarrel's dropped. By Earl Simon, no doubt, for ever, with no look behind. But the king never forgets. Now he feels himself strong enough to rid himself of this chain of the reform round his neck, soon he'll be bringing back all the Poitevins, elbowing the new sheriffs out of office one by one, and putting back his own men in their places. I'll tell you a thing not everyone even among his own counsellors knows! He has applied to Pope Alexander for formal absolution from his vow to support the Provisions. His best clerk, John Mansel, has gone to Rome on his behalf, to plead for it. And he will get it,' said Cynan.

I said: 'He will still find all the lesser folk of England in the other camp. They have had a taste of getting brisk and impartial justice, through the knights of the shires and the justiciar's perambulations, of seeing mal-practices hunted out and punished, even of seeing right done to the lesser man against the greater. Will they give that up easily?'

'It will be done slowly and gently,' he said, 'and by one who believes in his absolute right. But more impor-tant, it will be done by a power very well backed in arms.'

'If it rests with the feudal forces of England,' I reasoned, 'they may well be very evenly divided. Sup-posing, of course, that it ever comes to arms, of which at present I see no sign. Surely this Easter affair was a false alarm bred in the mind of a sick man, and one easily frightened.'

He acknowledged that it was so. Sitting there with me among the bushes, deep in the woods upstream from the ford, he made a strange figure, that smooth, well-combed man in his brushed gown, and yet he was as much at home as in his own office. There was but one change in him, that here, so near to Wales, the rounded softness of his face had sharpened to show the strong Welsh bone beneath the flesh, and his eyes had length-ened their look, and had the narrowed brightness of the mountaineer.

'Keep fast hold of your truce,' he said earnestly. 'Keep fast hold of it and draw it out as long as you can, for it will not always be the feudal host you have to face. The old order grows stiff in the joints, like an old man. The feudal host serves so many days, and goes home, and gladly. Earl Simon may not have brought any French mercenaries into the country, as he was rumoured to have done. *But King Henry did!* And so he will again, Gascons, Poitevins, whatever offers. It is a living, like any other; there are plenty of men who have skills to sell. A paid army does not go home in the winter, or put down its bows and lances to get in the harvest. Times are changing very quickly. So a king who feels he has the pope, and half the nobility, and enough of the paid soldiers of Europe on his side may not greatly care if the common folk of England are against him.' He dropped his white, ringed hands into his lap, and there they knotted suddenly into a grip as still and as hard as stone. 'Or the common folk of Wales!' he said.

All that I had heard from Cynan I related to Llewelyn. We had our truce, we had our peace, so far as it went. Two years is better than one. But the turmoil of England had now become more than our danger or our opportunity, for those ideas that moved men there were surely valid for men everywhere, and moreover, there were not many in the eastern parts of Wales who had not kin upon the other side the border.

Before Christmas, of that year twelve hundred and sixty, Edward was in Gascony. He had been allowed to stay in England until the keeping of the Confessor's feast, the thirteenth day of October, a festival dearly loved by King Henry. There he had knighted a great number of young men, among them the two eldest sons of Earl Simon de Montfort, and then, with several of the new knights in his train, he left for a long jousting tour in France, on his way to his regency in Gascony.

'It is exile!' said David, moved and angry. 'The king is turned idiot, if he conceives that Edward would ever do anything to harm him. Why, even as a child he talked of his father as a gentle simpleton who must be protected. And now he accepts this injustice because it comes from his father. Do you think he would tolerate it from any other?'

'You know him,' said Llewelyn. 'I do not.' And he watched his brother along the table with eyes aloof and attentive, for David had known a life at the English court which was closed to him.

'I do know him,' said David vehemently. 'The best and the worst of him I know, and if you think I am harking back to a childhood affection and seeing him all white, you are greatly mistaken. I never did see him so – nor any other man, for that matter. But of all the things Edward would not do, this is the most impossible. And it is gross injustice to send him away out of the country, like an exiled offender too noble to be put on trial, but too dangerous to be left at large about his father's court.'

'He is going in considerable state,' said Llewelyn, smiling, 'and to a court of his own. And if things go on as they have been threatening in England, you may well see the king beckoning him back to his aid in a hurry before long.'

That proved a true prophecy in the end, except that it took longer to fulfil itself than he had supposed. For the year that we were then about to welcome in saw a deal of change in the situation in England, but all in the king's favour. The shock of the supposed plot had had its effect; Henry had only to play the same strain again and again to keep the greater half of his magnates in more horror of seeming to countenance treason than of continuing to countenance mismanagement and corruption. As for the common people, they were not consulted, or the issue might have been very different. They had tasted a kind of diligent and honest rule that was very much to their liking, and they wanted to keep it, but the process by which it was gradually whittled away was so subtle and oblique that they hardly realised how it was slipping out of their grasp.

It was not further into the year than March, when William de Valence came back, bringing his train of officers and friends with him, and was welcomed at court, for by this time King Henry felt his position so strong that he could boldly set them back in their old position in his favour. Especially did he take courage after the end of May, when John Mansel, his clerk, returned triumphantly from Rome with Pope Alexander's new bull. Cynan had prophesied truly. As the pontiff had refused all countenance or aid to the reform, so now he took his warfare a stage further, for the bull absolved the king from his oath to keep the Provisions, and very shortly afterwards Alexander went further still, releasing not only the king, but all those who had taken the oath, and threatening any who tried to force their constancy, or used any violence against them, with excommunication.

The king made gleeful preparations to announce this decree to his people. He had a large force of foreign mercenaries and levies privately raised at home and, thus fortified, he installed himself in the Tower of London, and thence made public proclamation of the pope's judgments. With the temporal and spiritual power on his side, he was no longer afraid, and when he was no longer afraid he would begin to be vindictive, and also to presume too far on his luck.

The first we heard of this reversal was in late June, when the king wrote to Llewelyn in virtuous jubilation, saying he was now free to consider talks aimed at peace, being firmly established again in his royal authority. As though only the business of the reform had kept him from accepting the prince's offers of peace earlier, though we knew well enough that only the same vexed business had twice, at least, kept him from making war upon us.

'We have nothing to lose by talking,' said Llewelyn warily, and certain exchanges of letters did begin, which if they did nothing else provided us with regular news from England and beyond. And very odd some of those items seemed to me, if any pattern of sense was to be looked for in them. As, for instance, that at the end of May Pope Alexander died, as though the hurling of those two bulls against the reform movement had drained the final energy out of him, and within three months there was a new pope in St Peter's chair, and the parties were at work all over again arguing and angling for his favour as before. Or that King Henry, in the over-exuberance of success, nearly stumbled over into disaster by moving too fast, hunting out of office all the newly-appointed officials he did not like, and replacing them with his own favourites, some so objectionable that even the moderates demurred, and for a while it looked as if the new sheriffs of his appointing would be able to take over the royal castles only by force.

Thus things stood when the autumn began, and we, having made the most of our immunity and a very favourable year, were packing the fruits of our harvest into the barns and thinking ahead to the provisions for winter. Trade being free, we had no lack of salt, the summer having been hot and full of flowers we had honey in plentiful store. And Anglesey had provided a good grain harvest, which we were at pains to house safely. And I thought, I remember, viewing the shorn fields around Bala, when the work was done and the pale gold of stubble shone strangely in the sun, that this was a more blessed life than fighting, and that we were a happy land. If we had few riches, we had few needs. If we lacked power over others, we had a stronghold in ourselves. If we could not command the splendour of popes, we had the small, pure and homely holiness of the saints in their cells, who laid their prayers over us like sheltering hands, instead of hurling bulls of damnation against us. I would not have changed for any land upon earth, so beautiful and particular to me was this land of Gwynedd.

But into this contentment, not mine alone but embracing us all, came the envoy of death, that takes away blessed and banned alike. He came in the person of a squire of Rhys Fychan's galloping into Bala lathered and weary and stained, with the entreaty that we would forward his message also to the Lady Senena and David in Neigwl. For his mistress, the Lady Gladys, Rhys

Fychan's beloved wife, was brought to bed prematurely of a dead child, and slowly bleeding to death of that unstaunchable wound, in the castle of Carreg Cennen.

CHAPTER IV

The Lady Senena, scorning the slow ease of a litter, mounted a round Welsh cob, astride like a knight and with skirts kilted, and came like a storm-wind from Neigwl with David attentive and patient at her elbow. For though he used her very lightly when times were good, cheating, teasing and cozening her as best suited him, nonetheless he dearly loved her, and at her need reined in hard all his own indulgences. Now in her age she loved and leaned upon his raillery, as old women banter love boldly with young and comely men, in a manner of elegant game kindly and flattering to both. Threatened with bitter loss, his presence beside her reminded her of her remaining treasures. How much she understood of his ways with her, that I do not know. There was nothing he did not understand.

She let herself be lifted down in Llewelyn's arms, and wept upon his breast. Such a condescension she had not vouchsafed to him or any within my knowledge of her, for she was a very masterful lady.

'Mother,' he said, holding her thus, 'we go every one by the same narrow door. One before, and one a little later, does it matter if the way is the same?'

I was standing beside David then, and I felt him grip my arm with his long and steely fingers, and looked aside in time to see the blinding contortion of his face, bitter and brief like a shattered smile, as if he questioned whether the narrow door did not open wider and more generously for some than for others, and whether the

93

way, if not the end, did not bear a variation as extreme as the severance between dark and light. But he never made a sound, and I think he did not know he had clenched his hand upon my arm.

All we set out together to Carreg Cennen, except for Rhodri, who sent word that he was delayed on important business and would follow us and, as ever, came late. For though he was the one who had most attached his mother to him in childhood, perhaps after the Lady Gladys, by his very weakness and a tendency to ill-health, yet he was the one least disposed to family feeling, and most suspicious always that he was being slighted and disparaged. Nor could he bring himself to show as self-centred as he was, as I think Owen Goch, the eldest, might have done had be been a free man, but must always do the correct and ceremonious thing, but always grudgingly and with little grace.

We could not wait for him. Llewelyn had already sent forward a courier to have changes of horses waiting for us along the way, and this time the Lady Senena rode pillion behind a lightweight page of the escort, on a big, raw-boned rounsey, well able to carry the double load, for the lady was somewhat shrunken in her elder years, and had never been a big woman. Thus we made forced time, for the time left to the Lady Gladys was measured now in hours, not in days, unless the physicians found some way to stop the slow drain of her blood, which no draughts or potions could replace.

It was near the dusk of a September day when we came into the foothills of the Black Mountain, to that crag that rises above the river Cennen, and climbed the long ridge between the gate-towers, and in the inner bailey Rhys Fychan came out to meet us by the flare of torches. He was drawn and hollow-eyed with lack of sleep, his fair beard untrimmed and his dress untended. He looked at us all as we leaped down at his door, and said only, in a voice cracked with weariness: 'She still lives. Barely lives!' Then he took the Lady Senena in his arm and led her within, and we followed to the antechamber of the room where the Lady Gladys lay.

I did not go in with them, but waited outside the doorway, but the wide door was left open, and what was within I saw clearly, for the bedchamber was small. The evening was warm, and the window-spaces stood uncovered to the afterglow in the west, so that the single lamp by the bedside looked pale and wasted as the face on the pillow. They had raised and propped the foot of the bed, and beneath the sheepskin cover that draped her from the waist down she was swathed and packed with cloths to quench the flow that would not be quenched. She had on a white, loose gown, its sleeves no whiter than the wasted wrists and hands that lay beside her body like withered and discarded flowers. Between the heavy coils of her blue-black hair, as dark as David's, her face was waxen and translucent. It was as though I could see, clear through the delicate, blue-veined eyelids, the dark eyes that once had lifted upon King Henry's face in the hall of Shrewsbury abbey, and charmed him into smiling. For indeed she was, even thus in the awesome pallor of her strange death, a very beautiful lady.

There was a woman sitting on a low stool beside the bed, and when Rhys entered with his visitors she started up and made way for the Lady Senena, drawing back into the shadowy corner of the room. Thus I saw Cristin again in the presence of death, as I had first met her, and as then her influence was a palpable blessing, though she kept silence and stillness, and her calm was unshaken. She watched as the Lady Senena took within her strong hands the pallid hand that lay nearer to her, and nursed and fondled it, and still the face on the pillow lay mute and marble-cold. The mother crooned endearments over her one daughter, and for a long time was not heard, but at length there was a faint convulsion of the large,

95

pale lids, and a flutter of the dark lashes on the ashy cheeks. Rhys Fychan shook even to that omen, but with little hope.

'She has been like this more than a day and a night,' he said, low-voiced, 'growing ever paler. But sometimes she has spoken to me. She may to you. It will be but a thread, you must lean close.'

So they did, the Lady Senena on one side, Llewelyn on his knees on the other. And he also began gently talking to his sister, whether she heard him with the hearing of this world or of the world to come. He told her that all they who were close kin to her would care for her children as their own, and that he would be a heedful lord and a good uncle to Rhys Wyndod and Griffith, and in particular to his godson and namesake, the youngest of her sons. And whether it was the deeper notes of his voice that reached her even through the folds of her sleep, or whether the time had come when she must make her last rally and bid the world farewell, she stirred and opened her lips, and her fragile eyelids lifted from the dimmed darkness of her eyes. One on either side they leaned to her, either holding a hand, though she paid as little heed to their touch as if death had already taken all sense from every part of her but the mind and the spirit.

Something she said, for her lips moved, but sound there was none, and whoever would might interpret her last message to his own liking, and twist it, if he would, into his own name. But I think she was already speaking only with God. For her eyes closed again, and opened no more.

Through most of that night she breathed, though ever more shallowly, and all they watched with her. Rhys's chaplain came again to pray, though he had already ministered to her last wants. And in the hours before the dawn, the time of departures, she departed. I saw the very breath that was but half-drawn, and there halted,

96

leaving her with pale lips severed, as though about to speak, or smile.

It was a calm and quiet going, altogether seemly. It would have been a violation to make any outcry of grief or protest. The Lady Senena with a steady hand drew a kerchief over her daughter's face, and then those two women rose up and sent the men out of the room, closing the door against us, and presently there was running of maidservants with water and cloths, and an ordered and reverent bustle in which we had no part.

And now that his wife was well asleep, Rhys Fychan also consented without murmur to sleep, and Llewelyn saw him to his bed, for he had not closed an eye since the lady miscarried. Like one stunned he fell, and with the semblance of another death he slept.

David came forth with the rest, grave and silent, moving as though he walked in a dream. He drew me away with him to find a corner where we should be in no one's way, and a brychan to stretch out on side by side. He seemed more in wonder and awe than in sorrow, for in truth he had never been so close to death before except in the hot blood and impersonal clashes of battle. He lay on his belly among the furs beside me, his chin in his hands, and stared with wide eyes the way his sister was gone. He was still dusty and soiled from the long ride, and pale in reflection of her pallor, and he looked less than his years then.

'I had not thought,' he said, 'that it could be so gentle. But we have seen only the close, and perhaps even for her it was not all easy and without pain. I have always thought of death as the settlement of a debt – of all the debts in a lifetime. Though truly her account might well be very light and easy to pay. What harm, what wrong, did she ever do to any? Every one by the same narrow door, my brother says.' He smiled. 'I can well see him, when his time comes, riding boldly up and knocking, and the gates will fly open and let him in destrier and all.

Me, I doubt not, death will cram piecemeal through the bars of a closed wicket, a long and bloody business.'

I hated to hear him talk so, all the more as this was not said in the black mood that sometimes visited him, but deliberately and with grave thought. And I told him roughly not to be a fool, for he had no more on his conscience than most of us and, moreover, was insistent upon paying his debts as he went, so that he might well find the door open and the record clean when he came. Which would be forty good years yet, I said, to add to his present five-and-twenty.

He looked into me and through me with his dark and lustrous smile, and said: 'You little know what I have in my mind sometimes, and I would never have you know. But God keeps the tally.' And then he said, in the same considering tone, like one earnest to find exact truth in confession, and more concerned with truth than with contrition itself: 'Samson, I am afraid of death.'

And though he said it with an even voice and unblinking eyes, like a man measuring the odds and choosing his ground before a battle, with no intent of giving back or avoiding, yet my heart lurched in me, knowing past doubt that he spoke the truth. So I reached and jerked his palms from under his chin, and pulled him down with me into the hides of the brychan, and he uttered something between a laugh and a sigh, and lay where I had tumbled him, with his forehead in the hollow of my shoulder. And so, presently, he slept.

The castle of Carreg Cennen lay in mourning, and the Lady Gladys, waxen-white like a fine candle and frozen into such distant beauty that nothing of her remained ours, was laid in her coffin. Rhys Fychan arose from his long, deathly sleep refreshed and able to live again, made himself finer than usual in her honour, and took his eldest son by the hand to show him the last of the earthly part of his mother. The boy was twelve years old, in reason somewhat older, being bright and forward of understanding, and he went gravely to the lady's side and kissed her on the forehead in farewell, though the cold of her stung him into fright for a moment, and he clung hard to his father's hand. The younger ones stayed with their nurse, and she told them what all nurses tell their charges when it is certain they will see their mothers no more. But what that is I never enquired.

In this matter of the children David was at his best, for he had kept enough of his own boyhood, when the dark mood was not on him, to make him the most acceptable of us all to such tender creatures, and his play with them was worth a legion to that sorrowful household. So we passed not too painfully through the time of the lady's burial, for which Rhodri arrived just in time, and inclined to feel aggrieved at finding his sister had not waited to take leave of him. We took her to the abbey of Talley, and there she sleeps, we trust, in peace, for she was a good daughter, a loyal and loving wife, a devoted mother, as witness the honour her lord paid to her memory.

Afterwards, when we sat all together in hall in Carreg Cennen, with the whole household below us, and the business of life not so much waiting to be resumed as continuing in indifference to mortal comings and goings, then we took up the duties and anxieties we had laid by for a moment. For the rites of burial are designed less to lay the dead to rest than to set the living in motion again, there being no release from the world short of death.

On the eve of our departure the Lady Senena, who had spent her time mainly with the women and children, and had kept Cristin close about her ever since the two of them had tended the dead together, said to Rhys Fychan at table in the hall:

'There is a request I have to make of you, dear son, that I think you will not refuse me. For my dead daughter's sake, let me have her waiting-woman and take her into my own service. I should like to have by me for the rest of my days one who was so close and kind with Gladys.'

I think Rhys Fychan was not greatly surprised at this. But to me this speech came like lightning out of a clear sky, stopping the breath in my throat for desire and dread. And I looked down to the place where Cristin sat with Godred beside her, and found her looking fixedly upon me, though she was far out of earshot. Our eyes met in that look I had been avoiding hour by hour and moment by moment among the teeming hundreds of the castle, using the very stables and mews, and such places as the women seldom frequented, as shelter from the pain of beholding her. Sombrely and straightly she looked into my face, and it was I who first turned my eyes away.

Rhys said readily: 'I shall be happy to content you, mother, in anything within my power. If Cristin is willing to go with you, it might be best for her, for of late years her lady has been like a sister to her, and she will feel her loss sadly. You know what risks she once took for Gladys, and what reason we have for valuing her highly. But there's her husband to be thought of, too.'

'David will find a place for him in his own bodyguard,' said the Lady Senena firmly. 'We have truce now in Wales, but even if you should find a need for armed men, you have only to send to Gwynedd to get both Godred and whatever more you need.'

David, hearing his name, leaned along the table to enquire what was said of him, and she told him, as one taking consent for granted. For one moment he was mute, and his eyes opened a little wider, and flashed one sword-blue glance at me before they looked within, consulting that secret vision he enjoyed, or suffered, in the confines of his mind. A closed world he had there, intricately furnished with good intents that went hand in hand with impulses of malice and mischief, and reckless elations that held up mirrors to forebodings of black intensity.

'Why not?' he said with deliberation, and smiled upon whatever it was he saw within that private room. 'I'll gladly find a place for a good knight, if he says yes to it. And my mother will cherish Cristin. So will we all,' he said, and his smile turned outward towards us, and became human and sweet. But he did not look again at me.

'We'll put it to the pair of them,' said Rhys Fychan, 'and they may choose whether they wish to go or stay.'

So after we left the hall he sent for them to come into the great chamber, where the family sat retired with the cooling embers of their grief on this last evening. And it was David who did the messenger's part and went to bring them.

They came in side by side, but not with linked hands or in any way touching each other. Only once before had I seen them so close, and closer still, when he opened his arms to her in the narrow inner ward of Dolwyddelan castle, and she walked into their embrace with her eyes fixed ever over his shoulder, upon me standing distant and helpless, and never looked away until he stooped his head to kiss her, and then she closed her eyes, to see nothing more. Now they stood before their lord and mine, and waited with mild enquiry to hear what was required of them. He so fair, and agile, and fine, with that smooth and comely face ever ready for smiling, and she so dark and still and erect, seeming taller than she was by reason of her willow-slenderness. She had the bright, white skin that white flowers have, and hair as black as her lady's, but without the blue, steely sheen, and its raven silk was bound up then in a net of silver filigree. A wide, brooding mouth she had, wonderful, dark red as any rose, and eyes like running water over a bed of amethysts, now deep grey, now iris-purple. At this and every face-to-face meeting with her in my life I sought in vain for words to define what she was, and found none exact enough. But still I do not know, after all these years, whether what she had should be called beauty, or whether it bore by rights some other and rarer name.

Rhys Fychan bade them sit, and offered wine. She accepted the stool, but not the cup, and sat with such braced and attentive stillness that I knew she was not privy to this proposition, and did not know what was coming. Godred took what was offered. It would always be his instinct, as bees never say no to open flowers.

Rhys Fychan told them what was proposed. Godred was taken by surprise, but his life was an easy stream of surprises, most of which he welcomed. His brows went up, and his brown eyes rounded. It was not hard to see the wheels of his mind working busily upon the chances. David was brother to the prince of Wales and close to the seat of power, and there was glory and diversity and profit to be had around him. Why not? It was a fair enough estimate, and he had a right to pursue his own interest where no other person's was threatened. I did not blame him.

'I am at my lord's disposal and at my prince's command,' said Godred at his most melodious, 'to serve wherever I best may. But this choice is for my wife to make, since it is her service that is so kindly desired by the lady of Gwynedd. With Cristin's decision I will go.'

'Well, child?' said the Lady Senena, with her knotted, elderly hands quite easy in her lap, never doubting to have her own way. 'Will you come into the north with me? You shall be chief among my women, if you will.'

Cristin sat motionless and silent for a long moment, looking at her with wide eyes and parted lips, while it seemed that she hesitated what to answer. Then in a low, clear voice she said: 'Madam, I rejoice in the honour you do me, and am grateful that you so value whatever service I have been able to do for my lady, who is dead. Such service as I may I will do also for you, lifelong. Yes, I will go with you to Gwynedd.'

'Then I also consent,' said Godred heartily. 'If my lord

grants me leave, I will enter the Lord David's service.'

Pleased at gaining her wish, the Lady Senena begged
Cristin to put her belongings in order in time to ride
with the party the next day, and offered the help of one
of her maids to pack those possessions which could follow
more slowly. Godred, too, had much to see to, if he was
to accompany us, and so they went away to make their
preparations. I, who had stood withdrawn all this time,
having no part to play in the matter, whatever my longings and fears might be, remained still as they passed me
in leaving the high chamber, and willed not to be noticed
by word or look. Cristin went by me with a fixed and
resolute face, from which even the tremor of surprise and
wonder was gone, a marble face. It was Godred who
flashed me a jubilant smile and a sidelong gleam, as one
confident of an intimate friend who must share his
pleasure.

'Good!' said David, when the door had closed after
them. 'So that is settled to everyone's satisfaction.' And
he looked at me, and slowly smiled his dark, secret smile.

Late in the evening I went about the copying, for Rhys
Fychan, of certain small legal agreements of which he
required English versions, until I was called away from
the work by a page bringing me a mesage from David,
who desired me to come to him in the store-room where
were the linen-presses and chests belonging to the Lady
Gladys. There was no occasion for me to pass through
the great hall, where half the household was already
sleeping. I went instead by the stone passage, dimly lit by
a few smoky torches, and so into the antechamber of
the room where the Lady Gladys had died, and by the
curtained door into her store-room. Though what David
could be doing there, or what he could want with me at
this hour, I found hard to guess.

The light there was from two candles in a sconce on
the wall, and no brighter than in the passage, yet bright

enough to show that the figure bending over an open chest was not David. Nor was there time to withdraw unnoticed, for I had swung the curtain aside without any care to be silent, and as I entered the room she had heard me, and straightened and turned, without alarm, to see who it was who came. She chilled into perfect stillness. The hands a little outspread above the folded gowns in the chest hung motionless, every finger taut. The candles were slightly behind her, and her face was in shadow, yet I felt the burning darkness of her eyes fending me off. So I knew that she had had no part in this, that it was David who had done it to both of us.

It was not my own pain that caused me to draw back from her, it was rather the clear intimation of hers. Time that had done nothing to comfort me had brought her no comfort. In that moment I hated and cursed my breast-brother for his arrogance in meddling with us. And I said, through lips so stiff I could barely speak:

'I ask your pardon! I have been called here mistakenly. I had not meant to intrude on you.' And with that I turned from her, with what an effort I cannot express, and groped my way to the doorway.

I saw her stir out of her marble stillness just as I swung about and grasped at the curtain. Behind me she said sharply: 'Samson!' And when that word halted me with the latch in my hand: 'No, do not go!' she said, in a gentler tone.

I turned about, and she had come a step towards me, and the ice had melted out of her flesh and bones, and it was a live, warm creature who stood gazing at me. 'Come in,' she said, 'and close the door.'

'To what purpose?' I said. 'This was none of my seeking. David sent for me here.' And that was a coward's word if ever there was, but I was angry with him for daring to play God's part with us, and so wrung that I did not know whether it was mistaken affection for us both that moved him, or pure black mischief, to provide himself with entertainment, now that his sport in fighting was taken from him.

But Cristin said: 'David can be very wise. Even very kind. Do you think I do not know you have been avoiding me all these days? All these years! What profit is there in that, since you cannot avoid me for ever? It was time to resolve it. How much of this silence and pretence and avoidance do you think my heart can bear? In the name of God, are we not grown man and woman, able to hold whatever God fills us with? If I am to come north, as I have chosen to do, what future is there for us, if we cannot meet like ordinary human creatures, treat each other with consideration, do our work side by side without constraint?'

In the course of these words all that was ice had become a gradual and glowing fire, and she was as I had known her in the beginning, so gallant and so dear, the heart failed, beholding her. I stood mute in my anguish and my bliss, helpless before her.

She took one more step towards me, since I would not go to her, and now she had but to reach a hand a little before her to flatten it against my heart and feel how it thundered, with what desire and despair. And I but to stretch out my arms and gather her like a sheaf in the harvest, but that her troth and mine lay between us like iron bars. Her face was turned up to me, earnestly searching me. I never knew her to use any wiles upon me or any other. She had her own proud and purposeful chivalry. When she opened her eyes wide, thus, and poured their wit and intelligence and enquiry into me, she also let me in to the deep places of her own nature, and gave me the courage to enter there.

She said: 'Why did you turn away from me at Dolwyddelan, and leave me without a word of farewell, after all we had done and known together? You had no right!'

I said: 'For reason enough. I had no right to stay. You are my brother's wife. You knew it before ever I did.

You saw the ring I had from my mother, the fellow to his.'

She moved neither towards me nor away, but held her place. Her eloquent and generous mouth lengthened and quivered, and her eyes darkened into iris-purple. In a slow, hard voice, just above her breath, she said: 'Tell me the truth! Is that all I am?'

By what wisdom of David or mercy of God I do not know, in that moment my heart opened like a flower that has long been bound by frost, as if the sun had come out to warm me, and the rain to water me. I saw her mine and not mine, neither to be taken nor left, by reason of the barrier of duty and faith, by reason of the bond of love and worship. As I was bound not to despoil, so I was bound not to forsake. And I had done ill all this while, in depriving her and myself of what was ours and wronged no man.

I never touched or troubled or enticed her, but stood to face her as she stood to face me, God seeing us. I said, with all my heart and mind and soul: 'You are my love, the first one, the only one, the last one I shall ever know. I have loved you from the first night ever I knew you, before I knew if you were maid or wife. I loved you then without guilt or shame, and so I love you now, and shall lifelong. There will never be any change in me. To the day of my death I shall love you.'

Such ease I got from this utterance, I marvelled how I could have kept from making the avowal long before. Nor was it the ease of surrender and despair, but of release from bondage. And she stood before me so flushed and warmed with the reflection of my release that she was like a clear vessel filled with light.

'Now,' she said, 'you do me justice indeed, and I will do the like for you. Why should you or I go hungry for want of what is ours to feed upon without harming any man or committing any sin? When first I learned to know you, not knowing myself whether I was wife or widow, I loved you for your great gentleness and goodness to a dying man who owned he had used you ill. It may be I did wrong to choose you, but choose you I did, for once lost to me you might never be recovered, and I tell you now, such an election happens only once in any life, and in most lives never. If it was a sin, the sin was mine, and there is no man can blame you. I went with you because it was more to me to have your dear companionship than any other man's love and worship. God he knows I hoped for more, but I have had hopes before that came to grief, and the lot laid on me I could bear. But when you took from me even your dear companionship, in which my heart rested, that I could not bear.'

'I do repent me,' I said, 'that ever I did a thing so weak and so unjust as to abandon you. My love and worship is yours only, and yours lifelong, even if I never speak the words to you again. And my service and loyalty I can offer freely, before all the world. Forgive me, that ever I did you so great a hurt.'

'You have healed me,' she said. 'I give you my pledge for yours. I shall never love any man but you.'

'Yet we are taking from Godred what is rightly his,' I said, though I meant no protest against what was now past changing, but only to make all things clear between us, that we might know what it was we did.

'We are taking from Godred,' she said steadily, 'nothing that he has ever possessed. I was wed to him when I was fourteen years old; I never saw him until the match was made. And we are taking from him, I swear to you, nothing that he values, even if he had once possessed it. I am a dutiful and serviceable wife to Godred, all he has asked of me I have been and done, and will do, and will be. And I have no complaint of him. But my love he never sought, or needed, or regarded. I do him no wrong.'

Behind her the candles guttered, and a thread of tallow ran down from the flame. The curtain swung lightly, for the door behind it was still open. I felt the chill touch of the night wind, as though someone trod close on my heels. But when I stilled to listen for a moment, there was no sound. And such doubt and fear as remained in me I spoke out then, saying it would not be easy, that if she wished to take back her decision and remain in the south I would still be her faithful lover all my days, though apart from her, and such comfort as there was in that knowledge she might have without the heroic pain of nearness and silence. But all she did was to smile at me with that wild radiance making her face glorious, and to ask me: 'Is that your wish?' And there was nothing I could do but say, no! Her peace I desired. My own was safe in her hands. My wish was to see her and to serve her and to be at her call if ever she needed me. But that if it cost her too dear, that I could not endure.

'My mind is as yours,' she said. 'I will not willingly go a month, a week, no, not a day if I had my way, without the sight of you, and the sound of your voice. What you can endure, so can I. If you can make a sacrament out of your sorrow and deprivation, so can I. What I cannot do is to cease from loving you, and I would not if I could. It is the best gift God ever gave me, to love you and be loved in return.'

In these high terms we made our compact, Cristin and I. And then it came upon me that no more must be said, that the time to set the seal on so lofty a purpose was now, when all the words had been uttered that were needed between us, once for all time, and it remained only to prove what we had sworn, and make it binding for ever. And the way to do that was to bid her goodnight and commit her to the blessing of God, and so go from her without so much as the touch of hands, or too lingering an exchange of looks, as if we still had doubts, who had none.

So I did. And she, with as deep an understanding, gave me my goodnight back again, and turned to continue lifting the folded gowns from the chest. From this night on we were to meet before other people, and carry our daily burden, encountering and separating as our duties moved us, demanding nothing, repeating nothing, and even if by chance we met without witnesses, there would be no such exchange again, as none would be needed. Neither would there now be any resentment or any loneliness or any greed, for if we had not that great bliss of love fulfilled in the flesh, yet a manner of fulfilment, stranger and after its own fashion more marvellous, we surely had.

I went out from her like one in an exalted dream, and did not look back, for her image was within me. And I thought myself both blessed and accursed, but if the one was the price of the other, of what then could I complain?

In the inner ward of Carreg Cennen there was a faint silvering of moonlight, and on the wall I could hear the feet of the watch pacing. Out of the shadows near the great hall a man came walking lightly and briskly, and whistled as he came. When he drew near to me he broke off, and haled me cheerfully by name, in the voice of Godred.

'Samson!' said he, as though surprised to find me still among the waking. 'You work late tonight.' And since he halted in friendly fashion, I was obliged to do the same, though I would gladly have avoided him then. 'I am looking for my wife,' he said. 'Surely she cannot still be packing her gowns and bliauts? But you're the last man I should be asking – the prince's own clerk, and a bachelor, is hardly likely to be involved with a matter of stuff gowns and linen wimples. I must go and find her.'

Yet he lingered, eyeing me with the intimate smile I had observed in him ever since the turn I had done him at Carmarthen bridge, when he was unhorsed and in danger of trampling.

'I've had no chance to speak with you,' he said, 'since this evening's news, there's been such bustle to be ready to leave tomorrow. But I hope you may think it, as I do, a most happy chance that Cristin and I are to come and serve close to you, in Gwynedd. True, Cristin will be mainly at Neigwl, where the lady makes her home, but it's none so far, and we have peace now to travel and visit. And since David is often in attendance on the prince, I shall hope to be close to you very often during the year. Are you pleased?'

So pointblank a question, and in a tone so warm and trusting, what could I do but own to pleasure? Which I did with the more heart, seeing it had its own enormous truth, out of his knowledge, which yet did him no injury.

'So all things work together for good,' he said. In the light of the moon I could see the fair smoothness of his face, boyish and bright, and the round, candid eyes limpid brown under his tanned forehead and silvery-fair hair. 'I rejoice at being able to serve near to one who has once salvaged my life for me – and once, more precious, my wife! I feel you,' he said, in that high, honeyed voice that made speech into song, 'closer to me than a brother. Forgive me if I presume!' And he linked his hands in most becoming deprecation before his breast, in the full light of the moon, and the fingers of his right hand played modestly with the fingers of his left, turning and turning the ring upon the little finger, a silver seal bearing the image of a tiny hand, severed at the wrist, holding a rose. I had no need to see it more clearly, I knew it well. Once I had worn the fellow to it, my unknown father's solitary gift to my mother. I watched the silver revolving steadily, quite without the spasmodic motion of agitation or strain. 'Closer than a brother!' said Godred, softly and devoutly.

'You make too much,' I said, 'of services that fell to me by pure chance. There is no man among us would not have done as much in the same case.'

'Oh, no, you wrong yourself,' said Godred fervently. 'There are many who would have done less. And perhaps some,' he said, 'who would have done more.' This last in the same honeyed tone, too cloying, as honey itself cloys. 'Now in the north I may be able to repay all. All!' he said, and uttered a soft, shy laugh. 'But I must go find my wife,' he said, and clapped me on the shoulder with the hand that wore the ring, and so passed on, silvered by the moon.

I would have held him back from her then, if I could, to spare her the too sudden and too apt reminder, yet I knew that she was armed and able. It was not that that clouded all my ecstasy as I went slowly to my bed. But I could not help seeing still the slow, measured spinning of that silver ring, white in the moonlight, and hearing the soft insinuation of his voice. And I remembered too well the flickering of the candles in the draught from the door, and the chill of some presence treading hard on my heels. And my own voice saying in its own excuse: 'You are my brother's wife. You knew it before ever I did. You saw the ring....'

I prayed hard and slept little. And the next day we rode for Gwynedd.

I said to David, when he brought his tall English horse to pace by my pony on the way: 'Well, are you content with your work?' For still I bore him some ill-will for the trick he had played me, even as I rejoiced, pain and all, at my great gain by it.

Said David, shrewd and shameless: 'Are you?' And he looked at me along his shoulder, smiling. 'You have a look of achievement about you, you and Cristin both. Did you come to a satisfactory understanding?'

'Not as you suppose,' I said sharply, for I was sure in my own mind of what he had intended, and it was galling enough to have one brother soliciting me like a pander, leave alone my breast-brother joining in the game.

'Never be too confident,' said David, 'of what I am either supposing or provoking, you might go far astray. But if you think you could have gone on living in the same

111

world with her and utterly estranged, for God's sake, man, get sense. If *you* could, in your holiness, why should she have to endure the like?'

I own that any smart I felt against him, by that time, was but the reverse of my gratitude, and I admitted to myself that he might well be honest in his concern. But I had to ask him one more thing, for it was on my mind and I could not put it by.

'Tell me this, did you follow me there to see what passed between us?'

'No!' he said, indignant. 'What do you think I am, that I should spy on you?'

So if he had not, another had. But I did not say so to him, for there were already possibilities enough for mischief. 'Closer than a brother!' rang the soft voice in my memory, and still I saw the silver ring revolving with delicate intent about the long finger.

CHAPTER V

———

Llewelyn moved his court to Aber in the middle of November, as was customary, ready to keep the Christmas feast there, and at the beginning of December Meurig rode into the llys, on his way to his own winter quarters at Caernarvon, for he was thin in the blood, and liked to burrow and hide himself like a hedgehog through the frost and snow. He brought us all the news from England, having come direct from Shrewsbury and, sitting snug by the fire like a little grey cat, talked familiarly of kings and earls and popes, and the building and dismemberment of the grand dream of the Provisions.

'King Henry has gnawed and tunnelled like a rat, and prised gently like frost among the ranks of the reformers, crumbling them apart with his papal bulls and his royal French alliance. He called all his barons to a conference at Kingston at the end of October, feeling himself ready to play the winning stroke. He offered everything possible in reason and magnanimity, amnesty for all who would accept the findings of the meeting. They have given in,' said the old man, scornfully grinning, 'and come to the king's peace, every man of them. He has been gracious and kingly. He has them all in his hand.'

'All?' said Llewelyn sharply.

'All but one,' said Meurig.

'Ah!' said Llewelyn, satisfied, as though his own honour had been vindicated. 'And what had the earl of Leicester to say at Kingston?'

'Never a word, my lord, for he never went there. He and the closest who remained staunch were out in the shires, setting up their own wardens according to the Provisions. I do believe the lesser gentry in the country-side and the common people were ready to stand and fight if need be, but the barons were not. Half they feared what they were doing and what they had already done, and half they craved their old ease again, without too much need for thought, and believed the king's blandish-ments and swallowed his bait. First Hugh Bigod, that was formerly justiciar, and a good, fair man, too, but over-persuadable, he slipped away and spoke for com-promise. Then the earl of Hereford, and then even Gloucester. So in the end they all went to Kingston as they were bidden. All but Earl Simon. And he spoke out on them for a generation of changeable and slippery men he could not abide, when they had sworn every one to do these things and see them done. He has shaken off the dust of England in disgust, and gone away into his French possessions, for he will not touch this mangled rem-nant they are busy concocting out of the grand design.'

'Then King Henry has won his war,' said Llewelyn, with concern and misgiving, for though the desultory exchanges over peace had continued, they showed no sign of coming to anything, and a king triumphant and vindictive and in full control of his affairs again was less likely, for all his professions of goodwill, to want to conclude a genuine agreement with us.

'I would not say his war has so far even begun,' said Meurig, musing. 'He has brought the great lords of the older sort to heel – all but one – but he has not given any thought yet to the lesser ones, or to those young men who were not consulted when the Provisions were drawn up, and have not been consulted now when they are swept away, but who may very soon find that they have come to like what was begun, and miss it sadly now it's done away with. It's too early to say anything is lost, or anything won.'

So things stood in England that winter. But at least

we in Gwynedd received a Christmas gift rather more to our liking, for about the feast of St Nicholas, after Meurig had left us, a messenger rode into the maenol from the castellan of Criccieth, and his news was matter for sober celebration. Meredith ap Rhys Gryg, still kicking his surly old heels in captivity, had at last given in, and indicated his willingness to renew his homage and acknowledge Llewelyn as his overlord.

'True,' said Llewelyn, gratified but undeceived, 'I doubt if his mind towards Rhys Fychan or me has changed much, and once before he swore fealty and did homage, and was forsworn within the month. But at least he shows some sense at last. And we'll see what safeguards we can bind him with this time!'

So they brought Meredith ap Rhys Gryg out of his prison, to a great meeting of the council of Wales at Conssyl. The old bear reappeared before us somewhat fatter and slower for his two years of confinement, but little tamed, though he behaved himself with stolid submission, and contained whatever rage he still felt. The agreement that released him we had drawn up with care, to protect the rights of his neighbours and kinsmen, and he had to give up his prize of Dynevor intact to its rightful owner again, and also surrendered his new castle of Emlyn, with the commote belonging to it. But otherwise he got back all his ancestral lands in return for his homage and fealty, and was received into the prince's grace and peace.

As for the safeguards, they were hard but fair, and no one ever came to hurt through them. Besides the loss of his one castle – for Dynevor never was rightly his – he surrendered his eldest son for a time to live at Llewelyn's court, and was pledged on demand from the prince to render up to him twenty-four sons of his chief tenants, whose families would be sureties for his loyalty should it come into question. And if he broke any of the terms of the compact, he quitclaimed to Llewelyn all his inheritance and rights in Ystrad Tywi, which might be stripped from him without further ado.

To all this he swore, and plumped down on his stiff old knees to do homage. And doubtless much of what he was forced to speak tasted of gall to him, for he was a wild, proud man. Yet by this simple act of submission, which was but returning to what he had freely sworn in the first place, and to one to whom he owed so much, he regained all his own but for the castle and commote of Emlyn, which I think was no harsh dealing. And his son, a grown man and with more sense than his sire, gave his parole cheerfully and had his liberty in Llewelyn's court, and hawked and hunted with the prince to his heart's content while he remained with us.

So this, the prince's first traitor, came to his peace as an example to all others both of firmness and magnanimity. And the only note of regret was struck by Llewelyn himself, saying, after Meredith had departed to his own country, and the news had been sent to Rhys Fychan in Carreg Cennen: 'They will be riding home for Christmas, Rhys and the children. Pity, pity it is that Gladys could not have lived to take her boys back in triumph to Dynevor. It was her favourite home.'

The new year of twelve hundred and sixty-two was barely seven weeks old when the new French pope, imitating his predecessor, issued a bull supporting King Henry in all points. Pope Urban, it seemed, was determined not to allow the king to revive his son's claim on Sicily, for he thought to do much better with another candidate, but because of that he was all the more anxious to satisfy him of his goodwill on all other issues. Earl Simon, though forgetting nothing and abandoning nothing of his ideals, still morosely absented himself in France, and it seemed that everything in England was going tamely King Henry's way.

Thus fortified, he sent out letters to his sheriffs

denouncing all those ordinances made in the name of the Provisions. As for those who still feebly contended for a measure of reform, their position had been whittled down stage by stage until they gave way altogether at this blow, and wearily agreed to let the king's brother, Richard of Cornwall, king of the Romans by election, act as arbitrator on such matters as were still at issue. And decent man though Richard was, and sensible, yet he was Henry's brother. It did not take him long to restore the king's right to appoint his own ministers and sheriffs without consulting council or parliament, which was the whole heart of the matter. But at least he strongly urged on his brother the absolute necessity of coming to amicable terms with the earl of Leicester, and warned him to observe good faith in coming to such an agreement, and to adhere to it strictly once it was made.

He was spending wisdom only to see it blown away down the wind. For King Henry, who was always exalted into the clouds or abased into the kennel, was in his glory now, and no way disposed to be lenient to his enemies. In the summer he set off for France, to clear up matters of family business and to employ King Louis' good offices in making the advised overtures to Earl Simon. Louis urged moderation, as Richard had done, and with as little effect. Instead of approaching his sister's husband in conciliatory mood, King Henry dragged out of the past all his old hates and complaints against the earl, and instead of appeasement there was nothing but bitter rancour, which Earl Simon's hot nature could not but reciprocate. So nothing was healed, and nothing satisfied, and the wounds festered.

As for us, we kept our household and minded our own business, to good effect, for without difficulty we procured a renewal of our truce in the month of May, on the same terms as before, and again we gained not one year of grace, but two.

*   *   *

That summer was the time when Richard de Clare, the great earl of Gloucester, died in the month of July, a few weeks short of his fortieth birthday. He left a son turned twenty years, Gilbert, ripe and ready to be an earl, and fretting and furious when, because of the king's absence, he was kept out of his honour month after month, and received no seisin of his right.

David came visiting as soon as he had word of the earl's death, very bright of eye and expectant, for he was restless for action, and weary of the mere daily labour of managing his lands, which, though he could do it very shrewdly if he pleased, he could as well leave to his mother. He had Godred among his retinue, as eager as himself.

'I thought I should have found you in arms,' said David. 'Here's Richard of Clare gone, and no provision made for proper rule in his lands without him, and young Gilbert disparaged and kept waiting. The whole march is in disarray, we could pick off all the Welsh edges of it without trouble or loss, and an occasion for shaking the truce a little is not far to seek; you have only to goad Gilbert into lashing out first. I could do it within the week, and put him wholly in the wrong.'

'You'll do no such thing,' said Llewelyn smartly. 'There's a small matter of my word and seal in the way, even if we had anything to gain by setting the march on fire, and we have not. If I wanted occasions, there have been any amount without goading from me. So far I've had satisfaction by legal means. They meet us, on the whole, fairly enough; the measures of conciliation work.'

'They've worked in the past,' said David, discontented. 'Things are changing in the march, or have you not been informed? There's something in the wind among the young men. There isn't a castle down the border you could not pick like a flower now if you had a mind to.'

'I know it,' said Llewelyn calmly. 'I have been following affairs, as well as you. Old men are vanishing from the scene, and young men take views of their own, and are less happy with King Henry's ascendancy than their elders. Certainly this is an opportunity, if I had no restraints. But I have. A few months ago I pressed the king again to come to a formal peace with Wales. I know he is holding me off, with excuses about Prince Edward's absence and the need to consult him, and I know I could go on taking what I want, while I wait for him to recognise me and all my gains. I choose not to, for more reasons than one. But one is enough. It is barely two months since I set my seal to the new truce.'

David gave him a sidelong glance, and said provocatively: 'The king thanked you in so many words, did he not, for refusing to take advantage of England's household troubles? Are you so anxious to stand well with him?'

'No, with myself,' said Llewelyn, undisturbed. 'Though I believe he has done his best to keep the truce and make amends for infringements. Take him all in all, he has played reasonably fair with me, and so will I with him. Let Gloucester's lands alone.'

'He is not Gloucester yet,' said David, 'and they're in no hurry to invest him. That's one more disaffected lordling their side the border.'

'And one on mine?' asked Llewelyn, and laughed to see him flush and bite his lip, until suddenly David laughed, too.

'Not so bad as that! But I could be at home in such company, I don't deny it. You know they're ranging about Kent with Roger Leyburn at their head, holding tournaments? And in the marches, too. The justiciar is in a sweat about it, with orders to call in the churchmen wherever they plan a round table, and try to prevent it, but he has his work cut out. There was a great meeting at Gloucester itself – I tell you, I was in two minds about putting on false coat-armour and riding to issue a challenge there, as in the old tales. If you won't find me work to do, why, they might find me very good play, and nearly as rough.'

'Rein in for a little while,' said Llewelyn, 'and there may well be both work and play rough enough even for you.'

This movement of the younger barons had begun in the general uneasiness and discontent after the Provisions were seen to be enfeebled and abandoned, but the spark that set light to the disquiet was a personal one. The Lord Edward had the very able and fiery Roger Leyburn as his steward, and had some cause in his absence, or had been led by his mother to believe he had cause, to suspect his officer of peculation. Roger being of no mind to be made a victim, and stoutly asserting his own good faith, had returned to his estates and drawn round him all the restless young lords like himself, many of them from marcher families. Roger Clifford of Eardisley, John Giffard of Brimpsfield, Hamo Lestrange of the Shropshire family, and Peter de Montfort the younger of the English house, son to that Peter de Montfort who had conducted us to the parliament of Oxford – these were among his allies. Now, according to rumour, Gilbert de Clare was joining the brotherhood, and even the name of Henry of Almain, Richard of Cornwall's son, had been mentioned. There were northerners, too, a de Vesci of Alnwick, a Vipont of Appleby, all young men who had not accepted, as their elders had, the revocation of all the measures of reform. Most had been friends and companions of Edward, many David had known at court, as mere boys. If these young sparks were at violent play in the marches, and David was prevented by truce from working off his energy against them in honest battle, what wonder if he ached to go and join them and spend his fire in their company? Yet their movement was not play, and it had another effect, upon men graver and more earnest than they, for it drew into its current the hopes and longings of the small gentry, the yeomen, the citizens, all of whom had accepted the proclamations of reform with faith and eagerness, and then seen King Henry dash the cup from their lips.

Thus a casual confederacy may become a party almost without its own knowledge, and grow into a cause almost without its own will.

For want of warfare, at least Llewelyn found David some good hunting. They were often out together late into the evening, and ranged far in the hill forests with the hounds. So it happened that when the weather broke suddenly after a clear day they came home drenched and cold, as often rain brings on great cold after a long settled spell. In hall afterwards Llewelyn ceased to eat, and put his hands to his head, and before we left the table he began to shake with the marsh sickness, and soon fell into a terrible sweat. He was unused to illness, and would not believe or tolerate what was happening to him, until he fell in the drooping fury of helplessness, and had to be carried to his bed.

David sat by him into the night, and so did I, for it took him hard, so that he sank away from us and lost his senses at times, and again returned into shuddering consciousness, turning and tossing, muttering through chattering teeth, and ever soaked in sweat. His face grew hollow and grey, and his eyes sunken. When he opened them it was clear from their burning light that he knew us, but the words that came from his lips were broken and meaningless.

'This is my fault,' said David, distressed and bitter with himself. 'I wish to God I had agreed to turn back earlier, and get home out of the storm. Why should it fall on him, and not on me? There's no justice in it.'

Towards morning he said, as he wiped the sweat from the prince's forehead: 'It is very evil. He may die! I should go for our mother, she will be his best nurse.'

So he spoke with Goronwy, and as soon as it was light he rode, not entrusting the errand to any other. But it was a day before the Lady Senena came, and a grim day for us, for the prince sank even deeper into his wanderings, and the flesh watered away from his bones as fast as ever I saw. I stayed with him all the time, for he had about him at this pass no mother nor brother nor sister, and never had I felt him so solitary and so committed to my care. His physician came and went, but Llewelyn was past swallowing draughts, and we knew there was little to be done but help his strong and resolute body to do its own fighting. So we continued stubbornly replacing his soaked bedding and bathing his tormented face, keeping him wrapped when he was racked with shivering, and cooling his body with distillations of herbs when he burned. When he could not endure the heat of the bed I held him raised against my shoulder, and was nursing him so when for the first time he fell into a shallow but real sleep.

Afraid to stir for fear I disturbed this respite, I held him more than two hours, while his sleep, though troubled at times, yet continued. In the dusk of that day he opened his eyes, that looked at me with recognition, and essayed to smile, saying: 'Samson?' And when I answered, low, that it was I, he whispered: 'Again the same small favour! Harder than parrying a knife!'

Before it was fully dark David returned with the Lady Senena, and they came in at once to the bedchamber. And with them, entering silently on her lady's heels, came Cristin. The Lady Senena came to her son's bedside, felt his brow, and turned back the covers from his throat, that was still and ever running with sweat. But I saw by the way her grim face eased, no matter how slightly, that she found him in better case than she had expected, and that she would fight for him with a good heart. I looked beyond her, and found Cristin gazing with a still and serious face upon me, and upon the sick man in my arms.

Her eyes smiled. Not her lips. She spoke no word to me, but I knew she was remembering another bedside, in a hut among the snowy woods of the Black Mountain. That patient had been past our saving. This one I knew then would not be lost to us.

'It is not so bad as it might be,' said the Lady Senena, turning back her sleeves. 'He has slept? An honest sleep?'

I said that he had, for two hours, and that he shook now less than before. 'You have done well by him,' she said, 'but now lay him down gently and leave him to us.'

So I did, and myself slept for a while, being sure in my heart by this time that I might do so without fear, for he would live. The attack, which had been rapid and violent in its development, passed no less swiftly from him. Within three days he was able to get up out of his bed and walk a little in the sun, gaunt and shaky, but again his own man. When first he arose, uncertainly smiling like one entering in at a doorway to a world unknown, or almost forgotten, he leaned upon David, whose steely, arrogant strength was well able to sustain him. But before he lay down again he called me to him, and asked me to play my crwth, since he was too weak to put his senses to any harder work than listening to music. And so I did, and to my music he slept, which his mother said firmly was the best occupation he could have for some days yet.

So it went until he was stronger, his mother and David and I vying for the frail attention he was able to bestow. Only Cristin fetched and carried, cooked and nursed, without any ambition to take him from us. And she gave orders, too, with authority, to me as readily as to another if I happened to be at hand, as often I was. And that companionship in his service, quite without greed or insistence on personal recognition, was marvellously reassuring to me, and beyond belief rewarding.

123

But it was not long before the prince himself undid the half of our good work. He would ride before he was well fit, for it enraged him that his body should have the mastery over him, and he came back from his ride sweating again and shivering, tried too far too soon. Then there followed an anxious night when the fever racked him again, and at intervals, as before, he wandered, muttering confused words. His mother would have insisted on watching the night through with him, had not Cristin with authority taken her place, and even then she would have a man stand by, for should his state become worse he was too heavy for Cristin to lift and handle alone.

That duty she laid, by custom and without question, upon me, and without question I accepted it. And this befell in hall, before the Lady Senena withdrew to her rest, and all those about the tables above the fire heard it, among them Godred.

His duties being with the guard, and not within doors, I had seen but little of him during those days, yet I knew that when the whole household gathered his eyes were constantly upon me. So they were then, and I saw their knowing brightness. He came to my side as we left the hall, stepping lightly and walking close, and looking at me full with his open, round-eyed smile he said softly:

'I trust you'll have quiet watch tonight. And no occasion to call for other help. No one will dare disturb you uncalled, that's certain, not in Llewelyn's own chamber.'

I understood but would not understand him. And he, as though he talked at random and lightly, following a wanton thought that touched us only by chance, laughed and said: 'That would be a fine romantic scene for a geste – two secret lovers set to such a night-watch together! I wonder how long their continence would last through the night!'

I would not follow him down any of these devious

124

ways he led me, but took my arm from under his hand, and said I had no time or mood for fooleries while the prince was sick, and I must be about my business for him. Godred laughed again, very confidently, and laid the hand I had rejected upon my shoulder for a moment. 'Ah, there'll be time for plenty of changes of mind before morning,' he said in my ear. 'No need to carry your sword for a cross all the hours of darkness, like a new knight at vigil, nor lay it between you and temptation night-long, neither. Life owes you a sweet bed and a warm one now and then. I am expert in your deserts. I owe you so much myself, and you never will give me occasion to repay.' Still softer he said, and giggled: 'Nor her, either! We feel our indebtedness, indeed we feel it!'

And he dug his hard fingers into my shoulder, and so slipped away from me without looking back. And I went to watch by Llewelyn's bed with a chill of misliking about my heart, for there was something changed in Godred, and not for the better, something that went even beyond his shameful urging of me towards his wife. That I had heard from him before, but in a fashion somewhat different, lightminded and fulsome at the same time, anxious to have my favour and stand well with me, by whatever means served. All this was present still, but with a bitter after-taste, all the sweetness somehow underlaid with a note of cruelty and spite. Towards her? I could not think so. Towards me, then? He had no occasion more than before, and if he had spied on us at Carreg Cennen he knew it. Nor should he have any occasion this night, or any night to come.

So I put him out of my mind, and went to my duty. And I forgot him in my lord and my love, those two people I most revered in this world. Llewelyn lay uneasily between waking and sleeping, now and then babbling into his pillow and tossing weakly, great beads of sweat gathering and running on brow and lip, but

125

this time he was not turned inward away from us. He knew us, and at moments spoke to us, feebly but with knowledge, even with kindness and humility, begging pardon for the trouble he gave us, and the grief, and thanking us for our care of him. Towards midnight he panted and sweated most, and I lifted him into my arms and held him so, while Cristin bathed his face and neck and shoulders and breast with a cooling infusion of herbs, time after time until his shivering stopped, and he breathed more deeply, and lay more easily in my arms. And so he fell asleep as before, truly asleep, the fever ebbing away. Cristin spread a clean linen pillow under him, and I laid him down, never breaking his sleep.

'It is passing,' she said almost silently over his body. 'Now he will rest.'

In that bedchamber, small and bare enough, there was a little rushlight burning, set back behind his head that it might not trouble his eyes. The hangings on the walls were of woven wool, and we had young branches of pine fastened there, to make the air sweet and spiced. The summer was mild, with little troublesome heat, but the curtained door we left open, to let in air. The window-opening was full of stars. There she and I hung over Llewelyn's sleep together, one on either side of the bed. And by the grace of God we thought not at all of each other, but only of him, until his sleep deepened and eased into a wondrous freshness and grace, and the fever ebbed even out of his bones and left him clean. Then we looked up, our faces but a little way apart, each into the other's eyes.

In the anteroom to the bedchamber, scarcely wider than a passage, there was a brychan drawn close up to the doorway, put there when first Llewelyn began to mend, so that whoever watched with him overnight could get some rest and yet hear any sound from within the sickroom. I said to Cristin in a whisper, rather by signs than by words, that she should go and lie down there,

126

for she was weary, and I would sit up with the prince, and call her if there were any need. But she only smiled at me and shook her head, feeling no need to give any reason, as I felt none to ask for any. I could as well have withdrawn into the outer room myself, for the protection of her good name, even though none but the one person in all the household would ever have dreamed of calling it in question, and there watched out the night at her call, but I did not do it. For such moments as we might have together lawfully were beyond price, and the gift of a night was food for a hungry year to come.

So we trimmed the flame of the rushlight low and clear, and sat with him all night long, his body and bed the sheathed sword between us. Twice he roused a little, not quite awake, and made the wry movements of dry lips that signified his thirst, and then I raised him, and she put honeyed water to his lips, and a fresh, cool cloth to his forehead, and he swallowed and slept again. Such words as we spoke to each other were not of ourselves, but of him, and they were wonderfully few. All night long I never touched her hand. And all night long we were in peace. To be in her presence, unassailed and sinless, was more of bliss than I had believed possible.

In the dead of night the silence was so profound within the llys that every murmur of wind in leaves from without came to us clearly, and towards morning, but long before light, bird-song began in a sudden outburst of confidence and joy, so loud and brave that I marvelled how such fragile instruments could produce such notes without shattering. Then the first pre-dawn pallor appeared in the east, and the first footsteps were heard in the bailey, the creakings and murmurings of men arising unwillingly from rest. And Llewelyn opened his eyes, sunken but clear, and asked for wine.

I went to fetch it. If I had not leaped so gladly to answer his wish I should not have seen the curtain of the outer door of the anteroom still quivering from the hand that had just let it fall hurriedly into place, or heard the light, furtive footsteps fleeing, tip-toe, along the stone passage without.

The brychan was drawn close against the open door of the bedchamber, its head shielded by the tapestry hanging. I stooped and felt at the blanket draped upon it, and in the centre it was warm to the touch.

I did not linger then, but did my errand, neither seeing nor expecting to see on my way that person who had kept us company unseen and unheard during the night. For there were many ways out into the bailey and the wards from that passage, and outside in kitchens and stables and byres the household was already stirring. But afterwards, when I came again, and when the Lady Senena had bustled in to take charge, the first ray of sunlight piercing clean through the bedchamber and the open door showed me two more evidences of what I already knew. A tiny mote of sun danced upon the blanket, where all else was still in shadow, for there was a small hole in the tapestry, low towards the head of the brychan. And in passing through that chink, the light irradiated a single shining thread among the dark colours still further darkened by smoke, and I drew out in my fingers a long, curling hair, pale as ripe barley-silk.

I said no word to Cristin or any other. Nor to him, when I met him in the armoury, and he greeted me gaily after his usual fashion, and asked me how the prince did, and if we had had quiet watch. I answered him simply, as though I took him and all his words and acts for honest. Better he should never be sure that I knew anything more of him than the sunlit outer part. Nor could I discern anything in him changed towards me, in voice or face, until I left him there and, leaving him, for some reason looked back. Still he stood smiling after me, all innocent goodwill, with no more of parody in his manner than was usual with him. Only his eyes,

128

so wide and round and brown, and full of speckled golden lights like the shallows of the river where I had first encountered him, were become blind brown stones in his comely face.

After that day the prince mended, and this time he paid better heed to advice, and waited for his strength to come back before he tested it too far. By the time September came in, and we were busy with the harvest, he was himself again, a little leaner but as hard and vigorous as ever. And the Lady Senena, satisfied with his progress and his promises, returned to Neigwl and took Cristin with her, and shortly was followed by David and all his retinue. So I was rid of Godred, whom I was farther than ever from understanding, and robbed of Cristin, whom day by day, in presence or in absence, it seemed to me that I knew better, understood more profoundly, and loved more irrevocably.

During the prince's illness, of which rumour had spread far and wide as it always does, the state of lawlessness in the marches had grown worse, and the breaches of truce were many. And still, by Llewelyn's order, his officers held them in check as best they might, and refrained from turning the frequent incidents into major battles. True, the Welshmen along the border were not saints, either, and from stoutly defending themselves may well have passed, where a tempting opportunity offered, to local revenges, and even to raids of their own. But by now the retinues of the marcher barons had very little to restrain them, and the prince's patience, no more inexhaustible than that of any high-mettled man, soon wore perilously thin.

I think what held him back, where it might well have urged on another man, was the news that came through to us from France of the disaster that had fallen upon King Henry's court there. For in Paris there was a great epidemic of plague, which someone had unhappily carried in among the king's officers. Many died there, and King Henry himself and young Edmund, his son, were also stricken, and lay dangerously ill for some weeks. Rumours that the king was dead, or likely to die, did nothing to restore order in the marches. But late in October we heard that he was out of danger, and allowed to get out of his bed and walk a little.

'Poor wretch!' said Llewelyn. 'I have been in the same case myself. Why should I add to his troubles? As long as he forbears with me, so will I with him.'

But that was before Meurig rode into Aber from Shrewsbury in the early days of November, making for his winter nest earlier than usual because he carried urgent letters that concerned Wales very closely and bitterly.

He did not know what it was he carried, for the roll was sealed; he knew only that it had been brought to him secretly by a Welsh friar, the last of a chain of messengers conveying it not from Westminster, but from King Henry's own court in Paris. Thence it had travelled by the same ship that brought reassurances and orders to the justiciar in London, but in the care of a Welsh seaman. The covering letter was from Cynan, greeting us fresh from a sick-bed which had barely missed being his death-bed, for he was among the royal clerks in attendance on the court, and had been brought down with plague like almost all the rest, though by the grace of God he was mending well when he wrote. There were two enclosures, both copies in Cynan's own hand, though shaky still from his illness, so that Llewelyn frowned over the cramped Latin, and followed a slow finger along the lines.

'He says only his sickness has kept him from sending these earlier, for he could not trust them to any other, or let any other know he possessed copies. The first is not dated. The second, he says, follows it and will date it for us.'

The first letter enclosed was short, and for want of its original seal Cynan had written the name of the sender at the foot, and the name was Griffith ap Gwenwynwyn of Powys. Llewelyn read it through with a frown that changed as he went into a grin of somewhat sour amusement.

'Listen,' he said, 'what Griffith ap Gwenwynwyn writes to his patron King Henry. He greets his lord, and informs him that he has been making enquiries about Llewelyn's health, and it is bad. The prince rallied enough to take exercise, but then twice relapsed into the same sickness, and is said to be very weak, and unlikely to recover. Griffith will send further reports if he should grow worse.' He laughed, disdainfully rather than angrily, for there was nothing unexpected in this. We knew from long since that Griffith was the royal spy on our borders, just as we had Cynan and others in England. Yet there was all the width of the world between a Welsh-born prince slavishly reporting to England on the health of the prince of Wales, and a Welsh clerk in London risking livelihood and life itself in the service of his own country.

'Poor Griffith,' said Llewelyn, 'he has no luck, for all his industry. Here am I alive and dangerous, and the king laid low in his turn. Griffith must be biting his nails now which way to go.'

He unrolled the second scroll, which was longer, and raised his brows at sight of the superscription.

'It is from King Henry himself to his justiciar. The date is the twenty-second of July.'

It was the day he first walked out into the sun again after his relapse. I remembered it, and so did he. He leaned on my arm that day, looking out over the salt flats to the sea.

He read with a darkening face, that struggled with its own betraying thoughts, but mirrored most of them. A long, dour reading it was, and at the end of it he suddenly cursed aloud, and then as abruptly laughed even

131

more loudly, though there was outrage and anger in his laughter.

'His Grace has heard the news of Llewelyn's death! He writes in great haste – he was whole and well himself, then, his turn was still to come! – to make plain his plans for the succession in Wales. Llewelyn is unwived, and without issue, but with a vigorous brother named David ready to pick up the burden he let fall, and that must never be permitted, no, at all costs not David, who would be as single and vehement as his elder. His Grace has an answer to David. Owen Goch is to be freed from his prison and set up in half of what the king proposes to leave of Wales. But he'll gain very little, for Henry means to recover for himself the homages of all the other Welsh princes, leaving Gwynedd at its narrowest to be divided between Owen and David. And how is he to contrive all this? By force of arms! This, while he writes to me piously of peace! The barons of the march are to assemble their arms at Shrewsbury to conquer Wales. He looks for help from certain impressionable princes, not forgetting Meredith ap Rhys Gryg. Well? Those are King Henry's plans for Wales, when he thinks me on my death-bed, or dead already. It is not my word, it is his. Here in plain script. Under his own seal.'

It was as he had said, in every particular. How Cynan ever contrived to get a copy of the letter I could not guess; it may well be that he memorised it complete from another clerk's account, for he was not so close to the crown as to be dealing with such correspondence himself.

'To be fair to him,' said Goronwy, always the most temperate of us, 'this is no proof he was in bad faith in talking of peace with you, or thanking you for your forbearance in his troubles at home. True, he may well have been pursuing that path because he saw no alternative while you lived. It's when he thinks you dead that he feels it a possibility to conquer Wales. After his

132

fashion he is paying you a compliment.'

'A compliment I could well do without,' said Llewelyn, between laughter and rage still. 'How long is it since I heard much the same rumours of him, and held my hand from taking any advantage? When did King Henry ever make the least gesture of generosity towards me and mine? When we were hard-pressed, then he bore harder still on us and took whatever he could. Now I doubt not he would like this letter buried deep, knowing I am well alive. He shall know it even better yet. I tire of my own restraint, seeing he observes none. It is time to show King Henry how exceedingly alive I am!'

What plans the prince would have made, and where his deliberate blow would have fallen, had not others provided occasion, was never made plain. He summoned his host and his allies at leisure, calling David from Neigwl, while he considered the courses open to him, and weighed their advantages. This was the first time that ever he set out of intent not merely to breach the truce but to destroy it.

Occasion, amounting in itself almost to prior breach, was not far to seek, though we did not then know what was toward. The many and increasingly grave raids on the borders had alarmed and enraged others besides the officers of Gwynedd. In particular the Welshmen of Maelienydd, in the central march, uneasy neighbours to Roger Mortimer, were angry and unhappy when they saw that he was thrusting his border forward into their territory and building himself a new castle on the hill of Cefnllys, and thinking it politic not to speak first, but to act, for fear Llewelyn should continue to counsel moderation, raised a force of their own and took the castle by a trick. They had no wish to occupy the site themselves, only to prevent it being used as a base against them, and accordingly they razed the walls and the keep, and so left it. As soon as he heard the fate of his fortress,

133

Roger raised a strong force, helped by his neighbour Humphrey de Bohun, and rushed to Cefnllys to rebuild it. Too weak to attack so powerful a company, the men of Maelienydd did what perhaps they should have done earlier, and hurriedly sent a courier to appeal for aid to Llewelyn.

By a happy irony the messenger arrived on the first day of December, a single day after the arrival of a letter from King Henry himself, still weak and ailing in France, but stirring himself to deal, even from that distance, with the many disorders that plagued his realm, and should, if he had been wise, have kept his mind off meddling with any other prince's territory. Among the many complaints to assail him was one from Mortimer, it seemed, bitterly accusing the Welsh of the assault on his castle, and indicting Llewelyn by name. Which accusation King Henry duly passed on to the prince, requesting explanation for the breach of truce.

'Having got over his disappointment at finding me still alive,' said Llewelyn, 'he's forced back on the old approaches. How gratifying, to be able to write with a clear conscience and deny the impeachment. I have not laid a finger on the truce – yet.'

And he dictated a mild, noncommittal reply, acknowledging the letter, stating that as far as his knowledge went he had not in any way broken his truce with the king, and offering amends for any proven infringements to date, provided the same justice was done to him.

Next day came the man of Maelienydd, in his turn complaining to his prince, defending the action of the Welsh with many and voluble legal arguments, some of them sound, and appealing for help to prevent the reinstatement of Cefnllys.

'We have our occasion,' said Llewelyn, and laughed. 'We even have a case, should we need one. He had no more right to build contrary to the truce than I have to raze what he has built. Maelienydd is a very fair country, and we are courteously invited in; it would be unmannerly to refuse.'

That was the first time that we had meddled so far east, except in our own northern lands, and it says much concerning the situation in those parts, and the fears and hopes of those who lived there, that we were indeed invited, not only by the men of Maelienydd, but after them by those of Brecknock, and welcomed like deliverers when we came.

We made our usual vehement descent, outrunning our own report, with a force greater, as we found, than that Mortimer and de Bohun had furnished for their rebuilding. They were encamped within the broken walls of the castle, and we came so suddenly and unexpectedly that though Cefnllys stands on one end of a lofty ridge, we were able to occupy positions all round it without hindrance, and settled down to hold them under close siege.

It was plain that they had only limited supplies, and that they were advanced so far from Mortimer's base at Wigmore as to be very badly placed for breaking out of our trap, all those miles of hostile Maelienydd separating them from reinforcements. We could starve them into submission in a week or two. But Llewelyn had a better use for those seven days.

'Now let's see,' he said, 'how practical a man Roger can be. For he knows his situation as well as we do, and I think has the good sense to recognise and admit it. I have no great ambition to fight with him, and I would as lief have him out of here and out of my way while I secure Maelienydd.'

He told us what he proposed, and David laughed, and begged to be the ambassador to the besieged. He rode into the enclosure attended by a single squire, and laid before Roger Mortimer, no doubt with a demure and dignified face, the prince's offer. Since it was clear that surrender was only a matter of time, and relief exceedingly improbable, why expend men and resources in post-poning the inevitable? Llewelyn had no wish to fight with his cousin. If Mortimer would accept it, he and his army were offered free and unimpeded passage through Llewelyn's lines and across the border, intact to a man, with all their gear.

That was no easy decision to make, but Mortimer was a big enough man, and honest enough with himself, to shrug off what many a younger and rasher captain would have seen as disgrace and dishonour. Indeed, later he was plagued with suggestions in many quarters that he had been in league with the Welsh in this matter, which I can testify was quite false. He could have stayed and fought, and seen many of his men wounded and killed, only to surrender in the end. Instead, he chose to take his whole force home in good order when he was given the chance. For my part, I respect his common-sense, and so, I think, must the wives of his soldiers have done when their men came home unmarked.

We opened our ranks to let them out, and saluted them as they marched by, for we had nothing against them, and the message they were taking back to King Henry was more galling than a bloody defeat would have been.

'I call that good housekeeping,' said Llewelyn, watching their ranks recede towards Knighton. 'We've spent little to gain much, and he's preserved what could be preserved. No fool squandering of men for spite or stubbornness, as your thickheaded heroes would have done. I approve him.'

'I doubt if King Henry will,' said David, grinning. 'Are you sure he'll go tamely home to England?'

'He'll go,' said Llewelyn confidently. 'Not only because he gave his word, but because he's seen how many we are, and how many more we can call out of the ground here. The men of these parts do not love him. And now we're rid of Roger, we'll settle Maelienydd first, and then push on towards Hereford. This border country,' he said, looking across the rolling hills and cushioned valleys with appreciation, 'is very much to my mind. Let's add as much of it as we can to Wales.'

And to that end we laboured, and with much success. The men of the land were with us, our numbers grew by their willing adherence, we had nothing to do but pick off, one by one, the English-held castles that were outposts in this marcher countryside, and that we did briskly and thoroughly. Bleddfa first, and then over the hills into the Teme valley, to take Knucklas, and so sweep down-river into Knighton. The castle there hangs over the town on its steep hillside and, below, the valley opens green and fair. That winter was not hard, there was but a sprinkle of snow before Christmas, and the meadows in that sheltered place were no more than blanched as in the harvest. Thence we moved south to secure Norton and Presteigne, and everywhere the chieftains and tenants came to repudiate their homage to the king and urge it upon Llewelyn, together with their soldier service. Like a ripe apple Maelienydd dropped into the prince's hand, grateful to be gathered so, and overjoyed to be Welsh.

It was at Presteigne we heard, from a merchant who traded wool into Hereford, that King Henry had at last recovered sufficiently to make the sea crossing, and had dragged his still enfeebled body as far as Canterbury, where he meant to spend the Christmas feast, now close upon us.

'Well, since Roger is so quick to call my name in question with him,' said Llewelyn, 'we'll repay the favour in the same terms.' And he sent another letter, politely and formally complaining that Mortimer and de Bohun had occupied with a large force a castle within the seisin of the prince of Wales and, when surrounded and beseiged by the prince's army, had been generously allowed passage through the lines to withdraw to their base, though it would have been easy to compel their surrender. And again he offered amends for any proven breach of truce, provided the barons complained of would guarantee the same. And he ended with a sly reminder that it was wiser to hear both sides of a case before proceeding to judgment.

With this whole region established behind us, we swept on to the south, into the Hereford lowlands as far as Weobley and Eardisley, fat country full of cattle that we rounded up and drove off with us, and barns that we plundered. Very easy farming these lowlanders have, and very well they live. We drew so near to Hereford that the Savoyard bishop, Peter of Aigueblanches, as well hated as any cleric in England, flew into a panic terror and ran for his life into Gloucester, groaning though he was, so they said, with an attack of gout, and from there wrote indignant letters to the king. Henry paid dear in his own convalescence for his glee over Llewelyn's supposed mortal sickness. In that winter the prince was at the peak of his powers, and blazed down that border like a chain of beacon fires.

'He surely knows by now,' said Llewelyn, 'that I am man alive.'

At Hay-on-Wye came messengers from the chieftains of Brecknock, begging him to go into their country and accept their homage and fealty. Never before had we moved thus down the very fringe of the march, eating into those lands claimed and occupied by the marcher lords, where Welsh and English contended always. Surely he added one fourth part to his principality before the Christmas feast of that year.

I think King Henry truly believed at that time that the Welsh intended a great invasion of England itself, but if so, there were few others who took the situation so seriously, and certainly Llewelyn never had any such intention. When the king issued feverish orders to the lords marchers to forget their quarrels and unite against the enemy on their borders, and called them to muster at Ludlow and Hereford in the following February, the exhortation fell on deaf ears. Pitifully King Henry wrote off to Edward in Gascony, reproaching him for his lethargy and indifference in face of Llewelyn's threat, and urging him to come home and lift the burden from his poor old father – as though he himself had not as good as banished the young man into France in disgrace, and ordered him to devote his energies to running his province there, and keep his nose out of English politics.

Nonetheless, we had to pay heed to all threats of mustering the feudal host against us, whether we greatly believed in them or no. So at Christmas we parted company, half of our forces pressing on southwards towards the rich fields of Gwent under Goronwy, with the levies of the southern princes joining him, while Llewelyn with a sufficient company halted long enough to receive the homage of all the princes of Brecknock, and make dispositions to hold what had been gained, and then withdrew at the turn of the year into Gwynedd.

Of how Goronwy fared with his force, that can soon be told, for in the first months of the new year he carried Llewelyn's banner to the very gates of Abergavenny, and only there was the victorious rush to the Severn sea halted, by the stout defence of that same Peter de Montfort who had once conducted us to the parliament of Oxford. He was King Henry's officer in that region, and the only one who held his own against us, until he was joined by John de Grey and a great number of other marcher lords hurriedly massed to his relief. After a skirmish with this army, Goronwy withdrew his men into the hills, where the English were reluctant to follow them, and even the local Welsh tenants, who otherwise would have borne the brunt of the inevitable revenge, took their chattels and made off into cover and into the monasteries, where they had sanctuary. Our thrust went no farther, but turned to consolidation of our great gains already made. And it should be said that in this gathering of the princes of the south once again Meredith ap Rhys Gryg, according to his renewed fealty, brought his levy and fought for Llewelyn and Wales alongside his nephew Rhys Fychan, at which Llewelyn was glad. But whether it was out of duty and good faith, or because the pickings in those parts were fat, I do not venture to judge.

As for us of the prince's party, we returned to Gwynedd in the first days of January, and at Bala we were met by a messenger from Rhodri, who had been left nominally in charge with Tudor in the north.

His news was in his face, for envoys bearing word of sickness and death have a special way of approaching those to whom they are sent. The Lady Senena, who had brought her immediate suite to Aber in the prince's absence, convinced that no one but she could properly oversee the affairs of Gwynedd, had been taken with a falling seizure on the night of Innocents' Day, and though she still lived, she was helpless in her bed, unable to move any part of her left side, foot or hand, and her countenance fixed. She mended not at all, and her time could not be long.

Thus the third sally death made that year, after discarding Llewelyn and King Henry both, was made against the lady. And the third sally was mortal.

CHAPTER VI

⎯⎯⎯⎯

They gathered by her bed, those three brothers, as helpless as most men when the hour strikes that cannot be avoided. She lay stiff and still, like a figure already carved on a tomb, though she could move her right arm, and the right side of her face still flushed and paled, and was human flesh to view. It was marvellous to see, now that she lay still who had seldom been still when she stood, how small she was, to have borne all those tall sons. Her grey hair was braided, to save her from irritation where it touched, and she was warmly wrapped against the winter cold in fine wool and under well-cured sheepskins. Her level brows were still black and formidable, and the eyes under them bright and wise. Also bitter, for death she resented, as all her life she had resented what curbed or enforced her will.

Cristin stood at the head of the bed, and she was in command within that room, as if she had received into herself some measure of the lady's mastery to add to her own. 'My lady's mind is clear as it ever was,' she said, 'and she sees plainly, and knows all that passes. She can speak, but it gives her trouble and wearies her. You must listen well.'

Llewelyn went straight to the bedside, and stooped and kissed his mother's forehead. David came more slowly, his eyes great, and I saw the fine beads of sweat stand on his lip, and remembered how he had said, not retreating from it: 'Samson, I am afraid of death!' He also kissed her, on the cheek that still lived. It cost him more. He had not Llewelyn's bold simplicity.

The Lady Senena's eyes followed all their movements until they drew too close, or went beyond her range, and those eyes burned with intelligent purpose still. When she spoke, half her mouth moved freely, the other half resisted, like a log dragged by a strong tide. Her voice was a fine thread, but a clear one. She said: 'Where is Owen?'

Llewelyn said: 'He will come. We'll send for him.' He never flinched or avoided her eye, that was accusing enough.

'Soon!' she said, and it was an order.

'This hour,' said Llewelyn, and smiled at her without shame or dread. 'I leave you,' he said, 'only to do what you wish.' And he turned about and went out of the room on the instant, and sent an escort to bring Owen Goch out of his prison at Dolbadarn to bid farewell to his mother. And then he came back to her, and told her that it was done, and within a day she should have her eldest son with her to close the circle. When he addressed her it was without constraint. Truly I think that while she had her full wit and senses she knew herself nearer to him than to any, for he alone reverenced, loved, challenged and defied her, ever since he was twelve years old, and went his own way without ever grudging her hers.

Owen Goch had been held in Dolbadarn castle then for more than seven years, so long that it was often all too easy to forget that he lived, and his coming to Aber was an event calculated to shatter our peace of mind. Llewelyn had occasionally visited him in captivity, but of late years infrequently, and usually at Owen's own instance, for the prisoner was quite capable of proffering vehement requests and complaints concerning his comfort and well-being. The Lady Senena had visited him regularly, and never ceased to plead his cause, though it was the one thing on which Llewelyn would not be persuaded or softened. Perhaps she was even surprised at his instant acquiescence now, for she was not of a temperament to use her own death-bed to wring concessions out of him. What he denied her, sure of his own justice, when she was hale, she would not find it unreasonable or unfilial in him to deny when she was sick.

However, she accepted his gift without comment, and by mid-morning of the next day Owen rode into the maenol, unbound but strongly guarded. In the years since he rose in civil war against his brother, and so lost his liberty, he had grown soft and fat, being confined for exercise to the castle baileys, no very extensive ground, but he looked in good health, if somewhat pallid in the face, and was princely in his dress, and very well mounted. Like his father before him, he was a heavy, large-boned man, liable to run to flesh, the tallest of the brothers, and his hair and beard were still of the flaming red of poppies, untouched by grey. He had also his father's rash and violent temperament, though without his redeeming openness and generosity, for Owen brooded and bore grudges where the Lord Griffith would have forgotten and forgiven. So even after seven years he would in no wise accept Llewelyn's lordship or agree to any terms, standing obdurately on his total right in Welsh law. Indeed, he had grown more irreconcilable during his imprisonment, and long since ceased to remember that he owed it in large part to his own act.

Llewelyn went down into the courtyard to meet him as he dismounted, approaching him directly, without pretence that their relationship was other than it was, without relenting, without constraint, certainly without any affectation of love. The long ride, on a fine wintry morning with only a touch of frost, must have been most grateful to Owen, and had brought fresh colour to his face. He eyed Llewelyn warily and coldly, but he accepted the wine that was offered on alighting, and asked: 'Our mother still lives?'

143

'She lives and is waiting for you,' said Llewelyn.

They went to her together, but Llewelyn came out at once, and so did Cristin with him, and left those two alone.

'She cannot last the day out,' said the physician. And before nightfall all those four sons were gathered about her bed, for it was clear she had not long, and her will was the thing about her now most alive, and struggling with bitterness against the compulsion of dying. At that last meeting I was not present, but Cristin was, in constant attendance on her lady, and from her I know what I know of the last hour.

'She could still speak,' said Cristin, 'and be understood, if you attended closely. When the priest had blessed her to God, she blessed them all, one by one, and commended them to behave brotherly to one another, as they hoped for God's mercy. Then she fell into a wandering of the mind for a while, her one good hand straying about the covers, and she talked more clearly then – it might be better if she had not! For she was back in the old days, and they were children to her, and she babbled of David and Edward in the same breath, and so reminded them of the days they spent at court that Llewelyn was like a stranger among them, the only one speaking a different language. She even reproached him, that he forsook his father and his mother, and brothers and sister and all, to go with the uncle that wronged and disparaged them. Is this all true history?'

I said that by the Lady Senena's measure it was, and told her how it befell, and how in my eyes it did him great credit and honour, for he was but a child when he chose and acted like a man.

'And he bore all, and gave no sign,' she said, 'though I know he felt it deeply. For in dying men return to what holds them most, and she was in Westminster with all her brood, excepting only Llewelyn, and he was the outcast, and alone.'

144

I said that in those days so he was, but it did not turn him from what he meant to do.

'Nor now,' she said, 'right or wrong. For Rhodri was in tears, and David too wrung for any such easy way as tears, but Llewelyn sat by her and watched and listened, and took all as it came, as though he never expected any other. Or perhaps – it may be so – he has an understanding with her that the others have not, on his own terms. His father I never knew, but *I* think he is *her* son, through and through.'

That was truth, and so I told her. The two who most favoured their father were Owen and Rhodri. As for David, God alone knew from what mysterious forbears, from what perilous and resplendent women, he took his being.

'And then,' said Cristin, 'she rallied, and was with us again, out of the past. She left dandling Edward and riding in the queen's retinue, and came back very sharply to this day, and then she looked for Llewelyn, and even moved her good hand towards him, so that he took it up and held it. Her eyes were fierce and bright again, able to match with his. She said: "Son, do justice to your brother!" and he said: "Mother, I will do right to all my brothers, according to my own judgment." And he smiled at her, and I think, however twisted that mouth of hers, that was a smile I saw upon it. It was the last fling of her spirit, and she challenged him, and he stood like a rock and let her take or leave him as he is. And I do believe she took him, all his offences and failings and all, and was glad of him. But what they made and will make of it, God knows. She has shaken them to the roots.'

It was not strange. So forceful a person could not be withdrawn suddenly out of the world without some tearing of the living tissues, and every one of those four, as various as they were, was fonder of her and more deeply twined into her being than he knew.

'She never spoke word again,' said Cristin, 'nor uttered

sound. I think there was another such stroke passed through her, for she stiffened, and her hand gripped on his suddenly, and all the flesh of her face seemed to be drawn in like shrivelled leather to the bone. Her eyes rolled up, and she died.'

She was filling her arms with fresh linen from a chest in the great hall when she told me this, and with these sheets and with knotted bunches of dried sweet herbs she went back to the death-chamber to make the Lady Senena decent and comely for her coffin, which the masons were even then cutting. But as she left she said: 'If she had known they would be her last words, would she have spoken them? "Son, do justice to your brother!" Perhaps! She was bred in the old ways, and lived and fought by them, and at the end she clung to them. But what a stone to cast into that pool among those four, at such a time!'

There was but one place then where the royal women of Gwynedd were fittingly laid to rest, and that was in the burial ground of Llanfaes, in Anglesey, that Llewelyn Fawr dedicated to the memory of his great consort, Joan, lady of Wales, and founded beside it the new house of Llanfaes for the Franciscan friars, the closest of all the religious to the old saints of the pure church.

There we bore the Lady Senena on a grey, still January day of the new year, twelve hundred and sixty-three, down from Aber over the salt flats and the wide sands of Lavan, and ferried her across to the Anglesey shore, there to rest after all her triumphs and tragedies. The sea was leaden that day, the tide heavy and slow, and in the stillness of the air the voices of the friars were dulled and distant, as though the world had receded from us as far as from her, though outside this solitude of sand and sea and vast, shadowy sky the tumult of events thundered and shook, waiting to devour us when we returned across the strait, and even followed us there secretly like a smouldering

146

fire in the hearts of those four brothers. For she was gone into the earth, who after her fashion had held them tethered into a loose kind of unity, however they strained at it, and in departing she had turned back to invoke the very spell that severed them.

It began in hall that night, before all the household, and I think it was David who began it, though the voice that set the note was that of Rhydderch Hen, the oldest of the bards, who played and sang the lady's commemmorative hymn. I may be wrong, the spark may well have come from Rhydderch himself. But David sat so tense and strung that night, and himself spoke so little, that I cannot but wonder. For he knew how to put thoughts in men's minds and actions into their hands that they never fully intended. Moreover, these three days spent again in the company of his eldest brother, brought from prison inevitably to return to prison, had pierced David deep in the conscience softened and rent by his mother's passing, and the words with which she left this world.

Rhydderch began with the praise of the Lady Senena, and the recital of her troubled fortunes in her marriage and her chosen exile with her children, all that old story made gentle and acceptable now even to those who had been torn by contention then. He sang her faithfulness to her sons and her lord, her great strength of mind and will. Then he turned to the subject of filial duty and family loyalty, of the sacredness of a mother's last wish and prayer, and the obligation of a son, prince though he might be, and the greatest of princes, to reverence and observe it. For he sang that even where wrong had been done, brother should forgive brother, as he hoped for forgiveness.

It was not the first time the bards had made known their desire for Owen's release and reinstatement, and that was no great wonder, for they were old men and wedded to the old ways. But this was the first time it had been pressed with such force. Owen Goch himself, who was sitting beside Llewelyn in the centre of the high table – though he knew and we knew his guards were never very far away – began to flush and glow with gratification, and to give forth sparks of hopefulness, but I do not believe he had known beforehand what Rhydderch meant to do. And David burned like a slow and secret fire, and watched Llewelyn's face every moment. But the prince sat unmoved to anything more than a smile of slightly grim tolerance, and thanked and rewarded Rhydderch for his singing.

Soon afterwards Llewelyn, of intent, signalled to the silentiary that he would leave the hall, and withdrew into the high chamber with his brothers, and would have me attend him there. Since Goronwy was still absent in the south, there was no other with us at that meeting, for he foresaw that one or other of them had things to say better said only between themselves. Me he never shut out, since first I came in curious circumstances into his service. I was the silent witness, yet informed enough to make balanced judgments, and I was the recorder if such were needed. So he would say, but I think truly he wanted me because there were moments when he felt himself alone, and I was a brother at one remove, a brother without claims on him, and all the more indissolubly bound to him because there was nothing but my own will to bind me.

The door was barely closed between us and the hall when David said, not aggressively as I had feared, but with a white and quiet passion: 'You have heard our mother's voice, and the voice of the bards echoing it. I know you cannot be indifferent. It was her last wish, her last warning. All of us heard it. Llewelyn, you cannot send Owen back into captivity. You said you would do right to him. Keep your word! Set him free!'

Owen Goch stood gathered up tightly into himself, in that big, lusty body running to fat with such long

148

inaction, and his eyes strayed from brother to brother in uncertainty and watchfulness, reading every tone, every quiver of a face. Doubtless there was a great hope in him, but also a great and obdurate sullenness, at least as far from reconciliation at heart as ever Llewelyn was.

'By what right,' said Llewelyn mildly, and looking only at David, 'do you make yourself our brother's champion, and ask clemency for him? He has made no such claim on his own account.'

'By right of the clemency you showed to me,' said David, and his face was so drawn and shrunken with passion that he looked as one starved. 'Why to me, and not to him? Did not I offend as grossly as he? And yet I am free and indulged, and he is still in ward and landless and solitary, after seven years. You cannot justify it! What has he done that I have not?'

Llewelyn said: 'You have done somewhat that he has not. You offered me, voluntarily, your homage and fealty, and have kept them ever since.'

'You never gave to him,' said David, burning like a tall and bitter flame, 'the chance to offer the like. Me you took, and him you left. How will you answer for that in the judgment?'

'I will answer for it now,' said Llewelyn. And he turned and faced Owen Goch, who glowered upon him uneasily through the red of his bush of hair and bush of beard, 'I offer it now,' he said. 'The same you chose of your own will to pledge me, David.' But he did not look at David, or speak directly to Owen. At the one he looked, to the other he spoke. 'I say to him,' said Llewelyn, 'that I revere my mother's memory and intent, and I stand in her sight, by God's grace. If Owen will do homage and swear fealty to me as David did, acknowledging me as prince of Wales, if he will quitclaim to me, in return for what lands I assign him, all his claim to sovereignty in Gwynedd or in Wales, then he may go free from this moment, and be established in a fair portion. Fair,' said

Llewelyn hardly, 'considering all that has been, and the council shall be the judge.' For the first time he addressed Owen Goch pointblank. 'Will you do so?' he said.

There was a long moment of silence and struggle, as though all those there present held their breath, and fought for air and life. Then Owen Goch heaved himself clear of the hush like a salmon leaping, and said through his teeth: 'No! I have my rights! I keep my rights! You are my younger, and you rob me. I appeal to Welsh law. This land of Gwynedd is partible, every yard of it. I demand my own!'

'You had your own,' said Llewelyn, 'portioned to you by the council of Gwynedd, and fully equal to mine. You were not content with it, you struck for more and lost all. And even if I grant your claim in this land of Gwynedd, where do you stand in this land of Wales? That *I* have won, that *I* have made, that *I* have created with my bare hands? What part have you in that, and what right? None! You are seven years out of date, Wales has outrun you. You may do homage to me and hold lands to the full extent of your claim as my vassal, or you may go back to Dolbadarn and nurse your ancient right in prison. It has no reality anywhere else.'

So he said, forcibly but without any anger or venom, hammering to make all plain, though I think he had little hope that Owen Goch would accept the undoubted grace he was offered. For grace it was. He might then have come to the prince's peace, as many a better and greater had come, and been confirmed in all his holding, and protected under the prince's shadow from all encroachment. But he could not get over the fixed notion that he was the elder, and held equal right, no matter what he had done to imperil it, no matter what Llewelyn had done all this time to assert his better right, by virtue of the efficacy of his rule and the pre-eminence of his arms. For there is no question but Wales, to give it that glorious name, was his creation out of chaos.

'I will see you damned and in hell,' said Owen Goch, through a throat so crammed with hate he could hardly speak, 'before I will do homage to you or pledge you fealty.'

After a moment of bleak silence Llewelyn said evenly: 'I will not hold you to a decision made in heat, that may be regretted when the blood is cooler. Sleep on it overnight, and think what you do.' And he struck his hands together, and called, and the guards came softly in. There was not another word said between them. Owen Goch had enough sense of his own dignity to fend off the affront of being held or enforced. He stalked through the doorway without a look aside, and they closed gently after him and herded him away to his guarded sleep.

'If either of you has anything to say to me,' said Llewelyn then, with arduous calm, for I knew he was more distressed than he was willing to show, 'say it. I am listening.'

David was silent, but so taut and black of brow that I knew he had much more boiling within him. But Rhodri spoke up with all the loud, indignant righteousness of those who move upon the surface of events, and understand little of what goes on beneath. Nothing of what tormented David was known to him. He had neither betrayed Llewelyn in his warfare for Wales, nor helped him after, as David had. All he saw and felt was the narrow current that moved his own boat. But in the elucidation of that current he had read and brooded over all the law books of the old men, centuries gone.

He went into the assault with such desperate courage that Llewelyn was astonished, and at another time would have been amused, for he never took Rhodri very gravely.

'Owen does right,' Rhodri said vehemently, 'to hold strictly to law, and you do wrong to flout it, and have been doing wrong all these years, as you well know. Nor is it any answer to hark back to what is gone, and say that Gwynedd was fairly divided, and Owen sacrificed his rights by acting against you. He did what he did in defence of David's rights and mine, which had never been fairly met, and never have since. It would be honourable to write off what was done then, and begin afresh to do justice to us all. You have the true occasion now to do what should have been done long ago. No one will point the finger at you, or see any weakness in such an act. The bards will approve. It would be fitting, as a memorial to our mother, who made her own will plain before she died.'

He was very pale with passion, so that his reddish freckles stood out darkly over his cheekbones and nose, and his hair, that was a bleached red like ripe wheat-stalks, shook down over his high forehead. Surely he had been brooding for years and preparing what he had to say, and had wanted the courage to begin until the Lady Senena's dying words braced him to the deed. And now that he was launched, he poured out his arguments with such frenzied fluency that it was plain all his reading had been directed to one end, the urging of his own case. For though he was careful to bring in always the matter of Owen's freedom, with much more ferocity did he press the point that all the sons, from eldest to youngest, had equal rights to land, all of which was by law partible.

'Which land?' said Llewelyn with ominous mildness. 'The land of Gwynedd or all the land of Wales? What came to us by inheritance was the shrunken domain of Gwynedd west of Conway. Am I to divide that equally in four and share it with you?'

'The lands of Gwynedd east of Conway have also been recovered,' said Rhodri, well primed with his studies in law, 'and are also partible.'

'Recovered by my hand,' said Llewelyn flatly, 'though I grant to David, with hearty goodwill, that he did his share gallantly there. But where were you? And for the rest of Wales – barring the marcher lordships, and those are matter for action hereafter – there are princes with claims of their own, claims I have been the means of satisfying and guaranteeing, and though they may have done homage and fealty to me, never think they have waived any of their rights in their own commotes, or are likely to look kindly on any claim you may advance on them. No, confine your pleas to Gwynedd west of Conway, where they might – I say *might*! – have some validity.'

Rhodri was thrown somewhat out of his stride, but having begun he could not leave off, for he might never have the force to open the matter again. So he drew furious breath, and went at it with stammering passion, shooting legal quotations like arrows, and so voluble that it seemed he had learned most of the code off by heart. And the longer he went on, the less did he mention Owen's rights, and the more his own, though still he cried out absolutely for Owen's freedom. He needed Owen, if he was to achieve anything, for he was always uneasy at standing alone, and David, though he had begun this, stood by with a dark face and a bitter eye, and said no word now in his support. So Rhodri pressed hard on the theme of his mother's dying wish, and reviled the impiety of rejecting it. And when he was out of breath and words, Llewelyn said:

'Owen still has a choice, if he cares to use it. Don't prejudge what he will do. But I tell you this, if he goes free he goes free as my vassal, owing me homage and fealty, and with the law and the council ready to deal with him if he betrays me. It has been too late to plead the old law of inheritance in Gwynedd ever since our grandfather's day, when by consent it was put aside. You cannot turn time back. I will not give you or any man licence to dismember what I have made into one.'

'You are spurning justice,' flamed Rhodri, made bold by despair, 'and flouting our mother's prayer!'

'In your judgment,' said Llewelyn, 'doubtless I am. Certainly my answer to you is no! No, I will not release Owen as an act of mindless piety, without his submission.

No, I will not give you a full fourth share in even the western part of Gwynedd. The lands you hold were apportioned to you by the council, and held to be a fair endowment. You will get no more from me.'

Then Rhodri cried out against him for an unjust tyrant, a spoiler of his brothers, and flung away out of the room in a fury. I thought, then, he was half afraid of what he had already done and said, and wishing to be elsewhere when Llewelyn's patience broke. But now I think he had another idea and another reason, and made use of his rage as cover for his withdrawal. 'I will not stay in your court,' he cried from the doorway. 'I take my people home tonight.' And so he was gone, and when we heard great hustle and bustle and clatter of hooves in the wards somewhat later, no one wondered at it.

When the door had closed on his going, with a slam that shook a faint drift of dust out of the tapestry curtain, Llewelyn stood somewhat wearily looking after him for a moment, and then said, more to himself than to us: 'God grant that may be the end of it. Who would have thought he had it in him, though! If he could bring half the vigour to the interests of Wales he brings to his own we should have a paladin at our service.' And he poured wine, and drank gratefully, and looked across at David, who remained where he had stood throughout, his eyes burningly intent on his brother's face. 'In the name of God,' he said, 'even if you have more to say, need it be said bolt upright? Or are we still at the bar of a law-court? You, or I?'

'Both, it may be,' said David, darkly smiling, though it was more like a grimace of pain. 'I am sorry, but you have not finished with me. All that I said to you I say again. And neither you nor Owen have answered it.'

'My offer to Owen,' said Llewelyn, 'is still open. Even if he is of the same mind tomorrow, and still rejects it, it will remain open. He has only to submit, and he can have his freedom and his lands again.'

'You know he will not,' said David, and his face was riven suddenly, as though its composure fell apart from some terrible convulsion of pain, until he forcibly reimposed upon it its normal severe and haughty beauty. Only then did I begin to perceive how deeply he was torn by his mother's passing, and the manner of it, and how it had set him at odds with his own heart and mind and conscience. Not often in his life did he turn to do battle with the creature he was, though always he knew its lineaments perfectly, without shame or self-deceit. 'I am not asking you for bargains, or bleating of justice,' he said, 'I am asking you for a gesture of princeliness at your own risk. If you are not afraid to deny what my mother prayed for, I am. I am, because I am the instrument of his misfortune, and I feel the load upon me like a curse. You can deliver me, as well as Owen, if you will.'

'Fool!' said Llewelyn with affection. 'You wring your own heart for no reason. You have paid off your indebtedness time and time again, you owe nothing to me, and nothing to Owen. Unless he accepts his position as vassal to me, how can I control him, how protect the union I have made? His voluntary submission is vital, not for me, but for Wales, which he could otherwise destroy. Do you think I will imperil that?'

'He will not submit,' said David, with the certainty of despair.

'He will. Though it take him years yet, he will come to his senses. If I can wait, why not you?'

'While I go free,' said David, marvelling, 'and in your trust, and in your bosom!'

'Why should you not? You, whom he enticed into his revolt against me, barely nineteen years old, torn two ways between brothers, and knowing him better than you then knew me? He should have been ashamed,' said Llewelyn hotly, for it was something he had held against Owen from that day, 'so to have seduced you.'

'Sweet Christ!' said David, so low I think Llewelyn

did not hear, but I did, for I was closer to him, and much wrung between them, being friends to both. Then he raised his voice, and said harshly: 'You do us both wrong, we were not as you supposed, Owen and I. It was for *my* right he struck, whatever he believed he stood to gain, and it was *I* who put it into his head, and provided him all that argument he broached with you. He was the seduced, and I the seducer! Me you should have loaded with chains, him you should have loosed. What could Owen do against you, with no wits but his own?'

All this he said with such weighted and laborious force that I knew how much it cost him, but to Llewelyn it had, I can well understand how, the sound of argument composed in obstinacy, word by word as he devised it. He looked upon his brother hard and long, between sternness and affection, and said bluntly:

'Those are bold and generous lies, but still lies, and unbecoming between you and me.'

'No lies,' said David, quivering, 'but truth.'

'I do not believe you. If it had been true, you would have spoken up long ago, even if you lacked the courage after Bryn Derwin. It is no way to help Owen by slandering yourself.'

David saw then that he was caught in his own skills as in a net, and could not break through them, but would still have to carry this load of guilt upon his heart. For once before, but then of deliberate intent, he had spoken the truth in such a way that it could not be believed, and now the same fate, unsought, was visited upon him as a requital. He tried, but even for him now words were hard to find, and his persistence in a confession that was taken to be simply a mistaken act of chivalry, a weapon for enforcing his will even at his own sorry cost, at last pricked Llewelyn, who was tired and wrung, into flashing anger at such obstinacy.

'Stop this!' he cried. 'It is unworthy, and I will not witness it. I have said on what conditions Owen goes free, and the reason you know as well as I, and it is not a mere matter of land. There is one cause I care about, and it is Wales, and not for Owen, nor for you, nor for any other will I put Wales in peril after the old fashion. Only a few months since you saw yourself what King Henry intended, if I had been wiped out of the world — to divide and devour, to split up the land and consume it piecemeal, to play brother against brother in the name of Welsh law, which he despises but can still quote for his own purposes! He could not ask for better advocates than I have heard tonight! What does he need with armies if he can get his work done for him by Welshmen without ever unsheathing a sword? And for no pay but promises he need never fulfil!'

'Are you saying,' asked David, whiter than his shirt and stiff as a lance, 'that England has bought me?'

'Not so! There was no need. But if you had been bought, and at a high price, too, you would still be very good value to England. Half your heart,' said Llewelyn unwisely, 'was always in doubt where it belonged, between King Henry and me. I thought that severance had healed. Now I wonder! In the matter of Wales, he who is not for us is against us. It is time to ask where *you* stand!'

If he had not been driven so hard he would not have said it, and it was done to put an end to a colloquy he could no longer bear, but it went in like a sword, all the more because there was, then as always, a degree of truth in it. David stood staring at him for a long, aching time of silence, while he gathered a voice so thick and heavy with outrage and grief that it stuck fast in his throat, and he had to heave the words out of him like gouts of blood. His face was ice, but within he burned, and his eyes were pale blue flames, both fire and ice.

'I stand in the presence of my liege lord,' he said, 'and above the grave of my mother, and confronting the prison that holds my brother, whom I misled and cozened and abandoned. And you expect me to be whole? You under-

157

stand nothing, you care for nothing, but Wales. Very well, keep your Wales, hold it together with your hands, bind it with your blood, marry Wales, beget Wales, have Wales for brother and mother and all, and cease to be troubled with us mortals. I have done!'

He turned on that word, and flung away out of the room, so violently yet so silently that neither of us had time to say a word more or reach out a hand to him. I heard his footsteps in the stone passage outside the door, and they were swift and hard and steady, as though he knew what he had done, and where he was going, and did not repent of it, however mortal his pain.

'Dear God!' sighed Llewelyn wearily, and passed a hand over his face. 'Was it I did that, or he?'

'Shall I go after him?' I said.

'No. To what end? I am of the same mind still, and so is he, what can we have to say to each other yet? Nor have I any right to call him back. He is a free man. He is gone of his own will, and in time he'll come back of his own will. Have we not seen him stalk away in the same fashion many a time before?' And he looked at me very searchingly, and asked me: '*Was* he lying?'

I said: 'No.' What else was there to say, and what to add?

'The more reason,' said Llewelyn heavily, 'for letting him alone until he pleases to come to. I have been remiss. Too much a prince and too little a brother. Now there's nothing to be done but hope that Owen will think better of his refusal by tomorrow, and save David's countenance and mine.'

For whatever regret he felt, it was not for his decision, and whatever he might take back, it was not the sentence of continued imprisonment. David was right, he was married first to Wales.

David slept at Aber that night, if indeed he did sleep, but in the morning early he collected all his household and rode, himself with a handful of knights going ahead while the rest followed later. The vanguard made no farewells. The rest were ready to march by midday. Rhodri had taken himself off with all his retinue overnight, and Owen, still obdurate, rode with a tight escort for Dolbadarn soon after Prime. For he utterly refused to abate any of his full claims under Welsh law. Aber was emptying fast, and for all it would have happened so even without the quarrel, still that disintegration seemed to me a sad, symbolic thing.

Godred being with David's knights, I was able to speak with Cristin before she left with the main party, and I told her all that had passed. For she was as secret and stout as any man, and had always a steady fondness for David, alone of all women being able to meet him as equals and friends, without illusions and without reservations.

'There are times,' she said, 'when he speaks with me almost as he does with you.' And she flushed, as though by that notice he acknowledged, and she recognised, the bond there was between us. 'If by any means I can help him,' she said, 'I will. For your sake and his.'

Other than that, we said never a word of ourselves. Or of Godred. Above all, never of Godred.

It was towards night when the escort that had taken Owen back to his prison rode again into the maenol at Aber. They came three men short of their number, and several with the bruises of battle. Cadwallon, their captain, sought audience at once of Llewelyn, and made report to him.

'My lord, first I make it plain, the errand you gave us is successfully done. But not without hindrance. When we came down towards the lake-side, where there is cover close about the track, archers in hiding among the trees loosed at us, and then mounted men rode out on us from either side the way. They were more than we, and had

159

the vantage of surprise. Who looks for an ambush about the prince's business in Gwynedd itself? We lost one man killed, and three were wounded, before ever they closed. But we beat them off, none the less. My lord, this was an attempt to take away the Lord Owen Goch out of captivity. No question! They tried to cut him out from among us, but vainly. He is safe in Dolbadarn.' And he said, to be just and make all clear: 'He was not a party to it. Surely he would have gone with them if he could, but I saw his face when it began, and I know he was as much at a loss as we. There was no foreknowledge. It was the other who planned it.'

'The other?' said Llewelyn, as tight as a bow-string, and his voice unnaturally gentle that it might not be unnaturally harsh.

'My lord, pardon the bringer of unwelcome news! We took captive four of the attackers, before the rest broke and fled. Three are lancers of Lleyn. The fourth is the Lord Rhodri, your brother.'

I was by Llewelyn's side then, I saw all the lines of his face and body ease, warming slowly into life. He had expected another answer.

'Rhodri!' he said. 'These were Rhodri's folk, then?' And he drew cautious breath, and his hands upon the arms of his chair slackened, and flushed with blood over the stark bone.

'Yes, my lord, no question. We have taken them into Dolbadarn with the Lord Owen, and there they are in safe hold. Also our wounded we left there to be tended. But for a few scratches the Lord Rhodri is not hurt. And your castellan holds him safe until he receives your orders.'

'He shall have them,' said Llewelyn, 'tomorrow. You did well, and shall not be forgotten. For the man you lost, I am sorry. Bring me his name and estate, and if he has a family, they shall be my charge. It was too much to spend,' he said, more to himself than to us, 'for my

160

failure.' And he dismissed Cadwallon kindly, and sat a long time brooding after he was gone.

'Well,' he said at last, 'I must work with what I am and what I have. Rhodri shall have fair trial, and the law that he so loves, not I, shall say what is to be done with him. And till he has a day appointed him we'll keep him safe, but not in Dolbadarn. Two so like-minded in the one hold might be all too well able to buy a messenger and means. In Dolwyddelan he should be safe enough.'

He got up from his chair and paced a little between tapestried wall and wall, restless and troubled, and looking round at me suddenly he said: 'Here I stand, to all appearances at the zenith, not a Welsh prince against me but one, all the reality mine, nothing remaining but to get England's recognition, and that no longer quite out of reach. Yet it seems, Samson, I have stripped myself of all my kin, mother, brothers and all, in one day. As though a cloud had come over the sun. You remember Rhydderch's red-gold dragon in the noonday? It may be this is God's reminder to me that after the zenith there is no way for the sun to go but down.'

I said stoutly that he made too much of it, for to say the blunt truth, there was but one of his brothers had ever been of much value to him, and he was not at fault here. 'You heard Cadwallon,' I said. 'David was not there.'

'Not in the flesh,' said Llewelyn drily. 'By his own admission and yours he knows how to get others to do his work, even in his absence. Why should he not use Rhodri, if he did not scruple to use Owen?'

Then I understood the heart of his loss, and how it reached out beyond David to touch me in my turn, since I had known all these years, or possessed a conviction so strong as to be almost knowledge, of David's greater guilt at the time of Bryn Derwin, and had never said word to him about it, either in extenuation of Owen's crime or in warning against David. But neither could I

161

speak a word now for myself, while he said none against me. Nor was there any blame or reproach in his face or manner.

I said, and it was true, that it would be simple to send a courier and examine in David's household, without accusing any, at what hour he and his knights had returned, and whether he or any of them could possibly have been in touch with Rhodri's company after they left Aber. For surely this attack had not been planned beforehand, and we knew that Rhodri had ridden away in dudgeon before ever David left the prince's presence. Llewelyn shook his head and smiled.

'No, we'll not send spies to question my brother's grooms and servants against him. We have not come to that. Unless Rhodri accuses him, in my eyes he is clean. Guilt is no simple thing. It may be my own hands are in need of washing as much as any, and that's a salutary thing to have learned. I shall never again be sure – altogether sure – of any man.'

He halted there for a moment, and I thought and dreaded that he was about to add: 'Not even you.' Though my deserts were never more than other men's, yet my need of his trust was extreme. But as I waited he ended, as one accepting, wryly but without grudge, what he saw and recognised: 'Least of all, myself.'

Towards the end of that month of January the council of his peers brought Rhodri to trial for his treason, and committed him to imprisonment at the prince's pleasure until he should purge his offence. He was taken to Dolwyddelan, and there kept in secure hold. As for David, Llewelyn would not pursue him, but waited all the early months of the year for him to return as impulsively and vehemently as he had departed, and take his place among us as before. But even at the Easter feast, which we kept at Bala, we waited and looked for him in vain. David did not come.

CHAPTER VII

About Easter the Lord Edward came hurrying back to England in answer to his father's plea, and was ordered promptly to go and look after his intended heritage of Wales, and he did indeed hasten to Shrewsbury, where he made his headquarters and kept contact with the justiciar of Chester, and tried to enforce the better steward-ship of the marcher castles. But all he did in Wales, and that we let him do, was to relieve and reprovision his islanded castles of Diserth and Degannwy. The time of the proposed February muster had gone by unhonoured, for no one stirred to carry out the order. And it was not long before King Henry hastily called his son back to his side, and left us watching from a distance the mad dance of events in England.

At the feast of Pentecost, towards the end of May, a young man rode along the coast road into Aber, watched from a distance as he came. When he drew nearer the watch recognised his arms, and sent word in to the prince. For the second time he welcomed into Aber young Henry de Montfort.

He came unattended, and on urgent business, and Llewelyn received and made him welcome. Goronwy was then not long back from the south, having seen the Welsh gains consolidated as far as the borders of Gwent. I was present with them at that meeting as clerk, as was usual.

'My lord,' said the young man, 'I come to you this time as envoy not from king and council, but from an assembly of those lords, knights and free men who stand firm in

163

support of the Provisions. An assembly most fittingly held at Oxford, where first those principles were set forth and agreed. We are a party believing strongly in that fair and ordered form of government, we desire to uphold it still, according to oath, and to see it established in the realm for the good of all. We have many of the younger nobility with us, and the yeomen of the shires solidly behind us. And that you may know who leads us – my father, the earl of Leicester, is back in England, and presided at this gathering. Those who hold with him begged him to come home and be their leader, and he has again taken up the burden. It is in his name that I come.'

'In his name and in your own,' said Llewelyn, 'you are very welcome. What the earl of Leicester has to say to me I am all goodwill to hear.'

'My lord, when once we spoke of these matters I do believe you were interested and moved. I think we had your sympathy. Do we still hold it?'

'My position,' said Llewelyn, 'is as it was then. As between king and commons I do not presume to intervene. As between ideas I may certainly choose and prefer. But my business remains, as it always was, Wales.'

'Then I am sure you, of all men, know,' said the young man eagerly, 'that the present chaos in the march cannot in the end benefit Wales, whatever short-term gains there may be to be had. Also that King Henry came home at the year's end looking upon you as his arch-enemy, by reason of your campaign in Maelienydd, and bent upon making war upon you, and even now has not abandoned that theme. It is no secret that he is still contemplating calling out the feudal host against you this summer, having failed in February.'

'I have been expecting it,' agreed Llewelyn, smiling. 'And you do not regard me as an enemy?'

'No. Your business is Wales, ours is England. We will not betray ours, but neither will we fail to respect yours. And those who have a common enemy have much to gain by being friends.' He caught the import of what he had said, and blushed, as it seemed he still could, amending with dignity the ill-chosen words. 'It is not the king who is the enemy, it is the old order, and those about the king who seek to fend off all changes. The king is a victim, manipulated by some whose whole concern is to protect their own interests.'

'And how do things stand at this moment,' asked Llewelyn, 'with your own strength?'

De Montfort named names, very lofty names, and strange to note so many of them young. This was no old man's party. There was hardly a man among them of Earl Simon's own generation, except for his faithful friend Peter de Montfort of Beaudesert. The old, those who dug in their heels against change and resented that great lords should be asked to curb their privileges, or common men seek to enlarge theirs, were all with the king. 'The Earl Warenne is with us, Gilbert of Clare, Henry of Almain, Roger Clifford, Leyburn, Giffard of Brimpsfield ...' The list was long. 'We return absolutely to the Provisions, declaring all who oppose them, but for the king and his family, to be public enemies. And these demands we are sending to the king.'

'He will not agree to them,' said Llewelyn with certainty. 'And what then?'

'I do not accept that his refusal is certain. But we are prepared for it. If need be, we shall move against those who urge the refusal upon him.'

'In arms?' said Llewelyn, eyeing him steadily.

'In arms.'

'And what is it,' Llewelyn asked mildly, after a moment's measuring silence, 'that you want from me?'

'The chief part of our confederacy is in the marches, and from this base we must move. If it comes to war, we must secure the march behind us, with all the passages of the Severn in our hands, before we move east into England. Your presence in arms on the west bank of the river would be worth an army to us.'

Goronwy looked at Llewelyn and smiled, knowing his mind. 'The bridges at Gloucester and Worcester and Bridgnorth would need to be held,' he said, 'and certain fords. It could well be controlled from the west. It is in our interest to keep ward on that border for our own sake, in such troublous times.'

'You shall have what you ask,' said Llewelyn. 'I will take my host and hold station along the border, within your reach whenever you call on me. And in the south Rhys Fychan shall keep ward in the same way. We had best arrange codes and signals I can send out to my allies, we have a long frontage to guard, and you may have need of us in haste, at any point.'

So we were committed, and yet not committed, for out of the confines of Wales he would not pledge more than raiding units of his army, and within Wales he moved upon his own land, and could not be questioned or held to account. But with that the young man was content, it was what he had come to gain. And he dined with us, and was good company when he could call back his mind and spirit from where it habited by choice, somewhere far away in the city of London, in that Tower which I remembered from my boyhood, where that very day, perhaps, Earl Simon's envoys confronted the king with the high demands of the reform.

The council conferred long that night, and when the planning was done those two, Llewelyn and Henry de Montfort, sat privately over their wine even longer, and talked of all manner of things, growing close and eager, for they had much in common, being of that open part of humanity that does not hoard its light, but gives it forth upon other men, sometimes too rashly. And so I heard, for I attended them for a brief while, how they spoke also of that letter King Henry wrote when he believed Llewelyn dead, and the plans he made for supplanting him. And young de Montfort said, after some thought:

166

'But surely he has put his finger upon your weakness, the only one he could find, saying you are unwived and without issue. With such a princedom as you have to conserve, I do marvel that you have not married and got sons. If I presume, rebuke me but forgive me. For I do know of marriages made, and marriages that could not be made, for reasons of true affection. My father,' he said, with that ardour that possessed him always when he spoke of his parents and kin, 'never thought to aspire to the king's sister, when he came to England, and she in her child-widowhood was pledged to life-long chastity. A wicked folly, I think, to induce a young girl to swear to such a penance, with the whole world before her! But when they met it was a fatal thing, for each desired the other, and no other thing in this world. And she was gallant enough to withstand all the pressures put upon her, and to be forsworn of her oath for his sake. I am their firstborn, and I tell you, whatever the churchmen may say, I think God did not disapprove their love.' So he said, and flushed with pride in those two who begot and bore him. So he well might. They say she was a proud, demanding, difficult lady, this boy's mother, but none ever dared to say that she fell short in her devouring and devoted love to that man she chose and married.

'I would wish to you and to any man that I revere,' said young Henry, 'so proud and single a choice. It may be that you are also waiting for an Eleanor.' And he laughed, softly and hazily, for he was a little in wine, and because of Llewelyn's silence he feared he had trespassed on an unwelcome theme, where indeed I believe the prince was mute only in surprise at his own want of forethought, that he had never before given serious consideration to a matter of such patent importance as his marriage, and the provision of heirs after him. So the boy went on talking to fill a moment's silence and escape into safer pastures.

'My only sister,' he said, 'the youngest of us, is also

Eleanor, after my mother. She'll be eleven this year.' And he looked at my lord with a face like a flower wide open to the sun, ardent and vulnerable, and I, for one, considered and marvelled what the sister of such a one might not promise of beauty and gallantry.

Llewelyn had judged rightly, King Henry in the Tower indignantly refused the demands of the reform. He was still so blind to the real enormity of what was happening in his own land that he even persisted in sending out his writs for the muster against Wales at Worcester on the first day of August, but long before that day came, the tide of events had swept on and left the summons awash in its beached pools, like weed cast ashore on Aber sands. For as soon as the word was received of the king's rejection the young marcher confederates struck in arms against their enemies down the border, capturing the bishop of Hereford, shutting him up with all his Savoyard canons in Clifford's castle of Eardisley, and plundering his rich and coveted lands. He was the first and the most hated of the implacable foreign royalists, but after him they turned to others, long since marked out for vengeance.

By then we were on the border as had been promised. Llewelyn sent out his writs to all his vassals and allies on the day that young de Montfort left us, and by the middle of June we marched. Within one week more we had companies deployed from Mold in the north to Glasbury in the south, from which positions we could move easily into action anywhere in the middle march, according as we were needed.

The writ went also, as customary, to David at Neigwl, but because of the extra distance he had to bring his men we did not wait for them, but went ahead and set up our base at Knighton, whence we could very rapidly pierce into England by the Teme valley. The orders sent to David were to follow us to that place with his own muster as quickly as he could. And in the brisk excitement of action it never entered Llewelyn's head or mine to doubt but we should see David within three days, for he could never get into the forward ranks of battle fast enough to please him. It was shocking to awake suddenly to the truth that five days were gone, and no sign of any detachment from Neigwl, and no message.

'Surely,' said Llewelyn, startled, 'he cannot still be hating me so much that he will not even fight beside me?' But when another day passed, and still no sign, he was displeased in earnest.

'This is not to be borne,' he said. 'He has a right to hold off from his brother as bitterly as he will, but when his prince calls on him for service due he shall meet his obligations like any other vassal, or pay for his neglect as any other would pay.'

I said, though with a doubtful heart, that there might well be some good reason for the delay, and that we should not judge him unheard.

'Nor will I,' he said heavily. 'I am too well aware that I was not without blame in my handling of him.'

It was about that time that we were called on, by the signal agreed, to advance into English territory far enough to seal the western bank of the Severn at Bridgnorth, while the young marcher lords closed in and secured the town from the east, and Llewelyn had his men massed to march, and himself would go with them.

'I would not send an officer after him like a bailiff after a defaulter,' said Llewelyn fretting, 'not until I know what occasion I have to treat him so. Samson, do you go! Of all men he'll listen to you, if he will to any. Go as his friend and mine, and bid him come where he is missed and wanted.'

That was a time when I was very loth to leave him, but his need of a better understanding with his brother seemed greater than any need he had of my moderate ability in arms. So I said that I would go, and as soon as

169

his company had ridden, fast and hard along the river valley towards Ludlow, the footmen following at their tireless summer pace, I also rode.

I had his seal, that I might get a fresh mount along the way wherever I needed. Nor did I hurry, for at every mile I hoped to see the dust of David's column bright on the sunny air ahead, and it was my care to keep the way he would be most likely to use with a body of armed men. I found excuses for him very easily, for if he had first been delayed by some accident, and then kept the foot pace, he had a case for his lateness. But I confess what I believed most likely was that he still burned with resentment against his brother, and was bent on absenting himself.

At every place where roads met I made enquiry for him and his men, but nowhere did I hear of their passing. Other news I did pick up along the way, but none of David. At the abbey of Cymer there was a drover halted, returning from England, and he told me that Earl Simon with his army had struck south-east to cut off London from the Channel ports and so from France, so that no more foreign mercenaries could be brought in, and though Richard of Cornwall had hurried to try and intercept him, not in arms but with blandishments, the earl had swerved southwards and left him standing helpless and unregarded, and was now in Kent, where all the knights of the shire had rallied to him joyfully, and all the seamen of the Cinque ports welcomed him with open arms. Three reformer bishops, they said, of London, Lincoln and Coventry, had been sent to the king with a form of peace even while the army was on the march, and since the king was isolated in a London very unfriendly to him, and severed from the aid he had hoped for from France, he would be hard put to it to hold out very long. The speed and force of Earl Simon's movements had won the war before it began.

There was other news to be gleaned when I reached

Mur-y-castell, for the seneschal had a daughter married to an armourer in Denbigh, where news from Chester was easily come by, and she had sent him word of what went forward in London, to the great perturbation of the royal garrisons elsewhere, which were helpless to do more than look on from a distance. They said that the Lord Edward, when he saw the drift of events, rushed to the Temple and broke open the royal treasure-chests, and took away all he could to the castle of Windsor, together with a very strong garrison of mercenaries from France, whom he had brought over with him in April, and there he was determined to create a centre of resistance against the reformers. Doubtless he saw them now not as reformers, but as rebels against his father's rights and his own, and there was much to be said, if not for his good sense, at least for his bravery and determination. Certainly he was safer in Windsor than were his parents in the Tower, and the queen had tried to make her escape by water to join her son, only to have her barge attacked by the hostile citizens, and to be forced to take refuge ignominiously in the precincts of St Paul's, to avoid actual violence to her person. Poor lady, she was not accustomed to such usage, and there was indeed a terrifying quality about the affair, so far did it delve into final disorder, shocking to both sides and to us, looking on from afar. The king, they said, had already given way so far as to order Prince Edmund to surrender Dover castle, and it was but a step to his total submission.

After I had crossed the sands of Traeth Bychan and turned into the peninsula of Lleyn I refrained from asking word of David, for this was drawing near to his own lands, and I no longer believed that he had ever set out, or intended to set out, and I would not make public what was amiss, to make it harder to heal. So I came at last down from the hills into Neigwl, to David's llys. It was late afternoon when I entered the gate, and the court-yard seemed its summer self as I remembered it, only a little listless and unpeopled, like a household when its lord is away. The maids looked out, as always they do, to see who came, and before I set foot to ground the castellan was out to greet me. He was an old man, and lame, no longer fit for a war party. He knew me, and knew from whom I came.

I asked for David, and his officer gaped at me in puzzlement. 'Master Samson, the Lord David rode yesterday, with a company of picked men. Have you not met with them along the way?'

I said I had not, and told exactly by which way I had come.

'He said when he left that he meant to make a stay at Criccieth, for he had certain troopers there to add to his company. Did you enquire there? And it may be he had another such halt beyond, before heading for Knighton to join the prince.'

So he said, and clearly Llewelyn's order had been received, and was known to the household here, and it was believed that David had set out to obey it. I do not know, even now, why I did so, but I asked whether news of the Lord Edward's movements and King Henry's humiliations had been brought into the llys after the prince's summons was received. He said yes, that they had heard from Criccieth how the queen was hunted out of her barge, and how Edward had made an unavailing dash across country with his mercenaries from Windsor to Bristol, intending to make a stand there in his own headquarters, but the townsfolk of Bristol had closed the gates and refused him entry, sending him back to Windsor with his tail between his legs, like a scolded hound. And that, said the old man, was no pleasant hearing to one prince, when another was so humiliated, and the Lord David was indignant and disturbed, and short to question or approach.

My heart misgave me then, but I would not make public my doubts until the disaster was proven and irremediable. I asked how many men David had taken with him, and their names, and Godred was among them, at which I breathed more freely, for at least I could speak with Cristin without risking the poisoned attentions of her husband. I asked for her. Since the Lady Senena's death she had stepped into the office of châtelaine here in Neigwl, David being unmarried and having absolute trust in her. It was strange that he, who trusted so few and had no illusions about himself, yet was seldom mistaken in those he did trust.

She came to me in the high chamber, and I told her how matters stood. She was alarmed in the same manner and measure as I, and understood even what I had not had time to say.

'I knew,' she said, 'when he received the prince's writ, that he was in no mood to make any haste, yet he did begin preparations. I thought he would take his own time and keep his own distance, and yet he would go, and be reconciled once he was there. After there was so much talk of Edward being shut out of Bristol, and his mother insulted and abused, then he was blacker in mind than ever I knew him, and withdrew from us all. But still he called his men, and the muster went forward. Only it seemed he reduced their numbers, and chose with care. And the foot soldiers he countermanded.' She looked at me with wide, wild eyes. 'Wait!' she said. 'I have all the keys, of his treasury, too. No, come with me!'

I went with her through David's bedchamber, and into the small room which was his treasury. She unlocked the great chests there, and uncovered the hurriedly discarded hangings and plate and garments that remained, all tossed back at random after the rest was removed. She knew, not I, what should have been there.

'He has taken all that was easily portable,' she said, staring at me wide-eyed across the debris of his flight. 'All the gold and minted money he had, all his ornaments and jewels. And documents! What should he want, carrying his wealth about with him, to join his brother's army at Knighton? It is not to the Severn he's bound with all his best men, it's to the Dee! If you had enquired at Criccieth they could have told you when he was there, and which way he rode from there, since it was not towards Cymer.'

But she knew, and so did I, which way David had ridden. North-eastwards for Llanrwst, Denbigh, Mold and Chester, into the arms of the English garrison. Why else should he take with him all the valuables he possessed, and choose with care those companions who would welcome the change of allegiance and not betray him?

'He must not!' said Cristin. 'It means his ruin, and Llewelyn's bitter grief. He is mad!' And she said, seeing clearly and charitably that part of his act which redeemed it in a fashion: 'No one can say he did it for his gain! His brother's fortunes have never stood so high, King Henry's never been in such disarray. He is gone to an Edward bereft of friends, back to the troth of his childhood. His mother's wanderings have haunted him.' But she said again: 'He must not! He will never forgive himself or be forgiven.'

I took her by the hands a moment, forgetting not to touch in her distress and mine, and oh, the touching even of her fingers was such fiery comfort. I asked her to get me food and wine to take with me, while I got a fresh horse saddled in the stables, and to say no word yet to any of what we knew. Not until there was no help for it.

'There is no help for it now,' she said. 'You cannot overtake him.'

'I may. I doubt if he expects Llewelyn to make the first move, and he has no reason to believe anyone will be sent to enquire after him. If he stopped to add to his company in Criccieth, so he may again at Denbigh or Mold. Let's make the attempt, at least,' I said.

'May God give you wings,' she said, and ran to get

174

me bread and meat, for in this ride there would be no halting but to question and to get a fresh mount. A whole day's start of me was more than enough, he could well be in Chester with all his men, and out of my reach, but since he had no reason to expect pursuit, and every reason to take his best men with him, and make himself as welcome a gift to the English as possible, he might well have moved with deliberation. While there was a hope, I could not relinquish it. I was mounting in the courtyard when Cristin came back with the pack, and I stowed it in my saddle-bag, and touched her hand, and rode. There were others around, not a word was said but the most current of farewells.

At Criccieth I took heart, for on making enquiry I learned that David's company had halted and passed the night there, and left, augmented by three more troopers, with the dawn. If this pattern held good, he might well have stopped again overnight with the same object in view. I had still a long while of daylight left, and no need to spare my horse, having the order that provided me with new on demand. And I rode hard, and got another mount at the settlement of the Knights Hospitallers at Dolgynwal, and went on through the night, over the mountain road to Denbigh. There were other roads he might have taken, but since I could follow only one I chose the most likely, and prayed I might choose aright.

David had an interest in Denbigh, and there was a small timber keep there, and a garrison of his men. And there was also the point that remounts for so many would be harder to come by than my single rounsey; it would be better economy to stay overnight and rest the beasts. So I hoped, and reasoned, and prayed, and came by full daylight to Denbigh. And yes, they told me, the company I sought had spent the night there, and left in the early dawn.

It was now a matter of perhaps two or three hours between us, instead of a day, which was better reckoning, and if they made a stay for a meal, whether innocently in hall at Mold or furtively in the woods by the wayside, I could overtake them yet. I pushed hard towards Mold, through that fine, rolling, forested country that declines into the flats and sands and meadows of the Dee. Once I had fled from Shotwick, on the far side of that river among the salt marshes, with Owen Goch, to confront the boy Llewelyn at Aber, newly bereaved as he was by his uncle's death, and become his servant and friend lifelong. Now I rode that same track, but in the opposite direction, to pluck back, if I could, his best-loved brother from the murderous act of treason.

At Mold they had no word of him. I had to be adroit with my prevarications, not to betray him before the game was played. So now, was I ahead of him, or not? Or had he chosen not to be seen so close to this border, and circled the town in cover, to move towards Chester still ahead of me? In doubt as I was, I pushed on towards England as though I knew what I did, though by this time I was so weary and sore that I reeled in the saddle, and dismounting was great trouble and pain. By God's grace I knew the road here very well, and knew of a place close to the border where it threaded a low but abrupt outcrop of rocks among woods, before the last descent into the levels of Dee began. For this spot I made with all the force and faith I had left. And on the way to it I saw, thin and silver and tall out of the woods on the left of the road, the smoke of a camp-fire going up erect as a larch into the blue morning air.

It was July, the highest of the summer, and still as sleep, hardly a breath of wind. The column of their fire was no more substantial than a hair, but stood braced straight as a plym-line and high as heaven. Then I rode by with a thankful heart to my little defile among the woods, certain that I was between David and England.

I had not long to wait, which was as well, for as soon as I halted and took station in the shade, sleep crowded in on me. I dared not stay in the saddle, or sit down in the grass when I had painfully alighted, but paced stiffly back and forth in cover, at a spot where I could watch the road without myself being observed. A packman went by on his pony, and a local cart, creaking and slow, but there was no other traffic until they came. I heard the broken, soft thudding of many hooves, the mounts of riders going purposefully but at ease. They were close to the border now, they had no reason to hurry or fear, there was no force in these parts, after Mold, that could stand in their way. It was not force that could stop David, even had there been enough men to match his. Either he would turn of his own will, when the time came, or he would not turn at all.

I saw them emerge in loose file from the trees, some way from where I was, David in the lead and alone. He had perhaps some thirty well-mounted and well-armed men in his company, a considerable gift, for I knew what the English court paid for good horses, and what pains they took to import them. And no doubt he had selected his men well, to lend added weight and stature to his own person. And yet he rode, as I saw when they drew nearer, with a face as bleak and dark as midwinter, all his brightness caged and battened within, into a smouldering ferocity. What he did was done with bitter resolution, but quite without happiness. And at that I felt some hope within me.

At the right moment I clambered again into the saddle and rode out, clumsy and dull with weariness as I was, into the middle of the track, and there took station facing them.

He saw me, and his hand gripped and tightened on the rein, and his knees clamped close, every muscle in him stiffening, so that his horse checked and tossed in a shiver of uneasiness. His head was uncovered to sun and breeze, a squire carrying his helm, and he wore only the lightest of hauberks. The wind had ruffled his black hair into curving feathers about cheeks and brow. Though he was burned brown as a nut, all the bones of his face were drawn in golden pallor that chilled into the blue-white of steel or ice as he stared at me. I think he was not surprised at seeing me, only enraged. Beneath the black and level brows his eyes were sharp and mortal as swordpoints. And after a moment he shook the rein and edged his horse forward towards me, until we sat almost within touch of each other, but not on a level, for he always liked a very lofty horse, and my rounsey borrowed at Denbigh was sturdy and fast, but not large.

I gave him greeting as I would have given it at any other time, and it was no lie that I was glad to see him, though he had no such feeling then towards me, and pretended none.

'What are you doing here?' he said blackly.

'I am sent to you,' I said, 'with a message from the prince, your brother. He bids me tell you that they have marched on Bridgnorth, and entreats you to come soon where you are missed and wanted.'

I thought the lines of his icy mask blanched still paler, but his look did not change.

'I am going,' he said, 'where many are missed and wanted, and I, perhaps, not at all. But I am going. Where he told me my heart hankered to be, and secretly belonged.'

'You wrong him,' I said, but very low, for I wished to speak only to him, since speak I must. 'You wrong him, and you injure yourself, for he never said so. I heard, as you heard, what he did say, and a part of that was ill-judged from weariness and grief, yet it was not what you make of it. He did not send me to spy or rebuke in his name. He sent me to call you to him as his valued brother. And if you betray him, you betray your own heart. You know it as well as I, it is in your face, in your eyes, in the very bowels that knot and ache in your belly. Turn back now! It is not too late. There is no one knows but Cristin and I, both your true servants and lovers, and both devout in secrecy. You still have your freedom.'

I could no more, for they were too close. I said in a whisper: 'Call them off, send them back a little! At least talk with me!'

They were all eyes and ears at his back, greedy with curiosity. Perhaps some were shaken, and pondered their best interests. Only he, however tortured, was never turned from his chosen path. How great love, envy, reverence and hate there was in him for Llewelyn I never knew until then. There was no other could so drive David to despair, or inflame him to murder. There was no other could so draw him by the heart that in defence of himself he would tear himself and go the opposing way. And also to be reckoned with here was that Edward, with the giant frame and the furtive, drooping eyelid, the companion of his childhood, driven and hunted from Windsor to Bristol and back again, a demigod born, and now harried and derided and witness to his mother's humiliation, such a heroic, outcast figure as might well fire David into partisan action. I do not know the half, even now. Not the half! He was so deep, there was no plumbing him.

He made a gesture of his left hand, without turning his head. He said aloud: 'Go back! Wait on my order!'

I heard the horses stamp and sidle, edging backwards, heard them turned and walked to a distance, doubtless with many a rider's chin on his shoulder. David said: 'It is for you, not for him, I offer this respite. Say what you have to say to me. I am listening.'

So he was in the flesh, but in the spirit not at all, he was fixed and damned, unable to return. Nevertheless, I said what I had to say, with all the urgency I could command, calling him back to us not only in Llewelyn's name, that most wounded and most alienated him, but in mine, and Cristin's, and above all in the name of

179

Wales, the mother of us all. But he said he had had a mother, and knew word for word what she had demanded in dying. Then I prayed his regard for his own fealty, freely given, and his own homage, never forced on him, but forced by him upon Llewelyn, who would have left him free. I cried upon his blood to compel him, and his breeding to make his way clear, and he said that he was bred as English and royal as Edward, and his mother who bore him found no fault in it. Then I was left with nothing to plead but Llewelyn, who meant more to him than Wales, who was the source and stumbling-stone in all this coil of loyalties. And in his eyes Llewelyn had failed and rejected him.

Then I was out of words and arguments, and he was like an unquenchable fire on which I played but a little, helpless sprinkling of rain.

'Are you done?' he said, with that terrible patience that was more malevolent than rage. And since I was mute: 'Then stand out of my way.'

'Never of my own will,' I said, and kept my place and though I was but a symbolic barrier between him and his own irrevocable act, he did not thrust by me and leave me standing. 'I keep my troth, if you do not. I tell you in your teeth, your place is here. Either turn back with me to your duty, or kill me.'

'Stand out of my way!' he said again, even lower and more gently. 'Or I take you at your word.' And he loosened his sword in the scabbard and half drew it out, then as deliberately slid it back again and unslung the thongs that tethered the scabbard to his belt, and hefted sheath and all in his right hand, like one trying the balance of a mace.

'Do what you must,' I said, at the end of my resource. 'As long as I have breath and force I will not take my body from between you and treason.'

He moved so suddenly and violently my eyes never followed what befell, though I know he rose in the stirrups to loom tall as the trees, and the blow itself I saw and did not see, as though a great wind had hurled a broken bough past me too fast for vision. He struck me with all his skill on the left side of the head, and swept me out of the saddle into the dust of the road, and under that thunder-clap mind and eyes darkened. I felt the grit and stones score my cheek. I heard him snap his fingers and call peremptorily to those who waited and watched at a distance: 'March forward!' And doubtless he himself set manner and pace, riding past me without a look behind. I remember there was a kind of distorted light for a few moments, in which I saw the hooves of the horses stamping past my face, before I went wholly into the dark.

When I awoke to the thunder in my head, and the burden of pain that told me plainly enough I was still in the world, it was night, but not darkness, for the nights of midsummer after glowing days are full of a light of their own. I saw trees arching over me, and stars between their leaves, and I was lying in my own cloak on thick, dry grass. There was the smoke of a wood fire in my nostrils, and the glimmer of its flame, bedded low with turfs, not far from my left side. I heard the soft stamp of hooves in mossy ground, and the lulling sound of a horse grazing at leisure. In the glow of the fire there was a man sitting cross-legged with his chin in his hands, gazing steadily at me, but my eyes were not seeing clearly, and I could not tell who it was, except that it was not David.

He did not observe that I was awake and aware until I tried to lift one hand, heavy as lead, to feel at my head. Then he slid forward to his knees beside me, and put the wandering hand back to ground.

'Let be!' he said. 'He has broke your crown for you, but not past mending. I have cleaned the wound and bound it, and the best you can do for yourself now is sleep the night round, if you can, and let time help you past the smart. Here, drink some wine! There's bread, if you can swallow. If he had struck lower he could have snapped your neck, but he was gracious enough to leave you a throat to drink with.'

He brought a flask and held it to my lips, raising me with a hand indifferent but deft. It was then, when he leaned close to me, that I knew him for Godred. As fair and subtle and smooth as ever, smiling in the firelight, Godred nursed me.

'I see you have your wits and your eyes again,' he said as he laid me down. 'Six hours, after I moved you here into cover, you lay snorting like a bull, so that I feared your skull was broke in good earnest, and then you slid off sidelong into sleep. He never meant to kill, or you'd be a dead man this moment. Never stare so,' he said, grinning at me, 'I'm flesh, and damned to this world, and so are you. No vision, either of heaven or hell.'

In some surprise to hear my own voice clear and firm enough, I said: 'You were with his force, bound for Chester.'

'So I was,' he said, 'and none too happy about it, either. I owe you yet another debt for the reminder how long the prince's arm is. I have thought better of my allegiance. I have read the omens, and made my propitiation accordingly. Here am I, the saviour of Llewelyn's own familiar. I look for a handsome welcome.'

I thought then that he was in some mistake about the state of my faculties, or he would not have talked so airily and bitingly at large in my hearing. He was talking rather to the night and his own reason than to me, breathing out his doubts, his spleen and his pleasure in his own skills aloud, sure that none but a stupefied clod heard him, and safe and satisfied with that audience where he could not have been content with none. And I was unhappy in the role he assigned me, and to appraise him of my, perhaps, too acute attention, I said: 'How did you slip your collar and win back here?'

'Very easily,' said Godred, unabashed, and giggled over the bread and meat he was breaking. 'Every man has his needs. As soon as we were well in cover and the afternoon ebbing, I went aside to attend to mine. By the time any one of them looked round to wonder why I delayed, I was halfway back to where he left you lying. A pity I had not the best of his horses, but the one I have is none so ill, he'll be welcome where we are going, you and I.'

'And I was still where he had left me lying?' I asked.

'Some country kern had moved you to the side of the road and tumbled you there. Not wanting,' said Godred simply, 'to burden himself with some powerful man's discard. Can you blame him? You were bleeding from the scalp like a spring in spate, and all it wanted was a handful of cloth to staunch it. It's clean and drying now.'

'It seems,' I said, 'that I owe you my life.' For such a creature, abandoned in such a case the night over, might well have died for want of staunching, for want of warmth, for want of a draught of water.

'A debt I had to you,' said Godred softly, and his full brown eyes, golden-innocent in the firelight, burned brightly into mine. 'Now it is paid, perhaps. If we need talk of debts and payments, being close as brothers.' He leaned and folded the cloak closer around me, for the small hours of the night brought a pure, silent chill into the air. 'How could I ever have faced Cristin,' he said with measured sweetness, 'if I had let you perish by the roadside?'

Close as brothers we were on that journey we made together, Godred and I. For two days I could ride but for a short time, and we made slow progress down the border, and often were forced to halt for rest. And after his fashion he looked after me well, though for his own practical ends. For having decided his best interest lay in abandoning one master, he fully intended to ingratiate himself as quickly as possible with a new one. As for Cristin, it was plain to me, while all else was a cloud and a dream, that she played no part in his decisions, and counted for nothing in his plans, except where she could be useful to him. For he had left her without a word when he made up his mind to go with David to England, and he made no effort to go back to her or set her mind at rest now that he had changed his purpose. It was I who made shift to write a letter, when we halted at Valle Crucis, and beg the prior to have it sent to her at Neigwl, telling her both Godred and I lived, and were on our way to the prince in Maelienydd. I told her also that David was gone into Chester. There was no help for it, soon it would be common knowledge through Wales, and a national shame.

In those summer nights Godred and I spent together, out of doors, we two alone under the moon, he sat close and watched greedily, either with his shoulder warm against mine, or eye to eye with me across our little fire. There was no escape from him, for I was his key into a new chamber in fortune's house, and he was ever busy with the latest wager and the new-fangled hope. But there was more in Godred's kind and solicitous care than that. For he who never thought to write word or send message to Cristin never ceased to talk of her to me. Of her qualities, of her charms, of his luck in having her to wife. The darker the night, the more his tongue ranged into the intimacies of love.

'They say,' he said, softly marvelling, 'there are wives who have no love for being loved, but only suffer it as a duty. Not so Cristin! Welcoming and warm she is, a true consort. And who sees her only clothed, he cannot know how beautiful!' He leaned so close that his flaxen hair brushed my temple, and sighed his blessedness into my ear. 'Pardon me, if you feel I offend in speaking so of my bliss. I do so only to you, who have rights in her and me both. I could wish you the same happiness I enjoy. Who deserves it more?'

So it went, and ever I put him off with stony indifference, whose heart he pierced and parted and played with as a musician with an instrument. And ever it grew upon me that he tortured not only me, but himself also, and seeing how little he considered or seemed to value her, that was a thing incomprehensible to me. Can men be jealous of what they hold so lightly? I had never thought so. But perhaps when they perceive that another creature treasures what they despise, then the possession held in so slight esteem becomes a jewel to be guarded. But then I was also lost, for no man knew so well as I that he had suffered nothing by my means, for Cristin was as I had first found her, pure as crystal and gold. And it seemed to me that all his intent, increasingly frantic and greedy, was to urge on me the possibility, the desirability, the necessity of possessing and spoiling that purity. Nor did he urge it now by way of wooing my favour, as once he had lightly and pointedly offered her to me, but with the fury and furtiveness of one begging for the only food that might keep him from dying.

I was still too innocent then in the complexities of love, which had been to me as simple and clear as it was mortal, to understand that to such a man as Godred, who had cuckolded many husbands in his time with never a second thought, it might not be a matter of great moment to be cuckolded himself in the same manner. In the flesh! But to be cuckolded in the spirit, to behold his wife loved without sin and loving sinless in return, this was the width of hell beyond forgiveness. Godred desired the lesser offence, to have her his equal and me his fellow.

I think in those days he even ran the risk of growing to the point where he might have become her equal, for

I think that never before had any experience of his life been able to enlarge him to contain such suffering. Of his mind and motives I understood nothing. His anguish was an open book to me, the mirror image of mine. And daily and nightly I perceived how like we were to each other, he the bright image and I the dark of the same impress.

Sometimes by our camp fire he sat turning and turning the silver ring on his little finger, until it seemed to me that he and I were bound within just such a circlet, breast to breast, and could never get free one from the other.

But this uncomforted companionship ended, mercifully, earlier than we had expected, for at Strata Marcella, expecting still to have a day's march between us and Llewelyn, we rode into a courtyard full of his men, and a guesthouse peopled with his officers. The first we encountered in the stables told us that all the river crossings were secured, the army of the reform moving methodically eastwards into England, and the prince, at their earnest desire, was pushing north by forced marches to besiege and destroy the long-spared castle of Diserth, to prevent the garrison of Chester from making any move to alleviate the pressure on the royal forces elsewhere.

'He has been asking for you at every halt,' they told me. 'Go to him quickly, he'll be glad of you.'

But not of my news, I thought. And then, as I had not earlier because of my confused brain and the grief of my body and mind, I realised how slow we had been on the way, and knew by their faces that there was very little I had to tell Llewelyn. The news had reached him first not from Wales, but from England, by word from his allies in the march. What I could add might well be some alleviation of what had been done to him. For I knew, better than any other, that it had been done not in self-interest, and utterly without joy.

'Take me in with you,' said Godred eagerly in my ear. 'Speak for me now!'

186

I said I would speak for him, but not now, that for this moment he had no part. But only very reluctantly did he leave go of my arm, and let me go in without him to the guest-hall of the abbey, where Llewelyn was.

He had left the great chamber, and made use of a small office there, for there were some civil complainants from those parts who prayed audience with him. When I came in he sent the last of them away, and made me sit down before him, for I was still bandaged about the head, and no doubt showed in no very glorious case. He held me pinned to face the light, and eyed me hard, and when he took his hands from my shoulders and turned away from me it was with a rough, abrupt movement, as though in anger.

'There is little you have to tell me of him,' he said, not looking at me. 'I know where he is. The word came into Shrewsbury faster than you could bring it, marked as he has marked you. My bailiffs already administer his lands, and his tenants have pledged me their fealty. Nevertheless, speak, if you have anything to tell me. I am listening.' And again he said, not harshly but with a bleak simplicity that pricked me more deeply: 'The truth, this time. I want no shielding lies.'

I said, with a steadiness at which I myself marvelled, that I had never lied to him but by silence, never even kept from him what was knowledge, only what was misgiving and suspicion.

'Have I no rights even in those?' he said.

It was just, and I was ashamed. For if I was indeed his man, as David said with bitterness, I owed him even my doubts and fears, and his armour was incomplete without them. I said, faintly by reason of my weariness and self-reproach: 'In anything that is mine you have rights, and nothing that is mine will I ever again keep from you, not even my despair.'

'God forbid,' he said, 'that you should suffer any so extreme grief as despair, and not share it with me. Never

187

deprive me, Samson, of what is mine by alliance. You are the closest friend I have, and damage to you is damage to me.'

I said that I accepted that gratefully, but that I had yet somewhat to say to him, in all good faith both to him and to David, as God watched and judged us all. And thereupon I told him, as fully as to my own soul, all that had happened between David and me. What there was to say for him, I said, yet not urging. Llewelyn must take his own stand, but at least upon all the evidence.

He heard me out without question or exclamation, with darkened but quiet brows and attentive eyes. He said: 'You know where we are bound now?'

I said that I did, that we went against Diserth and Degannwy, to destroy them, and to pin down the garrison of Chester from moving south to King Henry's aid. And David was in Chester and a part of that garrison. By the prince's face I knew his mind.

'With the better will,' he said, 'since he is there. I am a bolt loosed at his heart now, for your sake and for mine, and no use to tell me that you forgive him, for I do not forgive. Both those castles I will raze, and drive on to Chester if I can, and if he move on somewhere else I will go after him there. Once he stirred up civil war against me, and I mistakenly held him a misguided tool, who by his own confession was the contriver of all. Now he betrays me and Wales together, and if you think I burn only for Wales, Samson, you do me too much honour, for I am flesh like you. He has not only turned his coat and discarded his fealty, he has preferred Edward before me when it came to the proving. And if he come forth out of Chester in his new cause,' said Llewelyn with soft ferocity, 'and cross my path, I will kill him!'

And truly he believed utterly in what he said. I was the one, not he, who knew that he neither could nor would be the death of his brother. Far more likely, far, that by some fatal, circuitous road David would be the death of him. And since I was pledged now to keep nothing from him, and he to receive and consider whatever I so delivered, I spoke out what was in my mind.

'Have you still in remembrance,' I asked him, 'what he said to you after the field of Bryn Derwin, when he stood unhorsed and bruised and at your mercy? *"Kill me!"* he said. *"You were wise!"* Not defying, not challenging, rather warning and entreating you for your own life, knowing what he had done against you, and might do again. Do you remember?'

He said: 'I remember,' and his eyes burned upon me, their deep brown quickening like fanned embers.

'So much he knew of himself,' I said; 'even then, and so much he valued you and desired your better protection in his own despite. It is all the justification he has, but it is enough. He knows himself and you. Neither you nor I will ever know ourselves as he knows David, or each other as he knows Llewelyn. As often as his right hand launches a blow against you, his left hand will reach to parry it, and his voice will cry you warning: *"Kill me! You were wise!"*'

'You read this,' said Llewelyn darkly, 'as a reason why I should not kill him?'

'Far be that from me!' I said. 'It is fair warning enough of perpetual danger, and the best reason why you should! But it is also the absolute reason why you never will.'

Howbeit, we marched upon Diserth, which the men of the Middle Country were already joyously investing, having leave now to go to extremes. That unlucky garrison had stores for a few weeks, but no more, and their courage was not heightened when they heard how the government of the reform, strongly in command in London, had diverted the king's muster against the Welsh to London itself instead of Chester, to ensure against a

189

defiant stand by the Lord Edward in Windsor, and to enforce the evacuation of all his French mercenaries from England.

That was the most ferocious insult so far offered to the crown, though phrased in the king's name. And Edward, with what bitterness I could imagine, did not wait to be besieged and declared a traitor, but surrendered Windsor and saw his paid soldiers ushered out of the country, and himself stripped naked and helpless. By which time we had taken Diserth, escorted the captive garrison out of it, and razed the walls. Thence we went on to Degannwy, but by September, when we were encamped around that fortress, Earl Simon's party was in complete control in Westminster, King Henry had accepted their demands, and both parties were willing to halt all warlike operations, and spare Degannwy the fate of Diserth.

They urged a brief truce with us. Had it been any other voice that spoke then for England, I doubt if Llewelyn would have heeded or agreed. But though the seal might be King Henry's, the message was Earl Simon's, and the charm of his name and person worked magic wherever it reached. Llewelyn agreed that Degannwy should be revictualled at need, and he would not hinder. But so far was England gone in confusion then that it was never done. We offered passage, but no stores came. By the end of September the starving garrison surrendered, and Edward had not one yard of ground left him in north Wales.

Then there was peace, or at least a great quietness.

And all this time such forces as ventured out from Chester against us were English, every man. They never let David come forth to fight; he ate out his heart within the city. Doubtless at that stage they feared to use him here against the brother he had abandoned, for fear some of those with him might think better of their wager, and turn their coats again. Such was David's fate, that

190

always he sold himself at less than his value, and redeemed himself at more. But what his value was, if every man had justice, that I dare not essay to judge. I leave it to God, who has better scales for weighing, and a more perfect law.

CHAPTER VIII

Now concerning the final months of that year twelve hundred and sixty-three, and what befell then in England, I tell only with the wisdom of hindsight, for to us, patrolling the rim of the march, it seemed then that nothing at all was happening, beyond a confused harrying of individual lands according to the harrier's allegiance – or, all too often, according to his hopes of a quick gain at his neighbour's expense. For Earl Simon's terrible uprightness was no bar to the lawless ambitions of lesser, greedier and more unscrupulous mortals, such as mount in the train of every successful movement merely to share in the pickings. And much injustice was done, some in too hot enthusiasm, some coldly and cynically, to lords who had never turned against the Provisions, but only held back in doubt or timidity from too much zeal in their cause.

After September, when king, bishops and magnates met in St Paul's, and the king's consent to the settlement laid before him was published and approved, it seemed for a time that Earl Simon had truly won, and that the new parliament called to meet in October offered a blessed prospect of repeating the fervour, unity and reconciliation achieved, for however short a time, at Oxford. But aside from the many grievances by that time clamouring for redress, and the many defections and changes of heart caused by them, there were other factors making against the earl, and eating away at the supremacy he seemed to enjoy. For timid and pliable men like King Henry, who cannot be broken, cannot be defeated, either, since they are incapable of despair.

With all his soft, uncrushable obstinacy he clung to hope, and wound about to clutch at every thread that offered. He was tired and in distress, he said, and he desired above all to confer with his dear cousin of France. And to maintain his position he declared, over and over again, publicly and in private, his adherence in principle to the Provisions, the sacred book of the reform. He did so because he had a quick ear for the public pulse, and he knew that the great mass of the people clung to that hope as to holy writ, and if he declared openly against it even that support he enjoyed must dwindle rapidly away. But by affirming piously his own faith in it, and asserting only that it must be subject to discussion and amendment by consent, he was able to show as a harassed and hunted monarch of goodwill, pressed unreasonably hard by men more unbending than himself.

He had his own mild, devious wisdom, for this stand began to work effectively upon many of the older barons close to his throne, who felt affection for him as a man, and some compunction at seeing him hustled and bewildered. So many turned gradually to the king's side again.

I think no man knew better what Henry could do in this kind than Earl Simon himself, but he was utterly bound by his own nature and his own inflexible honour. He could not be a tyrant, and he struggled with all his powers against those hard circumstances that were forcing him into tyranny. So though he knew how the king could twist and turn and break his word, he was compelled to take that word as he expected his own to be taken, and he accepted Henry's promise to return faithfully for the October parliament, and let him go to meet King Louis at Boulogne. And he himself with his foremost allies also crossed the Channel to that meeting, believing in Louis' goodwill and influence, and earnestly desirous of coming to a genuine reconciliation under his guidance. For since Earl Simon could not move against the king's person, or take his royal prerogative from him, it was clear that no order could be restored, no progress made, until king and earl could work together in amity.

Such were his hopes and aims, but it fell out very differently. For in France the Savoyard and Poitevin exiles had for months been building up a strong party of royalist feeling, and as soon as the emissaries of the reform landed they were arraigned as in a court of criminal justice, and found no goodwill at all to discuss or compromise. I will not say this was done with King Louis' approval, but certainly his efforts at mediation did little to amend it. The pope also, who had coldly refused the appeal for a papal legate to give spiritual aid and wise counsel some years earlier, now hurriedly appointed Cardinal Gui to that office, and despatched him to the coast, not, I think, as a mediator, but as accuser and judge. And so thought the barons of England, for they made shift by legal delays to deny him entry to the realm, and he never got nearer England than Boulogne, for all his credentials.

In the face of this treatment Earl Simon repudiated all dealings and returned home. And so did King Henry, in time for parliament as he had promised, but he left the queen in France to work with the exiles. Nor did the parliament produce any relenting on either side, but only bitterness. That, and the first revelation of a third power looming large beside those two who already held the eyes of all men. And that was Edward.

It was Earl Simon himself who provided Edward with his first weapon. He was deeply anxious to have a better understanding with the prince, whom he respected and liked. So during that autumn the earl made many approaches through the young men of his party who had been Edward's closest personal friends, Henry of Almain,

Roger Leyburn and such, several of them from marcher families. But instead of these persuasions working upon Edward, Edward worked upon them, and to such good effect that he won most of them back to his side. And as I know from Cynan since that time, his best argument in their ears was the threat from Wales. For a shadow they were throwing away the substance, leaving the way open for the constant enemy. So he prevailed and convinced them where their true interest lay, with him and with the crown. Man after man he wooed back to him, in and out of that parliament. And when he was ready, having quietly prepared and provisioned Windsor, he withdrew there and took his father with him, leaving Richard of Cornwall and certain others, chosen in desperation as mediators, to try to arrive at some compromise that should at least make government possible.

Doubtless Richard tried to be fair, but his judgments came down heavily on Henry's side, yet again restoring to his hands the main offices of state. Thus Henry won the compunction and loyalty of the old, and Edward seduced the affections and ambitions of the young. And from this time forth it was not Henry who ruled and schooled Edward, but Edward who nursed, cherished and governed Henry. So much must be said for him, in extenuation of the deceits and lies he employed without shame later, that he was fighting for his father, and made use of whatever weapons came to his hand.

I remember what David once said of Edward, after we had ravaged the lands bestowed upon him in Wales. 'He has had his nose rubbed well into the mire,' said David, 'and that was never a safe thing to do to Edward, man or boy.' So it was now. All that had been done against him, by the citizens of Bristol who locked him out of his own town, by the order to the host to muster against Windsor if he did not surrender it and disband his French mercenaries, by the London mob that chased his mother into sanctuary in St Paul's, by us who had captured and razed his last two Welsh castles, everything any man had done against him and his he remembered and recorded, and for every act he would have revenge. But all he attributed to Earl Simon, whom once he had followed and admired. And now that he had turned against him there was no limit to his animosity. The measure of his former love was the only even approximate measure of his new and implacable hate, and that measure fell far short.

Safe in Windsor, King Henry issued letters under his privy seal, and took back the chancellery and the exchequer into his own hands, while Earl Simon held the Tower. They say that Henry of Almain, the best of those young men, at least faced the earl and took a personal farewell when he deserted him, pledging himself with earnest grief never to bear arms against his former idol. But Earl Simon was without tolerance for those who looked back, once having set their hands to the plough, and he told him with cold contempt that it was not his prowess in arms for which he had been valued, but the constancy with which he had once been credited, and that he was at liberty to go, and to take his arms with him and use them as he would, for they inspired no terror. So he departed, and went to Edward.

In spite of his protestations and pieties, King Henry showed his hand early in December, when he suddenly made a sally to the south from Windsor, most likely at Edward's urging, to attempt to regain Dover castle, so precious to any monarch hoping to import soldiers from France. But Richard de Grey, who held the fortress, would not hand over his trust, and the king was obliged to retreat again upon London. Earl Simon at this time had retired to his castle of Kenilworth, to leave the mediators free from his shadow, but when he heard of the king's journey he hurriedly came south to London to see what lay behind it. He had the earl of Derby with him, and a limited following, and as they entered London from the north, the king, returning empty-handed, approached from the south.

King Henry conceived that at last he had an opportunity to seize his enemy, and sent in haste to order the citizens of London to close the city against 'the troublemakers'. And certain of the rich men of the town did indeed plot to close London bridge behind the earl, who had entered Southwark, thus leaving his force exposed while the royal army encircled and captured him. But the common people of London, discovering his danger, broke down the gates and brought him safely out of the trap. Virtuously the king denied all ill intent, or any design of bringing in foreign soldiers. But I think it was this adventure that convinced Earl Simon that without reconciliation England was lost to chaos, and he must make all possible sacrifices to obtain a compromise in which all could work together. So he was the first to agree, when the mediators proposed that the final arbitration should be referred to King Louis, and his judgment on all points should be faithfully accepted by both parties.

But he would never, I think, have accepted this but for the king's assurances that the Provisions themselves were not at issue, being generally accepted by all. Less surprising, King Henry also jumped at the proposal, and the road was prepared for a solemn assembly at Amiens in January of the coming year.

As for us, we guarded the march and waited for word, receiving news of all these things after the event, and the fate of England was decided before we knew anything of it. And in singular contrast to that sad confusion beyond the border, the fate of Wales shone steady and bright as a lamp, its unity crowned at last. For about the same time that the men of London were escorting Earl Simon out of the king's net, Llewelyn at Aber received a visitor he had hardly expected, and one who came in state and bearing gifts, with outriders going before him to smooth his entry, for he was a stranger to Llewelyn's court, and bent on ensuring his welcome now that he had made up his mind to come.

His herald came into hall where we were at meat, and made his reverence before the whole household.

'My lord and prince, the Lord Griffith ap Gwenwynwyn, prince of Powys, desires audience and grace at your court, for he comes to speak with you concerning his reception into your peace.'

Llewelyn rose from his place, astonished but wary, and asked: 'How far behind you does the Lord Griffith ride?'

'My lord, in a breath he will be at your gates,' said the herald.

'Then he shall not enter ungreeted,' said Llewelyn, and went out to meet him and bring him within, and there was haste to lay the place for him at the prince's right hand.

I saw him ride in, a big, thickset man in English harness and apparel, with a heavy, handsome face and greying hair and beard, for he was about fifty at that time. He had quick, roving eyes and a wary, calculating mouth, and in all his accoutrements he was very fine, and in all his speeches very smooth and formal, for he came to heal up and swathe into forgetfulness an ancient enmity, having, as I suppose, summed up our situation and that of England, and come to the conclusion that fortune was on our side, and his best interest to make his peace with us. So thought Llewelyn, past doubt, but he willed to make the move as easy as it might be, for Powys was precious, and Wales needed it. Also it was his way to meet every conciliatory gesture with impulsive warmth, for he was by nature generous to a fault, and the first motion of appeal drew him into a response sometimes over-rash, and laid him open to betrayals in spite of all his wit. So while he smiled at himself and Griffith, nevertheless he sprang in person to hold the suppliant's stirrup, and hand him from the saddle.

At that time neither offered the kiss, which was too sacred for policy. But Llewelyn brought him in with his guest's hand upon his shoulder, lodged him, sent him water and wine, and waited upon him at the door of the hall, to bring him to his seat.

After the banquet, that same evening, they came to stark talk in private, Griffith being bent on an early understanding. He was a little uneasy in bargaining, being unsure of his reception, but melted soon, finding himself met with so much candour. It came to hard terms and firm guarantees, and so to an agreement. At a formal meeting two days later, Griffith offered homage and fealty, and received therefore all those lands by heredity his which Llewelyn had occupied. And as for the future, they entered into a compact against the English of the march, based upon the little river of Camlad, by which Griffith was to have all those conquests north of that stream, and Llewelyn all those to the south. For Griffith's chief neighbour and rival, Corbett of Caus, held to the north of the line, and it was not long before he felt the shock of the alliance. There was an old grudge there, that surely had urged Griffith to his submission.

However that was, he had submitted. And the year twelve hundred and sixty-three ended gloriously with Wales truly one, while England was torn in two. So we had our hour.

Whether things might have turned out differently if Earl Simon had been present at the great conference at Amiens is mere conjecture, and lost pains now even to wonder. But he never crossed the sea that winter.

On his way from Kenilworth to embark he turned aside to visit the house of Cistercian nuns at Catesby, where there was a chapel to the blessed St Edmund of Abingdon, and as he departed he was thrown from his horse and broke his leg, so that he was forced to have himself conveyed painfully back to Kenilworth, and there lay crippled and burning while others pleaded his cause in France. But his son Henry was there among the leaders of the baronial party, with Peter de Montfort, and Humphrey de Bohun and others, and no doubt they put their arguments well enough. They had expected a patient process of discussion upon detailed points, and were prepared to give and take. What they got was very different. In a few bare days, and without overmuch consideration, King Louis gave judgment against them upon every point, and declared everyone who was party to the case absolved from all obligation to maintain the Provisions. The pope had already annulled them, King Louis pronounced them void and illegal.

King Henry's voice at Amiens spoke another language from that he had used in England, where he had professed again and again his devotion in principle to the reform. Before Louis he claimed the right to choose his own justiciar – or indeed to dispense with him if he chose – and to nominate his ministers, judges, local officials and castellans without reference to council or parliament. He vowed that acceptance of the Provisions was not consistent with his coronation oath, and insistence upon them violated his barons' oaths of fealty. And king holds with king as against the people, however they may tear each other over territory and conquest.

At the news of that award such a howl of joy went up from all the exiles crowding the French shore that almost we heard it in the march, for now pope and king had declared for them and against the reform, all legality was stripped from it, and what was to hold them back now from mounting an invasion of England with the blessing of state and church, a holy crusade? The pope hurried to reaffirm his agreement with the judgment, and reassert the mortal spiritual danger of all who resisted it. But in England, when the word came like a wave of the sea inland over the shires, the common people and the small gentry, the friars and preachers, the wardens of
200

the peace, all those who had pinned their fervent faith upon the new order, gave vent to a great cry of rage and bitterness, declaring, surely with justice, that King Louis had exceeded the powers granted him, and moreover that they had never been parties to the decision to make him judge, and were not bound by his award. Everywhere they rose to attack those who held against them, and threatened them with the king's displeasure or the pope's ban. They had looked for a judgment that would restore peace, they got a crude blow that could only mean war.

In vain King Henry, upon Louis' advice, hastened to publish his willingness to receive to his peace all those persons who would accept the decision. His peace was not the peace they wanted, and they did not come. They looked towards the sea that alone held off from them the legate's menaces and the exiles' ships and mercenaries, and they began to band themselves together into companies, and exercise in arms, not at all quenched but perilously inflamed.

We in the march soon saw some local flares, for Roger Mortimer, most powerful of the royalist faction in those parts, began to make rapid raids upon certain of Earl Simon's manors in the west, and Llewelyn moved a company of his men to Knighton and another to Presteigne, in the expectation that they might soon be needed. It was not for us to assume the defence of what the earl was quite able to take care of himself, but Roger's lordship of Radnor was open to attack, and offered a way of relieving the pressure upon the baronial position if such a diversion should be needed.

We were at Knighton when a courier brought a letter from the earl. More than one such exchange had passed during that month of January, while Earl Simon seethed and fretted helplessly in Kenilworth. This letter came at the end of that month, and thus it was from the earl's own hand that we heard the news of the award of

Amiens. He had but just heard it himself. His sons were newly landed and making for the west to fend off the encroachments of Mortimer, and his request was that Llewelyn would move to meet them, and close in with them upon Radnor. As long as we kept the west, Earl Simon's army in those parts was ensured of supplies, a safe retreat when pressed, and support sufficient to protect it from pursuit.

'There is one more thing the earl of Leicester asks of us,' said Llewelyn in council. 'This combat that now bids fair to burst into the open has shifted its ground, and here are we back at the old game, the Welsh on one side, the marchers on the other, the strongest group King Henry has at his back. It's in the west this war will begin, and we shall have need of a very close understanding if we are to make it prosper. Earl Simon asks that I will accredit to him a trusted officer to represent me at his court, and with him a good messenger who can carry his reports back and forth between us while this stress continues.'

Goronwy and the council agreed that it was a wise move, for our own protection as well as for Earl Simon's, for much might depend upon an instant understanding if the threatening fire burned up in earnest.

'Samson,' said Llewelyn, looking up at me, 'I would have you go. A clerk it should be, to have the safe-conduct of his office, so far as any man is to be safe in such a realm. Will you go?'

I said what he knew, that I would do whatever he asked of me, and serve him wherever he willed. And so it was settled, and he gave me Cadell, a sturdy, reliable young man-at-arms to be my companion, and bade us choose what horses we would, and sent us forth on the journey to Kenilworth, with the earl's courier to guide us and give us cover by his lord's writ. That same day we rode. But before I set out, Llewelyn drew me aside, and very earnestly and hopefully asked me to do more than was in my commission.

'While you are with him,' he said, 'and if you may without offending, for God knows he has his hands full with all the weight of England, study of him these views he holds on kingship and right rule, for I am curious to know more of them.'

So indeed was I, and this charge I undertook most willingly. We were hungry, both, for a deeper comprehension of this great man my lord had not yet even seen. We knew of him that he had been and was the friend and confidant of saints, if not himself a saint, and that he found in kingship an element as purely sacramental as in priesthood. We knew his pride and rigidity, but had heard also of his unexampled humility and patience under reproof. And this was but one pair among the many seeming contradictions in him which I think were no contradictions, any more than the right hand denies the left, but rather the exquisite balances that kept him so whole and so upright. His high and overbearing temper with the strong, and his delicate courtesy to the weak, his unbending insistence on his own rights and devout concentration upon the discharge of his obligations to others. So much we knew of him, and desired to know far more. And I was grateful and bound to him all the more because, the nearer we had drawn to his cause, the less did Llewelyn look hungrily towards Chester, where David was, and the more towards this irresistible heat and brightness that drew men as the sun draws up dew.

One more reason I had to be glad of my mission to Kenilworth, and that was that it freed me for a while of the unrelenting companionship of Godred, who had wormed his way into a secure place among Llewelyn's guard. True it is that he could do whatever was required of him, and do it well enough, and was quick of wit and without fear, but also true that he did no more than was required of him, and necessary to keep him in good favour. And with the rest of his time and energy he frequented me, unswerving and tireless, waiting and watching for I knew not what, for me to die, or succumb to his proffered temptations, or to confide in him and give him power over me – no, I cannot tell. I know only that his absence was to me as a spring of fresh water in a burning day.

By Ludlow and through the forest of Wyre we rode to Kenilworth, such soft and gracious country even the late spite of winter seemed lulled by it, and bit but toothlessly, like a puppy. I never saw such green grass in the first days of February, or such a sun in the heavens, low though it lay and briefly though it stayed. And when we came to that great pile that stopped up the roads like a mountain, and fenced itself in with one broad, chill water defence after another, I was struck dumb with wonder, for such a castle I had never seen. I doubted then if it could ever be taken, but by starvation over many months, and later it proved so to the letter. I know no way by which it could ever be stormed or mined, for there was a lake, made by man, that covered three sides of it, and the fourth approach was so menaced by shot and cross-shot that no army could ever draw near enough to do it hurt. Guided and guaranteed by Earl Simon's courier, Cadell and I wound our way through the many guards into the wards of the castle. On all sides its towers soared over us, and the great keep blotted out the noonday. And yet it was a most fair spot, ringed round with softly rolling country like a maze of rich meadows in paradise.

They said to me as soon as I alighted that their lord waited to receive me, and begged my indulgence that he could not come out to me on his own two feet, for reasons I knew.

They brought me into a small but rich chamber in

one of the minor towers. I remember tapestried hangings that warmed the nakedness of the walls, and a brazier glowing, that gave the most light in that dark apartment, even in the mid-afternoon, before the dusk fell. And a low couch along the wall beneath the hangings, where the great earl sat propped by furs, with his broken leg stretched along the cushions in a bundle of wooden brace and linen bindings, like a weathered log. And I remember how dead that one limb seemed, and how live all else, from the single foot thrust large and vehement against the flags of the floor, to the reared Norman head that turned towards me as I entered, to bring to bear upon me those marvellous deep-set eyes, yet so large and wide and fearless that they seemed to stand out like rounded gems from the sockets. To this day I do not know certainly of what colour they were, they so burned and shone that they had no colour but radiance. I think he was even ill-shaven and somewhat tired when I first saw him in his own house, yet do not know why I should think so, since what I most remember of him is the cleanness, the outline, of all his person, as if he had been chiselled out of some metal too pure to be taken out of the earth.

His voice when he spoke to me was as mild, direct and open as his gaze, pitched rather low, out of the centre of his body, which as I saw him then was but of middle size, sturdy and square but lean. I marvelled, for I had thought him a taller man, what was within him so towered above the flesh and bone.

'I ask your pardon,' he said, 'for not rising to receive you, but you see my condition. Prince Llewelyn's envoy is most welcome to me. I pray you sit down with me.'

In this first of many audiences I had with him, I told him how I had left affairs on the border, and that Llewelyn's force would already be deploying its westward half-circle about Radnor, prepared to close in as soon as the earl's sons had drawn near enough to match the thrust from the east. He asked many and brisk questions concerning the land and the roads, and clearly he was well informed about the watch we already kept upon the fords and bridges over the Severn. In return he told me the latest news of the enemy, though never calling them so. Richard of Cornwall, the regent during the king's absence, was in Worcester by that time, and intended going on to Gloucester, where he meant to keep and hold the bridge if the remaining ones must be sacrificed. I asked after the Lord Edward, whose name, by consent, now took precedence of King Henry's in the tale of our foes.

'He is on the sea at this moment,' said Earl Simon, 'and the king with him. If this wind hold, they must land tomorrow, or very soon. He has sanction to strike now, he will not hold his hand.'

We spoke of where that blow, when it came, was most like to fall, but in speculation upon Edward's actions there was little profit. Yet we were at one in believing that he would try to secure the marches, since he had already lured back to him so many of the young marcher lords, and that he would use the same bogey to bring the rest to heel now.

'The Welsh threat,' I said, 'will be his theme. And Radnor will be his text.'

'No matter,' said the earl, 'so he comes too late to save it.'

I told him then what had already been said through his son, that in my view Llewelyn would never willingly commit his army in out-and-out war against the crown of England, though his sympathies were engaged. Beyond the Severn he would not take them, unless those sympathies swept him away, for his first duty was to Wales, and his first concern to retain the power of bargaining, for her sake, with whatever regime ruled in England. However heartily he might pray the victory of the reform, yet he had to keep open his freedom to deal with whatever England he might find neighbour to him in the future.

'That I understand,' said Earl Simon, 'and respect. He has his cause as I have mine. He is right to pledge to it everything but his honour.'

'And yet,' I said, watching him with intent, 'if you should ask him to take that plunge, and commit his cause to yours, I believe he might do it.'

Earl Simon understood me well, that I was not prompting but appealing. He said: 'Be easy! There are limits to my rights in any man. I shall not ask him.'

Before I rose to leave him on this first occasion, since it seemed all had been done that at this moment could be done, I ventured to speak to him of those principles of kingship of which we had heard, and of which Llewelyn desired a better understanding. At that his eyes shone, and he began to speak with passion of the well-disciplined body in which every member bears its true part, and thence of the body politic, a realm in which the same balance and harmony obtain, where kingship is a sacred trust, and rule not for gain or glory but for the right regulation of the affairs of all men, from the highest to the lowest. And thence again it was but a deeper breath and a stretching out of the being to comprehend a body spiritual in which every realm should be a member performing still its just function, and this should be the true Christendom. And he told me that he had had copied for his own use the tract on kingship and tyranny written by the late, great Bishop Robert Grosseteste of Lincoln, and he would lend it to me to make another copy, if time served, for Llewelyn's study. And so he did, and even marked for me those passages that most engrossed his own thoughts, in case there was too little time for copying the whole. And thereafter he spoke with me, whenever we had leisure from events, of those lofty ideas that so consumed his heart and mind.

As I went out from him the door of his chamber opened before I reached it, and I was face to face with a startled girl on the threshold. Her lips were parted, about to call to him even as she came into the room, and thus on the verge of speech she halted, half-smiling, astonished to be gazing up so closely at a stranger. She was tall for her years, and slender, and bore herself with the simplicity and assurance of her birth, so that it took me some seconds of wonder and admiration to realise that she was hardly past childhood, surely no more than eleven or twelve years old. All that brave candour and innocence that showed so excellent in her brother came to perfection in her. Such warmth and rounded sweetness of line I never saw in any face but hers, such wide, generous shaping of lip, such grand, gallant honesty of eye. She was fairer than her brother, the long braid of her hair a deep, muted gold, and the brow it crowned was ivory-smooth and great with gravity. But the lashes that fringed her clear, gold-flecked eyes were dark almost to blackness.

I stepped back out of her path and made my bow to her, almost too bemused to move or speak, and she, child-like in her courtesies, made me in return the reverence due to older people, however lofty or humble, and looked from me to the earl for guidance. He was smiling upon her, as well he might, if such a jewel was his.

He held out his hand, and she went to him, laying her own small hand in his palm, and looked back gravely at me.

'Be acquainted, Master Samson,' he said, 'with my youngest child and only daughter. This is Eleanor.'

In that teeming household of his, among the thousand souls and more that gathered in hall to meet, knights, squires, lawyers, friars, clerks, men-at-arms, armourers, scholars, gentlewomen and damozels, I learned to know the other members of his family, and knew his imprint even when I met it stripped to the waist in wrestling, or soiled and tousled in leather, whistling over the grooming of a horse in the yard. For the mintage was unmistakable, that face repeating itself with but trivial changes in all that came of his blood. His two eldest sons, Henry whom I knew, and the younger Simon who was as yet unknown to me, were away in the march, and within a few days of my coming they were inside Radnor town, and busy with Llewelyn about the razing of Radnor castle. But three more he had here with him, Guy, already a man grown and in his twentieth year, ready and eager to bear arms, Amaury and Richard still boys of about fifteen and thirteen. The same welcoming and challenging eyes gazed from every one of those Roman heads, yet there were differences between them. Amaury had the sharpest tongue and the most scholarly inclinations, Guy, I think, the most formidable wits and the least governed impulses.

The Countess Eleanor, whom I saw only in hall, and seldom spoke to, was a very handsome woman, as tall as her husband and as fierce and impetuous, but without that deeper part of him that could school even his own fire into humility. All his dreams and lofty aims she shared, but only because they were his, and often without understanding what she nevertheless would have defended to the death. She had a life-long grievance over her dowry, which had never been paid, and doubtless she was extravagant and had good need of plenty of money, but I think it was her right rather than the gold itself that she fought for. And in that she was like Earl Simon, for he would not abate one mark of what was due to him, though he was even more punctilious in paying other men their due. I grew to know and welcome those foibles in him, and those moods of depression and bile, that brought him down to the same earth as ordinary mortals.

To Llewelyn I wrote despatches as often as we had news of movements upon the king's side, and Cadell carried them at speed, with Earl Simon's safe-conduct to shelter him and get him horses in England, and Llewelyn's in Wales. Thus we got word to both English and Welsh forces in Radnor when King Henry and his son landed, and Edward with all the men he could muster rushed westwards, while the king followed more slowly as far as Oxford, where he entrenched himself and gathered all his supporters about him. We were even able to get word to the march when Edward diverted his attack, and instead of charging upon Radnor as we had expected, struck deep into Brecknock, into the lands of young Humphrey de Bohun, one of the few marcher lords who continued on the side of the reform. Earl Simon's sons had therefore to expect his attack upon them, which must follow, from the south instead of the east, and with the importance of the Severn always in mind, they drew back their force towards that river, with Edward in pursuit. They had done what they had set out to do in Radnor, and left Mortimer's lands in disarray; they withdrew out of immediate range of Edward's force, and moved upon Gloucester ahead of him.

Our couriers were in furious activity then, for the whole of the march was in motion, and we were occupied in conveying to every force in the field upon our side the movements of every other, as well as of Edward's army. For Robert Ferrers, the young earl of Derby, one of Earl Simon's most daring and ingenious allies, but also one of the most self-willed and moody, brought his muster sweeping south to storm Worcester, intending to join forces with Henry de Montfort after the fall of Gloucester. This we made known instantly to the de Montfort force, for if the move succeeded we held the vital stretches and crossings of the Severn.

I observe that I have begun to say 'we', though my own lord was now left behind nursing the western rim of the march as before, to afford cover for his friends at need. So closely had I then identified myself with Earl Simon's ends and dreams, yet I felt no divided loyalties within me, as if the two I served were one.

And ever, when chance offered, I bathed my eyes and

refreshed my heart in the delight of watching that other Eleanor, artless child and great lady in one fine, fair body. And sometimes I had speech with her, for she had a child's licence to make friends where she would, with a woman's grace to hold the acquaintance in balance. And whether her brother had talked eloquently to her of what he had seen in Wales, or whether her curiosity was native to her by reason of her generous heart, and she desired both to please me and to benefit by the presence of the stranger; however it was, she would know what I could tell her of the ways and customs of Wales, and soon, caught by my decided attachment, she asked particularly of our prince. Doubtless I presented him as an object for love, seeing I loved him.

Now this matter of the struggle for Gloucester, which we witnessed helplessly from afar in that month of March, best demonstrates the mood and temper of the Lord Edward from that time forth towards his opponents and all those who held with them and comforted them. For in the first week of the month Henry de Montfort, by a daring trick played by two of his confederate barons, who certainly risked their lives in the frolic, captured the city of Gloucester, but not the castle, which was strongly held for the king. For these two young lords got themselves up as woolmongers, and came up to the west gate with bales on their backs to gain entry, and thereupon dropped their loads and showed their arms, and held the gate while Henry marched his men within. But I will not say that the town of Gloucester, as opposed to the guard, was sorry to be so invaded by the armies of the reform, for the evidence is that they gave in very willingly, and suffered for it thereafter.

But very shortly after this the Lord Edward came with his army, and was privily let into the castle by the garrison, and he had good need to fear when Earl Robert of Derby came scything south from Worcester to join the

Montforts. This was when he showed both his wit and his faithlessness. No one knew better than he that Earl Simon's cause was hamstrung by its own goodwill, for the half of its support was bishops and such benevolents, who above all things desired peace and reconciliation, while the other half knew only too well it had no choice but to resist in arms á l'outrance. So at this pass Edward sent piously to the bishop of Worcester, that good man, devoted to the Provisions but also to peace, and so prevailed upon him that he went to Henry de Montfort, who held the town securely, and offered in Edward's name, and clearly in good faith, a truce that should lead on – such was promised under oath – to a permanent peace, if Henry would withdraw from the town with his army.

The bishop was honest, no question, he offered what he confided in as in the Host. And as in the Host, young Henry received, revered and believed. Edward's word he took, as he would have expected Edward, with better reason, to take his. And he withdrew from the town.

For his complaisance and gullibility, may God forgive him! For his innocence, honour and purity, may God reward him!

Edward occupied the town, ravaged it to misery and despair for its forbearance to his enemies, fortified and garrisoned it to the utmost, and swept out of it to join his father at Oxford. No more was ever said of truce or peace.

May God also deal so with him according to his judgment. I say no more than that. For we know, every man of us, that there will be a judgment, even for princes.

Young Henry, when he knew how shamefully he had been tricked, left his brother to lead their joint force towards Northampton, where the baronial levies were massing to secure their ground in the midlands, and came hurrying home in person to confess his innocent folly and face his father's anger. He was spared nothing, for the blow was very bitter. In his own defence he said only, with simple truth: 'I took the sworn word of the heir of England. How could I suppose I was dealing with a liar and cheat? Sir, you would also have believed him a man of his word.'

'I should never have considered his terms,' said Earl Simon heavily. 'His truth or falsehood would not have been put to the test. Now you have lost me the west, and sent Ferrers fuming back to his own country in a rage, having wasted his capture of Worcester.'

'I own it,' said Henry, stricken. For the earl of Derby, an insubordinate and wayward man, had withdrawn from his capture and quit the Severn, marching back in a fury to his own country. 'I am at fault, and what I have done cannot be put right now.'

And he submitted without protest to the earl's reproaches, though for my part I could but think how like he was, in his lesser way, to this same proud incorruptible who chastised him, and how justly he could have turned and charged: 'You might well have done the same in my place.' For there is no remedy against the tricks of the devious for those who are themselves men of honour, and at that very time Earl Simon had consented again to one last attempt at conciliation, through a French nobleman who was in England on King Louis' financial business, and as friend to both parties begged to try what he could do to avert war. And what had young Henry done but consent to the promise of just such an attempt? It was not his fault that Edward's faith was rotten. Moreover, Earl Simon later committed even such acts of generous and high-minded folly himself, and lost by them more than his son had lost for him at Gloucester. A man can act only in accordance with his nature, and the weapons of the tricksters outnumber by far the arms of the honourable.

But the boy made no complaint, only bowed his head to the storm and set his jaw at the future.

'I do but scold at my own infirmities,' said the earl at

213

length, sighing as he turned to behold himself in the mirror he had made. 'You did nothing so ill, though ill came of it.' And to me he said: 'It will not be so easy now to keep touch with the prince, since the west is out of our hands, nor is he so likely to be needed and drawn in. I cannot answer for what course this year will take, but it seems we are thrust off into the midlands, and it's there the struggle must come. If your lord would rather that you return to him, I cannot fairly lay claim to you further.'

I wrote therefore to Llewelyn, telling him how matters stood, how the king's host was summoned to Oxford at the end of March, and the earl's forces massing in Northampton, and though the French arbitrator was hard at work trying to bring the parties to discussion with him at Brackley, and both sides had assented to the meeting, there seemed but little chance that anything would come of it. The bishops who spoke for Earl Simon and the reform had offered concessions on all points except the king's right to appoint aliens to his council and offices without reference to the community of the land, but King Henry, though paying lip service to conciliation, would not give way one inch upon this or any other item. I saw no possibility in the end but war, and it seemed that the field of battle had moved into the centre of England, away from the march. Then I sent this despatch by Cadell, and awaited my orders.

I had half expected and half wished to be called home, yet I found I was glad when Llewelyn replied that I should continue with Earl Simon, so far as I judged it safe for me, wherever he might go, and still keep as frequent touch as I might with Wales. By this I knew that even if he would not commit his heritage, his heart was committed.

While the royal army lay at Oxford, the main baronial muster at Northampton, and the hopeful French agent ran back and forth between the two from Brackley, which lies midway along that road, Earl Simon, though still crippled by his injury, which had not knitted well, could rest no longer, but determined to go south to London, which was unswervingly loyal to him. And I went in his retinue, and Cadell along with me, eager and curious at every mile, for he had never been beyond the march until we came to Kenilworth, and London was a marvel to him. The earl could not ride, but he had had a light, four-wheeled chariot made for him, and in that he rode, driven by one of his grooms, or sometimes driving himself. So we made that journey to London, and again I saw that great citadel they call the Tower, that had such long and grim memories for me. There the justiciar had his head-quarters, and there Earl Simon took up residence.

The whole city had drafted its people into armed bands, under a constable and a marshal, ready to muster when-ever the great bell of St Paul's should be rung to call them out. To tell truth, the results were somewhat disorderly, and before Earl Simon arrived there had been some ill-advised local attacks upon royalist lands, notably on Richard of Cornwall's manor of Isleworth, that did nothing to help the cause of conciliation. When a city as great and populous as London seethes with excitement and stands to in unaccustomed arms, even an Earl Simon may find it difficult to control.

But as to what happened next, and who first invoked absolute war, and in what circumstances, I tell truth as we knew it. Certain it is that the Frenchman's negotia-tions, however barren, had not been broken off. For proof, on the second day of April a safe-conduct was issued to Peter de Montfort as baronial envoy, to meet the royal proctors at Brackley, and this safe-conduct was to remain valid until Palm Sunday, which fell on the thirteenth of that month. Yet on the third day of April King Henry suddenly marched his army out of Oxford, taking with him his war-standard, a dragon with a tongue of fire, worked on red samite, and made straight for

215

Northampton at a forced pace, to lay that town under siege.

The news came to us in the city, and Earl Simon at once set out to relieve the garrison, though we did not fear any disaster, Northampton being so full of trusty levies and so well supplied. The only danger, we thought, was a long siege, which we had the power to break. But we had got no farther than St Albans when we were met by a messenger on a lathered horse, who croaked out his ill news from a dusty throat beside Earl Simon's chariot.

'My lord, Northampton has fallen! Your son's made prisoner, and the lord of Beaudesert and his two sons with him, and many another. All taken! By treachery! The town was entered and stormed in the night. By now I doubt the castle has surrendered. There's rapine and murder in the streets for your sake. Another Gloucester!'

It was so stunning a blow that Earl Simon was knocked out of words and breath, but the greater the disaster that fell upon him, the more quietly and immovably did he rally to resist it, all his furies being spent on things by comparison light. He questioned in few words, and took from the man all that miserable story.

'My lord, at the priory of St Andrew, by the north gate, the prior is a Frenchman, and of the king's party. He had the brothers make a breach in the walls of their house, and by night they broke through the last shell of the town wall, and let the king's men in. In the darkness they made their way by parties all about the town, and struck before dawn. It was so sudden we had no chance. The guards were surprised and overwhelmed first, many of us never had time to lay hands on our weapons. Some companies contrived to fight their way out, and will muster as best they can and come south to join you. But Northampton's lost, and many of your best knights with it, and God help the folk in the town, for Edward is taking revenge on them all.'

Earl Simon made no murmur over his loss of son and

allies and arms, fronting what seemed almost a mortal blow to his hopes with a granite face. Quietly he ordered the return to London, and back to the Tower we went, and there he took from those who managed to reach us the full story of the sack of Northampton, and the long list of the prisoners. For several days news came in. The valuable captives were whipped away into the hold of various castles in the marches, to remove them from the immediate hope of rescue. There was now no means of recovering them but by bringing this war to a successful end, for now beyond question this was war.

'It might be worse,' said the earl grimly, when we knew what the king's next moves had been, and Edward's. 'If I have let my chance be wrested from me, he is throwing his away.' For King Henry had moved on to Nottingham, elated by his easy success and neglecting to follow it up energetically, while Edward, though displaying energy enough, was tossing it to the winds by careering north to harry the lands of the earl of Derby.

'He is letting personal hate affect his judgment,' said the earl critically.

While Henry kept Easter in Nottingham, and Edward pursued Robert Ferrers in Derbyshire, Earl Simon turned south. For in France it was certain that the queen and archbishop and the royal clerks were massing soldiers and horses and arms, and sooner or later would try to land them in England. Whoever held the Cinque ports held the narrow seas. And the young earl of Gloucester, Gilbert of Clare, had not been in Northampton, but by reason of the dangerous state of the march was at his Kentish castle at Tonbridge, with a strong force. Between them he and Earl Simon could hope to take the royal castle at Rochester, where was the only substantial royalist force in the south at that time. In the event they took the town, but not the castle keep, and when both Henry and his son came rushing in alarm to raise the siege, Earl Simon pondered briefly whether this was the

217

time and place to stand and fight, and decided against it.

'No, not here,' he said. 'I need to secure London behind me, and keep it safe out of his hands. Let him have such as he can take of the ports, he will not get Dover, nor will he have the goodwill of the seamen or the men of the Weald. We go back to London.'

And back to London we went, leaving Rochester to be re-occupied by the king's army, and even sacrificing Tonbridge, for Gilbert of Clare returned with Earl Simon to the city. Not to sit in the Tower and wait to be attacked, but to re-order and enlarge his army with all the trained bands of London, ready to move again with an impregnable city at his back, before King Henry should have any chance to settle or enjoy his scanty hold upon the coast.

Thus those two armies, at last dressed for battle and no longer postponing, began to move together in the early days of May, the king returning from the coast to the town of Lewes, where Earl Warenne of Surrey had a strong castle, and Earl Simon marching south from London to intercept him. Now no one sought to avoid, but rather each observed, by way of scouts, the course his enemy took, and guided his own force to strike forehead against forehead.

No man can say for certain, but for my part I believe it was Edward who had decreed that attack upon Northampton, while proctors and agents still talked conciliation and issued safe-conducts. It accords well with the tenor of all he did at this time, for his every act shows that he did not consider himself bound by any considerations of honour or good faith in dealing with those he held to be rebels. And I think also that it was Edward who now thirsted to dash against his enemies and destroy them. For Earl Simon had said rightly of him that his hatred unbalanced his judgment. Not that we dared build upon that, for if there was one thing certain about Edward, it was that he could learn. Not that he would therefore hate less, but that he would be better able to control and channel his hate to do the greatest and most terrible harm to those he hated.

It was a temperament Earl Simon did not know, except by rote, for it was out of his scope. Though he used the word freely when he blazed against pettiness and inconstancy, I doubt if he ever hated any man, for in all innocence – no, I do not like that word for him! – in all purity he never found, of his own measure, any that were hateful, but only such as he reverenced, willing to sit at their feet like a scholar guided by his master. But they were legion whom he knew how to despise.

It was the eleventh day of May, and a Sunday, when King Henry's army reached Lewes and camped there. We were at Fletching, ten miles north of that town, in the forest country above the valley of the Ouse, and by our forward scouts we knew when they came, and their numbers, which were certainly greater than ours. It mattered not at all that it was so. The middle of May is not summer, yet in our camp by night there was a warmth upon us like a benediction and, as I think, it arose from a most rare essence, the unity of some thousands of minds at one and at rest.

Three bishops we had with us, of Worcester, London and Chichester, one of them as near a saint as mortal man can reach outside the canon, and he the most intimate and faithful friend of the demon-saint who led us. But that was not our secret. The great calm of ordinary, well-intentioned, reverent and humble blessedness was upon us, of mortal men doing what they devoutly believed to be right and true. There is no other grace needed, for this grace comes of God, without benefit of pope or priest. And I well remember that night, after so long, for the absolute peace of the spirit that lay upon it.

I went out between the camp-fires, muted and turfed by reason of the dry weather and the thick brushwood, up to a little spur of the downs, that lifted out of forest into the sky and was roofed over with stars, and there I said my office in the utmost calm, without fear or hope, both impurities, aware only of this blessedness.

In resignation of soul that was pure joy, I made my prayers for my lord, and for my country, and for my love, and from all three I was far distant, and yet I felt them very near. And it seemed to me that I saw them all the more clearly from this small hillock in the far south, as though the starlit air between touched my eyes into clarity beyond mortal, so that my love swelled in me into such grandeur that I could hardly contain it, and it welled into the night and made itself one with the silence and the calm. Then, believing myself alone, I said aloud the first, best prayer. And one in the shadow of the trees behind me said: 'Amen!'

I turned about, and he was there in the darkness of the trees, seated upon a bank of turf that clambered into the knotted roots of an old beach-tree. And so still that I had not marked him when I came, though there he had surely been in his own solitude, apart even from those three holy men who upheld his spirit and blessed his cause. By his voice I knew him, and by the shape of him, like a part, a buttress, of the great tree, or a bastion shielding the wall of a city. He could walk by then, leaning upon a staff, or with a page's shoulder under his hand, but not for too long, and as yet could not sit a horse without pain.

'I ask your pardon,' he said, 'for intruding upon your devotions. I could not move to leave you without disturbing you.'

'My lord,' I said, 'next to God and Llewelyn, there is no creature in heaven or earth I would so willingly trust with my prayers as you. This night I could believe I have been heard as compassionately there as here.'

His voice in the great starry spaces of the night was low and still and utterly assured, for we were all come to this marvellous stay, as upon a rock. Very seldom in a lifetime can men be so sure of what they do, and of their resignation and rightness in undertaking it.

'You know,' he said, 'as every man here knows, that this matter is now come to the issue. There is nowhere further to go, for beyond this point, if he will not bend, we cannot.'

I said that I did know it, and was at peace with it. And I said, in some wonder, that this must be the mark of a holy war, that it brought its soldiers to a high certainty of peace.

'Yet while we have life,' he said, 'and have not clashed forehead against forehead, I must still strive even for the world's peace. Tomorrow I propose to send to the king by Bishop Berksted, and make one more attempt to sever him from those who misuse and delude him. Then if that fail, there is no way to go but forward into battle. Master Samson, I have given some thought to your situation. If we march on Lewes, you will remain in the service of the bishop. I will place you officially in his household, and his hand and your own clerkship will protect you if my fortunes go awry. Very loyal and serviceable you have been to me, and I have been glad of you, but this quarrel is neither yours nor your lord's, and I would have you clear of blame.'

Such was Earl Simon, at the crisis of his greatest obligation still able to give care and thought even to the least. I thanked him for his kindness, but said I could not accept his provision for me.

'Thus far I have come with you,' I said, 'at my lord's will, and the rest of the way I will go with you at my own. Though I began as a clerk, I can take the cross like any other man and, if you will use me, I can use a sword. I could not go back and look Llewelyn in the face again if I forsook you now. He is bound in his own person, but free in mine, and what he cannot do, I can, in his name as well as my own. But for my man Cadell, if he will accept it, I welcome your good thought. I will write

221

some lines to my prince, and send them tomorrow by Cadell, if you will furnish him a safe-conduct, for by way of London he can still reach Wales safely. And I will have Llewelyn keep him there this time, and not return. After tomorrow,' I said, 'if the news be good, I will carry it back to my lord myself. And if not,' I said, 'I shall be troubled with messages no more, and it will be all one to me who carries him word of my death.'

'Either you are very well prepared for dying,' said the earl drily, 'or your faith in my cause is great. Or it may be both,' he said, musing. 'Who am I to tell?'

'I can think of worse ways to die,' I said, 'than in your cause and your company. And whatever the outcome, I will not turn my back now.'

I had thought he might be angry at being denied, for he was not used to being crossed, and indeed he had the right to give orders and dispose as he saw fit now that we were in the field. But he did not refuse me. A moment he sat silent, thinking, and then, dark as it was, I saw him smile. He reached out a hand to me, and said:

'Will you lend me your arm back to my tent? The way downhill is harder going than the climb.'

So leaning on me he raised himself, and with my arm under his on the lame side, and his staff helping him on the other, we descended to where the bedded fires loaded the night air with their green earthen scent, and the low murmur of voices and stirring of movement from company to company made a forest quickening, like the awakening of bird and beast before the dawn. Patient beside his tent the young earl of Gloucester waited for him, and took him from my arm to bring him within. But for some long, sweet moments of that night I had heavy and vital upon my heart the greatest man ever I knew, and but for one the best and dearest, and on May nights I feel that weight yet, and am back in the forests of Fletching, in the days before the battle, with the stars above debating secretly my life or death, and the fate of England.

CHAPTER IX

When the morning came, he did as he had said. In council with his barons he composed a letter to the king, assented to by all, and had it sealed with his own seal and Gloucester's. It was a letter altogether devout and courteous, but unyielding, declaring the unswerving loyalty to the king of all those consenting to it, though they were resolved to proceed to the utmost against his enemies and theirs, the evil counsellors who deformed his government and urged him to injustice and unwisdom. This letter was carried by a number of knights and clerks, and the embassage was led by the bishop of Chichester with a party of Franciscan friars. The bishop was entrusted with the matter of argument, and the elaboration of the letter, for the earl was still willing to discuss amendments and adjustments, as he had been all along. Only on the one great thing he was adamant. The Provisions were sacred, for he was bound by oath to them, and could not break his troth. Yet the Provisions themselves could by agreement be modified, and it was his proffer that they should be considered by good and wise men, theologians and canonists, whose recommendations he promised to accept.

This was the mission of the party that set out from Fletching on the twelfth day of May, and rode down the valley of the Ouse to the king's camp at Lewes.

It was middle evening before we saw them returning. The day most of us spent in resting, and refurbishing weapons and harness, and the earl and his captains in their own grave preparations, considering in detail the lie of the ground, and the nice balance between the advantages of surprise and caution, between going to them and waiting for them to come to us. As for me, I wrote my despatch to Llewelyn, thinking to do all words could do to bring him close to me, and acquaint him even with the curious, sweet and ominous calm of my mind at this pass, for greatly I desired to have him share what otherwise I thought, for all his generosity, he might grudge me. But in the end I used less words and balder than was common with me, and set down only the bare bones, and after some struggles with myself and with these intractable letters I let it remain so, trusting him to read on the vellum between the script what had not been written. And I delivered the letter to Cadell, and gave him his orders as though this was a day like any other, and nothing of great moment toward. He was young and of easy condition, and he made no demur, as willing to go as to stay, and of that I was glad.

The earl came out of his tent when they brought him word that the bishop's company was in sight below in the river valley. He had Gilbert of Clare at his elbow, and others of his young men came to gather at his back as he stood and waited. For young they were all, many newly come into their honours, recently knighted or expecting knighthood on this field of battle. His was the party of the future. Only his bishops and officials were of his own generation, and perhaps half of the feudal following of archers and men-at-arms. And even some of those young men who had abandoned him, like Henry of Almain, had done so with rent hearts and deep grief, unable to hold out against Edward.

I think there was not a man among us who expected anything to come of the bishop's embassage, and the sight of his face as he dismounted, grave and very weary, made much clear before he spoke. Behind him the knights also dismounted. They bore two scrolls for the earl's reading. He took them without a word.

224

'I bring you no comfort,' said Bishop Stephen heavily, 'but the comfort of something worthy at least attempted. The king refuses all further dealings, and rejects what he has been offered. I have done my best, to no avail. They have stopped their ears against reason. To the word that reverend and wise men should arbitrate, they reply with fury and scorn. They are the nobility of England, are they to submit their affairs to the judgment of clerks? They are themselves the experienced and the wise, are they to be charged as evil counsellors, enemies of the crown? The first of the scrolls you hold, my lord, is a challenge to battle, on behalf of all the king's captains, sent to you by Richard, king of the Romans, and the Lord Edward.'

'Who, no doubt,' said Earl Simon with a shadowy smile and a certain resigned sadness, 'was loudest and fiercest in his defiance and rejection.'

'I fear you will not find the terms of his challenge moderate. And had you chosen other words, he would still have found another means of discovering offence in them, for he wills to be offended.'

'I know why,' said the earl, without hatred or blame.

'And the second scroll, my lord, is the king's own reply. The gravest he could make.'

'I know it,' said Earl Simon, and with a strong movement broke the seal. 'I have spent six years staving it off, to no purpose, it is almost welcome to me now. It is the formal act of *diffidatio*. He has renounced our homage and fealty, and withdrawn his overlordship from us. He is no longer our king, and we are no longer his men. But it is his act that severs the tie, not ours.'

He stood before us all, and read it aloud, the denunciation of the solemn obligations of kings towards their vassals, his own excommunication from the body of the realm, along with all the barons who held with him. Even the youngest of those lords, unawed by the spleen of an ageing king for whom they felt mild liking and much

225

impatience and exasperation, grew solemn of face under the banishing stroke of kingship itself.

The earl stretched out his hand to the bishop, and smiled. 'Come within, and take your rest. I have worn you out, body and mind, to no purpose here, but God records the gallantry and the good faith elsewhere. Though I must send to King Henry again tomorrow, and return his courtesy if he will not withdraw it, that I will not do by your hand. I have cost you enough.'

And those two went in together, the lame lord and the gentle and steely bishop, quietly about their remaining business here. And so did we all, knowing now the best and the worst, and those who had not witnessed the return of the envoys, having duties elsewhere, got the word from us who had, and in turn set about making all ready for the morrow. There was little said that evening, but not out of any clouded spirits. Rather every man settled to his own particular task with a single mind, like practical citizens bent on getting the best possible out of tomorrow's market. Armourers went over harness already furbished to its peak, fletchers viewed the reserves of arrows and did their final re-flighting and balancing, lancers sharpened their blades, archers trimmed new shafts and waxed their strings, swordsmen whetted their edges, squires and grooms and boys walked all the horses, and I went to borrow mail and buckler to my size and weight, and to find myself a place, if I could, in Earl Simon's own battle. Not that my prowess or privilege were such as to earn for me an office close to the highest, but only that I desired it, and felt it no sin to bid for it. And Robert de Crevecoeur, a Kentish lord whom King Henry had tried to woo to his side only a few days previously, for the sake of his formidable archers of the Weald, accepted me cheerfully into the ranks of his mounted men, and made no question at welcoming a Welshman. He was very young and blithe, and dearly set upon knighthood at the hands of Earl Simon above all

226

men, and on the morrow he got his wish.

So this night went, and we slept without dreams, and waked without fears, however the meaning of the dawn rushed in upon us. For the potent enchantment that held us all enlarged somewhat beyond the bounds of our own flesh and spirit did not break, but carried us still, as long as we had need of it.

When the day was come, Earl Simon also committed to parchment his solemn renunciation of his homage and fealty to his king, in response to the repudiation pronounced against him, and did so in the name of all those King Henry had denounced. But this final severance he gave into the care of the bishops of Worcester and London, to deliver or withhold according to the reception they received from the king. For he would not move without attempting all that could be attempted with honour to avoid out-and-out war, though he knew, barring a miracle from God, that he should meet with no response but contumely. And so we all knew. But his dignity, for all his occasional passions flaring like tinder, was not vulnerable by the scorns of littler men. I speak of the soul and the heart, for of the body there were then few men living, as I suppose, so large as the Lord Edward, who most reviled and detested what he had sometime inadequately loved.

So those two bishops rode down the valley to their own ordeal.

They came back in the late afternoon, empty-handed, the renunciation of fealty delivered. For King Henry, buoyed up by the greater numbers he commanded, and the brimstone hatred of those nearest to him, who were sure of victory, would not retract anything he had said or done, but denounced Earl Simon as his felon and traitor, and refused all contact with him. So his great vassal formally withdrew the fealty that was no longer valued or desired, and took back his freedom.

'Get your rest now,' said the earl, 'for we muster at

nightfall.' And he issued his orders quietly, and went to his own brief rest. And so did all those young men of his, the buds of the nobility, many of them in arms against fathers and kin, some against elder brothers, all with alliances upon both sides. They did his bidding and copied his example with clear, white faces grave as angels and bright as stars, and after his pattern they composed their lives to passion and prayer, whether to live or die being a lesser thing. And if they knew many more such days in their lives, however long, that I question, and if they did, they were visited by God above other men.

Before the afterglow had faded, the horn summoned us, and to that solemn sound we stood to, and went every man to his place in the ordered companies. Almost in silence we assembled, only those words were spoken that were needful. Earls, barons and knights came forth to join their men half-armed, to be ready for any event and yet go lightly through the night, and they wore on their surcoats the white cross of the crusader. Behind the ranks of fighting men, drawn close in the woods, the sumpter horses gathered with mail, arms and supplies. In the faint remnant of the light the boles of the trees stood ranked like the pillars of a great church, and we were still as pilgrims at their journey's end.

The bishops came forth with Earl Simon. Bishop Walter of Worcester said mass for us all, and gave us solemn absolution, for we had come to this place and this hour with eyes open, and were as men voluntarily dead before our deaths in the quest for the thing we believed in and desired. Then we marched.

There was never such a night's march as that. Some ten miles we had to go, at the speed of the foot soldiers, and before dawn we had to be in possession of the ground Earl Simon had chosen. Therefore the pace was fast and steady, to have time in hand for ordering our ranks at leisure when we reached our stay. And silently we went, except that some of the footmen raised a soft murmur of

228

singing that helped to set the stride. I never made proper reckoning of the numbers we had in all, but estimate that there may have been nearly two hundred knights, as many again of other mounted soldiers, and about four thousand foot soldiers, archers, lancers and swordsmen, including a great number of the trained bands of London. We knew from our outriders that the king had greater strength, notably in knight service. I think it may be said that our scouting was better done than theirs, if, indeed, they did any at all, for in the event our advance passed quite unmarked. They had not expected us to move before day.

But what I chiefly remember is the beauty of that May night, cool and fresh and still, with a few drifting clouds that made shadows in the open spaces even under starlight, after the moon was down, and the green, spring scent of burgeoning bushes and the first may-blossom. And after we came into the track along the river-valley, close to the water-meadows that were brimming from the April rains, the overwhelming fragrance of meadowsweet.

Earl Simon rode that night, the first time he had tried his ill-knitted bone so hard, and I think not without pain, but to use the chariot here was impossible. For some time the old track along the river ran straight, and the going was smooth, but well before we drew near Lewes we turned aside to the right, into the woods, and climbed up the flank of the downs in a long traverse, in cover all the way. We had the best of guides, for Robert de Crevecoeur and his men of the Weald knew this countryside as they knew their own palms. The only danger was that King Henry or some shrewder soul in his company might belatedly have stationed a brigade on the high ground towards which we made our way. But we heard no rumour of men or movement but our own, and came before full light to the chosen place.

We emerged upon the great, bare shoulder of the

downs, and wheeling to our left, saw below us in the pearl-grey dawn the town of Lewes, a mile or more distant and deep below us, in the bowl where the river valley opened out into broad fields and soft, marshy hollows. We had made a half-circle about it in cover, and by the position of the sun, not yet risen but turning the sky above it into an aureole of thin, greenish gold, we stood now almost due west of it. For when we looked over the pool of delicate mist that hid all detail in the town, we looked full into the promise of the morning, and that we took in our hearts for an omen.

'In good time!' said Earl Simon, and without pause turned to draw up his array, before the sun rose. He was singularly alone in his leadership, however gallant and devoted those young men who followed him, for without exception they lacked all experience of deploying an army for battle, or making use of the ground afforded. And he was forced to go, with fierce patience, from one end of his station to the other, and place his companies himself, with clear orders. His host he had divided into four sections, brigading a company of foot soldiers and archers with each body of horse. Three of his sections were drawn up as centre and wings, the fourth he held in reserve, to follow at a little distance when we moved down.

When all was ordered and ready, Earl Simon called together those who were not yet knight among his young captains, and himself conferred that high order upon them, and girt them with the sword, as was customary before battle, and in particular before so sacred and responsible a battle as this. The list of their names was long and proud: two earls among them, Gilbert of Clare and Robert de Vere of Oxford, de Burgh, FitzJohn, Hastings, Crevecoeur, de Lucy, de Munchensey, and many another, all received the accolade at the hand of a man greater than kings.

I was among Crevecoeur's mounted men in the centre

battle then, watching the film of mist dissolve from over Lewes town, as though a hand had removed a veil of gauze dropped into the hollow of a green cushion. The towers of Earl Warenne's castle rose on a hillock in the centre of the town, the grey shapes of the priory more to the south, a house of Cluny, and very rich. Though all was still in shadow, being low in that sheltered bowl, the air was clear between, we could see the pattern of a street, and the tower of the church, and the roofs of the houses were honed sharp as daggers. In the hills beyond, the sun showed its rim, and the faint gold flushed into rose. Then the first long ray reached out across the bowl like a burning lance, touched us where we stood, and blazed upon the burnished helm of Earl Simon as he rode back to his own battle.

Out of their dimness below some watchman saw that light, and doubtless cried out and ran to sound the alarm in haste. We heard the first trumpet, shrill and small, then another and another taking up the peal, and all that quiet scene below began to boil and heave, jetting out running men from every part like spurting blood. The barking of dogs we heard, and the rolling of a drum in some high place, perhaps the church tower. Out of the castle men came pouring, and out of the priory, and everywhere about the town there was this festering excitement, as King Henry's host clambered into its harness and tumbled out into the dawn to form its array in furious haste. Whether we on our hilltop, glittering in sunlight while they scurried in shadow, appeared to them as the host of hell or heaven, certain it is the sight of us fell on them like a lightning-stroke.

Yet they had some little time to muster and form, for we were a mile and more distant from them, and must keep our foot pace most of the way, and they lay close and easy about the town, with ample room for movement once the alarm was given. They were more than we, and they had not marched ten miles in the night, but we were awake and aroused, and had the upper ground, through their folly in leaving it unoccupied. We counted the day well begun as Earl Simon gave the signal to march forward, and our three battles began to move steadily down the slope.

We went upon a broad, open spur of ground that kept an even descent aimed at the heart of the town below, but lower down, this ridge narrowed somewhat, and was split into two by the hollow of a little brook, and to keep even ground under them our left wing continued downhill upon the eastern spur, divided from us by the hollow. And as we went it was strange how clearly we saw, and how calmly, those great powers massing against us. The rays of the sun still did not penetrate into the bowl far enough to prick out for us the bright devices of the king's men, yet their colours came to birth gradually in glowing shadow, and many we knew by their coat-armour. And as they watched us descend, so did we watch them as they gathered and took shape in their three battles, and with solemn, ponderous majesty moved forward out of the town to intercept us.

Their right wing was perfect the first, and first to move, forming up under the castle, where they had been lodged. Even before the sun came up fully, and awoke the colours of the banners, I knew by the fashion of the leader who marshalled them what name belonged to him, for I doubt if there was another such giant among the nobility of England. On a raw-boned horse, leaner built and faster than most destriers but huge like his rider, the Lord Edward wheeled his battle into position against our left, on their severed spur. And having excellent eye-sight and a long memory, doubtless he recognised the levies of the city of London, which had sided against his father, several times foiled his own plans, and hunted his mother out of her barge into cowering sanctuary in St Paul's. For grievances, humiliations, grudges, his memory was even longer than for services rendered, as long as life itself.

He spurred his horse, sent his standard forward, had his trumpeter sound, abandoned his foot force to follow as they could, and launched all his mounted strength headlong up the severing hollow and crosswise into the advancing Londoners, driving them eastward across the foot of the ridge, to scatter like spray before his hurricane into the river flats beyond.

It was out of alarm and compassion for his city allies, I think, that Earl Simon loosed his main battle in the charge when he did, for though it served well in the end, for preference he would surely have held his hand a while longer. But loose us he did, to ease the thrust that swept those hapless burgesses sidewise from their ranks, and bring Edward back into the true fight, where he belonged. But Edward had not yet learned, his hatred still ruled his judgment, instead of his judgment honing his hatred into a deadly weapon, as later it did, to all men's bitter peril that ever crossed him, and to the rue of the kin of all such, down to half-grown brothers and unoffending sisters, and the children in their cradles. That day he did but kill and kill whatever he could reach, never stopping to reason how to kill the most of us, or the greatest, only the nearest, and those from London. So we gained and lost by him.

For Earl Simon gave the order to sound, and we set spurs to our horses and drove down the hill into King Henry's central battle, labouring up the first slope towards us. We struck them hard and truly, and swept them back down the hill with us until we hit the first houses of the town. Crushed between us and the adamant walls, they fought back as long as they could, but were gradually shattered into particles that drew back among the buildings as they might, and thus were hunted along streets and alleys, first hotly, then without haste, later even with moderation, seeking to pen rather than to kill or harm. It went not so rapidly as I have made it seem, for so we

233

laboured until near noon, though it passed like a breath, for we were exalted above ourselves, and knew no want nor weariness. I remember marking with astonishment, towards the middle of the day, how hot the sun was, and that the grass was no longer wet with dew.

I think I killed none in that battle, and wounded but few, as I got but a scratch or two in return. And truly I was glad it should be so, for there was about our cause some holy reluctance to hurt or hate, even though we could not give ground. The foot soldiers had heavier losses, but few knights died in that onset, the first among them Earl Simon's standard-bearer. The life of such an officer is always at any man's disposal, seeing his devotion is towards that he carries, and no more to his own defence than it is to the slaying of those that come against him. William le Blund died with the standard still aloft over him, and another took it from his dying hand and bore it forward. Thus we drove into Lewes, and gripped and held it.

Then I saw no more of Earl Simon for a while, for he drew back to watch the progress of the battle, and make use of his reserve to the best effect. The morning passed, and Edward still absented himself, hunting his unhappy Londoners about the marsh-land and into the river, and killing as long as he had strength in his arm, or his driven horse could go. We neither saw nor heard of him, and them we could not help. We combed the fringes of Lewes, pricking out at sword-point lord after lord, all those lofty names, Hereford, Arundel, Basset, Mortimer, even names more outlandish to me, for they came from beyond the border of Scotland, vassals out of their own country, Balliol, Comyn and Bruce, the keepers of the northern marches.

King Henry had given his left battle to the king of the Romans and his son, Henry of Almain, and only they, with a handful of their followers, made any headway up the slope of the down, and even succeeded in breaking through to its crest, only to find they were cut off from all the rest of their number, who were still entangled with the centre and pinned down in the low ground outside the town. Earl Simon's reserve closed the circle about those who had penetrated, and drew in upon them until they were forced to take refuge in a windmill which stood in a high spot there to take the weather. And there, encircled and under threat from the archers if they tried to break out, they at last surrendered and were made prisoner.

Then all was centred around the town, where baron after baron and knight after knight was severed from his support, surrounded and taken. Where we wearied, the reserve came in to relieve us, and Earl Simon used a part of that force, and especially the archers of the Weald, who knew their business and their country, to fling a cordon round Lewes and stop the ways out of it towards the south, for that way lay the easiest escape to the sea, and what was most to be feared was that King Henry might be whisked away, or some of his allies more dangerous than himself might reach France by that route, and add their strength to the invasion force we all knew to be massing there. As indeed a few did break through before the circle closed, and got away by sea from Pevensey, two of the king's half-brothers among them, William of Valence and Guy of Lusignan, together with Hugh Bigod, who had once been a de Montfort man and justiciar of England, and the Earl Warenne, the lord of Lewes himself. For the rest, we made a clean haul of them, all those great lords who parted England among them fell one by one into Earl Simon's hands.

To the north-east of the town he left the approaches open, but with reserves in wait wherever there was cover, for in the early afternoon Edward brought his gorged and sated troops back into the field, and no doubt expected that the day would have gone with his father and uncle as pleasingly as with him. Earl Simon let him in, and the circle closed behind him. Too late he saw the battle-field swept clear of all but puny, scattered clashes, like the last sputtering flames of a dying fire, and marked and understood the litter of harness, banners and arms that was left of King Henry's army, and knew that in gratifying his own revenge he had lost his father the battle.

He did not know where the king was, though by then we did, and had a strict watch all round the Cluniac priory, where he had fled to sanctuary. Earl Simon stood between Edward and the same refuge, and even to that angry and embittered mind there was no sense in trying to fight over again, with a handful of tired men on tired horses, the battle already irrevocably lost. Edward turned tail and made for the house of the Franciscan friars, and there took cover with the remnant of his following. As much a prisoner of Earl Simon as if he had surrendered himself into his hands, there he was suffered to stay, and his father among the monks of Cluny, for neither of them could escape.

So ended the battle of Lewes, that many saw as a miracle and the direct judgment of God, so complete was the victory. Yet not without cost. Friars, clerks and monks went about the river flats and meadows and the shoulder of the down after the fight, and reverently took up and buried the dead, to the number of six hundred, and of those it may well be more than half were men of London.

As for us, we secured the castle and made our camps, and gathered the spoils of arms and armour, and set guards, and did all that men must do as scrupulously after a victory as before. We saw to our horse-lines, fed and watered, tended injuries, the smiths repaired dinted armour and ripped mail, and the cooks and sutlers found us meat and bread and ale, and we ate like starving men.

The furnishings of Earl Simon's chapel went with him wherever he went. And most devoutly, that evening, he heard mass and offered thanksgiving with a full heart for the verdict of God, delivered in the blazing light of day before all men, in token that it behoved all men to accept the judgment. For the award of heaven is higher than the award of kings or pontiffs, and even they must bow to it and be reconciled.

CHAPTER X

After the men-at-arms had done their part, and while they slept after their exertions, the clerks and friars began their work, and for them there was no sleep in Lewes that night. Those who were not tending the wounded or burying the dead, ran back and forth all night long between the parties that had been brought to a stand, and must now be brought to a settlement. For complete though the triumph was, it could not do more than determine who now put forth the terms to be met, and since Earl Simon was not and never desired to be a monarch himself, or to displace the monarch that England already had, he was greatly limited, in what he could propose, by his own nature and his conception of duty and right. He aimed always at that which had been his aim from the beginning, an order of government such as had been begun at Oxford, with the consent and co-operation of all the limbs of the state.

By morning they had drawn up a form of peace, and both King Henry and the Lord Edward had given their assent to it, having little choice. It provided for the royal castles to be handed over to new seneschals responsible to council and parliament, for the proclamation of peace in the shires and the strict enforcement of law, so that no partisan upon either side should now molest his neighbour of the other side without penalty, and for the immediate release of young Simon and of the lord of Beaudesert and his two sons, taken at Northampton. The whole immediate purpose of this urgent accord was to ensure the order and safety of the realm, against the uncontrolled malice of faction in the shires, the opportunism of malefactors who thrive on discord, and the threat of invasion from overseas, for everyone realised that the eternal problem of reaching a final amicable settlement still remained, and was as intransigent as ever. And for the sake of law and order, since half the nobility of England was now captive, indeed more than half of the chief persons of authority in the marches, Earl Simon made a gesture no other man could have made, and upon their acceptance of the form already sealed by king and prince, ordered the release to their own lands of all the lords of the march, and also of certain others, the Scot, John Balliol, the sheriff of Northumberland, and a baron of Hampshire who was needed along that coast. They pledged themselves to go home and keep peace and good order, and attend in parliament when called. But bound as he was to accept other men's oaths as his own was acceptable, Earl Simon did not let all the weapons out of his hands, and no blame to him. He named two hostages who should remain in captivity as surety for the observance of all the terms of the peace, and those two were the Lord Edward and his cousin Henry of Almain.

With what bitterness and resentment the Lord Edward accepted his subjection I guess, yet he did give his word. With what weariness, discouragement and timidity King Henry resigned himself to his, that I saw and understood. But I use the wrong word, for resign himself he never did, being unable to despair of his luck. But very piously he subscribed to the terms, his only present advantage lying in assent, and very heartily he wrote to King Louis with a copy of the form of peace, and entreated him to use his good offices with the exiles to persuade them to acceptance, for the safety of the royal hostages, and the preservation of his own precarious rights. All the more since Earl Simon declared himself willing, secure in heaven's verdict for him and the general adherence of the

239

people of England, again to submit matters at dispute to the arbitration of King Louis and his best advisers. Believing as he did in the sacredness of Christendom and the common health of its component lands, no less than in the need for right and just government within each of them, he could do no other.

Thus far I saw matters unfold, with every promise of a good outcome. For shortly after the battle Earl Simon set out to take the king to London, and the young hostages to honourable confinement at Richard of Cornwall's castle of Wallingford, and that being my way also as far as the city, I went with them. But when we came to St Paul's, where lodging was prepared for the king, I sought an audience with Earl Simon, the first time I had been alone with him since the May night under the stars at Fletching.

He walked less lamely by then, but he was not free of pain, and seeing him thus closely, after many days of seeing him in the seat of power, far removed from me and controlling kings and princes with a motion of his sword-hand, I started and checked at seeing him worn away so lean and steely-fine, as though the spirit had fretted away the flesh from his bones. Those bones had been to me a marvel from the first moment I set eyes on him in Oxford, so purely drawn were they, and so taut and polished and private beneath the skin. He had no soft lines that could be manipulated, no pliable mask like King Henry's. What he was he showed to every seeing eye, like mountain, flood and fire, most beautiful and perilous. And still, revealing himself mortal and vulnerable, subject to ills of body and mind, he favoured his new-knitted leg, and eased its weight with a hand when he shifted it. So close and so far he was, and so distanced, and so drawn, I had discovered how to love him.

'I guess your errand,' said Earl Simon, 'and your longing to be home I understand. When you elected to go with me to the judgment, you said you would carry the news to Wales yourself, and so you should. With my blessing and my thanks, to your lord and to you.'

I said then, not with any great foreboding, but knowing that all things were still uncertain, that he might yet need a close liaison with Wales again before long, and that if he desired it and Llewelyn permitted it, I would return to him.

Then he bade me sit down with him, and told me what further moves the council of England had in mind, that Llewelyn might be fully informed without the committal of such vital matters to writing. The first need had been to establish reliable wardens of the peace in all the shires. The second, he said, was to call parliament as quickly as possible, and to ensure that those who attended it truly spoke for the people, and to that end writs had already been sent out. These were the first days of June, and before the month ended parliament must meet and ratify what had been done in the name of the whole realm, or demur and amend it.

'On the lesser people of the shires,' said the earl, 'much has depended, as you have seen, and much will depend on them in the future. I have learned to know them as staunch to their faith, and have leaned upon them hard in contention and battle, and they have not let me fall. Surely their voices should also be heard in peace, and their loyalty remembered. We are calling to this parliament, from every shire, four knights chosen by the shire court to stand spokesmen for their people. With their aid some form of council must be chosen to advise and direct the king's actions, until we can achieve a permanent peace and a proper constitution.'

I asked after the fate of the remaining prisoners of Northampton.

'You touch on a sore and tangled matter,' he owned. 'The marcher lords are being called to parliament and told to bring their prisoners with them, to be exchanged man for man against those we took at Lewes. We cannot

241

leave good men rotting in cells while all the legal arguments are hammered out to the end, but the exchange will certainly be bedevilled by questions of ransom and right. If need be they will have to be released on surety for their price, but we must have them out.' He caught my eye and smiled, reading me well. 'True, before the summer's out I may need every sword and lance I can muster. Neither King Louis nor the cardinal makes any move to call off the pack they have raised against us in France. Well, if we lean only on ourselves, no one can let us fall. Perhaps we should give thanks for threats from without, if they bind us so firmly together within.'

And that was truth, for even before council made any appeal, the men of Kent and Hampshire had risen themselves to patrol the coast and watch for alien sails, and the shipmen of the Cinque ports were prowling the seas on guard. And when later he called, every man answered.

'Yet I will not believe,' he said steadfastly, 'that it need be so. We are an organ of Christendom, how can we live and to what purpose, cut off from the body that nourishes us? No, we must prevail! When God has spoken for us so clearly, surely his vicar on earth cannot for ever shut his ears against the truth.'

When I was with him I shared his faith, so potent it was. Yet I knew, as he knew, that beyond the narrow seas more and more ships and arms were massing even as we spoke, and that the mood of the exiles was most bloodily bent on invasion. At Boulogne Cardinal Gui threatened excommunication and interdict, and although King Henry in his anxiety had written again to Louis, urgently begging for a conciliatory attitude and a helpful spirit, for the sake of the hostages if for no other reason, still the thunderous silence continued. Earl Simon had enemies more than enough, and none of them impressed by the vehemence with which God had stood his friend.

Nevertheless, and whether he willed it or no, this man

242

who sat quietly talking with me was the master of England then, towering above kings.

He gave me his hand when I took my leave of him, and his safe-conduct to get me service and security wherever his writ ran. And so I left him still embattled, since there was only one victory that could satisfy him, and that was denied to him by the obduracy of his enemies. And I rode the same hour, and set out for Wales.

Llewelyn was at Knighton, keeping a close watch on his cousin Mortimer's lands and movements, for it was clear to him that the march was no better resigned to submission than before Lewes, and though he had not yet all the details with which I could provide him, he already foresaw that all those turbulent young men might find their parole easier to give than to keep, even if they had begun in good faith, which was by no means certain in all cases. He welcomed me eagerly, and when I had told him all, as I thought, still found me many questions.

'You have been at the heart of things,' he said, 'while I have been sitting here like a shepherd guarding a fold.' And he took from me again and again the story of Lewes, and said that he envied me.

'But he will need us again,' he said with certainty, 'and soon, and in my country, not in the south. Even his virtues fight against him. He could not leave the march in disorder, for the sake of right and justice, where another would have let right and justice fend for themselves, and the barons of the march lie safe in prison, until all was better secured for his own cause.'

'His cause *is* right and justice,' I said, 'whatever errors he commits on the way. How, then, can he defend them by abandoning them?'

'I know it,' said Llewelyn, 'and he is discovering it. He wills to have all the estates of the realm taking their due part in its governance, and he finds himself forced by the times to take more and more power into his own hands. And I see no remedy. We have already heard how they are standing to in the south, all those sea-coast pirates and fishermen, and the archers of the Weald, expecting the fleet from France, while Louis holds aloof and the cardinal-legate threatens damnation. And I think in his heart the earl of Leicester knows, as I guess, that for all his offers and concessions upon the one part, there will be none on the other. What can he gain by all this to-ing and fro-ing of envoys across the sea, when all they will accept is his surrender or his death?'

'Time,' I said.

'Yes,' granted Llewelyn after a moment's thought, 'that he may. If he can weather the summer, they'll be less likely to put to sea in a winter campaign. And all the coastal castles, those he holds. However great the numbers they gather, they'll find it hard enough to land them. And if paid mercenaries don't run away home for the harvest, they'll take themselves off fast enough when there's no more money to pay them. Yes, every week gained is precious. You say young Henry is keeping Dover for him?'

I said that he was, and the Countess Eleanor was there also, with her two youngest sons and her daughter.

'The other Eleanor,' said Llewelyn to himself, and smiled. 'You have seen this child? Does she resemble her brother?'

I told him, as best I could, what manner of girl she was, of her radiance and simplicity as I had first beheld her, gracious, artless, as blazingly honest as her brother and her sire. He listened with a faint smile, as though half his thoughts were still upon the dangerous game being played along the marches, yet his eyes were intent and rapt. And at the end he said mildly, as if rather to himself than to me:

'And she is not yet betrothed, or promised to any, this lady?'

*   *   *

Before many weeks were out all Llewelyn's forebodings were justified, for in spite of all their oaths the barons of the march did not obey the summons to the parliament in June, or send their prisoners, nor did they surrender such royal castles as they held, Bristol among them. In July, while one more arduous formula of agreement was being hammered out at Canterbury, in the hope of finding favour, however grudging, with King Louis and the legate, Earl Simon was forced to come himself, with the earl of Gloucester, to deal with the troublers of the march, who were raiding and plundering their neighbours and building up their household forces in defiance of law. The earl sent an appeal to Llewelyn to aid him from the west, which he was glad to do upon more counts than one, for the turbulence of the marcher rule threatened us no less than England.

That was a short, brisk campaign, profitable to us and to Earl Simon also, for it added to his strength the castles of Hereford, Hay, Ludlow and Richard's castle, and gave us more land in Maelienydd, bringing Mortimer and Audley and their fellows to surrender at last at Montgomery, and to promise attendance at court with their prisoners. But so they had promised before, and broken their word, and so they could and did again.

Perhaps this time they had truly intended to keep it, if the approaches so patiently made to King Louis and the exiles at Boulogne had met with any acceptance. But though the envoys sailed back and forth tirelessly, still amending, still making concessions on all but the sacred principles, never did legate or king take one small step to meet them. On the contrary, Cardinal Gui reverted to the pope's original denunciation of the Provisions, and ordered the bishops who came as envoys to observe the papal sentence promulgated against the earl and his followers. They as firmly refused, and departed. Late in October the legate formally pronounced sentence of excommunication and interdict against Earl Simon and

245

all who held with him. So the saints fare always in this world.

This utter rejection at Boulogne revived all the vengeful defiance in the march. In that same month of October a band of knights from Edward's castle of Bristol, all intimate friends of his, made a great dash across England to storm Wallingford castle and rescue the prince, intending to carry him back with them to Bristol and gather an army round him. They took the outer ward of the castle by surprise, but the garrison turned their arbalests against them, and even threatened to give them Edward, since they had come for him, by hurling him from a mangonel if the attackers persisted, so that he was glad enough to be brought up on to the walls to beg his friends to give up their mad plan and depart.

The upshot was that Earl Simon, rightly alarmed at so daring an onslaught coming so near success, removed the two hostages into stricter keeping at his own castle of Kenilworth, sent peremptory summonses to all the marchers to attend at Oxford in November with their prisoners, and called up an army of barons and knights to muster there to ensure obedience. But in spite of all their promises, the marchers still did not come. Then the earl was forced to move against them a second time in arms, and sent again to Llewelyn to close in at their rear.

'See how the year has slipped by,' Llewelyn said, when we were in the saddle again, and marching east to match the earl's westward advance, 'and ours the only fighting, after all. If he has done nothing else, he has got England through the summer. They'll not put a fleet to sea now. And next year will be too late, they'll all have gone off to better-paid service.' For December was beginning, and a gusty, wild month it was, though with little frost or snow.

Mortimer, the boldest of the lawless marcher company, made a bid to hold the Severn against the earl, but changed his mind when the chill of Llewelyn's shadow fell on his back. He drew off down the river, but we kept pace with him, and crowded him into Earl Simon's arms for the second time that year, forcing another submission at Worcester.

So near we were then to the earl, and yet those two still did not meet, who were already so drawn to each other, and worked so well together. For time, of which we had enough, was then so wanting to Earl Simon that he was handling two or three desperate problems at the same moment, and we could not hamper his actions. We drew back and stood on guard for him, but he needed us no more then. He had made up his mind that the west could no longer be left to this endless chaos and misrule. All those lands held in the march by the Lord Edward, the palatinate of Chester and the town and castle of Bristol, he determined to take into his own hands, for they were too dangerous to be left to any other. In exchange for them he provided Edward with lands to the same value elsewhere, in less vulnerable counties.

He sent Llewelyn the terms of his settlement with the marchers, for we also were concerned in them. The offenders agreed to withdraw into Ireland for a year and a day, surrendering those royal castles they still held, and releasing at last the unfortunate prisoners of Northampton. Mortimer was allowed to visit Edward with the terms, for the exchange of lands required his consent and charter. And since his release from strict confinement, if not from all surveillance, depended upon his agreement, he had little choice but to agree. At least he might, at the cost of that exchange, be able to see his young wife again, and the infant daughter she had borne him only a few weeks after Lewes.

'Chester!' said Llewelyn, rearing his head suddenly, at gaze into distance, when he heard the terms of the submission. 'If the earl is to have Chester, where does David go?'

There was in his voice and in his eyes a kind of mild

247

astonishment, as though he had remembered something from long ago, once taken grievously to heart, and now recalled as curiously small and distant. He had not thought of David for so long that all the crust of hatred and hurt and resentment that had made his desertion bulk so large had dwindled away, and left only the human form, slighter than his own, of the young brother he had loved and indulged, and by whom he had suffered what now seemed only trivial wounds. Forgetfulness is sometimes easier than forgiveness, and achieves the same end.

'He is still there?' I asked, for I, too, had almost forgotten him. Strange, for he was memorable, if there had been no giants blotting out the light.

'He has been there with Alan la Zuche all the year, holding the town and county for the king. There'll be a new justiciar now, and a new garrison. And he has lost so much, and been left so far out on the fringe of events,' he said, almost with compunction. 'He could never abide to be out of the centre, and here he lies washed up on the rim. And his Edward baulked and prisoner. Poor David!' said Llewelyn, marvelling at the revenges of fate and at himself. 'I could be sorry for him! He is so torn. How could I ever have hated him?'

'I doubt you ever did,' I said in all honesty. 'It is not among your gifts.'

'It could be,' he said with a startled smile, 'if it were not such a waste of time. But with so many things better worth doing, hate is a luxury must wait its turn, and it dies of waiting. I wonder,' he said more sombrely, 'if his is dead, as mine is?'

And for a while I think his mind was again upon his brother, and the wrongs he had suffered of him, and also, perhaps, those he had unwittingly inflicted upon him. But that lasted no long time, for the very reason he had given. The fortunes of Wales were always foremost in his thoughts, and thrust David out of mind. Whatever the force of Llewelyn's sympathies in the long contest between king and barons, and with whatever willingness he took sides, there was no question but he meant Wales to do well out of the conflict, and intended to exploit it to the limit for her sake. And this was the greatest opportunity of all to secure his northern conquests, and make his boundary there inviolable, now that all the former earldom of Chester was being transferred into the hands of his ally, who owed him a share in the benefit.

'We'll turn homeward for the Christmas feast,' he said, 'and we'll see who comes to garrison Chester and rule as justiciar in Earl Simon's name, and what message he has for me.'

He left a moderate force in Maelienydd when we turned northwards, and since it seemed that we were somewhat ahead of the new officials at Chester, we went home to Aber for the Christmas feast, and then repaired to the castle of Mold, to be in close touch with events in the city. The word went round at the turn of the year that all the tenants of the county and honour, as well as the officers of the castle, had received their orders upon Christmas Eve to serve the earl of Leicester as they had been wont to serve the old earls palatine in the former days, before the line of Blundeville died out and the honour reverted to the crown. And Earl Simon's new justiciar was come, in the person of Luke Tany, and la Zuche, the king's partisan, was about to march out with his men and betake himself elsewhere, perhaps into the lands given to the Lord Edward in exchange. We waited but a day more, and a courier came from Luke Tany, bearing a letter from Earl Simon himself, appointing a day when his envoy would meet with Llewelyn at Hawarden, on the business of the northern march.

Mold is no more than twenty miles or so from Chester, and Hawarden halfway between. We made our way there in advance of the day, and the weather then being fine, with only light frost in the mornings, we had good riding in that pleasant, rolling land. Llewelyn was withdrawn and quiet, but restless and unable to settle, and turned his mount and his gaze towards Chester, and there being no enemy now to hold us at distance, rode as far as the river and lingered there, walking his horse under the very walls of the town, and watching the road that led south from the gate. Then I knew what had drawn him there, and that he had knowledge of it beforehand.

From our place in the rimy meadows we saw the long file of horsemen issuing from the bridge gate, the sun picking out their lance-heads and pennants in a shifting play like little flames. We could even hear the drumming of the hooves across the timbers of the bridge, so clear was the air, and pick out the devices of la Zuche and his knights, Edward's knights, banished to some less vital castle in the south. Llewelyn reared his head to stare upon all those riders, narrowing his eyes to bring them close, and I knew that he was looking for his brother.

So, indeed, was I, but it was Llewelyn who first found him. I knew it by the stillness that fell upon him, and following where he gazed, I saw David riding somewhat aside from the deposed justiciar, but level with him. He was not in mail, but cloaked in fine cloth and fur, and very handsomely mounted and equipped, and though he was but a small figure to us, too far off for his face to be more than an oval mask, by his seat and his carriage in the saddle there was no mistaking him. There was no reason why he should already have observed us, and he would have had to turn and look round over his right shoulder then to do so, since the cortège was moving away from us towards the south. Yet I believe he did know that we were there. Two horsemen motionless in those meadows against the pallid winter turf stood out like trees, and he knew Llewelyn's manner and bearing as Llewelyn knew his. If he was aware of us, he gave no sign. The tilt of his head and easy sway of his shoulders were as always, proud and assured.

They passed, and he dwindled gradually out of our sight, and it was over. Llewelyn wheeled his horse and rode back without a word until we drew near to Hawarden.

'Well,' he burst out then, between self-mockery and a kind of quiet fury, 'I have seen him! Neither sick nor sorry! I need not have troubled!' And he set spurs to his horse, and led the way in a gallop the rest of the journey home.

Earl Simon's envoy rode into Hawarden the next morning, well attended with knights, clerks and lawyers, and we saw with pleasure that the earl had sent us his eldest son to deal in his name. Llewelyn went out to meet him gladly, and embraced him.

'I thought,' he said, 'they had you walled up in Kenilworth as keeper to your cousins since you left Dover. There is no man I would rather see here in your father's place.'

Young Henry was grown and matured since first we had seen him, yet not changed. He had had to deal with many grave matters, and to make decisions even more perilous than the generously wrong decision he had made in trusting Edward at Gloucester, but still he had that straight and confiding eye, and the brightness that grave children have, willing at all times to seek and believe the best, and by reason of their own truth slow to look for lies. And I thought then that such creatures, whatever their gallantry and skill and wit, are at disadvantage in this world, where the current kind are wiser than the children of light. Yet he had learned, and his learning had saddened him.

'If all goes well,' he said, 'my cousins will soon be let loose to the king's care, under surveillance, and even if I must still be watchman, I need not be gaoler. At the parliament that's called for later this month we hope to find a form for easing Edward's captivity and mine.'

Llewelyn asked him of this parliament, for the writs sent out for it appeared to be on a wider ground even than in June, and clearly the impulse came from Earl Simon. All the bishops were called, said Henry, more than a hundred heads of the great religious houses, all those barons who were in due obedience and had not flouted previous calls to court, as the marchers had, from every shire two knights respected and trusted, and from a large number of boroughs two burgesses, for the towns had taken active part in the struggle for the Provisions, and willed to continue their aid, as Earl Simon was heartily glad to encourage it. Sandwich and the other southern ports were also sending four men. Though only God knew, said Henry, in the troubled state of many regions, whether all the members would reach the city on time, for the year, in spite of the welcome silence from France, opened in fearful uncertainty, and the marcher lords who should already have withdrawn to their banishment in Ireland were still in their liberties, upon one pretext and another. Nevertheless, a parliament there would be, and upon the writs issued, even if it meant delay.

'The boroughs, too! I see,' said Llewelyn, smiling, 'that your father's body politic grows more, and more agile, limbs with every year.'

'And all function,' said Henry. 'The lowest of men *are* men, of the same affections and infirmities as the highest. I have learned to marvel at what they can do. In the world of the saints and the religious there have been great men raised from the sheep-fold and the plough. I think there is too much waste of many who are wise without learning, and many who are able without power. We have leaned on such at need, in this cause, and they have not failed us. Only the great, established in power, have let us fall.'

That he could not have said, two years ago. He said it now with all his old simplicity, but the matter was new. And since I was come of the lowest, son of a waiting-woman and by-blow of a passing knight, I remembered his saying, and thought upon it often. I have seen dead bodies of the great and the mean stripped naked for tending to burial, and I know there is no way of knowing which is the prince and which the ploughman. Wherefore I think there are princes in all estates, and doubtless in all estates slaves also.

'And I?' said Llewelyn, eyeing his young friend narrowly.

'You have not let us fall,' said Henry, and smiled. 'I say no word of small or great to you. You have another way of ordering your realm, as it were a family, but carried to the ultimate degrees. Who is great or little in a family but by his generation? I think we have something to learn from you.'

'Not if you look for unity,' said Llewelyn fervently, and laughed, and went in with him. And I know they talked much and ardently of those matters at night, after the business was done and the clerks busy copying.

I would not say there was hard bargaining at that conference, for each side had an urgent end to gain, and they so marched together that the outcome was certain. Llewelyn gave what was required of him, and got what he required. What Henry wanted for his father was an absolute and assured peace along the Dee, so that Earl Simon need lose no sleep over his support in that region. And that he had, most willingly. What Llewelyn wanted was recognition for all the conquests he had made in these parts, and renunciation of all English claims upon them, his Saxon neighbour now being the earl himself, an ally instead of an enemy. And that he had.

'For every yard that I have taken back by force in my lifetime,' said Llewelyn, 'was Welsh land from time beyond memory. No part of it English but by seizure.'

'I am empowered,' said Henry, judicial and grave on his father's business, 'to acknowledge that ancient right,

253

and leave in your hands all that you hold along this march.' And so it was sealed and delivered in the agreement.

'And I wish to God,' said young Henry passionately in private, afterwards, 'that the southern march were as securely in your hands, my lord, as the northern, for so we should have quiet minds. If there were no marcher lordships between your power and the Severn in the south, with all my heart I believe we could control the entire border between us. But the marcher hold in the south is so strong, I dread what may go forward there.'

'I see,' said Llewelyn seriously, 'that you rate the vital balance as lying here in the marches. For you as for me.'

'In the name of God!' said young Henry devoutly. 'They are a third country. Except to themselves, they have no loyalties, and except for their own, no law. I am afraid of them. If that is cowardice, I have the wit to be a coward. And the need, bearing as I do this responsibility. United, there is very little they cannot do, to the west as to the east, to you as to me.'

'I will keep the north for you, and the centre,' said Llewelyn. 'I and mine – Rhys Fychan, Meredith ap Owen, all those who hold with me – will do our best in the south. So much I promise you. More I cannot do.'

'More I dare not ask,' said Henry with humility. 'Unless there could be more of *you*! Did you never think, my lord, of getting yourself a noble consort, and a generation of sons?'

'I am thinking of it now,' said Llewelyn.

Earl Simon's great parliament was slow in getting into session, for even at the end of February some of the knights of the shires had not arrived, and those who had, so said Cynan in a message he sent us during that time, were uneasy at the expense of their long stay, and had to be allowed funds from the public purse to maintain them. But in March the debate began, and to all appearances much was achieved. A form of peace was painfully produced, continuing the present provisional rule, re-uniting Henry and the lords he had repudiated at Lewes as king and vassals, and by a clever manipulation of legal forms placing the control of the greatest royal castles in the hands of the council, while not attempting to alienate the king's title to them, or his son's. Dispossession was never in Earl Simon's mind. His hope – a vain hope in this world – was always for final and universal goodwill, so that restraints should wear away naturally and cease to be needed.

As the promised part of this settlement, the Lord Edward was released from captivity, though not from surveillance. He took the oath to maintain the form of government agreed, to refrain from any act against those who had created it, and to forbear from bringing in aliens himself or allowing others to do so, all this on pain of disinheritance if he broke his oath. It seems to me that Earl Simon, even if he never admitted it to himself, knew the worth of Edward's word, and did all he could to bind him.

However that may be, the prince formally accepted all, and acknowledged that the baronage had the right to turn against him and repudiate him if he broke his oath. Then both he and Henry of Almain, his cousin, were released from their prison and given into the king's care. But Henry de Montfort, though no longer their gaoler, as he had said, was to remain Edward's constant companion, and ward on his honesty. And since the king himself was safely in Earl Simon's control, so were the two young men, at one remove.

'I see all manner of dangers crowding in upon him behind this seeming triumph,' said Llewelyn, pondering the outcome with a disturbed and sombre face, 'however bright the surface shines. Again and again it is plain here that he can trust none of them but his own sons and a handful of others, and if his mind does not yet know it, his heart does. Therefore he cannot choose but confide more and more of the needful work to those few, and the rest begin to murmur against his preference for his own, while they themselves are the cause of it. Even his insistence on justice works against him! He has called men of his own party to order, even imprisoned the earl of Derby, for offences against other men's lands, and for that all those who have followed him for gain will turn and hate him, fearing their own turn may come next. He has offended Giffard of Brimpsfield, one of his few supporters in the march, over the misuse of prisoners and ransom, and Giffard is airing his grievance to Gloucester, who sees himself as good a leader as Earl Simon if he had his chance, and may even be in two minds about making his own opportunity. The more Simon stands erect and tries to do absolute right as he sees it – for God knows no man in this world can hope to see it whole every day in the year! – the more the envious will envy and the greedy resent him. And the more certain they are that he will never go back on his word, the more they have him at their mercy. Even his devotion to bishops, the best of their cloth in the land, and their reverence for him, so far from convincing the pope, only turns Simon into Antichrist and them into heretics, in rebellion against Rome's authority. This is a fight he can win only one way, with the sword, again and again, and that is not the victory he wants. What can this world do with such a man?'

'Or with such bishops,' I said. For no less than nine of them, in full pontificals, had closed that parliament with the solemn excommunication of all those who transgressed against the great charter, the forest charter and the present statutes, the bible of civil liberty.

'Break them,' said Llewelyn bitterly, 'and put smooth noblemen from Savoy and Poitou in their places.'

I said, for I also saw the same stony barrier blunting

256

every attempt at advance: 'He may yet be forced to take the sword again. And with the sword he is their master.'

'If they can force him to hold down England with arms,' cried Llewelyn with sudden passion, 'they will have defeated him, as surely as if they beat him in battle. It is his dilemma. I pray it may not be his tragedy!'

It was as if I argued with my own heart. Every word he said I felt to be true. And greatly I marvelled how he, watching and fretting at a distance, had come by a sharper understanding of Earl Simon than I had gained in the earl's own retinue.

CHAPTER XI

Before the beginning of April we were reminded of all that we had said together, for Meurig came riding into Bala, where Llewelyn's court had removed while the shaky quiet held, with a scrip full of gossip he had collected about the horse-markets of Gwent and Gloucester. Yearly he grew greyer and shaggier and smaller, more like a seeding thistle, but he was wiry and tough as thorn still, and had very sharp ears for all the tunes the wind brought him.

'There's more goes on below the hangings than is known abroad,' he said. 'Gilbert of Clare took himself off from Westminster before parliament ended or the peace was made, and went home to Gloucester with all his men. Some say in displeasure over the earl of Derby's fall, for his own conscience is not altogether clear. Some say for jealousy of the de Montfort sons. There was to have been a grand tournament at Dunstable, a court function, on Shrove Tuesday – did you hear of that? – but they got wind of high feeling between the Clares and the Montforts, and found it easier to call off the occasion on the plea that all good men were needed at court to aid in the Lord Edward's settlement. They put it off until the twentieth of this month at Northampton, hoping the bad blood would need no letting by then. And John Giffard was not long after the earl in quitting London, they say for fear of the law reaching for him as it had reached for Ferrers. He's with Gilbert now, hand in glove. The latest word is that the council called on Gilbert to make good his pledge as guarantor, and see the castle of Bamburgh handed over, and Gilbert has sent a very left-handed answer, pleading that he cannot take any steps because he is fully occupied defending his Gloucester borders. Against *you*, my lord!'

'I have not so much as cast a glance in his direction,' said Llewelyn warmly. 'What can the man be up to?'

'That is what the earl of Leicester is also wondering. Nor is Bamburgh the only castle still detained.'

'I know it,' said Llewelyn drily. 'Shrewsbury, for one.' For we knew by then that David was there, still tethered on his long leash, it seemed, as close as he could get to Gwynedd, as though he had been tied by his heart-strings, as indeed perhaps he was.

'And others,' said Meurig, nodding his silvery head, 'and others! It cannot be overlooked for ever. If Earl Gilbert does not appear at Northampton on the twentieth to run a course among the rest at this tournament, I think the earl of Leicester will be forced to go and smoke him out of Gloucester in person. The young man has been his right hand ever since Lewes; he cannot afford to be at odds with him, or leave him to his sulks. Who would replace him?'

'And they have called another parliament in June,' said Llewelyn, listening and brooding. 'Will it ever meet, I wonder?'

When the prince laid all these considerations before his council, Goronwy put his finger on the heart of the matter.

'There is one man,' he said, 'who could resolve all this if he would, and only one. It is pointless affirming to King Louis and pope and cardinal that England is at one, and King Henry consents to his lot, when it is plain he consents only under duress, however many oaths he swears. But their arguments and their weapons would be blunted if the crown did indeed consent and work with

259

the earl and the council. All that the marchers and their kind are doing is done in the name of the royal liberties and privileges, and all the orders that issue from the chancery under the king's seal are all too clearly Earl Simon's orders, and can be denounced. But it would not be so easy to denounce them if the crown actively linked hands with the earl and repudiated the troublers of the peace. Aloud, voluntarily and credibly. King Henry never will, granted, he has fought every step of the road. But there's one who already carries more weight than King Henry, and shows as a more formidable enemy and a more effective friend. And once he was inclined warmly enough towards the earl and the reform. Surely it is only personal grudges, not ideas, that divide them even now. If the Lord Edward willed to make this government secure, he could call off the marchers, silence King Louis, and disband the invasion fleet, at one stroke. He might even convince the pope. He could certainly disarm him.'

Llewelyn looked to me for answer. 'It is true,' he said, 'I remember, not so long ago, he went so far in support of the earl as to bring himself into suspicion and disgrace for a time. Is there any possibility, do you think, that he may raise himself far enough above his grudges to discover some good in this new order, and give it his countenance, if not his blessing?'

I said: 'None! If he examined it in his own heart and found it perfect in justice and virtue, it would not change him, and he would not relent. Edward can be generous in friendship, even generous from policy, but once he turns to hating his hate is indelible. Edward will not lift a finger to make peace. But he will go to the last extreme to get his revenge.'

When the twentieth of the month came, the earl of Gloucester still absented himself from the tournament at Northampton. According to report, he was encamped with an ominously strong force in the forest of Dean, with John Giffard in his company, and this continued sulking so disquieted Earl Simon that he decided to move to Gloucester himself, and take the king with him, and sent out writs to the baronial forces of the border shires to rally to him at that town. The young earl was headstrong and inexperienced, yet he had shown himself ardent, brave and able, and Earl Simon was grieved at being at odds with him, and very willing to meet him in a conciliatory manner and discuss freely whatever matters rankled with him.

As soon as we heard that the earl had taken his unwieldy court to Gloucester, Llewelyn, restive and uneasy, called up his own levies and moved them down into the central march, to be on the watch for whatever might follow, and ready to act upon it at need. He had a little hunting castle at Aberedw, near Builth, and took up residence there, and he took care to send word to Earl Simon where he could be found.

In the forests and hills round Gloucester, Gilbert of Clare and his fellows camped through the first days of May, and while they received messengers civilly, and even sent replies, they held off from making any closer contact. Earl Simon sent conciliatory envoys to try to arrange a meeting, and Earl Gilbert replied with a long list of bitter complaints, no longer troubling to hide his jealousy, but pouring out all his grievances, over prisoners, ransoms, castles, and the preferment of Earl Simon's sons. This seemed to be some progress, at least, yet all attempts to bring him to the desired meeting were somehow evaded. To us, looking on from Aberedw, it seemed almost that Earl Gilbert was playing for time, while he waited for something to happen.

That whole dolorous court was there with Earl Simon, proof once again that in his heart he trusted none of them. The king, hemmed in with all the officers and ministers who controlled him and spoke in his name, went where he was taken, by then so discouraged and apathetic that I think only his obstinacy kept him alive. And I confess I understand how many who had truly believed in Earl Simon's ideals, but had not his endurance or his responsibility, turned to pitying a tired and ageing man, and felt revulsion at witnessing his plight. Yet I think Earl Simon was as much a victim and a prisoner as he, caught in the same trap, and with even less possibility of escape.

Edward was there, too, accompanied everywhere by his two guardians, Henry de Montfort and Thomas of Clare, Earl Gilbert's brother. No doubt a Clare was added to the warders to try and balance that enmity between Clares and Montforts that was splitting the younger reform party into two, but that must have been an unhappy partnership, damaging to all three. Thomas of Clare slept in Edward's bedchamber. No doubt those two had plenty of time to talk together, while Earl Gilbert was holding off in the forest, and setting the night alight with his camp-fires all round Gloucester.

With all his burdens, Earl Simon did not forget to keep us informed. We heard from him when the bishop of Worcester, eternally hopeful and ardent in the cause of peace-making, undertook to try and bring Gilbert de Clare to a meeting, and felt some relief when news followed, on the fifth day of May, that the young man was softening towards the idea, and had agreed to come down into the city if certain conditions were fulfilled.

'So it may pass over, after all,' said Llewelyn, glad but scornful. 'He's satisfied with the trouble he has caused, and flattered at having great men and reverend bishops running after him, and no doubt he'll enjoy being gracious after the wooing. We were wrong about him, he's lighter than we thought.' For he himself, at twenty, had been joint prince of Gwynedd, tried not only in battle but in the hard discipline of submission for the sake of preserving his constricted birthright, and labouring hard to restore its derelict fortunes. He had no time for tantrums.

So our minds were eased, and Llewelyn hawked and hunted over the uplands that day, without expectation of hearing more until the promised meeting should take place. And we were astonished when another messenger from Earl Simon rode into our narrow bailey the next morning, his horse ridden into a sweat, and his clothes whitened with the dust and pollen of a dry May. He stooped in haste to Llewelyn's hand.

'My lord, Earl Simon sends you word he is gone to Hereford with all his retinue, and begs you will attend him south on your side the border, for he may have good need of you.'

'I will well!' said Llewelyn heartily. 'But why to Hereford, and so suddenly? Is Gloucester at some new trick?'

'No, my lord, this is no contrivance of Gloucester's; he is still in camp, and has not moved a man. But William of Valence has landed from France in his lordship of Pembroke, with the earl of Surrey and a hundred and twenty fighting men. There'll be others following unless we turn back this onslaught at once. The earl is gone to block the roads into England and stay the flood.'

'You go to join him in Hereford?' said Llewelyn. 'You may tell him we shall not be far behind him.' And he sent the man in to get food and rest, while a fresh horse was saddled for his onward journey. When the prince turned upon me, I knew what was in his mind before ever he spoke, for it was in my mind, too.

'Samson,' he said, and his voice was so quiet and so current that it was strange to hear in it what I heard of doubt and entreaty, 'will you go back to Earl Simon with his messenger, and be my voice with him as before? I am not easy among these shifting tides. Go to him, and I'll keep pace with you my side the border. For I cannot go myself!' he said, crying out against what drew and denied him.

I said I would go. What else could I say? I did not
say, gladly, there was then no gladness, though there
may have been gratitude. I cannot tell. Within the hour
I rode for Hereford with Earl Simon's messenger, and
with Cadell beside me to be my courier with good tidings
and ill.

The king's court was installed in the house of the
Black Friars in the city of Hereford, and the strange
retinue of officials and army filled the town, from the
castle to the enclosure of the Franciscans, and spilled
into encampments outside the walls. Something of Earl
Simon's rigid discipline of body and mind had bled into
the veins of those who served him, and there was order
and purpose even then, when the foundations of their
brief and splendid world were crumbling.

When they let me in to him, on the morning of the
seventh day of May, he greeted me with a faint gleam
of pleasure that burned through his black preoccupation
for a moment, and warmed both him and me. I saw
him greyer than before, the close fell of brown hair,
like a beast's rich hide, silvered at the temples and above
the great cliff of forehead, and his eyes sunk deeper into
his skull than I remembered them.

He said: 'It is barely a year since you left me, after
Lewes. I have found that a man may do ten years'
living in one year. But you are not changed. I trust
your lord is well?'

I said that he was, and of his own will had again sent
me to be his envoy and hold the link close between
them. And he made me sit down with him, and told
me how the matter stood as at that time. As yet there
had been no move from the force which had landed in
Pembroke, his only information concerning them was
that William of Valence and the earl of Surrey had made
very correct and peaceable overtures to the religious
houses in Dyfed and Gwent, and seemed to be contem-

plating an appeal through some such go-between towards the restoration of their lands and right of residence in England. Their numbers were not great, and in themselves they were not a great danger, provided entry could be denied to any others hoping to follow them.

I told him that Llewelyn proposed to be ready to match any moves the earl might make, and keep pace with him on the Welsh side of the border, where he could be very quickly reached at any time. But I repeated yet again that his first concern was the unity and stability of Wales, and that he needed and deserved to have his position made regular by formal acknowledgement, which he would not jeopardise by military adventures into England itself. His stand, as one having no covetous designs on any soil that had not been Welsh from time out of mind, could not be abandoned.

Earl Simon smiled. 'I remember,' he said, 'you told me so once before, and warned me that it might be in my power to tempt him from his resolve. Be easy! I will not lure any man from his own crusade to accomplish mine. It is good to have such a man as the prince keeping my back for me. I ask no more.'

In those days of May letters patent and letters close poured out from the city of Hereford, first to the Cinque ports and all the coastal castles, alerting them against the possibility of further attempts at landing troops, then to all the sheriffs of the shires, to hold their forces on the alert to keep the peace, arrest preachers of sedition and rumour-mongers, and insist on the maintenance of the settlement. Then, as stories began to come in of local levies massing in the marches, and brawls and disorder resulting, the sheriffs along the border were ordered to search for and seize those marcher lords who had promised to withdraw for a year of exile to Ireland, but on one excuse or another had contrived to evade keeping their word, and were now openly repudiating it. Rumours were spreading like brush

265

fires along the borders that there was discord and enmity between the earl of Leicester and the earl of Gloucester, and these Earl Simon was intent upon suppressing.

'The man has his grievances, and has said so freely,' he said, 'and I have promised him redress if I am held to have done him any injustice. God knows I am not so infallible that he may not have just complaint against me. But he is a true man to the Provisions and the settlement, and I will not have his faith called in question because he finds fault with me.'

In this he was utterly sincere, for Bishop Walter of Worcester had indeed been successful in bringing de Clare to consent to a conference, but that the landing in Pembroke had caused that matter to be postponed in favour of more urgent business. Yet I could not get it out of my head that Earl Gilbert had been holding off for weeks from such a meeting, as though time, and not a hearing, was what he wanted. Time, perhaps, for the ships from France to put their cargoes ashore in Pembroke? He had not yielded to persuasion until the day before their coming was known, and to him it might have been known before the news came into Gloucester. I said so to young Henry de Montfort, on the one occasion when I saw him in the courtyard of the Dominicans. He bit on the suggestion with some doubt and consternation, as on an aching tooth, but shook his head over it after thought.

'How could he have foreknowledge of it? All the ports are under guard; you see they attempted nothing in the south, but went afield as far as Pembroke. And then, he has not made any move to try and join them, or they to make contact with him. We know he is still encamped where he was, close to Gloucester. I cannot believe he is in conspiracy with the exiles, or in sympathy with them, whatever his differences with my father.'

'Yet Pembroke's lands were in his care,' I said, 'and he should have been prepared to repel any such landing.'

266

'True,' said Henry, 'and he is certainly guilty of negligence, but surely of nothing more. He has neglected his duty to pursue his own quarrel, but he cannot have abandoned the cause he has fought for like the rest of us.'

So I pressed the matter no more, but I was not easy, for that very aloofness and stillness of Earl Gilbert caused me, as it were, to listen and hold my breath, as though both he and I were still waiting for some future event. However, there was nothing then to bear me out. The general alert continued, and so did the flares and raids in the marches, and the rumours of secret gatherings, but Gloucester made no move, and all the newly-landed exiles did at that time was to send the prior of Monmouth on a mission to the king's court, to plead for the restoration of their lands. A chill reply was sent from the council, saying that justice was open to all in the king's courts, and could be sought there at will.

That was a strange, sad Whitsuntide, in spite of the fair and sunny weather. The king, tired and unresisting, did as he was bid, and hated his own acts, council and ministers; Llewelyn patrolled his own side of the border, round Painscastle and Hay, and passed word back to us regularly, but there was no sign of any move from Pembroke. Earl Simon kept both hands upon the workings of chancery, and began to raise money where he could, from the Hospitallers and any who would loan it, foreseeing an urgent need to come. And Edward went to and fro in a controlled silence that was new in him, taking no part in any of the business of state unless his seal was expressly required upon some document, and then permitting its use with a bland but stony face, all his will and intelligence refraining from what was done with his supposed consent. And for the rest, he read, took exercise, rode, heard mass and music, as though what went forward in England then was nothing to do with him. In some such fashion, I suppose, he justified

267

to himself his oath-breaking and faithlessness, his will and spirit having absented themselves when his tongue uttered all those vows. After all this time I believe I begin to understand even Edward.

On the morning of the Thursday in Whitsun week I saw him ride out of the city to take air and exercise, closely attended, as always, by Henry de Montfort and Thomas de Clare, his keepers, and several grooms, and with a string of lively horses for his testing. They went out in sunshine by the north gate, towards Leominster, and what I noticed as they trotted out from the Dominican friary was that Thomas de Clare leaned to Edward, and said something lightly and gaily into his ear, and that Edward laughed aloud, and rode out laughing. The only grave face among them was Henry's, who did not love his wardship or his ward, and was showing the signs of his unhappiness in that unpleasant duty.

But it was Edward's laughter that lingered in my mind all that morning, for I had not seen him laugh since the days when I had known him as a long-legged four-year-old running wild at our David's heels. And what he should find to laugh about on this particular day, in a situation in which he so dourly maintained a face of grim indifference through all other days, was more than I could fathom.

Before that day ended, all was made plain.

It happened that I was in attendance on Earl Simon in the afternoon, one of several clerks standing by in case he should wish to consult us, for he had matters in hand involving both Wales and England. Bishop Walter of Worcester was at his side, as constantly he was in those days. If the earl found few men constant to his measure, those he did find were worth the keeping. Peter de Montfort of Beaudesert was also among them, and also with us that day. About mid-afternoon there was a flurry of voices in hurried and agitated speech outside the door, and then young Henry came bursting in and confronted his father with a stricken face and staring eyes. His riding clothes were dusty and disordered, and there was a long graze down one cheek, and a smear of blood on his forehead. Earl Simon rose from his chair at the sight of his son, even before the boy gasped out between gulps for breath:

'The Lord Edward – he has escaped us! He is gone, and Thomas of Clare with him. The thing was plotted between them – them and others!'

He had not got so far, when every man there was on his feet. The earl stood stiff and still, gripping the table before him. Yet he did not exclaim, and his voice was low and even as he questioned:

'Where did this happen?'

'About five miles north, climbing up from the Lugg to ride over the commons there. I left a groom at the place. Beyond the ridge there are woods between the river and the old road. I have guards and archers beating the woods now,' he said, but without much hope.

Nevertheless, Earl Simon sent out more searchers before he questioned further: 'How did it chance?'

The young man told the sorry story, grinding his teeth over his own failure, and wiping away the trickle of blood from his cheek with a heedless hand when it vexed him. And the anger and bitterness that had not yet blazed in his father burned fiercely in him.

'He had two spare horses with him, he wanted to try them over the hills there, so he said. He changed to the second, and only when we reached this place to the third. It was the best of the three, and of a creamy-white, a colour to show out well over distance. He tried its paces along the grass away from us, and came back to us again, once, twice, and then loosed it to a canter as far as the ridge, and there checked a third time where he had turned, as if to turn again. And on the top of the next hill, between the trees, a horseman rode out, and I saw him lift his arm and brandish a sword. And at that Edward struck in his spurs and was away headlong, and Thomas, who was close beside me, lashed out with his whip and struck my mare over the face and eyes, and she reared and threw me. When I got up from the ground the Lord Edward had vanished into the woods, and Thomas was over the ridge and climbing the slope beyond, and my mare was halfway home without me,' he said, writhing with fury. 'I took Edward's horse and went after them. Some of the grooms were ahead of me, and of them I'm sure, they were honest, they had no part in this. But they were not so well mounted, and the start was too great. And there are some of the laggards among them that I doubt whether they were not in the secret. I take the blame upon me,' he said with humble arrogance. 'I have failed in my trust.'

I saw Earl Simon's lips shrink and curve, between a smile and a contortion of pain, but he was not yet ready to comfort his son. There were more urgent matters yet.

'Thomas was in this, then,' he said. 'Surely not his brother, too? But they are gone north, you say.'

'Due north. He could not turn. I have hunters already on all the roads between here and where we lost him. To reach Gloucester, why start north? He could have chosen where he would for his ride.'

'And clean away from Pembroke and de Valence,' said Earl Simon. 'You are right. He is not gone to them. Well, let us improve on this hunt. We have sheriffs in the shires to the north, and a guard on the border.'

And he shook himself like a weathered and experienced hound surging out of the current of a river and questing afresh for scent, and set himself to cover all quarters leading out of Hereford that a fugitive prince might take. When all was done that he could do, he dismissed his attendants. But I did not go. I do not know whence I drew my awareness of privilege, yet I did not feel myself dismissed. I was still there, in the corner of his vision but not absent from his mind, when he sank back at last in his chair, and let his hands lie spread upon the table before him, great, practised, sinewy hands.

It was then I saw that these hands were already old before his face, having experienced and suffered so much, and carried such immense weights. He was then fifty-six years old, and his body a vigorous and powerful instrument that might have belonged to a man of forty. But his hands acknowledged their years.

His son had also remained, motionless and silent in the face of this calm. I believe I learned then how the sons of great men are themselves diminished below their own value, by respect, by fear of failure, by too great love and admiration. This was the best of his sons. Young Simon, the second, was then his father's deputy in Surrey and Sussex, busy watching the sea towards France, and he was bolder, more impetuous, and I think smaller than Henry, but he suffered the same diminution. It is not good nor easy to have a father who is both demon and saint. Had Henry been my son, as then and at other times I felt towards him the bowels of a father, I think he might have been happier, at least if ease is happiness.

He moved with a heavy lameness, tired with his fury of hunting and riding and humiliation, and shaken and bruised by his fall, and came like a child to his father's side, and there fell on his knees and leaned his head against the arm of the earl's chair. I could not see his face, it was in shadow.

'My lord and father,' he said, 'it is I who have failed you. I take the blame upon me.'

Earl Simon did not move his head or look down at his son, but I saw him smile, so marvellously and so mournfully I remember it yet. He took his left hand from the table, and folded it about the young man's head, holding him as in a bronze bowl.

'That you cannot,' he said, 'unless you will to be recreant and forsworn in his place. Child, if a man is

271

not bound by his own oath, believe me, there is no way on earth of binding him.'

He rested a moment, cradling his son, the eldest and dearest, and fashioned so closely after his own pattern. 'Sooner or later we should have lost him,' he said, and suddenly the great, arched eyelids rolled back from his deep eyes, and they were looking full at me, with the last glow of that all-illuminating smile in them.

'If it were not for your presence, Master Samson,' he said, 'I should be saying: Put not your trust in princes! But since you are present, sit down with me, and write in my name to the prince of Wales!'

So began the last correspondence between Llewelyn and Earl Simon, through my hand. What the earl most wanted was reliable information as to where the Lord Edward was gone, and who had been the instrument of his escape, beyond the suggestive complicity of Thomas de Clare. And Llewelyn, through his intelligencers in Knighton and Presteigne, might be better placed than we to get news of these matters, since the fugitives had ridden northwards. In the meantime, the earl took steps at once, calling up the entire knight service of England and bidding them travel day and night to come soon to Worcester. But the process of getting all those local levies into motion was always slow, even in emergencies, as the monarchy had acknowledged already by its increasing inclination towards paid soldiers, whose whole business it is to get into action with the least delay, and stay out their term without grudging. By the time the ponderous engine moved, there was a marcher army barring the passage of the Severn at Worcester, and the order to the knights was changed to call them to Gloucester, which the earl had left well garrisoned.

Thus things stood when Cadell rode into Hereford, and delivered us by word of mouth the news Llewelyn had not stayed to have written down.

'My lord, we have found him! The secret was well kept, but this is sure: The Lord Edward, when he fled, was met and escorted to Mortimer's castle of Wigmore, where the lady hid him while the hunt was up, and as soon as the way was clear sent him on to Ludlow. Geoffrey de Genevill is away in Ireland, and may not even know the use made of his castle, but his wife is a de Breose, and they are all kin, and all marchers. And there Roger Mortimer was waiting for him. And there, the next day, Earl Gilbert of Gloucester came to join them. Gloucester was in it from the beginning!'

'Gloucester – hand in glove with Mortimer?' said Earl Simon. 'It cannot be true! The man had agreed to parley with us! For all his waywardness, I trusted him!'

'It is true, my lord,' said Cadell. 'He was never worth your trust, for all these weeks he has been playing his own game and Edward's, holding your eyes and ears upon himself while this plan was laid and hatched. They are in the field now, all their forces joined, and moving down the Severn valley, and if they are not in Worcester by this, as they are certainly between you and that city, it is no more than a day or two before they take it.' And he said, awed by Earl Simon's face, which was still as stone and yet sick with grief, like a carved mourner on a Calvary: 'The Lord Edward himself has taken over the leadership of the army.'

Earl Simon in his own unaltered voice, courteous and low, thanked him for his pains and dismissed him. When there was no other with us in the room he said, as though to himself: 'Gloucester!' and hung upon the name again and again with incredulity and pain, for never had he learned to be prepared for the faithlessness of men. And suddenly he cried out against him, and against Edward, for the cheats, dissemblers and liars they were, and against himself for the trust he had placed in creatures so devious, and swore that Edward had deprived himself of all rights in land or revenue or privilege in England, and deserved to lose his claims to the realm, for he had of his own will taken the oath, under pain of that loss, and he must abide the consequences of his own act. And forthwith he burned into a passionate fury of activity, dictating letters setting out this same theme, and despatching them to the lords of Ireland, to the men of all the shires, and to the bishops, on whom he urged the solemn duty of renewing the sentence of excommunication against those who had betrayed the cause and shattered the peace. He also redoubled his efforts to build up by loans and other means a reserve of treasure to be laid up at St Frideswide's priory in Oxford, for clearly the greatest strength of his cause was in London and the cities and shires of England, and to reach London and rally all the scattered forces he must take the road through Oxford, which was invincibly friendly to him. The bitterness of his disillusionment never caused him to abandon hope or to give up the fight, even though he found the most of men hardly worth saving, and hardly deserving of the justice and good government he had wanted for them.

But before he moved east into England, as he knew he must do, there were certain things he had in mind to set right, that he might leave no loose threads behind him.

On the nineteenth day of June he sent for me. 'Master Samson,' he said, 'do you know at this moment where to find your lord? I would have you go to him yourself with what I have to say, and present my envoys to him. And they will be not only my envoys, but the envoys of England and of King Henry.'

I said that Llewelyn was no more than twenty miles from us, with the greater part of his force then marshalled along the border. He was encamped at Pipton on the Wye, due west of Hereford by way of Hay, and he had with him there a good half of his council and several of his chief vassals, Rhys Fychan of Dynevor and both the lords of Powys among them.

'So much the better,' said Earl Simon, 'if he is attended in some splendour. This is what I would have you say to him.'

And he taught me such a message as uplifted my heart with joy and eagerness, and had me also write a letter which should further expound his purpose, already in those few words made plain.

That same day I rode, with Peter de Montfort of Beaudesert and certain knights of his train, and also various clerks and chancery lawyers, and we came to Pipton before evening, and to the prince's camp in the rich meadows above the river Wye. In that summer country, with no close enemy, the camp lay spread among green fields and uplands, most princely, and when our party was sighted and reported to him, Llewelyn came out to meet us, glowing with the weeks spent in the sun, and splendidly attended.

When he saw me, and weighed the quality and gravity of those who followed me into his camp, I saw behind his composed and gracious face and warm welcome the wonder and curiosity that filled him, and I rejoiced to be the instrument of his glory and gain. For though he had waited a great while for this day, he did not foresee its coming even now, when it fell ripe into his hands.

We dismounted, and when I had made my obeisance I stood before Llewelyn in all solemnity, as the messenger of another lord to whom he had lent me, and delivered with a swelling heart the embassage with which I was entrusted.

'My lord, Simon de Montfort, earl of Leicester and ancestral steward of England, sends his greetings to the Lord Llewelyn, prince of Wales. By that style and title he addresses you, and he desires that you will receive the mission of these lords from the crown of England with goodwill, to the intent that the king of England and the prince of Wales may compound for a treaty of peace between their two countries.'

The blood so left his face, all his bronze blanched into the palest and clearest of gold, and his eyes burned from deep brown into glowing red with passion and gladness. But the hour was too great and too sudden for elation. Princely he bade them in to lodging, when I had presented them all, and feasted and served them, and sat down with them to hear their business.

Not then did I have leisure to tell him what the earl had said further when he sent me forth, though long afterwards I told him all. How he had said that before leaving Hereford to go to his testing, in the sure knowledge of his own mortality that ensured him here no steadfast stay, he would do right to the prince of Wales, whose loyalty to his word was a gem-stone in this wilderness of falsehood, who had never promised more than he meant to perform, or failed to perform what he did promise. Surely he meant to bind Llewelyn to him even more closely by this act, yet I believe it was not a price offered for future favours, but an acknowledgement of help already given, and more than all, a free act for his own soul's sake, as truly as largesse or prayer.

I think there was never a treaty so momentous made and ratified in so few days, and with so little argument. So I said later to the earl, and he smiled, and said that might well be because it was long overdue, and no one could well object to it as unjust. Yet afterwards there were many who did so object, blaming Earl Simon bitterly for conceding so much in the name of England.

When the lord of Beaudesert had had his say, Llewelyn set out his own terms.

'In the king's name I am promised recognition of my title and right as prince of Wales, with the overlordship of all my fellow-princes, the remission of any illwill the king may still bear to me, the repudiation of all documents that infringe or cast doubts upon my right and title, and the retention of all my present possessions. It is very fairly offered, and I have little more to demand,

276

but that little is important to me. My border is long, and in places vulnerable, lacking the proper protection of castles I can hold as bases. I ask for nothing which has not in old times been Welsh, but I do ask that I may have acknowledged title to such Welsh ground as I may still recover from the king's rebels in the marches. I have in mind such lands as were taken from my grand-sire Llewelyn ap Iorwerth, or my uncle David ap Llewelyn. I ask also for certain other castles which are vital for the protection of Wales, namely, Painscastle, Hawarden and Whittington. And in return I am willing to pledge my duty and fealty to the king, and to aid and support,' said Llewelyn with emphasis, 'the present law-ful government of England against all its enemies.'

There was some mild demur over these castles he named, and Peter de Montfort said, justly, that these were great concessions, and could not be lightly made. Llewelyn replied as courteously that he well understood that, and they were not lightly asked, for he was prepared to pay a fair indemnity for his gains. The price he offered was thirty thousand marks, to be paid over a period of ten years. It was a great sum, and they opened their eyes respectfully at it, as well they might. It must be said that Llewelyn's housekeeping was exceedingly able and practical; he could and did command large sums when he needed them, and his reputation for prompt payment was high, as the English acknowledged. I suppose no prince ever devised a means of moneying so perfect that it did not lean heavily on someone, but there were few complaints of injustice or misuse in Wales during his rule.

Since every man there desired the treaty, it was very readily made. There were certain elaborating letters written separately, though Llewelyn also stated the gist of them there and then.

'The agreement is with this lawful government, and with King Henry as head of it. If the king should default

277

from his adherence, which God forbid, my obligation to him ceases, until he shall again be in good faith with his magnates. And should the king die, and leave a successor who adheres to the settlement, then I will go on paying the indemnity to him, or, if the lawful community of the realm so desires, I will pay otherwise, but in all events, I will continue to discharge my debts.'

They agreed this was fair, and thereupon the documents were drawn up. We slept overnight in Llewelyn's camp, and when we left with the dawn, for time was short for Earl Simon's business, the prince drew me aside for the only personal exchange we had during that visit.

'Samson,' he said, 'there is one more thing I most earnestly request of the earl of Leicester, and that I would ask of him myself. Say to him that I greatly desire him to meet with me, and ask him to ride the few miles to the abbey of Dore tomorrow, or to appoint me some other place and time, or give me safe-conduct to come to Hereford if need be, for he is pressed, I know. But do not fail me. Unless you send Cadell with other word, I shall go to Dore tomorrow.'

I wondered but did not question, for he asked it as a young man asking favour of someone to whom he owed deference, and that was not his way, and his face had that bright intensity, and his eyes that wonder, that I had seen there whenever he looked within at his vision, as now he was able to see it openly under the sun, without turning his gaze into his own heart. Therefore there was still something secret to him still wanting, and all things else, all that triumph, remained at risk until it was won. So I said that I would press his wish, and was sure it would not be denied.

Nor was it. For when I preferred it to Earl Simon on my return to Hereford, he lifted his head from the letters he was studying, and looked at me with those deep eyes now so large and lambent in their sockets of bone, and said: 'I, too, have long nursed the same wish. Nor will it be time lost, even by the measure of England's need, for I can better plan my movements now with Llewelyn in person than by letter or courier. We go, Samson, south to Gwent as soon as this treaty is made fast, and if Llewelyn will go with me and keep my flank, the rest I will do.'

I was then so close with him, and so concerned for him, and he so acknowledged that bond, that I could and did ask him what plans he had in that southern march.

'To cut off de Valence and his force from crossing to join the rebels,' said Earl Simon, 'and to secure such of Earl Gilbert's castles in Gwent as I can, and cross by Newport into the safety of Bristol, and so to Oxford and London. Plainly I shall be dependent on the prince of Wales for supplies and support during that passage. I have sworn, and I will keep my oath, that he shall not be asked – never by me! – to put his Wales in peril by committing himself out of its bounds. But within those bounds he is an army to me. And I will go to Dore to meet him, with all my heart.'

He bade me ride with him the next day, for he would go otherwise unattended. To that great Cistercian house it was no more than ten miles, for him a breath of freedom in this punishing time. For Llewelyn it was a much longer ride, he must have risen before the sun. We went, Earl Simon and I, after morning mass from Hereford, but when we came to that glorious rosy-grey house in the blossoming valley, all gilded and green with summer, Llewelyn was there before us.

In the quiet courts of the Cistercian house of Dore, golden indeed that June, under a sky like periwinkle flowers, those two met and joined hands at last.

I watched them come together, I knew the desire that drew them, and the weight of wonder and thought that made their steps so slow and their eyes so wide as they crossed the few paces of earth that parted them. From the moment they set eyes upon each other they looked neither to left nor right, each taking in the other like breath and food and wine. And it seemed to me, when their hands linked and grew together, that there was in them, for all their differences, for they did not look alike at all, some innermost thing that set up a mirror between them, and showed each his own face. Also I saw that Llewelyn had come, like the earl, almost unattended, only one of Goronwy's sons at his back, and that there was a shining splendour upon him, for all this simplicity, that made him unwontedly beautiful and solemn. His dress, that was never planned to impress, was that day most choice in dark and gold. He looked as a prince should look.

'My lord of Leicester,' he said, and stooped to touch with his lips the hand he still held, as fittingly and royally he could, with the awareness of destiny upon him, 'I rejoice that I see you at last, and I thank you for this kindness. I have long desired your acquaintance, and I wish the times better favoured me, for I know I trespass.'

'No,' said Earl Simon, and looked at him long and hungrily, and saw, I think, as I saw, the heart's likeness that surely was there, for still the mirror shone between them. 'No, you refresh me. I have many times had need of you, and need you still. I had believed it was for a cause. I think it was also for my soul's sake. In my desert now there are not many springs.'

He had known deserts in his time, for he had been a crusader.

'My lord,' said Llewelyn, 'I desire all of your company that I may have, but my time is silver, while yours is golden, and I will not hamper your movements, not for my life. So I speak directly. Your son, my lord, I have known and loved some years. You I have loved without knowing you. Until today! My lord Simon, you have also a daughter.'

'I have,' said the earl, enlightened, and smiled, remembering her. 'She is with her mother and my youngest sons in the castle of Dover.'

'And she is not yet affianced? Nor promised to any?' He drew deep breath at the earl's nodded assent, and under his tan he was white to the lips with passion and diffidence, as he said: 'My lord, if it will please you to entertain and favour my suit, I would ask of you your daughter's hand in marriage.'

CHAPTER XII

————

What he asked, that he had. Earl Simon leaned to him and laid both hands upon his shoulders, and kissed him upon the cheek with the kiss of kinship, for acceptance and blessing.

'My daughter is yet young,' he said, 'not quite thirteen years. But there is no man to whom I would more gladly confide her than the prince of Wales, and none among all those not my sons I would so joyfully welcome as a son. With all my heart I promise her to you, and will record the vow here and now, if you so please.'

So simply was this match made, and so hard afterwards to make, so quickly closed with, and so long awaiting fulfilment. Those two went in together and exchanged their vows in the church of Dore, and from that moment Llewelyn's resolution never wavered.

Until the late afternoon they remained together in the hospice at Dore, and talked together of everything that bound them, first and most urgently of the earl's plans, and the stages by which Llewelyn would match them on his western flank, appointing certain places where messages could readily be exchanged, and further stores delivered for the provisioning of the earl's army. Upon such details they were both brisk and practical, and those few hours were well used. Then they talked also of what hopefully must become family affairs, and of the child Eleanor, on whom Llewelyn had fixed his heart, never having seen her.

'And I confess,' he said ruefully, 'I doubted my right

to ask for her, being so much her elder, but I promise you there could no suitor of her own years cherish and care for her as truly as I will, if she also willingly accepts me.'

The earl said, smiling: 'Master Samson, who has been in some degree her friend for a while, can tell you that she has already pursued him with many questions about you and your country. I doubt if she had marriage in mind, then, but you could hardly have had a better advocate to satisfy her curiosity.'

'You have not heard him,' said Llewelyn, 'on the subject of the lady! You do not know how closely I questioned him, or how I have pictured her out of his praises.'

Then her father also talked of her, with love and pleasure, and watching his face soften at the thought of her, I began to understand how great refreshment he found in this day stolen from his immense and crushing cares, all the more because the lady might not many years more have a father to provide and care for her, and it was ease and blessing to him to know that she would have a worthy husband to shield and love her after him. So I came to understand that he entertained ungrudgingly, in that proud, devout and humble mind, the daily possibility of his own death, and took thought for his responsibilities. His wife was the king's sister, and for all her fierce loyalty to the earl could not be allowed to miscarry, for the king's own credit. His sons were men, and could fend for themselves. His daughter was another matter. Lords marry their daughters for many reasons, most of them tied to property and land, and certainly it was no mean thing to be the princess of Wales, but this was no such betrothal for gain, nor was his consent given to persuade Llewelyn to more aid than had been freely tendered. The offer for Eleanor, coming from a man he respected and trusted, was pleasure and release to him. Each of them had come to that meeting

283

bearing a gift of great price.

By the time they parted, late in the afternoon, they had probed each other deep, and reached into those lofty places beyond the art and practice of government, where Earl Simon's visions still shone undimmed after all his disillusionments, half understood with the mind, half sensed with the heart and spirit and blood, no less valid because all men but one fell away from loyalty to them. And I think those two were content with each other, and that there was no falling short.

So we rode back through the early evening to Hereford, and Llewelyn to Pipton. And the next day King Henry set his seal to the treaty, naming Llewelyn prince of Wales, and Peter de Montfort of Beaudesert rode to Pipton and delivered it into the prince's hand.

The day after that we marched, all that great tangle of king, courtiers, officials, clerks, judges, soldiers, south to Monmouth. The last letter patent sent from Hereford was an urgent order to young Simon, in Surrey, to muster all the levies of the shires, and hurry north-west to his father's aid.

If young Simon had indeed been near enough to get his men to the eastern side of Gloucester before the castle fell, and Earl Simon had closed in to meet him from the west, they might well have broken Edward's army between them. But it is a long march from Surrey to the western border, and I doubt if the young man ever truly realised how urgently he was needed, and how much hung upon his coming. Even if he had, it might well have altered nothing, for about the time we moved from Hereford the castle of Gloucester fell, and there was then no crossing of the Severn left to us but by going south.

Only then, I think, did even the earl himself realise how desperate was his situation, thus cut off in the hostile marches from that solid body of support for him that habited in the English cities and shires. With both

Worcester and Gloucester closed against him, he hastened his march south, and attacked and took, without much trouble, the earl of Gloucester's castles in the vale of Usk, first possessing Monmouth and establishing a base there, then going on to take Usk, and Newport itself. And all this time Llewelyn with his main force kept pace with us, almost at arm's length, and supplied us all our needs.

As for the earl's first declared objective, to sever the force in Pembroke from all possibility of joining Edward, that hope was lost before ever we reached Usk, for William of Valence was already across the old passage of the estuary of Severn, and had added his strength to Edward's outside Gloucester. That formidable army, most formidably led, came surging south on the opposite bank, and occupied all the English shore.

The old passage of Severn at the opening of the estuary was well known to us, and quick and easy, given proper use of the tides, but it needed boats none the less, and under archery, and facing a landing upon a shore heavily occupied by an enemy, it was impossible. There could only be a massacre. Earl Simon sent out scouts, and accepted their bitter verdict. For him there was no way over into England by that route. Moreover, detachments of Edward's army were moving along the road between Monmouth and Gloucester, and there was no returning to Hereford by that way, either.

There was but one way he could go, and that was deeper into Wales, and that at least was made easy for him by Llewelyn's presence in force in the hills, where he had greatly strengthened his hold on the roadways that threaded the disputed land of Gwent. Cadell rode ahead as courier to inform the prince of our need, and he came down himself into the valley of Usk to meet and accompany the earl to a safe camp already waiting in the hills.

So those two met again, and though Llewelyn in delicacy held aloof from meeting king or officials, and confined his personal encounters to Earl Simon and his son, now his own kinsmen, nevertheless it was strange to see the court of England, sorry and suspect court though it was, guided and guarded and provided food and rest under the wing of the prince of Wales, and so shepherded back by stages in a half-circle towards Hereford. And safe they were under that guardianship, but ineffective. No man could touch them with impunity, but neither could they advance their own cause. No base in Wales could avail the earl to strike effectively at his enemies. No Welsh army, even had all the forces at Llewelyn's disposal been committed to him, could restore him to his severed support in England. The greater the numbers he had to spirit across the Severn, the more inevitable was a premature battle, before they could join hands with young Simon, hurrying north from Oxford.

That was a strange time, that journey through Gwent and Brecknock, like the quiet place at the heart of a great storm. For now the stream of ordinances and letters had ceased, as though all the business of state held its breath, and they were but a great multitude of ordinary men, making their way unhindered and unpressed through a summer country of hills and forests and heathland, camping in the calm and warmth of July nights, and listening, unstartled by rattle of steel or sound of trumpet, to a silence deeper than memory. And sometimes at night, when the wretched tired, apathetic king was sleeping, and the camp settled into stillness, Earl Simon sat with Llewelyn, and the talk they had was not all of wars and treaties and disputes, but of high, rare things that both had glimpsed and both desired to comprehend more fully, if all the ways by which they sought to reach them had not turned about treacherously under their feet, and brought them round in a circle, as now, to the place from which they had set out. For I suppose that this life is but the early part of the pilgrimage, and the search will continue in another place.

In the last days of July we came again to the uplands above Valley Dore, and saw below us, beside the stream in the blanched hay-fields, the rosy grey of the great church where they had first met.

'A month lost,' said Llewelyn ruefully, 'to reach the same place.'

'No month is ever lost,' said Earl Simon. 'Certainly not this. Whatever follows, I may tell you so with truth. But now you must come no further with me. For across the Severn I must go, by some means, however desperate, or there is no future.'

'I am coming with you,' said Llewelyn, 'as far as Hereford, for I have sent some of my men of Elfael, who know these parts and have kin on both sides the border, to spy out the state of the river ahead of you. It's high summer, and little rain now for weeks, there may well be possible fords where no one will think to guard. Our rivers are low, so should Severn be. And I have stores waiting for you below.'

'It could not last,' said Earl Simon with a grim smile. 'In Wales my cause cannot be won, nor yours out of it. And my men tire of your shepherd's table and long for their bread and ale. It is high time to go.'

It was past time, and I think he knew it already. But one last night they conferred together, with young Henry, and Peter of Beaudesert and a few others in attendance, and Llewelyn offered a company of lancers to be added to the earl's foot-soldiery, though without Welsh captains. Thus drafted into the English ranks, they did not commit Wales and its prince. And that reservation the earl understood, and did not blame by word or look. It was Llewelyn who agonised within himself, ashamed and tempted, torn between two duties that could not be reconciled, and no longer sure what was duty and what desire. And the next day his scouts came back with word that Edward was making his chief base at Worcester, expecting that crossing to be attempted, and also on the watch for young Simon's army, which was known to be approaching from the south, and thought to be heading for Kenilworth. At that the earl drew breath cautiously, and approved his son's choice.

'In Kenilworth we could be safe enough, and hold off siege as long as need be. If he makes all secure, and I can get my men across and reach him there, we have time to rally the rest of England. The Severn is the only bar.'

'My lord,' said the messenger, 'I have had speech in Hereford with the steward from the bishop of Worcester's manor on the river at Kempsey. The water is low, he says it might be forded there with care, the country people use it in dry summers. But it is barely four miles from Worcester, you could only attempt it by night.'

'There will be guides,' said Llewelyn, 'to show the way.' For the country people were always, without exception, silently but dourly upon Earl Simon's side.

So the army rested that night, and the next day – it was the last day of July – we left the Welsh forces behind, all but those lancers who were drafted into the earl's foot companies, and with a small party escorted the wandering court of King Henry some way beyond the border, and parted from them only when they were drawing near to Hereford.

They did not halt the march, but Earl Simon laid a hand upon Llewelyn's bridle, and checked and drew aside with him to a knoll above the road, and young Henry and I reined after them, and waited. Henry, being also a kinsman, and I, unasked, because I had here two masters and two roads to go, and was as doubtful as Llewelyn what was right and what wrong. So we sat a few moments watching the knights and troopers riding by, and after them the ranks of the foot soldiers. And I watched Llewelyn's face rather out of compassion than for guidance, and saw how he was torn. His countenance was set and still, but not calm. There was sweat on his forehead.

'Here you must leave us,' said the earl, and again, reining close, offered the kiss, and Llewelyn leaned to it and embraced him. 'For all your aid, and for your company,' said Earl Simon, 'I thank you, and with all my heart I wish you well.'

'In the name of God!' said Llewelyn in anguish, and still held him. 'How can I let you go to this trial without me?'

'You have mapped your own way,' said Earl Simon, 'and I approve you. In your place I would do as you have done. Go back to your own fortune, and bear your own burden. And take this with you,' he said, and shook out from the pocket in his sleeve a small rondel that caught the sun in a delicate flash of painted colours, like an enamelled brooch. 'I had forgotten I had it with me,' he said, 'until last night I made my peace, and destroyed all that I carried of regrets and vain memories. This is not vain. I give it to you as a visible pledge and earnest, against a future too dark to be seen very clearly at this moment. At such times it is well to see one thing clear.'

And he smiled, a sudden brightness as though his soul soared like a bird, and laid the rondel in Llewelyn's palm, and so would have wheeled away from him and spurred after the head of his column, but I reined into his path, for I, too, had rights and duties and desires.

'My lord,' I said, 'if my prince releases me still, I am still in your service, and I have not deserved dismissal.'

He looked from me to Llewelyn, who sat holding the earl's gift in his hand like the relic of a saint, but had not so much as lowered his eyes to it, so captive was he to the giver.

'No!' said Earl Simon. 'Neither have you deserved that I should take you with me where I am going, and you have no protection but mine, all fallible as it may prove. Go back with your lord, Samson, friend, and serve him as before.'

Then I, too, looked at Llewelyn, stricken and torn between us, and I said: 'He is my lord, and it is his bidding I take, and him I shall be serving. And his command I wait, my lord earl, and not yours.'

There was a moment while everything hung like a hawk before the stoop, and I held my breath, feeling my desire and Llewelyn's desire burn utterly into one, as we two shared the same stars at birth. And after a moment he got out of him: 'You have my order. I bid you go with the earl of Leicester, and see him to his triumph in my name!' His voice was sudden and vehement, yet quiet as the flood of a lowland river in spring. I knew then that he had understood me as I understood him, and in obeying him I took him with me wheresoever I went.

'So I will, my lord,' I said, 'and bring word to you again.'

Once before I had thought that Earl Simon might deny with anger, being so used to obedience, and he had not denied. Even so now he looked back and eyed us mildly, my lord and me, and found no fault. For he so felt the largeness and dignity of his own person that he could not grudge the same to others.

'In the name of God!' he said. 'So, come, and welcome!' Then he looked a moment upon Llewelyn, his head reared and his eyes wide to take in all that hunger and thirst that coveted me my place, and next he shook his rein, and was away after the slow-moving head of his column, and I as dutifully after him.

From the corner of my eye I saw young Henry de Montfort embrace and kiss with Llewelyn, I think without words. He overtook me soon. We fell into our places near the head of the marching column, and the last day of July declined slowly in sunshine and heat.

In the evening and night of the second of August we forded the Severn opposite the manor of Kempsey, making down to the water where there was cover from willows. Some of Bishop Walter's people had been on the watch for us, and stood by to show the best passage. The water was still high enough, but leisurely in its flow, and the bottom firm and smooth, without hazards. A slow business it was, but accomplished before dawn, and at Kempsey we had some rest before the sun rose, for the bishop's household was staunch like its master, and willing to take risks for the earl's cause.

Earl Simon asked urgently after any news of his son's coming with the reinforcements from the south, and the bishop's steward told him what he could.

'All we know,' said he, 'is that the Lord Simon's muster was reported to be nearing Kenilworth two days ago, and that same day the Lord Edward left Worcester with a large force and took them eastwards to try and intercept. Since then we have heard nothing, and last night I sent a groom to the city to gather what news he can. He'll set out for home again at first light.'

It is barely four miles from Kempsey to Worcester, and as we were breaking our fast after mass the groom rode in, and was brought to Earl Simon.

'My lord,' he said, 'forgive me if I waste no words to better what is not good. Time is too short. The Lord Edward returned to Worcester with all his force last night. My lord, they brought prisoners with them – noble prisoners!'

'My son?' questioned Earl Simon, low of voice and still of face.

'No, my lord, not he. He escaped them, and is in Kenilworth with the remnant of his following. But I saw the arms of the earl of Oxford, and there were others, barons and knights, all brought into Worcester captive. As I heard it, they surprised your son's force outside the castle, at the priory, where they had lodged overnight, reaching Kenilworth in the early dark, and thinking themselves safe, so near to home.'

'Folly!' said Earl Simon in a harsh cry, and knotted his hands in exasperation. 'To halt outside the walls, with such an enemy as Edward so close! He has lost me good men when I needed them most. How many got into the castle with him? Can you say?'

But there was no way of knowing, or of being certain who was free and who prisoner, nor was there any time to lament longer over losses and opportunities thrown away.

'He has not learned yet to recognise urgency, or to make sure of his intelligence,' said Earl Simon grimly. 'And Edward is already back in Worcester with all his force! I take that to mean he hurried back so soon for my sake. He believes me still on the far side of Severn, and thinks I must attempt to storm the crossing there, as my only way over. I have but one advantage left, that I am already on the English side. But only four miles from him! I could be happier if the four were forty. We are barely through his lines, we must move east as far and as fast as we may, clear of his shadow. In the middle of England I am his match, but here in the marches the power is in his hands.' He thought some moments and said: 'We march in three hours.'

They held brief council, and agreed it was our best policy to move rapidly, before it was realised that we were over the river and through the cordon. Eastwards we must go, and the earl chose to march for Evesham, to put his host on the best and easiest road either northeast from that town by Alcester, to join young Simon and the remnant of his force in Kenilworth, which was as near invulnerable as a castle could well be, or southeast by Woodstock to Oxford and London, for throughout those shires his following was strong and loyal, and there were enough scattered companies of his following to rally to him and make him invincible. Even though I dreaded that his treaty with Llewelyn might have angered some of his noble adherents, their pride being shocked at ceding so much to Wales, yet I knew that the hold he had upon the lesser nobility and the common people would not be shaken. Could he reach Oxford, then his cause was saved.

Nevertheless, we did not march at the third hour, as he had said, for when the time drew near, King Henry was so fast asleep, and so like a worn-out infant in his helplessness, that they had not the heart to awake him. Earl Simon himself went and looked upon him, intending not to spare where he himself and everything he held dear were not spared, but the oblivious face of his king and brother by marriage, stained and loose and exhausted with being dragged up and down the marches, and showing innocent and piteous in sleep, held him at gaze a long time, and turned him away disarmed and resigned. Surely he knew what he risked with every hour lost, but he said: 'Let him have his sleep out!'

Every man among us needed rest, for though we had the better part of this day, little of it was spent in sleep, most in tending our beasts, as jaded as we, making good all that was amiss with arms and equipment, and darkening what little was left bright about us, for the sun was glaring and cloudless, and would be so until well into the evening, and could betray us at a mile or more. We had marched almost ceaselessly since leaving Llewelyn, and this after all those weeks of scouring the borders south and west and north again to find a way back into England. Still we kept order, discipline and pride. No army of Earl Simon's could let go of those. But for the rest, we were by then a dusty, travel-worn, hungry and footsore company. We had few remounts, or none, only the handful of beasts the bishop's grooms could provide us, and many of us went on foot with the archers and men-at-arms by choice, to ease our over-ridden horses.

So we set out in the early hours of the evening, that third day of August, King Henry like a tired child still querulous and complaining, and those around him attentive and courteous but remorseless, for time trod hard on our heels, and we had learned to respect the efficiency of Edward's spies. From Kempsey on the Severn to Evesham on the Avon is roughly fourteen miles of rich, green, smiling country, full of cornfields and orchards, the grain whitening in the sun when we passed that way, and the meadows full of flowers. Laden as we were, we gave thanks when the sun declined and left us the cool of the night, and into the night we still marched, not knowing how far behind us the inevitable pursuit must be. It could not be long before word reached Edward that his enemy was across the river and brushing past his shoulder into freedom.

So we came, halfway through the night, into Evesham, dropping down from the softly rolling upland fields north-west of the town into the wide meadows about the abbey. And there we halted and rested while Earl Simon conferred with his close council in the abbey itself. He knew, none better, how urgent it was to press on, but he was in doubt whether to cross the Avon and strike south-west for Oxford, or turn north towards his own Kenilworth, and in Evesham he hoped to get word whether Edward had yet moved, and in which direction. The best of our horses had gone to his scouts, and they were appointed to meet him again at the abbey. This alone would have caused him some short delay, but indeed many of his commanders urged that, danger or no danger, the men could not go on further without rest and food, and the king was again drooping and weary. When the first of his scouts rode in and reported that Edward had moved from Worcester in fiery haste, but towards Alcester, clearly expecting the earl to attempt to join his forces with those of his son at Kenilworth, Earl Simon accepted the verdict of all, and agreed to a stay of some hours for food and rest before pushing on towards Oxford, the road it seemed he was not expected to take.

Neither he nor any other amongst us had yet experienced the speed and wit and ferocity with which Edward could think and move. It was true that he had made straight for Alcester to cut the road to Kenilworth, but at such a pace that even with this detour he gained ground on us, and hearing reliably that we had not passed through Alcester, immediately turned south and began to close in on Evesham, racing to cut us off also from the road to Oxford and London. We did not know it then, though the storm of his pursuit was in the air, a troubling of the night.

Howbeit, we rested in Evesham, and with the dawn we heard mass and broke our fast. And in the early light the watchman on the tower of the great abbey church sounded the alarm, and cried down to us that the sun on the uplands to the north had caught for a moment a distant glitter of steel. Then we mustered in haste and made ready to move, for the way to Oxford should still be open to us, and every mile that we gained along it would add to our strength.

But before we so much as moved off through the town, a messenger came galloping in wildly from that direction, and cried from the saddle: 'My lord, the road's blocked against us beyond the bridge! A yeoman from Badsey came in by that way not ten minutes since. He has seen them, a great force, moving round from the west to shut us in. He barely got by before they straddled the road. He saw the banner and livery of Mortimer!'

Then we knew that we were taken in a trap from which there was no escape, if Edward was driving down upon us from the north to pen us into the loop of the river that encircles the town, and Mortimer waiting for us on the southern bank. Between the moat of Avon and the ring of marcher armies the noose about us was complete.

I watched Earl Simon's face then, and I saw in it no surprise at all, as though in the inmost places of his soul he had already known this ending beforehand, and learned to contemplate it without lowering his eyes. The grief I saw in him was strong and stable and calm as a rock. And from that moment there was, in a sense, no more urgency.

For all that it was now possible to do, we had time enough.

'I had thought to bring you safely to a better stand,' said the earl, 'without committing you to a fight here against the odds. But since there's no other way now for us, let us see what manner of ending we can make. If we have nothing else, we have the choice of ground.'

As deliberately as at some noble exercise he might marshal the lists, so he led his army to the higher ground north of the abbey, to deliver that holy place from his too close presence, and there set out his array, mainly directing his strength against the north, from which Edward must come, but so contriving that we should be able to fight on all sides, for Mortimer surely would not stay out of the battle, though he might come too late to get much glory out of us. Such archers as he had, no great number, the earl placed flanking the lancers, to give what cover they might, for it was certain that Edward had far more knights and heavily armed troopers than we had, and it is ill for light-armed foot soldiers to stand up to cavalry charges. King Henry he set in the midst, with all his own chivalry ringed strongly about him. And when all was ready, he asked absolution for us all from the prior of Evesham, and bade us take what rest we could while we could, for since we could go nowhere, but were arrived at that place to which we had been travelling without our knowledge, there was now no haste to strain beyond, for what was beyond would come to us.

Then there was indeed a calm, however ominous, yet sound and true, and rest they did, on the grass in their stations, while they quietly whetted their edges and strung their bows, and hitched scabbard and quiver ready to hand, and the lancers dug themselves firm grounding for the butts of their lances. Earl Simon took some of his closest companions with him, and went up to the tower of the abbey church to view the approach of the army from the north, and happening to see me among his swordsmen, paused and frowned for a moment, and then called me also to go with them.

The sun was fully risen and high in the sky by that time, and clear in the distance along the dappled fields of the uplands we could see the faint, hanging curtain of glittering dust that moved steadily towards Evesham, and the sparks of colour, still tiny, that flashed through the haze. It was like the steady surge of a long wave on a beach, thrust by the incoming tide, as gentle and as irresistible. As it drew nearer, the colourings and the quarterings grew distinct to the eye, Edward's banners, and Gloucester's, Giffard's, Leyburn's, all those same young men who had banded themselves together in the marches in their hot discontent, and called Earl Simon back from France to lead them, not so long ago.

And yet I think they were not turncoats, nor traitors, though they could not keep the earl's steadfast mind. I do believe they tried to do what they saw as right, however hot blood and inexperience and self-interest and tangled loyalties confused them. And I know that he could find in him no hate or great blame for them as he watched them close about him like a mailed fist to crush him. When they opened their ranks, as they drew nearer, and formed their orderly array on the march, he looked upon them with approval, and smiled, and said: 'I taught them that.' And as if to himself he said, wondering and hopeful: 'If he can learn the discipline of battle, he can learn the discipline of statecraft, too. From his enemies, if need be. But even to a felon a prince should not break his word.' And I knew that he was making his last estimate, both just and critical, of Edward.

Then he shook himself, and turned to us whom he had called to attend him. To the justiciar, Hugh le Despenser, and his kinsman, Ralph Basset, who was warden of the shires in that region, he said seriously that they ought, and he so advised them, to take horse and escape out of this trap, for that was still possible for solitary riders, whom Edward would not break ranks to pursue even if he detected them. He said that they should remove in order to provide a voice for their cause at a better place and in a happier time, so that it should not be utterly silenced. And as one man they smiled, and refused him. He had said what he meant, but he would not urge or persuade. They had their way, and stayed with him.

As we went down again from the tower, leaving a watch behind to signal us from the distance the movements of those approaching, he took me by the arm, and said in my ear: 'Master Samson, this is not your fight nor your lord's fight, and he has a use for you for many years to come. Well I know I can give you no orders, you are not my man, but Llewelyn's and your own. But you are a clerk, and you have a right to sanctuary with the clerks that I have sent into the abbey. Go with them, and stand upon your right, and return whole to your lord. There is nothing better you can do for me.'

But with that fair example before me, out of which I believe he took as much comfort as grief, I also denied him.

'You heard,' I said, 'what Llewelyn said to me when he sent me with you. I am the custodian here of his honour and my own, and more than mere honour, of his love and mine. I will not leave you or separate my fate from yours while we both live. And God willing, I will carry Llewelyn word of your triumph as he bade me.'

'God's will,' said Earl Simon, 'is dark to us, but bright to those who will behold it afterwards. I am content. Do what you must.'

So we went down and took our places, every one. And he took bread and meat in his hands and ate as he stood, his horse gently grazing beside him, looking steadily towards the north.

The tips of the lances and the banners rose out of the crest, the mailed heads after them, all cased up in steel, then the steel-plated heads of the horses, and the turf vibrated and the earth beneath it shook with hooves. The line of horsemen spread and folded in upon us, a hand closing. Earl Simon wheeled his own knights into a fan, and all those braced spear-heads went down, levelling as one. And then there was a great shout, and they were upon us.

What can be said about that battle, so unequal and so brief? They came rank after rank out of the ground, growing from the grass like seams of corn. I suppose now that they were not so many as they seemed, yet they outnumbered us twice over, and they could come, and recoil, and come again, and we could but stand, or fall where we stood. Yet I remember clearly that Edward was the spear-head of the first shock, he was the thrust of the lance, and time and again he sprang back only to recover like the gathering wind and sweep forward again. Whatever any man may deny to Edward, I have seen his appalling gallantry, fitter to kill than to spare, more ardent to kill than to live. Nor did his hate run away with him, this time. No, it carried him, like a destrier not subject to wounds or death. He made a method of his hate, for now not only his heart and blood, but also his mind and spirit were in it. And I saw, and I testify, that at the third onset he detached the heaviest-armed of his knights, and hurled them at the vulnerable point where our lancers and archers met, with all their weight fresh and vengeful, and orders to scatter and kill.

That charge, avoiding the earl's mounted men, shattered the Welsh foot, driving in where their spears were not braced, and crumpling them rank by rank, thrusting the long shafts aside and trampling the men. What could they do but break? The archers who gave them their only cover were ridden down, though they took some toll before they fell. The spear-men broke, left without weapons. They were used to fluid hill-fighting, thrust and run, double and strike again, with tree and bush to harbour them. Instead, they were exposed in open ground, ridden down and ridden over, rolled up like soiled rushes, swept aside before the storm-wind. They broke and ran, what else could they do? They scattered like hares over that heath and turf, plunged for shelter into cornfields and gardens, that barely covered them and sheltered them not at all.

But Edward had learned since Lewes. He detached but a minor part of his strength to pursue, the rest he concentrated about our tightening circle, and bit with all his teeth to devour us.

The half our beasts were crippled or dead, more than half our mounted knights left to the sword or mace, having broken their only lances. Those whose horses still could carry them kept a thin outer circle about the centre where the king was, huddled, dazed and shrinking while the fight raged round him. Those barons and knights and other troopers now bereft of horses drew close into an inner circle, and held off the second charge, and the third, with the sword, and the archers who still lived picked off without mercy the mounts of the attackers to bring them down within hand-grip. It was less a battle than a massacre. We had known from the beginning that no retreat was possible. Neither was surrender. Therefore the only end there could be was when all of us were dead, disabled or prisoner, or, for the last few of us, fled the field when everything else was lost. I marvel it took them as long as it did, our broken foot soldiers being scattered and slain, to make an end with the rest of us.

They had remounts, and used them. They had reserves of lances and arrows, and made good, leisurely use of those too, until we were stripped of all but our swords and daggers, and stood among the ramparts of our own dead. And still Edward struck, and circled, and struck again, with fury but without haste, and dimly it came to me, as I wheeled still to face the next thrust, that I should know the arms of the knight who kept so lightly and

300

fiercely at Edward's left flank wherever he turned, and matched his movements like a twin brother. Quartered red and gold, the shield flickered before me here and there, a wandering sun, and was never still, until suddenly they drew off again to look for our weakest place in the circle, and for a moment my eyes were clear of sweat, and I saw on the red and gold the counter-coloured lions of Gwynedd. Then I knew the easy seat and the graceful carriage, though doubtless the harness he wore he had by Edward's grace and favour. Thus for the first time after two years I saw my breast-brother again closer than across the meadows of the Dee.

But that was near the end, and he did not see me, or if he did see me I was so streaked with sweat and dust and blood that he did not know me. Not then. The deaths of so many had levelled us all, man-at-arms and clerk and squire and earl all drew brotherly into the circle and kept one another's flanks faithfully as long as they could stand. Humphrey de Bohun the younger, the only great marcher lord who fought on the earl's side in that battle, went down wounded at my side. Peter de Montfort of Beaudesert, faithful from first to last without wavering, died trampled and hacked under Edward's final charge. So did Hugh le Despenser and Ralph Basset his kinsman, who had both refused to escape the slaughter and live for a better day.

We were then but the sparse remnants of the circle, drawing in ever closer, and in that last charge they rode us down and crashed into the centre. I was shouldered from my feet and flung some yards aside by the great war-horse of one of Gloucester's knights, and escaped hooves and swords to be stunned against the ground. When I got my wits again and heaved myself up to my knees there was a swaying tangle of men, mounted and afoot, where our ring had been, and I hung winded and dazed at the rim of chaos, witness to the ending I could not prevent.

301

I saw the blow, but do not know who struck it, that sheered deep into Earl Simon's shoulder and neck, and sent him reeling back with blood drenching his left side. I heard young Henry shriek as his father fell, and saw him leap to intercept the following blow, with only a broken sword in his left hand, and his right arm dangling helpless, and saw the axe-stroke that split his skull and flung him dead over the earl's body. And Guy, the third of those brothers, lying wounded almost within touch of them, vainly stretched out a hand towards his father's empty sword-hand, that lay open and still in the dappled turf.

And I saw, and still I see when the winter is harsh and the night dark and all men show as evil, how two or three of the knights of Edward's army lighted down like eager hunters from their saddles, and reaved off Earl Simon's helmet, stripping the torn mail from his neck, that was already half-severed, and hewing off with random, butcher's strokes that noble head that had conceived, and served, and almost achieved, a vision of order, justice and accord fit for a better world than this.

Then I could look no more, for everything was over.

I got to my feet, leaving my sword where it lay, and turning my back upon that dolorous sight walked aimlessly away, across the field littered with bodies and arms and cast harness and crippled men. And it was due only to the king that I ever left that field alive. There were some of Edward's men still coursing at large about the fringes of the fight, hunting down fugitives, and one of them might well have dealt with me, but suddenly all their attention was drawn inward to the swaying mass of men I had left behind, for King Henry, buffeted and ridden down unrecognised among the rest, shrieked aloud in terror of his life that he was their king, and no enemy. And someone – they say it was that same Roger Leyburn who led the young men of the marches when they called Earl Simon home – was quick enough to understand and believe, and haled him grazed and frightened out of the press.

Those who had heard rallied eagerly to him. No one had any eyes for me, straying like a sleep-walker between the corpses. And it chanced that the horse of one of those who had leaped down in such haste to the kill was also straying, unhurt, to where there was clean grass to crop. I slid a hand down to gather the rein, and at the touch life leaped again in me like a stopped fountain, and I remembered I still had a lord, and had even a vow on my heart to carry this fatal field back to him, for better or worse to share with him all that burden I had come by at Evesham.

A fine, fresh horse it was, and from the corner of my eye I saw the fringes of thick woodland away to the north, where the Welsh lancers, such of them as survived to get so far, might well have gone to ground. I set my toe in the stirrup and mounted, and crouching low on his neck, drove my heels into his sleek sides and sent him away at a gallop towards the trees. And if any of the many cries that filled the air behind me was an alarm after my flight, it was lost among all the rest, for no man followed me. So I fled from that lamentable place.

All that night they hunted us, and I did not keep that fine horse, for the roads were watched, where I could have made use of him, and in the forest north of Evesham, where I was forced to go to cover, he was only a means of betrayal to me. I turned him loose at the edge of the wood where no one was in sight, and sent him off with a slash of a branch behind, to be picked up as a stray from the battlefield. And I took to the deep thickets, and put a stream between me and pursuit, in case they brought hounds after us, and there lay up until night, when I trusted the hunt would slacken. For

Edward had his king to care for, and urgent matters enough to occupy his mind, and all those he most hated were already dead or captive, all the de Montfort race, all but the children with their mother in Dover, and young Simon agonising with dread and self-blame in Kenilworth, as yet unaware of his bereavement.

There were others of my own race there cowering in the bushes. The first I stumbled on drew a knife on me, and knowing him for what he was I spoke him quickly in Welsh, and he thanked God for me, and put up his weapon. Before nightfall we were seven living men who had thought to be dead. And to make but a short tale of this sorry escape, the hunt we had dreaded reached our station about dusk. We heard hooves on the narrow ride apart from us, and voices high and confident in victory, and the threshing of bushes. We were crouched in thick growth, and lay still as stones, but even so one of those riders checked, and pricked his ears and turned aside towards us. I never traced the moment when he dismounted and slid forward afoot, so lightly and silently he stepped, until a hand thrust through the branches and parted them right before my face, and a face looked down at me between the leaves.

Tall and straight and arrogant he stood, staring down into my face with eyes wide-open and light blue as harebells, fringed with lashes as black as his uncovered hair, for he went unhelmed and light-armed to this cleansing work. Even in the dusk the blue of those eyes shone. He knew me, and I knew him. I got up from my hiding-place and stood fronting him, and I knew he had a drawn sword in his right hand while the left hand held the bushes apart between us.

He never said word to me then, neither smiled nor frowned. His face was as still as marble, and as mute. Only when someone called to him from the ride did he utter a word. He turned his head, and cried back through the trees: 'No, nothing! Go forward, I'm coming!'

He had ears as quick as the fox in the covert, he knew there were more of us, though not, perhaps, how many. He held the screen apart between us a moment more, and as his hand was withdrawn I think the pure, motionless stone of his face shook with the wryest of smiles, before it drew back and vanished.

'Go safely, and give thanks to God!' said David, low-voiced, and was gone like a shadow, the forest hardly quivering after his passage.

CHAPTER XIII

It took us four days to get back into Wales, moving only at night, and we were twenty souls in company by the time we swam the Severn below Stoke, for we dared not go near Kempsey, knowing Bishop Walter must suffer by what had already passed, and could not and must not afford us any comfort now. Nevertheless, we came safely to Presteigne at last, and thence to Knighton. Some wounded we had, but them we sustained in the water between us when we were forced to swim, and nursed among us as we went on land. And often I thought how the news of Evesham must have gone before me, and pierced Llewelyn to the heart, and I not there to perform the duty that was mine. And yet I was bringing him twenty good men back for the price of my delay, and I could not but think that my debts were fairly paid.

As for thinking of what I had left behind me, or of what I had to tell, I thought not at all. I could not. Everything I had seen, and suffered, and done, was live within me, and I so full of it there was no room for thought. I lived and acted, and that was all.

Until I came at last into Llewelyn's presence in the hospice at the abbey of Cwm Hir, and saw his face, that was as ravaged as my own, and his eyes, haunted by what he had seen only within, in the anguish of his own heart, but I in the open light of day. Then indeed I thought on what was done and could not be undone, for the bare fact of it he knew, but it might well be that there was something within my knowledge apt to his need, and not yet known to him.

306

'I know,' he said heavily. 'They are dead, father and son both, dead and violated. All this land knows it. The heart is gone out of all those who followed and believed in him. It is over. And I let them go to their doom. without me! I believed in him as in the Host, but for my own cause I denied his. And now I have destroyed by that denial, since justice there must be, both his cause and mine.'

I had never heard him speak so, or seen that look in his face before, as though he had seen the finger of God write his own doom fiery and plain across the bloody field of Evesham. I said: 'God forbid!' and shook like a sick man, for the end of one dream I had seen, and that was bitter enough.

'God forbids,' said Llewelyn, 'that a man should hold his hand and forbear to commit his heart where he believes right and truth to be. How if God offered me that chance as a test, and I have failed it? Had I thrown in all my weight with his, I might have won both his battle and mine. Now it is but just if mine proves to be lost with his.'

All this he said with a fatal calm that chilled me, so far was it from any mood I had ever known in him. And strongly I set myself to compel him out of this darkness, all the more because there was some ground for it, for everything Wales had stood to gain by Earl Simon's friendship and recognition was indeed lost, or to win again. However tamely King Henry had set his seal to the treaty of Pipton, I had no faith in his will to honour his bond now that it was in his power to repudiate it. Yet Llewelyn's justification, if he needed any, was that Earl Simon had been the first to approve him, and so I said.

'Even had you been there with all your host to aid him, you could not have saved him. That was no battle for your people and mine, they could not sustain it. Even for him it was the wrong battle. The time when he lost his fight was when he failed to storm through Gloucester into England as soon as he heard that Edward was gone. He knew it himself when it was too late. Of two visions one may yet be saved. Do you think he would not urge you to the work?'

To that, as yet, he would answer nothing, but he asked me to tell him every detail of what had passed, and so I did, the whole sorrowful history from the moment we left him on the Hereford road. That narration took a great while, and the room darkened about us before it was done. Even so Llewelyn covered his face.

Afterwards he said not a word, at first, of what he had heard, or what he had learned from it, but only asked me to go with him to hear mass in the abbey church, and after it to watch with him for a while, which I did gladly, for there was that working in him that comforted me for his soul and mine. Together we two watched out the greater part of that night, and the grief we shared became a living fire in place of a hellish darkness.

When he came forth his face was clear, pale and bright. Under the stars he said to me: 'Well I know his enemies made use of his dealings with me as a reproach to him, that he gave away England's rights for his own ends, though I asked of him nothing, and he gave nothing, that was not Welsh by right, and lost to England only by force. The guilt I bear in holding back from going with him, when my heart and will desired to go, I cannot measure. That God must do. But if they think to have put him away out of reckoning and out of mind by dismembering his body and befouling his memory, they have everything yet to learn. Others will take up his visions after him, and bring them to veritable birth in England. But I know of two things I can do here to honour him, and those I have sworn to do. I will wrest from King Henry at liberty everything he granted to me under duress. And I will make

Earl Simon's daughter princess of Wales.'

The heart and spirit of the reform was broken after
Evesham, as well it might be. Castles were surrendered,
towns sued to come to the king's peace. Weary and sick
and seeing now no man to lead them, even young Simon
and the garrison in Kenilworth listened to the first
proffers made them, and were ready to deal. But though
at first there were hopeful signs for conciliation and
moderation, that soon changed.

It was Edward who sent out the first call to all loyal
prelates and barons to attend at Winchester in the first
week of September, and issued orders to the sheriffs to
maintain law, so that no man should despoil his neighbour under the pretext of loyal indignation, ordinances
worthy almost of Earl Simon himself. For the king was
so low, wounded and weary and dazed, that he was
carried away to Gloucester, and thence to Marlborough,
to recover from his ills. And only when the gathering
at Winchester convinced him that he was again royal,
and had real power in his hands, did he begin to feel
his own man. Had he continued abased and frightened
a little longer, things might have gone more wisely in
England. For when Henry was no longer afraid, he would
take vengeance on all those who had frightened him,
as a braver and stronger man need not have done.

But to us, watching from Wales, the first important
act that followed Edward's victory was his prompt march
to Chester. Llewelyn smiled sourly at that, and went
quietly to Mold to keep a watch on events. But at least it
proved that Edward considered us still to be reckoned
with, and was in haste to secure his city and county again
on our borders, and put his own men back into the seats
of power there. At Beeston castle, in mid-August, Luke
Tany surrendered Chester to him, and relinquished his
office to a new justiciar, James Audley. It was the reversal
of the scene we had witnessed less than a year before,

in the meadows by the Dee, and as we heard from our ageing friend the garrison horse-doctor, who kept his place through all reversals, David was close at Edward's side when he entered the city, and known to be in the highest favour and intimacy with him.

'I hear he did well at Evesham,' said Llewelyn bitterly. 'And got his pay for it! The king rewarded him with all the lands forfeited by some poor wretch called Boteler. Well, I never doubted his gallantry. And at least he has preserved some kindness for you.'

'Even for Wales,' I said, 'seeing he knew very well there were more of us, and all Welsh. "Go safely," he said, "and give thanks to God!" And a grain of thanks I gave heartily to him, also.'

'I have not forgotten,' said Llewelyn, and almost smiled. 'For that and other reasons, I grudge him to Edward. But this Edward himself – I see qualities in him that speak for David, too. To fight well and to think well is surely a promising beginning.'

In this I think he was right. For it was only at Winchester, where King Henry began to rule again, that the tone of the victors changed, and in place of conciliation there was nothing better than vengeance and spite, and hatred had its way. For there were too many others of smaller quality, like the king, who had felt themselves humiliated and disprized, and yearned to climb back into their own esteem by debasing those who had outmatched them. So tragedy was compounded for two years to come, and a great opportunity lost.

Young Simon in Kenilworth received letters of safe-conduct to go to Winchester, as speaker for all his garrison, and he went with a fair hope, for Edward's first approaches had been generous and large-minded. But at Winchester hatred prevailed, and the terms presented to him were such as he could not tolerate. So he returned unreconciled to his father's castle, and prepared it for a long siege, and so held it in defiance. And I think he

310

achieved his full growth only then, when he was left to uphold that lost cause without hope, but still with dignity.

At Winchester, too, it was concluded, and I do not quarrel with that conclusion, that whatever deeds, acts, grants, charters and other documents King Henry had enacted since Lewes, when he fell captive into Earl Simon's hands, were enacted under duress, and thereby invalid, and all were repudiated. So passed among the rest, as we had foreseen, the treaty made at Pipton.

'More than that I lost at Evesham,' said Llewelyn. 'So be it! Better by far I should bring him to such an act voluntarily. And so I will!'

For us this was the most meaningful of the business at Winchester. Yet we could not be unmoved by the ordinance made on the seventeenth day of September, the triumph of the vengeful, by which all the lands and tenements of all the adherents of Earl Simon were seized into the king's hands. That was the only test, that the defaulter should be ally to the earl, and who was to be the local judge of that adherence? Every man who coveted could cast the accusation. No manner of pure principle was a defence, no clear uprightness of life. All those of one faction were damned, whatever their virtue and goodwill. There was raised at Winchester a great, ghostly company of the dispossessed, by this infamous act of disinherison that was opposed, vainly, by all the wise and humane men on the king's side, Edward, I think, among them. They were outnumbered five to one by men neither wise nor humane, bitter for their former losses, and insatiable for their possible gains.

'Well,' said Llewelyn with grim calm, 'they have Chester secured, their treaty and the royal seal dishonoured and discarded, my ally disposed of, and me, as they think, checked and subdued into caution. They think they can turn their backs on me and set about the despoiling of others. I have two ends to serve. Once before King Henry wrote me off his accounts as dead, and found me very much alive. It's time to remind him once again.'

Deliberately he called up the local muster to add to his own guard, enough for his purpose, and rode out from Mold towards Hawarden, that same way we had ridden a year ago to see Edward's garrison march away and give place to Earl Simon's men.

'Hawarden I was promised,' said Llewelyn, 'in his name, and if they deny it now to me, so will I deny it to them. Edward's garrison there threatens my valley.'

In one swift and unexpected assault we took that castle, drove out the household, such as were not worth keeping as prisoners, and stripped roofs and walls low enough to make it uninhabitable. It was done with economy and precision, and it was a hoisting of his standard on his border, as a warning that he had suffered no setback, and had a power that could stand of itself, without confederates.

When it was done, we drew back to Mold, and he called in a reserve force, expecting that some action must soon be taken against him. And in the month of October it came, a very strong army loosed against us from Chester under Hamo Lestrange and Maurice Fitz-Gerald, two marcher lords both experienced and able. But Llewelyn struck hard before they had reached the position they desired, or ordered their array to the best advantage, and broke and scattered them so completely that they fled back into Chester piecemeal, we chasing them to the very gates. They began to talk anxiously of truce with us, and though in the general confusion in England this came to nothing, what we had was as effective as truce, for wherever anything was attempted against us it was quenched at once and without difficulty or loss. So he taught England that Wales had lost no battles, nor been defeated in any wars.

London had submitted to the king before that time,

and been fined and penalised and plundered like a conquered city. Disputes and lawsuits over lands seized from the disinherited arose even among the victors, and in many parts of England companies of rebels betook themselves to lonely and difficult places like the eastern fens, and there held out month after month against the king's peace. Worst of all, there was a bitter division between those of the victors who were for mercy and moderation, and those who wanted to crush the defeated utterly and drive them into the wilderness. So the state of England in those days was worse than before Evesham, and though the old cause was hopelessly lost, its surviving adherents had still to put up a rearguard fight for their lives and livelihoods and lands, and some remnant of justice.

During those autumn days Llewelyn kept anxious watch in particular on the distant fortunes of those de Montforts who were left. For the Countess Eleanor, still fiercely loyal to her dead lord, held the castle of Dover, and her daughter was still there with her. Her two youngest sons she had succeeded in shipping away to France, fearing captivity for them if they should be taken. The third son, Guy, wounded at Evesham, lay sick and prisoner at Windsor, and young Simon still defied siege in Kenilworth, though later he slipped away out of that fortress, leaving it well manned and supplied, to join the gathering at Axholme, in the fens.

All this year through we had had no word from Cynan, for we had been nearer to events than he, and moreover, left behind among the minor household clerks in London, at such a time of malice and suspicion, he had been forced to look to his own life and observe absolute caution in his dealings. Now with the monarchy re-established he breathed again, however regretfully at least more easily, and finding a venerable and reliable messenger in a Franciscan of Llanfaes on his way home from pilgrimage to Rome, he sent us in September a full and enlightening account of what went forward in the south.

'They are waiting, it seems,' said Llewelyn, reporting Cynan's news in council, 'the arrival of the new cardinal-legate at Dover. There's no bar to his landing now, he'll be welcomed with open arms. God knows they have need of good and sane counsel to bring order out of the wicked chaos they have made. And this man, since he took over the mission, has at least hurled no more thunderbolts and curses across the sea.' For Cardinal Gui, who had been kept so long in holy wrath at Boulogne, had been called away some months since to become pope under the name of Clement, the fourth so styled, and in his place a new man was appointed, of whom at that time we knew nothing. 'The exiles are on their way home, the queen is expected to make the crossing in the legate's company, and soon. A Genoese, a lawyer, and of good repute,' said Llewelyn, pondering Cynan's usually acute judgment with interest, 'and he comes with wide authority, to preach the crusade, to make peace and reconcile enemies and assuage grudges in all the land of England. And why not in Wales, too? I will gladly use any man of goodwill, and be thankful for him.'

In this manner we first heard of the approach of Cardinal Ottobuono Fieschi, who did indeed enter England with goodwill, and with very good sense, too, as we later found, though he had a hard struggle of it. Had the most implacable of the victors paid heed to him, England could have been pacified very quickly. But then he was no more than a name to us.

'Cynan writes further,' Llewelyn said, 'that Edward has left the king resting at Canterbury, and is setting out for Dover himself, not only to meet his mother when she lands, but to try if he can get possession of the castle from Countess Eleanor, first. By persuasion!' But he made a wry face over that word, for something we had seen of Edward's persuasion.

'She is his father's sister,' said Goronwy sensibly. 'He cannot for his good name offer her any offence. But he will not need to. What can she do but make her peace? There is nothing left to defend.'

He spoke truth, there was nothing, except a memory and an ideal, and the integrity of her love. Yet I know that Llewelyn feared for her, and waited in great uneasiness for the next news of her forlorn and solitary stand. There was no possibility as yet of making any approach to her on his own behalf, her situation was so piteous and so difficult that even if there had been a means of sending to her, he would not have done so. She had lost a husband most deeply and passionately loved, and her firstborn son, and was separated from two more sons whose fate she could not aid. It was no time to send proffers to her for her daughter.

'She is very young,' said Llewelyn, steadily looking towards the south-east. 'As yet it could have been only a betrothal. And I can wait. Until her mother is free of this last burden, and has her remaining children back, or at least knows them safe and free. There will be a right time for it!'

So he waited with patience. And in the early days of November Cynan sent another letter. I was at work among the documents of a dry civil case at Mold, when he came into the room with the parchment unsealed in his hand. His face was bleak and still, but his eyes were wide, far-looking and calm. The wound he had received was sharp enough, but short of mortal, because he would not acknowledge it. The first thing he said to me was simply: 'I have lost her!'

I looked up at him in some doubt and wonder, for he had not the look of one admitting loss.

'I have lost her – for a while,' he said. 'Edward is in Dover castle, and the Countess Eleanor is out of it. The prisoners she held there broke out and captured the keep against her, but even if they had not, what could she have done? If she had fought, it would have been the worse for her and for others. And for whom should she hold it, now Earl Simon is dead? Edward has received her into grace, but all she has asked of him is that the gentlemen of her household shall be maintained in all that is theirs, and not held felon for their loyalty, and that he grants. She has accepted his peace, and undertaken to withdraw herself from all activity against him and against the crown and government of England. I doubt if she can love, but she will not oppose him. Poor lady, what is the world, and justice, and the well-being of the realm of England to her, now Simon is gone?'

'It is safely over, then,' I said. 'You would not have had her resist?'

'No, God knows! I dreaded she might,' he said.

Yet I saw that it was she who had dealt him the blow that was twisting his heart so sorely at that very moment, while he kept his will and his countenance. This pain was not all for her. And in truth, deprived though she now was of all her rights, since the king had already bestowed the earldom of Leicester upon his second son, Edmund, and though she stood bereaved of husband and son, solitary in her grief, yet I thought her rich and exalted above all her sisters. Better Earl Simon, dead and abused, the king's felon and the pope's pestilence, the people's hero and the poor men's saint, than all the living and vengeful lords that served in King Henry's retinue and enjoyed his favour.

I said, I doubt not with some taint of blasphemy: '"Blessed art thou among women..."', and Llewelyn said: 'Truly! But the greater the blessing withdrawn, the deeper is the desolation left behind. She knows little of me, and nothing of this betrothal. He never saw her again. My bride is only a child. I cannot touch or trouble either the one or the other in their sorrow.'

I said that the lady might be glad, for what future

was there now for her daughter? And he laughed, rather
ruefully than bitterly.

'Glad? She, whose whole peace now depends on the
sanction of brother and nephew? She, who wants nothing
but to turn her back on the world as it is, and remember
it in secret only as *he* wanted it? No, she will never be
glad of me. But in time – in time, God knows, not now!
– she may learn to bear with me. When I am no longer
a reminder to Edward of an old alliance that cost him
dear, and a marriage with me ceases to be the imagined
threat of a new alliance as perilous as the old. No, I
can wait! The time will come when she will forget, and
he will cease to suspect and fear. But not yet. Even if
I could reach her now,' he said in a soft and grievous
cry, 'and I cannot!'

I asked him in dread: 'What has she done?'

'She has shaken off the dust of England for a witness
against them,' said Llewelyn, 'and set sail for France
with her daughter, one day before the Queen landed with
Cardinal Ottobuono at Dover. They say she did not
want to see her brother's detestable wife, and has said
she will never set foot in these islands again. She is gone
to Earl Simon's sister at the convent of Montargis, and
has taken the other Eleanor – *my* Eleanor! – with her!'

When he had thought long, and come to terms with
his situation, he said: 'I have two vows in my heart,
both debts due to his memory, and if I cannot yet do
anything about one of them, let's see how quickly the
other may be brought to fruit. One thing at a time!'
And he turned his every waking thought to the re-estab-
lishment of the settlement he had briefly enjoyed after
Pipton, absolutely resolved to compel the recognition of
the unity and sanctity of Wales.

Cardinal Ottobuono came to London and set up his
office there without delay. On the first day of December
he held a clerical council to declare his mission and

317

display his authorities, and to receive oaths of obedience from bishops and abbots, though four of the most saintly bishops of the realm were soon suspended by reason of their devotion to Earl Simon's cause, and so would Bishop Walter of Worcester have been, but that he died, old and tired as he was, before his case ever came to be examined. Howbeit, it did appear that the legate truly intended generosity and mercy, and desired to ensure that justice should not be defiled by malice and self-interest. Llewelyn, encouraged, called his council and proposed, with their approval, to present the Welsh case and his desire for an amicable settlement, without waiting to be invited to do so, the cardinal's brief being all-embracing.

'He'll be beset with petitioners clamouring for their own ends,' he said disdainfully, 'and we'll not press him, but at least we'll let him know that we are here, with both offers and claims to make, civilly waiting for his attention when the time serves.' All which the council heartily endorsed. So he wrote requesting letters of safe-conduct, that envoys from Wales might come to pay his respects, and in the middle of December they were granted.

'If I am to seek a friend at court,' he said, 'it shall be the highest.' And he chose the best and wisest of his lawyers and clerics to go as envoys. Before Christmas they came back to report a very willing hearing, and a degree of interest and sympathy, though the legate's preoccupations at that time were naturally with the most pressing distresses in state and church. 'The more pleasure it must be to him,' said Llewelyn hopefully, 'to hear of one petitioner who has learned how to wait, and who desires peace on present terms, and not the slaughter and ruin of all his enemies. And he shall not forget us, we'll make sure of that!'

In this same month of December young Simon and his company in the fens at last submitted to Edward, who had them securely penned there at a disadvantage, and who, to do him justice, promised, and this time kept his promise, that if they placed themselves in the king's grace they should have no fear for life, limb or liberty. Lands they might and did lose, and they had to find sureties for their submission, and await the king's pleasure, but they fared better than many others later, who still held out in forests and hills.

Having done all that could be done at this time, Llewelyn turned homeward to Aber for the Christmas feast, according to custom, feeling secure enough to remove his forces from the border for the first time in many months. Since my return from Evesham I had scarcely been twenty miles into Wales. Now at last I came at his side along the coast road once more, and under the mountains, gazing across Lavan sands at the shore of Anglesey, with a sprinkling of snow over the salt marshes, and the gulls wheeling and screaming above the tide.

It seemed to me then that I had been away from this place far longer than a year, and had travelled an infinite distance across the world to make my way back to it again. It was even strange to me, like a country seen in a dream, for the soft, rich green and soiled and sorry red of the vale of Evesham filled all the landscape of my mind. I had almost forgotten the faces of people here, and the very echoes were unfamiliar to me. I came as a stranger.

We rode into the gateway of the maenol, and out of every doorway the household came running to welcome us. And the first person I saw, crossing from the mews to the hall with her arms full of fir-branches, and a hood drawn over her black, silken hair, was Cristin.

I was speaking to Llewelyn at that moment, and I broke off mute and stricken in the midst of a word. I know I drew hard on the rein and my horse baulked in offence, marking the break. I had thought she was in Neigwl, safe, distant, delivered from my shadow and delivering me from hers, while I died a little with Earl Simon, and grew a little English in desperate, perverse tribute to him. Last Christmas she had not been here either to trouble or fulfil me. I had not seen her for two whole years. For many months I had not thought of her consciously, but only with my blood and bones, she being for ever part of me. The compact we had between us was for all time, and did not waver, but the sudden vision of her was more than my heart could bear of bliss and pain, I was not large enough to contain it. Face and voice failed me. And Llewelyn saw. I knew it then, though he never said a word until later. His mind, also, had ventured into far places among alien people, he was shaken as I was, and he saw with newly-opened eyes.

She was then approaching thirty years of age, but time was of no moment, except that she grew finer, more purely-drawn and to me more beautiful with every year, the whiteness of her skin like sunlit snow under the raven hair, and her eyes iris-grey and clear as light at dawn. So contained and perfect she was within her body, the soul was visible within. Wherever else I had been, whatever else I had done and seen and known, whoever else I had loved after my fashion, for love is an enlargement of the being and lets in other loves, there was no end nor limitation to the love I felt for her. When we were together, brushing arms about our work like other men, I could deal with it and be at peace, but when I saw her newly after so long, and without warning, I doubt it burned in me like a lantern, blinding all those who saw, or all who had eyes to see.

She looked at us and she stayed, her long mouth curling like a bent bow, and her eyes widening and glowing darkly purple. At me she looked, and it was a renewal of vows, and the strong curve of her lips became a smile to be remembered long. Then she went on where she was going, into the hall.

I awoke, and Llewelyn's eyes were on me, waiting courteously and patiently. He had reined in to keep pace with me. I said: 'I did not know she was here. I thought she was still in Neigwl.'

'Last spring,' said Llewelyn, 'after you were away from us, I sent a new castellan to Neigwl, the old man being ill and needing to give over such a charge. The new man had a wife. And Godred being now in my household force here, I thought well to send him to bring his wife to Aber.' So he said, and his voice was level and low and mild, forbearing from wonder or question.

I had not seen Godred, either, since returning from Evesham. Until then I had not remembered him. A strange year, maker or breaker, that had been to me. I said: 'That was right. I am glad to see Cristin here.' And I shook my rein and went forward into the court-yard, and there dismounted, he close beside me.

So we came home to Aber with all our gains and losses, to keep Christmas of the year of our Lord twelve hundred and sixty-five, the year of Evesham.

From the moment I saw her in hall among the household, with Godred at her side, it was as it had been with us beforetime, as close, as calm, as sure, as when we made our compact. We met and spoke each other and passed, with every look and every near approach uplifted and sustained, and the manner of our exchanges when we were alone was not different from the manner of them when Godred was at her elbow. The first speech she had with me was when she entered the hall, the night of our arrival, on Godred's arm, and gave me her hand with open and fearless warmth and bade me welcome from the heart, saying she had prayed for me all the days of my absence. Before all, and proudly and simply, she said it, so that he had not even the twisted satisfaction of conceiving that she feigned reserve and indifference. And when I met her alone in the store-

321

room, folding away newly-mended hangings, she met me
with pleasure and serenity, speaking only of the day's
work and the season's festivities, with never one word
he could not have heard, had he been crouching behind
the door again to listen, as perhaps he was. Not one
step towards me nor one step away did she swerve from
her path to gratify Godred's perverse longings.

But I think after that Christmas-time there were two
who watched us, instead of one, with motives and
missions as far apart as darkness and light.

All the following year the struggle in England continued, for all Cardinal Ottobuono's patient mediations,
as nest after nest of rebels was painfully smoked out of
forest and fen, and brought to submission. Young Simon
was ordered to leave England, and swear never again to
take action against the king or his realm, and Edward
took him in custody to London to prepare for his departure. But he was warned secretly that he could not trust
his captors, and his life might be in danger before ever
he embarked. How much truth there was in this warning we cannot know, for no man then trusted his fellows,
and even if Edward's intent was honest enough, as for
my part I think likely, it was no wonder that those who
wished young Simon well were afraid for him.

Whatever the truth, he escaped from the Old Temple
and made his way safely to the coast, where the independent men of Winchelsea hid him until they could get
him away across the Channel in February. Not many
weeks later his younger brother Guy, recovered from
his wounds, also made good his escape and followed
Simon to France. Some people thought that the escapes
had been connived at, as the quickest means of ousting
from England the last sons of Earl Simon, but by the
alarm that followed I think this was not so. The narrow
seas were full of reiving galleys sympathetic to the rebels,
and now the fear of invasion was turned about, and

King Henry dreaded that the Montforts might raise an army and a fleet to return and fight the war all over again. A vain fear, surely! All that remained was a few forlorn camps of desperate men living wild through that winter and defying the crown. There was no possible hope of a recovery, there was no army, almost there was no cause.

Two men were chiefly responsible for the gradual betterment of this state of disorder, and those two were the cardinal-legate and the Lord Edward. Nor was Edward's part all the fighting and none of the pacification. He did indeed fight, and formidably, and while the fighting endured he was unrelenting. But when he had taken and broken the town of Winchelsea, the most obdurate of the Cinque ports, he did not pillage and burn in revenge, but very quickly turned to offering the merchants good, sensible terms, inviting them to a new age of well-ordered and peaceful trade, and restoring them freely to royal favour and all their privileges. He did so, doubtless, because they were strong and could be either valuable or dangerous to him, and many of his conquered opponents who had not the same power behind them found short shrift and ended on trees. Nevertheless, he showed very shrewd sense, and the ability to rein in his grudges where that was good policy, as King Henry could seldom do.

But it may be that even the better part of Edward's wisdom came from Cardinal Ottobuono, who did truly endeavour for peace, mercy and forgiveness. So when the final siege of Kenilworth was planned in the summer, the legate still tirelessly haunted both parties and battled for a better ending. And in the meantime, there being a limit to one man's energy, ingenuity and time, our affairs in Wales had to wait.

What we chiefly noticed from our side the border was the growing rift between Earl Gilbert de Clare of Gloucester and Roger Mortimer. For Gloucester, though he had been the instrument of Earl Simon's fall, nevertheless was heart and soul for conciliation, and did his best to save his old associates from disinherison and utter ruin, while Mortimer, who had been absolute against the Provisions from the beginning, desired the ultimate in vengeance, and encouraged King Henry in his obduracy against all concessions. I think it was as a result of this enmity between neighbours that Mortimer took the step he did in May of that year, meaning to strengthen his own influence, to keep alive the king's resentment, and to remind him that Wales was held to be a continuing danger. For in the middle of the month he suddenly gathered all his men and made a determined drive into Brecon, intending to occupy those lands in the teeth of Llewelyn's lordship.

That was the only time we had to take action all that year. Rhys Fychan moved east from Dynevor to meet the attack, and we drove south through Builth, and between us Mortimer was crushed as in a closing fist, barely escaping with his life back to Wigmore, and leaving behind the greater part of his forces dead or prisoner.

'He chose his time badly,' said Llewelyn grimly. 'I might have been content to drive him off, if I had not to maintain before the legate a position I desire him to recognise. He shall be in no doubt whether I am the master of Wales, or whether I deserve the title to add to the reality. Also,' he said, 'I might have spared him if he had not been among the chief of those who dug Earl Simon's grave. If this display was for King Henry's benefit, I hope he draws the right lesson.'

Then we were again no more than spectators to the turmoil and tragedy of England, for no man raised a hand against us more. The long siege of Kenilworth began that June, and was not ended until December, and even then the castle was never taken. Doubtless the garrison at first believed, as much of England believed, that the earl's sons might yet return with an army from

France, but even when that dream was over they did not give in. And all that time, untiring, the cardinal-legate plied between all the parties, procured that parliament convened at Kenilworth, recruited to him all the moderate opinion and goodwill he could find in barons, officials and churchmen, and at last, against long resistance from the king, hammered out a form of settlement by which all who came to the king's grace within forty days should have pardon and indulgence, and those already dispossessed should be able to redeem their lost lands at a fee. Though this form was not all that the legate had hoped for, it was a great gain over anything offered before, and it put an end to retrospective revenges, and made a new beginning possible. Nevertheless, the garrison in Kenilworth fought on until the middle of December, when they gave up hope of aid from abroad, and at last surrendered on these terms. Sick, starving, ragged they marched out of Earl Simon's castle, and on their given word were allowed to depart to their own homes, with their pride and faith unbroken, as a last offering to the earl's memory.

But in the isle of Ely in the fens the rebels still held out, and it seemed that this last bitter sore was to be left festering, perhaps to start a rot within the whole body of the realm, if the earl of Gloucester had not gone beyond exasperation into action. He resolved to go to London in arms, and stop this long persecution, preventing the worst and most violent of the king's advisers from having their way with England. And shrewdly he made known his design to Llewelyn, and asked and received assurance of quiet on his borders while he went to work, and goodwill from beyond the march.

'God forbid,' said Llewelyn, 'that with such a task in hand he should have to look over his shoulder. But who would have thought,' he said, marvelling, 'that the same man who loosed Edward and won the war for the king

325

should now be the man who may save what remains of the reform?'

In the event it worked out not quite as we had supposed, or Earl Gilbert, perhaps, intended. He established himself in London, and some of the rebels from Ely joined him there, while the city itself rose hopefully to him, and again created that commune of London which had so strongly supported Earl Simon. For two months the capital city was a rebel camp, and perhaps that very outburst recalled all the forces in England to their senses, and made them aware with what dangerous fire they played. So in the end it served well enough, for king, prince, officials and rebels all were drawn together under the legate's guidance, and forced to come to terms at last.

Gloucester had come near to being himself a rebel again, yet it was he who put an end to the long-drawn struggle, by showing what was the only alternative, a new war. So he came home unscathed and in due fealty to the king, however suspiciously Edward looked sidewise at him from under his drooping eyelid. And he brought about the final accord that made life supportable and justice at least a possibility in the realm.

'They have been long enough about the affairs of England,' said Llewelyn, drawing satisfied breath, 'now let's see if they are ready to turn to the affairs of Wales.'

Courteously and dutifully he wrote to Cardinal Ottobuono, to remind him that we also waited patiently for his attentions, when he should be free to bestow them, and that we desired, as we always had, a just and lasting treaty of peace with England. His messengers brought back a very favourable and even grateful reply, promising early consideration of the request. King Henry also responded agreeably, declaring himself no less anxious than Llewelyn to have a settled peace. And this was the fruit of the prince's policy of confining his rule and his ambitions to Wales itself, and refraining from exploiting the wounds and dissents of England as otherwise he might have done.

'Perhaps,' he said, when I said so. But his eyes looked far and the shadow of Evesham gathered over them. 'How do I know,' he said, 'how can I ever know, that we could not have won both our battles, if I had had more faith? To the day of my death I shall be in doubt. Only in the judgment shall I come to know the degree of my offence, and whether God sees it through Earl Simon's eyes or mine.'

So I said no more then, for he was resolute in his self-blame, but the more determined to press home to a triumph the cause for which he had sinned, if sin it was. And the day of that triumph was near.

At the end of the month of August King Henry came in great state to the town of Shrewsbury, with Cardinal Ottobuono, the Lord Edward, Henry of Almain, and all the servants and officials of his court, and sent safe-conducts into Wales for Llewelyn's envoys to come there into conference. Llewelyn sent two very experienced men, Einion ap Caradoc and David ap Einion, and since the season was again summer, the golden end of the summer when the evenings draw in but the days are radiant, he took his court into camp in the green valley of Severn in its upper reaches, close to Strata Marcella, and himself lodged in the abbey. And there we stayed through the greater part of September, while messages went to and fro busily, and sometimes we fished, and sometimes we rode, our bodies at leisure and our minds at rest, for time was nothing to us. We had a position that could not be shifted, and we could afford to wait King Henry's yielding, for he needed that peace more than we did. Nor did we wish him any ill. Llewelyn wanted no more than his own.

The couriers who rode back and forth between Strata Marcella and the town of Shrewsbury, where the king was lodged at the Benedictine abbey outside the walls, brought us the current news as well as the quibbles and counters of argument requiring answer.

'My lord,' they let Llewelyn know, early in September, when the lawyers had barely fleshed their pens, 'your brother, the Lord David, is there in the abbey in the Lord Edward's own retinue. And very well found and attended, and with the prince's arm about his neck as often as not.'

'A passing heavy torque that must be,' said Llewelyn, and grimaced. 'Still, I thank you for the warning!'

The conference continued through three weeks of September, while the original proposals from both sides were rejected, amended, amended again, declined again and again rephrased, in the fashion to be expected of so large an enterprise. By that time each side knew what the other would and would not stomach, and the ground between was open to manoeuvre. That was the point when King Henry, never tenacious when it came to fine detail, turned over the whole negotiation to Cardinal Ottobuono.

Then it lasted but four days.

On the twenty-fourth day of September the envoys came with the last draft of the terms. Many items had been agreed already, but a few had been disputed, and some stipulations were only now put forward, though they had clearly been held in reserve until agreement was near.

'King Henry makes one exception,' said Einion ap Caradoc, 'in his willingness to cede to you the homages of all the Welsh princes. He insists on retaining for himself the direct fealty of Meredith ap Rhys Gryg of Dryslwyn.'

'Doubtless at Meredith's urgent entreaty,' said Llewelyn drily, for though the old bear of the vale of Towy had submitted to him after his defection, and kept out of trouble since, he had done as little as he could to aid

and support his overlord, and absented himself and his
forces from all our recent activities, and it was no secret
that he had still not forgiven the reinstatement of his
nephew Rhys Fychan, or the prompt punishment of his
own treason. 'I said when he came to my peace that he
loved me no better than before, and had not changed his
mind. This is his first opportunity to slide out of my
grasp.' And he thought it over, but briefly, and shrugged
the item by. 'It is not worth rejecting the whole for the
sake of one Meredith. Let the king keep him, since that
is what he wants. But let there be a clause permitting the
cession of his homage to me hereafter, if King Henry
should ever be so reconciled and reassured as to want to
part with it. I would have him if I could, I admit it. A
pity to spoil the whole.'

'The king would certainly insist on a further payment
for it, in that case,' said Einion, having now had considerable dealings with King Henry.

'He shall have it, if the day ever comes. And let's set
it high enough to tempt him,' said Llewelyn, 'since his
coffers are empty. I would pay five thousand marks for
the homage of Meredith ap Rhys Gryg.'

So that, too, was written into the draft.

'There is another matter,' said Einion, 'which has lain
somewhat in the background until now, though I own I
have scented it waiting there, and I believe, my lord, so
have you. The king requires that suitable provision be
made for the Lord David. That you give him again all that
he held at the time when he departed from you, or, if
reasonable Welshmen now think that portion too small
for his needs, that it shall be added to. A committee of
Welsh princes, it is suggested, could decide on what is
fit for a prince, and your brother.'

I was watching Llewelyn's face as he heard this, and
certainly there was no surprise in it for him. He smiled a
little, and again was grave, remembering, I think, two
other brothers he had, both in close ward, as both had

offended against him, like David, though these two had no royal patron to take up their cause.

'This he owes to Edward,' he said with certainty.

'It is true, the Lord Edward shows him great favour,' said Einion, 'and he has already been given lands in England. What is better worth thinking about, by this token it must be his own wish to return home.'

'In the teeth of my lordship and at my cost,' said Llewelyn, and laughed aloud without rancour. 'No suing for David! He makes his return, as of right and without penalty, the condition of my recognition. But he comes, if he comes at all, as my vassal. So be it! He surely does not think I will throw this peace away, after eleven years of pressing for it, simply to spite him? He rates himself too high! He has cost me somewhat, but he cannot cost me near so much as that.'

So that, too, was accepted without demur, even without regret. His hot hatred, if it had ever ranked so high, had cooled and vanished long ago. And the terms were written and agreed, and the whole sent back to Shrewsbury, where the next day king, prince and council also accepted it, and Cardinal Ottobuono breathed relief and joy, and blessed the settlement.

That same day King Henry sent back to Llewelyn letters of safe-conduct to come to Montgomery on the twenty-ninth of the month, to meet the king and do homage to him at the ford, to be entertained in the castle, and enter into his household as the greatest of his vassals and the closest of his fellow-princes. For though the treaty made him the king's liege man, yet his own principality he held as of independent sovereignty, with its own laws, customs and right entirely free and separate from those of England.

And these were the provisions made in that famous treaty: As to what Llewelyn gained, above all he gained the full recognition by England of his right and title as prince of Wales, to whom were ceded, for himself and his heirs after him, the homages and fealty of all the lesser princes excepting only Meredith ap Rhys Gryg. And of lands, he kept all of what he held, the four cantrefs of the Middle Country, Kerry, Cydewain, Builth, Gwerthrynion and Brecon, even Maelienydd so far as he could establish his present tenure of it, and also the castles of Whittington and Mold, though he agreed to release his prisoner Robert of Montalt, whom he had taken at Hawarden, and to restore that manor to him, but without the right to build a castle there for thirty years to come.

As to what he gave in return, there was the provision for David, his formal homage to King Henry as his accepted overlord, saving the rights of Wales, and a great indemnity to be paid in money, twenty-five thousand marks, though this was five thousand less than he had pledged at Pipton, the remaining five thousand being reserved to compensate for Meredith's homage should it later be granted to him. I doubt if King Henry had that sum, or anything near it, in his coffers at that time, and the treaty made very careful provision for the payment at certain dates of the amounts due, until all had been paid, for certainly in this bargain Llewelyn was helping to restore solvency in an England blighted and poverty-stricken from its long and bitter war.

For eleven years he had striven for this, fending off out-and-out war with truce after truce, paying what he promised, and, saving provocations from others and the occasional outburst of anger, keeping the truce unbroken, always desiring, always requesting, what he now held in his hands by the waters of Severn, peace with recognition, freedom to turn his powers to the arts of government in tranquillity.

In the church of Strata Marcella Llewelyn heard mass, and gave devout thanks to God.

CHAPTER XIV

On the twenty-seventh day of September King Henry
removed with his court from Shrewsbury, and took up
residence in the castle of Montgomery. Two days later we,
being so much nearer, rose and made ready early for the
day, and rode in great state to the meeting at Rhyd
Chwima, by the ford of Montgomery.

All down the river meadows the grass was seeded and
white with ripeness, full of moths, and the late flowers
nested in it like larks. The sun shone, and the trees were
turning gold, and over us the sky was deep blue without
a cloud, and we went gaily caparisoned as for a festival,
for that was a ride of no more than ten miles, a pleasure
journey along the great river all the way, under Griffith
ap Gwenwynwyn's castle of Pool, and so round into the
coil of the spreading stream between the willow groves,
where the gravel shone clear under the water, and the
woods and meadows on the further shore rose into the
folded hills that shield Montgomery.

They had pitched a splendid pavilion in the meadow
by the water, draped with cloth of gold, and king, legate
and court were there to meet us, a great assembly of
knights, barons and officers, and two sons of kings.
Edward, like his father, had consented fully in the treaty
of Montgomery, I believe in good faith and even goodwill.
He lost what pretensions he had to the title of prince of
Wales, but he was still the heir of England, and his
thoughts then, I believe, were fixed elsewhere, for the
new settlement had brought him in thankfulness to con-

sider taking upon him, as regards the legate's urging to the crusade, both his father's vow and his own. And he took the assumption of the cross, I grant him that, more gravely than did his father.

Down the blanched and rustling meadows Llewelyn rode, to the spit of sand and turf that ran out into the river, and all we after him. Into the shallow water he splashed, and the silver danced at his horse's heels. When he rode up the green sward on the further shore, towards where King Henry sat before the pavilion on a gilded throne, royal esquires came to take his bridle, and all we who served him dismounted with him and lined the shore. The king's knights kneeled to do off his spurs and ungird the sword-belt from his loins. He wore no mail and no gauntlets, and his head was uncovered, and thus he walked alone up the slope of green turf, his sombre brown made resplendent with scarlet and gold, and kneeled upon the gilded footstool at the king's feet, lifting to him his joined hands and his fierce and joyful face.

King Henry sat in shade, just at the rim of the pavilion's canopy, for the brightness of the sun somewhat troubled his eyes. But Llewelyn kneeled in sunlight, and when he raised his head the sunbeams blazed upon him and touched his sunburned face into minted gold, and the king paled and dwindled into a spectre beside him, like a candle in the noonday.

In a loud, clear voice Llewelyn rehearsed the oath of fealty, saving his own sovereign right within Wales, while the king's thin white hands, a little knotted with increasing age, enclosed his own. And thus he became vassal to King Henry and magnate of England, and also acknowledged prince of Wales, at sworn peace with his neighbour. And as he owed allegiance to the king, so did the king owe the loyal support and protection of his overlordship to Llewelyn, with right and justice in return for this feudal due.

I did not take my eyes from him until it was over, and

he rose and stepped back from the throne. As English knights had disarmed him, so Welsh princes, of lineage as long as his own, girded him again with belt and sword, and did on the spurs at his heels, and the lord abbot of Aberconway set upon his head the golden talaith of his estate, as royal a crown as King Henry's. It was then that I drew breath and stirred to look all round that brilliant circle of two courts, and my eyes lit upon David as birds fly home, as though no other in the ring of English faces bore any difference from his neighbour, and only he was marked out from all, the one Welshman upon the wrong side of the throne.

He was close at Edward's side, as they said he was constantly, but he had eyes for no one but his brother. Very wide and blue those eyes were, in a face intent and still, and I could not tell what it was I read in them, whether love or hate, regret for his desertion or resentment that it had achieved so little for him, and that little only at Edward's urging, and lightly granted by Llewelyn out of his own rich plenty.

Too lightly! I saw it then. So lightly that, though he knew as well as I that David must be present here in Edward's train, he had forgotten him utterly, and never looked for him among the bright cavalcade, even when he was riding up the broad track between the rising hills towards Montgomery, at the king's side. Not one thought did he give to him until in the hall of the castle, led by King Henry to the high table between the ranks of his barons and knights, he came face to face with his younger brother, and could not choose but see him.

They were of a height, the two faces eye to eye, and Llewelyn checked for an instant, astonished and reminded, but his flushed and joyful countenance never lost its brightness. I watched David closely then, for he looked as I had seen him look once, years back, before he fell senseless on the field of Bryn Derwin, of which he had been the sole and deliberate cause. Unsparingly he kept

334

his high and arrogant countenance, but behind the defiant stare of his eyes, blue and brilliant as sapphires, it seemed to me that there was another being gazing out from a private prison, and when he said, with the sweet insolence of which he was master: 'My lord, after all I see you do remember me!', what I seemed to hear, in the thread of a voice, warning and entreating, was: *'Kill me! You were wise!'*

I think there were some in the hall who held their breath, expecting a rough exchange and a flare of illwill to besmirch the feast. But Llewelyn clapped a hand upon David's shoulder, and said: 'Very heartily I remember you! Perhaps I can hope now to improve the acquaintance?'

And suddenly he laughed, wildly generous in his triumph, and leaned and kissed the marble cheek that suffered his salute like a blow, and burned where his lips had touched. Then lightly he took his hand from his brother's arm, and passed on to his place of honour beside the king. And David blazed and paled, all the blood forsaking his face, and slowly turning his black, glossy head, watched his brother go to his seat, and never took his eyes from him thereafter all that evening. As I know, for very seldom did I take my eyes from David, smouldering in black and bitter resentment, but to glance for reassurance at Llewelyn, who shone like a golden lantern with his joy and fulfilment.

There was much music that night in Montgomery, the king's music and the music of the bards. And we sat late, after the treaty was sealed and ratified, and as the wine flowed there were calls for this song, and that, and some of us went back and forth ordering the festivities as we were bidden. So I came late in the evening where David had withdrawn below his station and apart, altogether sober still, and from his shadowed place endlessly watching Llewelyn, with such fixed and famished eyes that I was drawn to go to him for pity and dread. Even then he was not aware of me until my shadow fell upon him, and then he shuddered, and his long gaze shifted and shortened to take me in, and was slow to know me, but knew me at last with such recognition as I found hard to fathom. There was compunction in it, and wonder, and a kind of drear self-derision. He said: 'What? Is it you? Now of all times I least need you to set me right.'

I thought, and said, that he well might need me more than he knew. And then he truly looked at me, who had looked through me before, to continue seeing Llewelyn. His face shook. Very strangely minded he was, that night. A little, and I think he would have wept, if there had not been so much anger in him. He said: 'Samson, how is it you haunt me still, seeing I slew you long ago?'

'Slew me and saved me,' I said. 'If you wanted me to remain dead you should have drawn the covert you spared to draw, after Evesham.'

'Dear God!' said David. 'Was it you taught him so to despise me?'

I understood then the ground of his despair and rage. 'Fool,' I said, 'do you not know how much that cost him?'

'It cost him no more than a pat to a hound,' said David bitterly, 'and he lets me back to him good-humouredly, as he would a hound that had gone off on a false scent, coming back shamed with his tail between his legs. He sighs and bears with me, like an experienced breaker with a useless pup. He values me not a pin!'

I began to exclaim against him that he judged well his own desert, but greatly misjudged his brother's largeness of mind and heart. But he cried me down with sudden breathless ferocity.

'Fool, if he had cared a toss for my desertion, do you think he would not have struck me down before all this company, and ordered me out of his sight?' And he spread his arms upon the board before him and sank his head into the crook of them, and shook terribly, like a man in fever, with grief and laughter. 'And I would have

336

let him!' said David, groaning and cursing into his brocaded sleeves. 'And I would have gone!'

Even then, though daunted, I would have stayed with him and made him hear me, but when I laid my hand upon him he started up, very tall and erect, and made his face marble-calm and smiling in a breath, and so turned and stalked away from me towards the high table and his own place, and his gait as he went was long and lissome and soft as a cat's, forbidding all concern or question.

After Montgomery we went back in state to Aber, and David did not go with us, which caused no man wonder, for his offences had been gross, and the requital needed time and a certain ceremony. There were even many, English as well as Welsh, who held that Edward should have kept his favourite out of sight on this occasion. The forms of courtesy have their values and uses. No one took this to be an easy matter, and the delicate legal exchanges concerning his stipulated lands were to go on for more than a year, that being an aid to healing.

Some miles along the great sea-road from Aberconway the men of the royal household of Aber came out to meet us, all the garrison and the bodyguard but for a few duty men, and among them came also Godred, my half-brother, my fair mirror-image, to remind me that my life had still a secret side where there was no victory and no achievement. I was aware that as soon as they met us he looked for me at Llewelyn's left hand, which was ever my place. And since we rode those last miles at joyous ease, keeping no formal order, he made his way to my elbow very soon, and clung there, close to my ear, out of reach of Llewelyn's. And there he spoke with his blithe, serpent voice, and smiled his smooth, guileless smile all the way into Aber.

'Now at last,' he said, 'I trust we may see more of you, now your missions are all done and the peace secured. Once before we hoped for it, and no sooner had we followed you into Gwynedd than you must be for ever wandering out of it. You became such a great traveller, there was no keeping pace with you. Now you and I are in the same service, with time and ease to live close and brotherly.'

I said that David might be returning to his old lands in due time, and would certainly require his old following. This with mild malice, seeing he had deserted David's service for his own advantage, and not at all out of any devotion to Llewelyn. But he laughed openly at that, sure that where the master's treason was wiped out the man's would not be allowed to count against him, especially as it could be represented as loyalty to the higher power.

'That will be a new beginning, for both high and low.' he said, 'with old scores wiped out. I don't know but there's something to be said for living in Lleyn.' And I think he began then, in cold blood, to weigh the advantages, as ready to leave one lord as another. 'I hear there's talk,' he said, 'of the Lord Edward making a rich match for David, now we're all at peace. There's some little kinswoman of his own, left widowed after one of Earl Simon's barons, before she's even properly a wife. They say he has it in mind to give her to David, along with the English knighthood he's already bestowed on him. If he sets up with a noble English wife, she'll need a household of her own. And David thinks highly of Cristin, and would be glad to have her companion to his bride. But it would be shame,' said Godred, wantonly smiling and soft-voiced at my shoulder, 'to take her even so far from you as Neigwl, now *you're* home.'

We were nearing the maenol then, and the women came out to greet us and bring us home in triumph, and I was so intent on looking for her among them that I made him no response, and hardly heeded his baiting. Yet I heard him whisper even more stealthily into my ear, a thread of sound, like a sharp knife slicing through the shouting and singing: 'You know, do you not, that she chose to come north with the old dame only for *your* sake?'

If I had not known it I might have made him some sign then of the depth of that wound, but I did know it, from her own lips, and there was no way he could move me. Moreover, I found her at that moment, a star among her fellows, half-grave, half-bright, wholly beautiful, all the more because she had found me first, and her eyes, like irises wide-open and glowing in sunlight, were waiting to embrace me.

Into that liquid light I fell and drowned, drawn into her being and one with her. How many times have I not died that blessed death! I think I did not halt nor check, nor did my face change, and I do not know how much Godred saw of what we two became before his eyes, or heard of what we spoke to each other in silence. But when I drew back into my body the soul she gently returned to me, and opened my own eyes to those about me, Llewelyn at my right hand rode softly with his chin upon his shoulder, and his gaze wide and deep and reflective upon me, as darkly brown and still as the peat-pools of his own mountains. When he saw me awake and aware he stirred and looked before him, and spoke me freely and cheerily, putting the moment by. But there was nothing he had not seen.

After the feasting and the mirth and the singing of the bards in Aber that night, I went out into the mild darkness of the courtyard, and there was so golden a moon that the sight of it was like a benediction. I walked through the cool stillness to the chapel, and there made my prayers, for that night was to me a home-coming of such power and magic that nothing on earth seemed out of my reach, not even my love, Cristin, Godred's wife. I had only to wait and be still, and everything would be added to me. Yet in humility I consented to forgo what

I might not desire, having the inexpressible bliss of what was already granted. For she loved me, and no other. And I prayed passionately grace and mercy for Godred, my brother, who had not that bliss, and only by its bestowal on me had learned to covet and begrudge it.

When I had done, I rose from before the lamp that burned on the altar, and turned towards the darkness, and there was a still and man-shaped shadow in the open doorway, that moved towards me as I moved, as the image advances in a mirror. So used was I to meeting my demon that I halted where I stood, and called him by his name: 'Godred!' Not dreading nor questioning, only in recognition, that he might have peace, if there was the means of peace in him.

'Not Godred,' said the shadow, very low, 'but Llewelyn.'

He came towards the light, and took shape as he came, and within reach of me he stayed. I think he had hardly touched mead or wine all that evening long, the burning within him was the fire of one aim achieved, and one still distantly beckoning.

'I did not follow you,' he said, 'but it was in my mind to send for you. And you were here before me. The dagger that strikes at me strikes also at you, the stars of our birth shone on us both. I have been blinded by my own concerns, but now I see. Forgive me that I did not see from the beginning. I must have cost you dear in your silence many a time.'

I told him what was true, that he had no need to reproach himself or compassionate me, that I had no complaint against man or God, that I would not change my fate if I could, that there was but one thing lacking to me, and that was not my love's love, for that I had in fullest measure.

'I know it,' he said. 'I saw her face, also. Did I say we shared one fate? Come here to the light, look on *this* face. I have shown it to no one but you.'

He laid a hand upon my arm, and drew me with him to the small, steady lamp upon the altar, and there he slid from the breast of his gown and laid beneath the light a small silver circlet, the size of a woman's palm, threaded upon a cord that he wore about his neck. The disc was enamelled with soft, bright colours and gleamed like a jewel, and I knew it for the talisman Earl Simon had given him beside the road to Hereford, a year and a half ago.

Some cunning artist had made this tiny image of a great beauty. A little face in profile, pure like a queen on a coin, with one large, confiding eye gazing before, a folded, dreaming mouth, and a braid of dark, gilded hair on her shoulder, the Lady Eleanor de Montfort, twelve years old, looked with a grave, high confidence into her future, towards a bridegroom and an estate fitting her nobility. A wonderful thing it was, but not wonderful enough, for it missed the warmth of her full-face gaze, that stopped the heart with its trust and its challenge.

'You have seen her,' said Llewelyn in awe. 'Is she truly so?'

I said: 'This is but the half. She is more. If this image could turn its head and look you in the eyes, and speak to you, then you would know.'

'And can this face,' he said, rather to himself than to me, and brooding upon the little medallion in fascination and dread, 'ever look upon me as I saw Cristin look upon you?'

It was not my response he wanted, nor even hers, for she was still barely fifteen years old, and a long way off in France, with more than distance dividing her from him. Rather he longed for a sign from God that he had the right to believe and to hope. And when there was no sign, he took that for a sign in itself, that the duty was laid in his own hands. He took the medallion into his palm and held it before him in the little circle of reddish light, and the face flushed into rose, as if the blood stirred under her pearl-clear skin, and the movement caused the lamp to quiver, so that its light trembled briefly over her folded lips and caused them to smile. He saw it, and smiled in return, in the night of his triumph, with the golden talaith gleaming in his hair.

'There is nothing you or I can do but wait and trust,' he said, 'but that we have learned how to do. I had two vows registered in heaven, to win the acknowledgement of my right, the birthright of her sons, and to lay it at her feet. The first is done. The second, God helping me, I will do, though I wait life-long. You see her, the bud of a royal stem, and the daughter of that tremendous man, better than royal. From such blood, what princes will spring! If they took her away to the end of the world, I would not give her up. Her father pledged her to me, and I have pledged myself to her. The more spears they array between her and me, the more surely will I reach her at last. I have waited but two years for her yet, and she is still hardly out of childhood. For Earl Simon's daughter I will wait as long as I must. Either I will have Eleanor de Montfort, or I will have none.'

So he said, and so he kept. For however Goronwy and Tudor and all his council, thereafter, urged on him his duty to take a wife, and ensure the succession to that throne of Wales which was his own perfected creation, he smiled and passed on unmoved. And however they paraded before him the names and persons of all the noble ladies of Wales, any one of whom he might have had at will, still he never took his eyes from the image of Eleanor, that shone like a private star to him day and night. And still he saw her twelve years old and in profile, waiting, like himself, for the miraculous moment when the bud would blossom, and she would turn her head and look him in the eyes, and reach him her hand upon their marriage day.